Hand of Glory

Hand of Glory

by

Susan Boulton

www.penmorepress.com

Hand of Glory by Susan Boulton

Copyright © 2016 Susan Boulton

All rights reserved. No part of this book may be used or reproduced by any means without the written permission of the publisher except in the case of brief quotation embodied in critical articles and reviews.
This is a work of fiction. Names and characters, places, events and incidents are either the products of the author's imagination or used in a fictitious manner. Any resemblance to actual persons, living or dead, or actual events is purely coincidental.

ISBN-13: 978-1-942756-80-4(Paperback)
ISBN -978-1-942756-81-1(e-book)

BISAC Subject Headings:
FIC031010 Fiction/ Thrillers/ Crime
FIC031070 Fiction /Thrillers/ Supernatural
FIC032000 Fiction/War Military

Cover work by Christine Horner

Address all correspondence to:

Penmore Press LLC
920 N Javelina Pl
Tucson. AZ 85748

Or visit our website at:
www.penmorepress.com

Dedication

To the real George Adams, who made it home in 1919.

Acknowledgements

A big heartfelt thanks to my family and friends, and especially to Donna Scott and Kathy Saideman, without whose help and advice in the early days, Hand of Glory would not have turned out to be half the novel it is.
And to Michael James, Midori Snyder and Lauren McElroy of Penmore Press, thank you for your help and guidance during the final stage of the journey.

Chapter One

Western Front–Passchendaele
3rd Major Battle for Ypres
Late October 1917

A military policeman indicated for Jim to fall in behind the slow procession of wounded making their way down the communication trench.

"Be alright," Jim said, winking at Archie.

It wouldn't be, not if that fucker Tennant had his way. The sod had been after them for weeks. Archie moved down the dark trench after his brother. He reached into his pocket, pulled out a battered packet of cigarettes and offered one to Jim. Jim looked at his escort. The man nodded and Jim reached out for the cigarette. He took it lightly between finger and thumb, rolling it slowly from side to side.

"Christ, Jim!"

"Arch, you take care of yourself, you hear? Remember what we talked of, just in case."

"Jim..." Archie struggled to speak. He had only been parted from his brother a handful of times. Jim always looked out for him. Jim was boss and knew the trade inside out. It'd been Jim's idea to join up and make a killing from dead men's pockets. The war, everyone had said, would be over by

Hand of Glory

Christmas. But things had bloody gone pear-shaped and they were stuck in the horror.S That hadn't stopped Jim. He'd come up with a plan to get them out of here with enough loot to get home and bribe a screw to get the makings. Jim intended them to be rolling in it within six months, and having the likes of officers licking their boots.

"Gotta go, Arch," Jim said, placing the cigarette in his mouth. He nodded in thanks as his escort offered him a light. The pale red glow illuminated Jim's face, tracing the dirt-engrained lines round his eyes.

Archie opened his mouth to speak again, but Jim turned away, walking with his escort towards the bend in the trench. Archie remained standing there in the dark, listening to the fading sounds of the men making their way down the communication trench. He was alone, surrounded by a pile of yes sir, no sir, arse-licking bastards.

*****

Archie didn't know how long he stood there. It began to rain. Thick, heavy drops fell out of a demon sky, bombarding the scurrying rats as they dashed down the duckboards seeking shelter.

Then.

Artillery.

Moaning Minnies.

Archie felt the vibration in his jaw as they started to come over. Jerry was indulging in his evening pastime of trying to find the latrines. The latest ones had been dug a week before and were well overdue for a hit. The air reeked of shit and churned mud. He swore and threw himself against the wall of the trench. The attack was inching back from the latrines along the line of communication trenches, the men who were moving to and fro from the front under cover of darkness now the target.

"Jim!" Archie screamed and ran down the trench, dodging men trying to escape the onslaught by pressing themselves to the walls, onto duckboards, and scrambling into already overcrowded dugouts.

Then the artillery stopped, as suddenly as it had started. Archie was running through *wet dust,* the flying, pulverised flesh and bone of what had once been men. He skidded to a stop. The walls of the communication trench had been torn open, the wounded tossed from their stretchers and assaulted again, their remains mingled with those who had been carrying them to safety.

Other figures appeared out of the dissipating human fog and began to search for survivors. "Archie?"

"Jim... Charlie, you seen Jim?" Archie could only think of his brother.

"Christ! Was he being sent down the bloody line tonight?" Charlie bent over the mangled body of the military policeman. "This bugger's still alive! Stretcher-bearers, over here!"

Archie crouched and shuffled forward. His gaze flicked from one lump of torn flesh to another. He stopped. His mouth opened to swear. Nothing came out. Bile, thick and burning, rose in his gullet.

There, was Jim.

There was not a mark on his face. His head was whole; so, too, his left shoulder and arm. But Jim's right arm and half of his chest were gone, as was the rest of his body below the waist. Just a ragged knot of burst bowels and strips of flesh remained. Archie knelt. He touched Jim's left hand. The fingers twitched. A hand within a hand. His and Jim's. The fingers moved again, half closing around his. He heard Jim's voice. Swore he did. Not bloody fucking well possible. Archie sobbed. He didn't hear the

Hand of Glory

voices around him, only the echo of Jim's voice whispering in the dark pit that had opened up inside.

*****

It had been just the night before.
One day.
One push over the top ago.

Archie twisted his hands together in suppressed rage. "That tosser did for Jim."

"Let it go, Archie," Charlie said. He rubbed his nose, smearing mud across the bulbous end. "Just bloody bad luck, that was all."

The two men stood in a funk hole, their backs against the sodden, foul smelling Flanders clay. Their rough shelter was cut into the side of a trench between the mud-cemented, rotting remains of a Yorkshireman—long considered just part of the scenery—and a rusting sheet of corrugated steel. An oilcloth pegged into position above their heads with bayonets acted as both roof and door.

"Every bugger lifts stuff. Tell me someone who doesn't."

"That's not the way the lieutenant saw it. He caught Jim red-handed; should've been more careful," Charlie said, half-heartedly, trying to put the other point of view.

"Fucking bastard!" Archie's eyes narrowed, making his apple-round face resemble a worn-out leather football. The lieutenant was a fucking gung-ho swine set on earning a few lengths of coloured ribbon at others' expense. Tennant deserved to be bumped off like all the other shit-faced, medal-hunting officers did. No one in B Company would miss the bastard, that was for sure.

Charlie eased his back off the muddy wall and stepped forward, reaching out a hand to push up the oilskin. He peered up into the dark, rain-laced sky, squinted, then ducked back in as a star shell exploded high over the trench system. Night had come to the battlefield, bringing with it the cries of those abandoned in no man's land.

"A Jerry shell killed Jim, Archie."

"That's not true, is it, Arch?"

Jim? No. Jim was dead. Yet it was Jim's voice.

Archie looked at his mate. Had Charlie heard? No. He couldn't have. The voice had spoken to Archie alone. The words echoed through his mind and sparked thoughts, making his upper lip twitch in a half-smile, as cruel and as dark as the idea forming in his mind. All he needed was half a chance. "I know, Charlie, but who put Jim in that sodding trench, huh?"

"Put a fucking sock in it, Archie." Charlie again peered out from beneath the oilcloth and then stepped out.

Archie could hear someone approaching. He joined Charlie in the dark trench. A small, half-shielded lantern, set in the wall by the corner of the man-made ditch, winked as a figure walked past. The man came to a halt a few feet away from Archie. It was the officer they had been waiting for. They had drawn the short straw and been ordered to be part of one of that evening's night patrols. Charlie began to stand to attention, Archie half-heartedly following.

"At ease, men. You know the drill. But I can't stress enough the importance of patrols such as ours. We need to cut as much of the enemy wire as we can and take at least one prisoner to send back for questioning. The chaps in intelligence are banking on our success."

The lieutenant swayed slightly as he spoke. He had his right hand on his belt, fingers tapping on the leather holster of his Webley revolver. He didn't look either soldier in the eye, not even acknowledging them as men. He addressed them as if they were no more than lead toy soldiers on the nursery carpet.

Hand of Glory

It was Tennant. This was a fucking turnaround, and no mistake. Archie believed he'd more than half a chance now: he was going to be alone in no man's land with the bastard. He patted his trench knife. The lieutenant smiled, taking this as a sign that Archie was keen to get at the Hun. Archie was keen all right: he'd just been given what he wished for on a platter. Tennant gestured for Archie and Charlie to follow him over the lip of the trench.

"Sod's going to get us fucking killed. You know it as well as I do–the bugger's a Jonah," Archie whispered to Charlie as they began to crawl through the muck towards the enemy lines.

"Shush... "

Archie could hear the fear in Charlie's voice. "You know he don't give a fucking damn about the likes of you or me. Time he was fucking well topped." Archie came to his feet. Now was his chance. They were on the edge of a huge shell-hole. He pulled the garrotte from his pocket and uncurled the thin, waxed cord.

"Archie? What the sodding hell–?" Charlie said, just as a star shell exploded overhead.

Archie ignored him. He looped the garrotte over Tennant's head and crossed his arms as the cord went round Tennant's throat. He pulled the garrotte tight, and shoved his right knee deep into Tennant's back. The officer tried to scream. His hands at first lifted upwards, fingers widespread. Then they turned into claws as he reached back to rend Archie, but he lost his footing. He tumbled forward and slid over the lip of the shell-hole, dragging Archie with him.

"Fuck!" Archie toppled, his hold on the thin cord slipping. The star shell was falling to earth, its light fast fading away. It cast warped and twisted shadows of the two men. Tennant was wriggling, trying to swim in the yellow mud. His arms came up as he reached backwards over his head, trying one more time to grab his attacker. His nails found Archie's right eye and gouged runnels in the surrounding flesh. Archie bit off a bellow of pain. He felt Tennant's body jerk forward. In the fast-fading light Archie saw Charlie pushing Tennant's head into the mud. He tightened the cord around his victim's neck, the veins bulging in the back of his hands: rivers of skin, outlined in mud. Suddenly he was straddling a corpse.

"Dead?" Charlie whispered, his voice shaking. Archie looked up and saw the trench knife fall from Charlie's hand. The bugger had knifed the sod. Or had he? The steel glinted in the light of the fading star shell as it fell: unsullied.

Archie sat back on Tennant's buttocks, letting go of the garrotte. His lungs hurt. He'd been holding his breath. "Good fucking riddance." He removed the cord, flinging it away into the depths of the shell-hole. His hand came out, fingers reaching for Charlie's unsheathed blade where it lay point down in the mud. He stopped, not at all sure why he was reaching for the knife.

He could hear Jim chuckling. *"Well done, Arch. You did for him. Hung the bugger. Bloody murderer deserved no less. You got the makings now. The right hand of a hanged murderer. That's just what the sod was. You can do it. I'll help you. It'll be just as we planned. We'll have a Hand of Glory and no bugger'll be able to stop us."*

His granddad had been thrown into jail for trying to get the makings, when he and Jim had just been lads. The plods had taken a dim view of grave robbing, even if the grave was that of a murderer. The screw his granddad had tried to bribe had shopped him. The days were long gone when a hanged man swung in the wind on a gibbet at a crossroads, and with those days had faded the Hawkins family's place in the world of thieves.

Archie reached again for the knife. It came out of the earth with a soft plop. He leaned forward, lying on the body of the

Hand of Glory

man he'd killed, and lifted up Tennant's right hand, chopping at the wrist like it was firewood.

"What you doing, Archie? He's fucking well done for, no need..." Charlie moved swiftly away, no longer wanting any part of this. His feet dislodged waves of mud, which slid splashing down into the foul water at the shell-hole's centre. His shadow vanished into no man's land, leaving Archie and his victim alone.

"Hand of Glory, hand of a hanged murderer!" Archie cackled, devilish, dark. He tucked the severed hand into his tunic. Another star shell burst. Archie quickly moved off the corpse, flattening himself to the ground, the foul yellow earth splashing onto his face. It burned. He raised his hand to his face, trying to feel the damage Tennant had done. His fingers traced wet, stinging lines around his right eye. He pushed hard at the body by his side. It slithered down the side of the large shell-hole, vanishing into the dark depths.

For a few seconds between the fading of the last star shell and the eruption of the next, Archie looked round the undulating sides of the man-made demon pit. Did he see movement to his right? No. There was no one there. Just food for rats hung on the wire. He patted the bloody trophy he'd taken and began to move off, inching slowly over the battered landscape. He needed to find somewhere to hide out until dawn, so he could think about how he was going get into and out of the front suicide trench.

His fingers wandered up to his torn face. How bad was it? Damn that bastard Tennant. Still, maybe if he crawled back in and told a sob story about the loss of the brave lieutenant, the corporal would send him back for treatment. It would be easy enough then to disappear among all the poor fucking sods working their way back to the main dressing station.

Susan Boulton

A star shell exploded high over the battlefield, banishing the darkness for the space of its short, spluttering fall to earth. In the flickering man-made light, hell was again visible, pockmarked and drowning in the late autumn rain. It was home to the living, the long and newly dead, and those like Giles Hardy who believed they belonged with the fallen.

He had been trapped since the previous dawn. Over the top he and his men had gone. Hardy still breathed, but he knew each expansion of his lungs was a lie: he was dead.

Mud, thick and hardened, made his face a death mask. He hung on an unravelling strand of the barbed wire barrier that criss-crossed no man's land. The wire twisted round his hand, shoulder, chest, and across his neck. It had him imprisoned, allowing the glutinous yellow mud filling the shell-hole to take its time devouring him.

Another star shell. Lower in the sky this time—a violent explosion of raw light which punched through the haze of rain. It illuminated for a few moments dark shapes on the edge of the shell-hole. Their sudden movement drew his lacklustre gaze. In the eerie light the figures squirmed along the top of the crater. He could see their feet fighting for purchase. Two soldiers grasped another, who fought the cord placed round his neck. He heard their muffled voices and saw a trench knife glitter in the fading, brittle illumination of the star shell.

Hardy felt a flicker of curiosity. Why was he interested? He was like the corpse the two shadow men were now hunched over. Their actions and pain, his, meant nothing anymore. Perhaps he was already in purgatory. Further down the trench system another star shell burst open. The light was faint, fast-waning against the sky. Had these men seen him there on the wire?

No.

Hand of Glory

One of them pushed away the remains of his mutilated victim and scuttled, a human crab, across the sea of destruction.

In the fading light Hardy watched the corpse slide at a forty-five degree angle down the side of the shell-hole. It inched its way round the side, then lurched upright into a sitting position as it hit the remains of a tree stump. The last dying drops of the night's downpour splashed the murdered man's face, adding fake tears to his muddied cheeks. Then the body folded over itself and slid into the thick mud. Brackish bubbles rose round the new addition to the shell-hole. For a while the corpse floated, a dark shadow, bobbing closer. The right arm, handless, was outstretched, as if pleading for aid. Then the corpse sank, banging against his legs as it did so. Hardy felt it come to rest under the surface, hard against his left calf.

His eyes closed. All was silence, then a sound close to his left ear. A voice he never expected to hear in this place. Not male. Not worn rough by warfare. The smell of burning autumn leaves. The scent that lulled the English countryside into its winter sleep. The scent of home. *Impossible.* No leaves here: just a sea of sour-smelling mud. Suddenly, it was hard to breathe. The fleeting touch of a phantom hand replaced the bite of the wire for a scant moment. He tried to dismiss it, but the sensation was there. The voice came again. His name: Giles. Spoken in trust and need. So close, yet no one was there. He was alone with the dead. His hand tightened on the wire, making it vibrate. The barbs cut deeper. Blood ran into his clenched palm, reddening the mud-stained creases. The voice began again and turned into murmured sounds of relief, even gladness. Then it vanished, banished by the soft clink of a rifle barrel being leaned against the wire.

"Captain?"

A face came nose to nose with his. The man's breath stank of tobacco and bully beef. Corporal Adams—dead, too? Should he reply? Be polite? Were manners expected in this halfway hell? His head nodded as he thought on the matter.

Adams took the nod as an acknowledgement. "Told the sarge no way was you a bloody goner; lying low, I told him. Crawl in when you had a chance."

Hardy wanted to say he could not crawl in; the wire had him and it would take him down as it had others before. Deep into the mud. Lost and forgotten.

"Sir..." Corporal Adams hesitated, torn between duty and helping his officer, "it's just that... well, got something to finish off first, sir..." After patting Hardy on the shoulder in an effort to reassure him, Adams inched up to the lip of the shell-hole. Here he became as still as the corpses littering no man's land, the only movement the remains of the night's rainfall dripping from the rim of his tin helmet. The butt of his rifle lay against his right cheek. Adams was waiting for his opposite number to begin the dawn hunt.

Dull and reluctant, the day began. The sound of the men in the front trench filtered across the battered landscape. The morning stand-to—Hardy knew the drill off by heart. Men sweating even in the cold. Their hands tightened white on their rifles. Feet on the forward step, eyes on the reeking stretch of land before them, they waited for the off, to plunge into the horror, or to repel the enemy Fritz, the Hun, coming out of the yellow-tinted morning mist. Man-Made, lung-burning, eye-destroying. A snake-cloud: when it touched earth or water it left its venom there to burn the flesh of the men scrabbling through both. Up to five days in a row, men would wait at dawn on the step. Then, their time in the line over, they would begin the nightmare journey back down the communication trenches to rest.

Hand of Glory

There was no dawn attack by either side today, but the men still stood on the forward step, a slight movement visible above the trench line.

A sniper's heaven.

A single shot rang out, followed by shouts, curses and the rattle of the enemy's machine gun on this sector.

"Yes!" Adams grunted as he slid back down the inside of the crater. "Got the bugger." As he lay on his back in the mud, Adams fumbled in his pocket, pulling out a battered tobacco tin. Carefully he pulled out a Woodbine. Adams's left elbow caught on a former member of the Shropshire Light Infantry, entering the man's shattered ribcage. "Sorry, mate,"–not that the lad from Newport minded, or was in any state to complain–"I needed a fag."

Hardy watched the soft plume of tobacco smoke curl out of the corner of Adams's mouth. The man lay back, eyes half-closed, enjoying the moment. Then he snapped upright into a sitting position, stifled a cough, and moved through the mud to Hardy's side. Adams offered the cigarette to Hardy. Hardy's mouth opened as if of its own accord. The crinkled paper was damp with Adams's saliva; it moistened the mud caked on Hardy's lips. He inhaled, drawing in the smoke. Once, twice–his head began to swim. Adams took the cigarette back, peeling it from Hardy's lower lip, and replaced it with the cold metal of a water flask. Hardy gulped.

"Easy, Capt...." Adams said, removing the flask. "Won't be a tick." With this, the stocky sniper scrambled up the side of the shell-hole and disappeared.

The sun gave up on its assault of the morning sky and cowered under a thick veil of low, grey cloud. More rain threatened. Wisps of smoke inched over the landscape, followed by the rattle of billycans as men supped their morning brew.

Clack, clack. A machine gun spat out a few seconds' warning, raking over no man's land. No attacks today, just a reminder. We are here. You are there. Death is between us.

"Get your fat arse down there." Adams's whispered snarl preceded the wet slipping noises made by the boots of the man he was cursing.

"You got no sodding right, Corporal…"

"Have, so put up," Adams snorted. "Bloody good job you bumped into Corporal Jones."

Adams slithered down the inside of the shell-hole after the three-man wire team and their unwilling hanger-on.

"Indeed it was; he was going the wrong sodding way, Corporal Adams." The Welsh wire-cutter winked at his fellow non-commissioned officer, then saw the predicament of his commanding officer. He inched his way to Hardy's side. His capable hands hovered over the twisted lengths of wire that held Hardy prisoner.

"Wasn't. You should've let me try and get back to my own company," the hanger-on muttered.

"Stop yon fucking moaning," one of the other privates said. He unslung a length of rope from his shoulder, snaking out the coils ready for use.

"Aye, enough. Though what your lieutenant is going to say about the matter of you getting sodding lost is anyone's guess," Corporal Jones said.

"Wasn't fucking well lost!" the interloper snarled, his voice rising in volume.

Adams drew his right index finger sharply across his neck, indicating for the interloper to cut his talk.

Clack. Clack. The machine gun's chatter repeated its message. All five men flattened themselves to the walls of the large crater. With breath laboured and hard held, they waited.

Hand of Glory

The gun fell silent, its latest warning given and understood by all who heard it.

With rough hand gestures, Corporal Jones ordered his men. The rope was quickly slipped round Hardy's chest and knotted firmly in place. Then Jones placed the thick hemp line across and halfway up the side of the crater, over the remains of the tree stump. The three privates picked up the end and took the strain, slipping in the mud. The interloper cursed under his breath.

Adams dug with his hands at the mud wall behind Hardy. Globs fell away, tumbling down into the fetid water. Disturbed, the water frothed a sickly yellow. It stank of chlorine; the water, laced with the residue of more than one gas attack, had become a foul and deadly cocktail. A rough hole made, Adams slipped his body in behind the captain. His arms joined the rope round Hardy's chest and he braced himself to take his commander's weight.

Hardy began to squirm. The movement awakened pain. His joints ached. Cuts and abrasions cried out as his chilled flesh moved.

"Easy, sir," Adams said.

"Aye, easy," Jones repeated as his wire cutters clicked shut.

The links round Hardy's hand were cut off, a small length of metal left attached to the flesh. *Snap. Snap.* Gone was the metal from round his arm, removed by Jones's hands. The heavy fabric ripped as Jones roughly pulled the wire off Hardy's khaki jacket. Small flashes of his clean shirt were exposed, bright and innocent, unmarked by the muddy hell. Hardy's body suddenly jerked downwards. The barbs round his neck bit deeper, clawing at the vein under the mud-caked skin.

"Shit and fucking damnation!" Adams's curse cut the air. His muscles bunched, heels digging in harder. The rope tightened, taking the strain; the tree stump groaned. All the men repeated curses under their breath as they scrambled backwards in their effort to heave Hardy free.

Jones's knuckles whitened as he cut the wire from round Hardy's chest. His own blood stained the metal as it slashed him. Then the metal cutter's teeth slipped round the length binding Hardy's neck. They pressed deep into the flesh. Hardy's pulse throbbed against the cold metal. Adams's arms tightened, constricting Hardy's breathing. *Snap,* the final length severed. The men shuddered as they heaved, slipping in the mud. Hardy rose from the thick, muddy soup, but not alone: his foot had caught on the body of his "companion" in the water. The murdered lieutenant surfaced with a soft gurgle. The body rolled over. Its mud-coated features gazed blind-eyed at the autumn sky. Mouth open, it expelled a soft sigh as escaping air from dead lungs bubbled from stained lips.

The interloper screamed at the sight of the rising corpse. He dropped the rope and scrambled up the wall of the shell-hole. His fellows tried to grab him, to silence him, but he was gone, his cries lost in the rattle of the machine gun.

"Oh, fucking well done, mate!" Corporal Jones snapped.

Hardy watched the corpse of the murdered man sink back down, returning to death, leaving him stuck between. His legs were numb from the cold, the skin under his well-made woollen breeches blistered by the acidic water. The agony gnawing at his limbs fought his mind's denial of it, for if he were dead then surely there would be no pain.

"Take it yon bit of flotsam was the lieutenant from B Company?" one of the privates asked.

"Must be. Sodding fool. Why'd he scream and run like that? You'd've thought he wouldn't take fright at just the sight of his lieutenant bobbing around in a shell-hole. Dead is dead—no fucking harm in the dead," his fellow remarked.

Hand of Glory

"Bloody funny fella. What was his name? Charlie?" the first private asked as he reached into his haversack and pulled out a tin of bully beef. The enemy was now watching this area. It was best for them to sit tight for a while and make the best of it. An improvised meal of pooled tins of bully beef, hard biscuits and water appeared from packs and pockets.

Hardy lay there, his breath coming in harsh gasps. Adams pressed a dressing pad round the metal barbs still embedded in Hardy's hand and checked for other hurts. Hardy was half-frozen in body, and numb in mind. He was still lost—observing those around him, but totally disconnected. Hardy tried to eat the tinned meat and biscuit Adams gave him, but found it thick and unwholesome on his palette. The water from Adams's flask was brackish and tasted of metal. It made him choke.

The day dragged on, the men—all save Hardy—chafing at their entrapment in the shell-hole. Soon the shadows across no man's land began to lengthen.

"Best make a move. Dark's coming," Jones said and checked his gear. His fellows did the same. One of the privates curled up the mud-coated rope, and then carefully placed it over the shoulder of his fellow.

"Take me smelly," Adams said, holding up his well-oiled Lee Enfield rifle. Jones nodded, taking the gun and slinging it on his back. "Can you stand, sir?"

"I don't know." Should he try? He did, but his limbs would not obey. They were still frozen from their time in the mud. Hardy could feel his skin ripping, coming away with the fabric of his trousers as the cloth moved. The metal in his hand rasped, inching deeper into his flesh. He gasped. Adams put out his hand to steady him, and Hardy gripped... hard.

"I'll carry you, sir. You sound a bit nervous, so you do." Adams bent down and, with Jones's help, heaved the officer onto his back.

Susan Boulton

A bit nervous. Hardy knew what Adams was hinting at. Shell shock. The unmentionable illness. The embarrassment. The paralysis of mind that unmanned even the strongest. Was he nervous? Or was he just dead and in purgatory? His hands clung harder to Adams as the man shifted his stance. His head was on Adams's left shoulder, his legs tucked high on Adams's hips and held firmly. A child's piggyback.

The three other men squared their shoulders, summoning their strength to face the hell above the lip of the shell-hole. They inhaled a few deep breaths and took off. Out of the pit they went into no man's land, zig-zagging, keeping low to the ground. Adams followed. They were thirty yards as the crow flies from the front trench. It would take them half as many yards again to get within spitting distance. Foamed waves of mud crashed from one shell-hole to another, overlapping, intertwining, gashes in the earth linked by wire and its accompanying dead, hung on the barbs like caught carrion on a farmer's gate.

The thud and the squelch of Adams's boots echoed into Hardy's mind. His eyes were downcast, watching with detached horror each placement of Adams's feet. Adams's right boot grazed the skull of a long-dead Jerry. The left plunged deep into the entrails of one of Hardy's men who had died the day before. Both of Adams's feet slipped in mud mixed with the blood of too many men. English and German. Enemies and friends. Zigzag. To the left this step, to the right the next.

Across the last few yards of no man's land Adams danced towards the relative safety of the forward trench. Hardy's body vibrated with each of Adams's hard-won breaths. His fingers tightened their hold on the man. Knees tried to grip, as if astride a prancing horse, but failed. *Just a few paces now.*

The cry of the Hun machine gun began. A rush of red-hot metal cut the air round the two men. Adams's upper right arm exploded in a mass of blood and fabric. It lathered the side of Hardy's face, coating his lips. Adams stumbled, grunting and cursing. Hardy felt a sudden sharp pain in his left thigh and dampness against his skin as the blood poured down, pooling at the top of his mud-encrusted, knee-high leather boot. He cried out, unsure if it was in denial or acceptance of the agony clawing its way up through his groin and into the pit of his stomach.

"No bloody fucking way you is gettin' us!" Adams bellowed as he flung himself and his burden down into the bottom of the British front trench.

*****

Cries filled the air, accompanied by the angry *clack, clack* of the machine gun. Denied its prey, it spat in anger along the top of the trench for a dozen more heartbeats, then faded away to wait for the next time.

"Bloody Norah, Adams! Watch me feet, you big, sodding ox!"

"Fucking hell, you're bleeding like a stuck pig. Grab the Capt, someone—Adams is going to drop him."

"That's it—lay him down. Gently, now."

"Seen Jones with me damn smelly?" Adams's voice cut through those of his fellow soldiers. He allowed them to sit him down on the step in the trench.

"Here you are." His Welsh counterpart passed the gun to the wounded man. Adams tucked the gun between his knees, butt to the floor. Jones stood watching as a fellow soldier cut away Adams's jacket to reveal the damaged flesh. "Lucky bugger, you are. Next thing we know you'll be walking on sodding water."

"You haven't messed it up, have you?" Adams said, ignoring Jones's remark.

"Jones wouldn't dare. Now, Corporal, let's get that dressing on and get you to the battalion aid post with Captain Hardy."

The company's senior officer, Major Grives-Thomas, strode into the middle of the scene. He looked round, then half turned and barked out orders. "Make some room here. Back to your duties. Stretcher-bearers, at the double!" Hardy began to shake, his heels drumming on the sodden duckboards as shock raced through his bloodstream. "Don't move; it will undo all Adams's hard work in getting you back. Tighten that belt, Sergeant Major; I won't have Captain Hardy bleed to death here."

The rough hands of the company sergeant major notched the belt tighter where he had slipped it close to the groin on Hardy's left thigh. The sergeant major then squeezed Hardy's arm in a fatherly way and turned his attention to applying a dressing to the wound.

"Good!" Grives-Thomas said in satisfaction as he crouched down by Hardy's head. The man's features were drawn. Haggard, even. He tried to smile at Hardy, to reassure him, but Hardy knew there could not be any reassurance.

Hardy's wire-impaled right hand slipped off his chest, fingers waiting for the touch of the mud-slick duckboards. However, he touched peat, cold and rough. The smell of a wintry English day, of burning leaves, again filled his nostrils. He tried to laugh at the jest this devil of a place was playing on him in his last moments. Hardy felt the peat under his fingers move, rasping, shifting as it sank from under his touch. Two fingers touched his palm. The nails were broken, breaking more as they caught on the roughly applied dressing on his hand, ripping it away in anxious haste. A hand was attempting to hold his. *Why not*? He closed his hand on the warm flesh, feeling the wire barbs embedded in his palm cut into another's. For a moment the two hands held on tight to each other, pain and blood joining, then the grasp was broken. Hardy screamed as a damp, slick, broken length of duckboard was prised from his damaged fist, leaving the rough dressing trodden in the mud as he was lifted quickly onto a stretcher.

Hand of Glory

*****

Through the advancing mental mist, images flickered. Trench walls of swollen sandbags and corrugated iron panels, glued together with mud. Men's faces, gaunt and haunted, their bodies hunched against the encroaching damp of nightfall. The back of his stretcher-bearer, arm muscles bunching under khaki sleeves, shoulders stooping, as the straps round them took their share of Hardy's body weight. Light fading, darkness seeped into the communication trench, down which the stretcher slowly moved. The bearers trod their uneven tread, taking care not to jostle the injured man in their care too much. The sudden flame of a match, red, then yellow. Adams's face illuminated by the fast-dying glow as he lit his cigarette. The rumpled length of paper-wrapped tobacco was offered to Hardy's lips, but this time he turned his face away. A faint haze of smoke rose round his face as Adams took away the untouched cigarette. All the sights and sounds were blending, becoming a crumbling wall of images. Pressing down and shutting his eyes, his mind decided it could experience no more and slipped silently into oblivion.

Chapter Two

Hardy came to in the rough dugout of the battalion aid post. The medical officer hovered over him. An orderly scribbled the doctor's dictated orders on an overlarge parcel label. "Wounds on right hand, arm and neck. Superficial. Cleaned and dressed. Bad gas blisters on the skin from the waist down. Gunshot wound to outer left, lower thigh cleaned and dressed. Bullet to be removed. Morphine given." The medical officer plunged the long needle of a syringe into Hardy's exposed right shoulder. "Sorry, old man, but it's going to be a while before we can risk moving you and the others down the line."

Hardy's mouth worked, but no words came from it. The medical officer smiled, nodding as if Hardy had thanked him, and moved on to his next patient.

His stretcher was quickly lifted off the trestles set in the middle of the dugout. These stood between the scant quarters of the medical officer and the slides: tiers, onto which the stretchers loaded with the wounded were slid. Wounded men layered and tagged for dispatch like parcels in a sorting office. Already another leaden stretcher had taken centre stage on the trestles.

The orderlies abandoned him on the lower rung of the furthest inside tier. Around him, men coughed, grunted and moaned. The walking wounded sat on benches, talking softly,

Hand of Glory

exchanging cigarettes, biscuits, and their evening rum ration. The brittle light of the acetylene lamps picked out the pale hue of their tired flesh and cast hunched shadows on the dugout wall. Hardy lay hemmed in by his fellow wounded. Shrouded in a rough blanket, he was succumbing to the morphine in his system and becoming lost in a maze of images.

"Sir?" Adams again offered a cigarette. This time Hardy opened his mouth. Adams nodded to himself, as Hardy's hand automatically came up and took hold of the rumpled length of off-white paper. Hardy was vaguely aware of Adams watching him. Adams nodded, as if content that his officer was as fine as could be under the circumstances, and settled on the bench at the foot of the tier.

Hardy was oblivious to the measured progress of time. He groped with the fact that the cigarette was finished. Ash peppered his uniform. Adams reached over and pinched the dog-end, partly extinguishing it. It dropped from Hardy's limp hand, hissing for a moment as it brushed the side of the stretcher before its small light died for good on the clay floor.

The dugout filled up with men. Stretchers now went outside after their turn on the trestles. There had been no major push today, but still men died and others were wounded.

A red-headed soldier came in, hugging his pack. A blood-soaked dressing covered the right side of his face. Just another of the walking wounded. But, hang on: he was familiar to Hardy. The way the man moved, turned his head, and the harsh brittleness of his voice. The man addressed the medical officer as he approached. "Private Archie Hawkins, sir. Was out last night with a patrol. We ran into the Hun and our officer was killed. We scattered and I got this." His words came out in a clipped manner, as if he had to underscore each in his effort to impress the medical officer that he had every right to be here.

The medical officer nodded. He was not really listening; he'd heard the same tale told a thousand different ways. He pulled at the dressing. The bandage fell away from the man's features. A deep wound lanced the man's eyebrow and upper eyelid. Then three cuts, as if drawn by claws, scored below his eye, making his cheek look diced.

"Doesn't look like the eye is damaged. You'll need to go down the line to the main dressing station just to make sure, but I think you'll be back with your mates within a day or two." The medical officer quickly re-dressed the wound and waved him towards the benches.

"Not a Blighty, then?" Archie asked, disappointed, his hands tightening on his bag. It was plain he had seen his wound as a ticket out of this hell.

"Not a bloody cat in hell's chance, with that little scratch," one of the other walking wounded remarked. He moved up on the bench to allow the newcomer to sit.

"Not for me, either," Adams laughed.

"Yon bullet made a mess of that arm, Corporal. It's for us to decide, though I think you will get a trip to one of the large hospitals on the coast, at least," commented the orderly, trying to impress his charges with his superior knowledge as he gave the new arrival a mug of tea.

"Don't fancy the bloody French seaside at this time of year. Can you arrange for me to go to Paris instead?" Adams took off his tin hat and ran his fingers through his black hair.

The orderly opened his mouth to retort, thought better of it, and continued on his rounds.

"Don't you want to go fucking home?" Archie asked Adams.

"Yes, 'course I sodding well do," Adams said and glanced round at Captain Hardy. "Both going to make it home, aren't we, sir?"

Hand of Glory

"If you say so, Adams," Hardy replied. His mind drifted for a moment into reality, before shifting back into its haze of dulled pain.

"Your officer?" The phrase was accusing, as if the man did not like the friendship he saw between the two.

"Aye, got caught in bloody no man's land. Was hung on the shitting wire in a shell-hole for more than a day. He was nearly done for; the cold had got to him something rotten. It's left him a bit nervous. Saying which,"–Adams peered at the regimental and company badges on the man by his side. The twisted knot of the county was bright and clear, the words *"East Staffs"* curving above–"you said 'patrol.' Think we saw your lieutenant bobbing about in that shit-filled shell-hole we pulled the captain out of."

"Anything's fucking possible," the man replied and stared hard at Hardy.

It was the voice. This Hawkins... was he the murderer on the lip of the crater? All circles. All tied together in this purgatory. Hardy felt a burst of insane laughter seek to tumble past his lips, but it got lost in the shallows, as the waves of morphine increased their grip. Instead, the laugh just came out as a harsh rattle.

"You alright, sir?" Adams stood, handing his mug of tea to Archie as he made to move to Hardy's side.

"Going round in circles," Hardy replied.

"Aye, sir," Adams said and sat again, reclaiming his mug of tea. His eyes sought out one of the orderlies.

The man came towards Adams, answering the unspoken summons. "You alright?"

"Aye, just the captain–he's a bit off."

The orderly moved past Adams and peered into Hardy's face. "It's the morphine. He'll drop off soon, hopefully."

Susan Boulton

Drop off. The words rattled in Hardy's head, becoming a machine gun, spitting out a haze of linked words and ideas.

*****

Snooze.
Sleep like a top.
Drive the pigs to market.
Have a kip.
Doss down.
Sleep, perchance not to dream.

Hardy did not know if he said the words aloud, or if they merely echoed in his thoughts. He was adrift on the wings of the drug, floating deep into the returning hallucination that had begun to haunt him. This time the vision was sharper. He heard the thump of an explosion. Felt the vibration under his feet, the earth shifting. A latticework of tree branches forming a gothic window of wood was in front of him, framing a scene from Dante's Inferno. Through the roar he heard a voice calling his name. A figure, its arms outstretched, was silhouetted against the flames. He felt a surge of elation and of victory. Then everything was turning upside down. The pain of his wounds came back. His eyes opened with a snap. The images that had filled his head were gone, leaving only a lingering sense of once being there, as if it were a waking dream, not wanted or welcomed.

The raw heaven exposed above his head.
Flashes of explosions.
The air stank of cordite, blood and mud.

Hardy was lying with his injured left leg twisted and trapped under him. It was caught in the remains of the stretcher on which he lay. On his chest lay the remains of one of his fellow occupants from the motor ambulance. A half head, the top and

Hand of Glory

back gone, with the lips pulled back. The teeth a brittle white, grinning in the illumination of the gun flashes all around.

How had he got here? Of course, they were sending him back down the line. Silly, really—he was as good as dead. He tried to move and free his left leg, but only succeeded in inching himself higher on the floor of the shattered vehicle. The half head on his chest jiggled, then rolled off and tumbled through the blasted-open rear doors of the vehicle, the lips still laughing at the world. Hardy's gaze followed the gory remains and was drawn to the unfolding scene outside his shattered refuge.

The enemy's barrage was creeping back towards no man's land, smashing at the communication trenches and support positions, then the zigzag maze of front line trenches. The sky was alive with flashes of light. Against the backdrop figures moved; they were searching the torn-apart convoy for survivors. Hardy could feel the throb of his pulse in his trapped leg. He decided to try to move again, but the pain sent him tottering to the edge of unconsciousness. A shadow fell across him. Fingers pulled at the buttons of his jacket, slipping into his pockets and removing the contents. The clink of two small coins as they fell—one on top of another, onto his stomach—brought his eyes and mind into focus. Archie Hawkins was standing over him. He had removed the dressing from his face. The scars round his eye glinted, wet with fresh blood.

Archie was roughly stuffing the contents of Hardy's wallet into his pack. The gold chain of a previously purloined pocket watch dangled against the pack's buckle, chiming a lament. He flung the wallet away, then bent again, his right hand reaching out for Hardy's left one. Hardy again tried to scrabble clear of the entangling stretcher. His heart beat faster. Archie was a thief, a corpse crow. He picked the dead clean, taking anything valuable and scattering their personal belongings, the thievery leaving nothing to identify them.

Susan Boulton

"You bloody bastard!" Hardy's left hand struck out at Archie's, but the blow had no power behind it. Hardy had no more strength than that of a small child. He struggled. He had to; he sensed that this was important. Something deep inside him did not want to be nameless, forgotten, left unknown, like so many in this sea of mud and blood.

Archie hissed between his teeth as his left hand reached behind his back for his bayonet, suspended on his Mills webbing. It was plain his intention was to take more than a wallet or watch.

The villain's fingers never touched Hardy. Corporal Adams's fist slammed into Archie's right cheek, splitting the wounds above and below his eye wide open. Archie staggered sideways with the force of the blow, into the broken door of the ambulance, feet scrabbling to keep himself upright. He bellowed and pushed himself forward, drawing his bayonet. Adams dived in low, rugby tackling Archie, his shoulder punching hard into Archie's stomach. Adams's good arm wrapped round Archie's middle, his fingers grasping the man's webbing, using his weight and the force of his attack to drag Archie to the mired ground.

Hardy forced himself up, his hands reaching out. He grasped the slats that had held the stretcher above him and heaved. Pain tore through his body. The shapes of the two men before him blended into one as they rolled on the ground. An arm broke free of the entwined ball of struggling bodies, then vanished into it again. Fingers reached out to gouge. A leg whipped out, the boot-clad foot fighting for purchase on the slimy ground. A rumble cut the air. The last dying gasp of the enemy guns. One flash, two. The glint of a bayonet held high in the pale moonlight. A bellow, swiftly followed by a scream, lanced the air. The two forms parted, one rising from the ground and shaking, doglike. The man's breath hissed through

Hand of Glory

his clenched teeth. The blood-coated bayonet in his hand came forward.

"I will have your watch now," Archie said, then bellowed in pain and began to double up, knees bending. Adams's body lay in a half-moon shape and his right boot was in Archie's groin, while with his good left arm he was hanging onto Archie's right leg like a Jack Russell terrier.

"Fucking hell, damn you!" Archie's voice rattled with pain. He sliced down with his bayonet, cutting at Adams's leg and hand. His heavy pack swung to and fro, the strap slipping down his arm and fouling the hilt of his bayonet. Archie swore and wrenched it back onto his shoulder. Adams took advantage of Hawkins's fumble and heaved himself half to his feet, trying to get his good hand round the hilt of the bayonet.

Hardy found his voice, "Let the sodding bastard go, George! It's not worth it!" He could feel tears coursing down his face. He managed to get himself sitting upright, then forward, his left leg bent back at an impossible angle. His hands were outstretched, trying to reach Archie to stop the long knife going down again into his friend's flesh.

A woman's voice carried across the hellish scene. "Orderlies! Here, now! I have wounded!" The ghostly figure of a nursing sister, a volunteer VAD with a lantern in her hand, appeared out of the dark. Archie stopped moving, frozen in the harsh, brittle beam of light. He slashed down with the knife one more time, shook off Adams's slack fingers and fled into the darkness.

Hardy tried to speak, but could not. He just stared at the young woman as, undaunted by what lay around her, she came forward and knelt in the mud alongside Corporal Adams. She carefully placed the lantern down by the man's head and took his bloody hand in hers. Other shapes appeared out of the darkness, illuminated by a maze of bobbing lights. Voices spoke words of comfort, mumbled the odd curse, even laughed, as the shapes of their owners mingled with the wreckage that had been the convoy.

"Thief. Tried to stop him, miss. His name... Hawkins... He's a carrot-top, can't miss him..." Adams whispered as he looked up at the young woman holding his hand.

"I understand," she replied. The nurse looked up at an orderly who had appeared by her side.

"Don't worry, mate, we'll tell the redcaps. They'll have him rolled up by tomorrow teatime." The orderly put the stretcher he was carrying on the ground and made to lift Adams onto it. The sister shook her head. The orderly replied with a nod of his own and glanced round. He peered hard in Hardy's direction, then bent down and picked up the sister's lantern. "Someone in there?"

"Yes, here! How is George, I mean, Corporal Adams? How is he?" Hardy asked urgently.

The silver beam of the light illuminated the devastated insides of the vehicle. The orderly whistled through his teeth at the sight. He reached down and pulled an abandoned blanket over the remains of one of Hardy's former travelling companions, then picked up a pay book discarded by Archie during his search of the corpse's pockets and put it on top of the blanket. He inched further into the debris and turned his attention to Hardy.

As the man spoke, his voice was gentle, as if comforting a child. "Don't you fret, sir, soon have you out of here. They won't be sending any more over tonight. We'll get you down the road to the main dressing station. Not far, just round the bend. We have hot water and pretty nursing sisters to ogle at, when the matron's not looking." The man spoke in a condescending, almost superior "mother knows best" tone as he hooked the lantern above Hardy and set about clearing the debris.

Hand of Glory

"Adams?" Hardy asked again as the orderly cleared his injured left leg and began to run his hands down it, checking the limb.

"Don't you worry. Sister Reed will sit with him awhile. Let's get you out of here first." At any other time Hardy would have railed against being smothered in such institutional cotton wool; now all he did was shut his eyes tight against the vision of Adams dying on the ground before him. His breath hitched, and a sob escaped his lips.

The orderly waved to one of his fellows who had appeared at the broken door of the vehicle. Together they lifted Hardy free and placed him on the stretcher next to Adams.

The dying man turned his head, as if he sensed his commanding officer and friend was there. A smile tugged at his mud-caked lips. "Got a Blighty, sir."

"Yes, Adams, a Blighty," Hardy answered, the words burning his gullet.

"Both going home, then, sir?" Adams coughed, his hand tightening on the nursing sister's.

"Yes, both going home," Hardy repeated, as the two orderlies lifted his stretcher and bore him away.

*****

Hustle and bustle.
Faces peering into his.
Voices addressing him.
Other voices talking about him.
The pain of dressings removed by small hands.
Uniform cut and dragged off by larger ones.
The prick of a needle in his arm.

All blurred together. Nothing was exactly clear to Captain Giles Hardy except for the flapping of the tent above his head. It rose and fell, as if it were the chest of an immense beast which ate men and vomited out their remains though various doors.

Hardy was not aware that time was running out for him. Thirty-six hours was the window. If treated in that expanse of hours, gas gangrene and sepsis had a high chance of being avoided. Hardy was on the fringe of this golden time. The doctors knew it, the orderlies and nurses knew it, and thus they hurried for him, for all those that came in through the mouth of the tent monster.

The tent was filling up fast. The young doctor, face old-man haggard, glanced at the tags accompanying the stripped wounded. "Pre-op, evacuation train, make comfortable." His words sorted the contents of the stretchers. No reply came from the men so dismissed, all too tired to complain, badly in shock and exhausted by their journey back from hell.

The snap of a clean white sheet over his body brought Hardy's eyes down from the expanding lungs of the tent overhead. "Pre-op, that leg, bullet wound lower thigh. Broken tib and fib." The words consigned him through one opening into another tent. He plunged into blackness.

Grit in his eyes.
Hard to breathe.
Hand in his.
Gladness at the touch.
Blood coating the join of two palms.
Adams's voice: "Don't you worry, sir, things'll be fine."

Fine? Things could never be that—Adams was dead, as was he... No? Yes? He wasn't sure. Hardy's mouth was dry. He felt sick. The tent monster was again breathing above his head. His whole body from his waist down felt damp, clammy, swaddled in soaked fabric, and this, covered with another layer, crackled like oilcloth as he tried to move.

Hand of Glory

A woman's voice spoke out of the blurred surroundings. "Easy, Captain, gently now. I know it's cold, but we have to do it. Nearly done, then Orderly Hammond will shave you. You'd like that, wouldn't you?" Hardy could feel hands peeling back the outer cloth, touching the inner, damp ones. Then the pain began, rushing through his legs and into the pit of his stomach. He began to shake. Tears came unbidden to his eyes.

A pair of larger hands gripped his shoulders. "Now, then, sir, I know it's bad, but Sister needs to change your dressings to keep the wounds clean. We're nearly done. Then a cup of tea, a shave, and maybe a haircut, eh?" The chill round his legs got worse. The stench of the solution rose. Chlorate of lime.

Hardy's eyesight cleared, his tears washing away the grit. A soft cloth wiped his face. He looked at the woman holding the cloth, then down his body. His lower half was wrapped in a mackintosh-type fabric. His left leg was elevated in a frame, also wrapped. His leg... was it still there? Was it important if it was or not?

"I'm sorry, Captain. It's a horrible thing, this dressing with Dakin's solution, but it's over now for a few hours. You rest. I'll see if the doctor will allow you some more morphine." The nurse placed the fabric in her hand down on a trolley by her side and straightened the edge of his pillow. She gave Hardy a sad, soft smile. Her green eyes crinkled at the corners. She patted his arm and turned her back, pushing her trolley of bottles, dressings, and large dressing syringes in front of her.

Orderly Hammond waited until the nurse had moved away before he came to the side of Hardy's bed, a mug of steaming tea in his hand. "Got a light touch, Sister Reed has. Between us we give our gentlemen the best care." Orderly Hammond, Hardy had noticed, was obviously the gregarious type, and deemed it his duty to keep the patients informed of the day-to-day events in their small, white-walled world. Hardy tried to smile and say thank you. It seemed correct to do so, but the words did not come, nor did the smile. Hardy felt annoyed at himself. Good manners cost nothing. Hammond acted as if they had been said nonetheless and held the tea to Hardy's lips.

Hammond continued to talk as he shaved and washed his charge, helping Hardy even with a bed bottle. "Now, as I said, Captain Hardy, here in Tent Seven you have, I believe, three of the best VAD nursing sisters about. Sisters Reed, Thomas and Marshall. Then there is myself—I'm Orderly Hammond, as you know—and my counterpart is Orderly Clark." Hammond pointed to sisters Reed and Thomas, and then touched himself on the chest as he said his name. The other nurse and orderly he had named were obviously off duty. "We take good care of our gentlemen; soon have them off to the coast, then Blighty. You'll be on your way soon, sir, once we're sure of that leg of yours." The man's strange conversation kept pace with the throbbing in Hardy's wounds. His eyelids flickered. "That's it, sir. You have a little kip."

*****

Days merged into nights, marked by the four-hourly changing of his dressings. Cold cups of tea abandoned on the stand by his bed. Faces close to his. Sometimes he recognised them. Fellow officers. The men under his command. The living and the dead. The orderlies and nurses asking questions he struggled to answer. Hardy wandered strange mental roads marked out by injections of morphine.

Laughter, the sun on his face.
Good company and an arm in his.
Contentment, feeling grateful for his lot.
A job well done, home all of them, not forgotten or lost.

Other times the pain took him down darker avenues: the whine and thud of shells, far away, then closer. The war was not far away.

Hand of Glory

Shells
Overhead.
Crashing down.
Flames.
The smell of gas.
Mud between his fingers, then the slender digits of another.
Anger for those gone, their memory trapped in mud, beyond the reach of those who should know.

*****

"Now, then, sir."

Adams? It couldn't be. Hardy forced his sticky eyes open. The weak, late autumn sun played through a crack in the thick canvas door of the tent, dappling the wooden floorboards. It traced the outline of the man who stood at the bottom of Hardy's bed.

It was Adams. Jacket off, hooked on the index finger of his left hand, slung over his shoulder. His right thumb was tucked in his braces and he had his soft cap on. The slightly greying edges of his dark sideburns were picked out by the harsh daylight. The corporal stood there with a soft smile on his face. No strain of the months in the mud showed in the lines round his eyes.

"Adams... George..." He scrambled to understand what he was seeing. Was this a result of being *a bit nervous*, the shell shock breaking down the barriers between real and imagined worlds?

"Aye, sir. Just thought I'd come and see how you're doing, make sure you're alright for the trip home to Blighty."

"Not going to make it home, George."

Adams frowned. "Don't be daft, sir, you will..." The man's tone changed, becoming concerned. "You have to, for all of us."

"Why?" The question tumbled into the air between them.

"Because."

"Because what?" Hardy snapped, suddenly annoyed. Adams did not answer, just looked sideways at the figure that had joined him at the foot of the bed. Sister Reed, her VAD nursing uniform plain and unflattering, nothing like the high fashion she would have worn before she volunteered to nurse the mangled men who tumbled endlessly off the battlefield. Yet Adams acknowledged her as if she were walking in the park in her Sunday best; he lifted his right hand up and touched the peak of his cap, saluting her.

She smiled, as if in acknowledgement, then turned her attention to Hardy. "Well, that's better."

"What's better?" Hardy snapped again. The sun had suddenly increased its brightness, making Adams's figure a shimmering silhouette.

"You, being annoyed with us."

Hardy's full attention was now on the VAD nurse. "And that's better than...?" He eased himself up on his elbows, glaring at the young woman. Her manner made him feel like a small boy who had refused to hold his nanny's hand in the park. Lank strands of his light brown hair fell in front of his face. He blew at them angrily.

"Being lost." As she spoke, her eyes flickered sideways to the empty space where Adams had been. At least, where Hardy had thought he'd been. Adams was dead. Gone. He could not have been there. *Shell shock. Tricks. Purgatory. Trapped between. Or was he?* "Lost" Sister Reed had said. What had she meant? Did she know he was as good as dead? Was she dead, too? His elbows gave way and he slumped down onto the bed, the air sighing out of his pillows.

"Am I lost?" Hardy asked, wanting an answer, yet dreading it. He could just hear her telling him such thoughts were stuff and nonsense.

Hand of Glory

Instead, Sister Reed left the foot of the bed and came to his side, her hand touching his wrist. "Do you think you are?" she asked softly, then added, "Who was he, the man whose name you just said?"

"Corporal Adams, George." The answer was out before Hardy could stop it. It had been Adams. She had acknowledged him, surely? No, she had just glanced that way for some reason. Adams was dead. Confusion began to bubble in Hardy's mind. "He was my friend. I, we..." Her hand squeezed his arm gently. "He didn't have to sign up in 1914. He was well over thirty, for God's sake. Had a family. Said it wasn't fair us younger chaps having all the fun. But that wasn't it. He wanted to watch out for us, protect us. The way he had when we were younger. He saved my life. I let them down. Let him down. They all looked to me, and I made a mess of it. Got caught on the wire... All gone. Lost. I should be with them, abandoned in no man's land. I... he... my friend..."

The words rattled out, all Hardy's natural reserve—especially with regard to the opposite sex—swept away by the swirl of emotions flooding through his mind. The phrases were harsh, brutal and lacerating. He deserved it, all this. His mistakes had killed them all. He would be at the bottom of the shell-hole but for Adams, a man he had known, befriended and loved. And Adams, too, he had killed. All for a damn watch. It had not been worth it. The officer on the lip of the crater killed by one of his own men, as he, Captain Giles Hardy, A Company, 2nd Battalion, East Staffordshire Regiment, deserved to be: dead on the wire. He did not deserve to be alive. Yet he was, and he had to live with that fact somehow, as Adams had said, because he was going home when so many were not. How could he learn to be alive and live with that fact?

Hardy's right hand came up, brushing at the tears on his face. He looked up at Sister Reed, concerned how she would react to such an unmanly admission of weakness. Her green eyes were glistening. She sniffed and squeezed his arm again. "It's the smell of the Dakin's solution." Her statement, so matter of fact, yet full of understanding.

"Yes it is," Hardy replied, suddenly feeling very tired.

"Anything up?" Orderly Hammond asked as he entered the tent and looked over the half-moon of beds holding his charges.

"No, just Captain Hardy is feeling a bit better today. He's complaining about the smell," Sister Reed said over her shoulder.

"Good on you, sir. Might be that you'll fancy some apple pie come lunch time," Hammond said, laying his left index finger against his nose like a conspirator.

"With custard?" Sister Reed asked, a note of surprise in her voice.

"Wouldn't be apple pie without," Hammond replied, and began readying the trolley of dressings.

Sister Reed gave Hardy's arm one more squeeze, and gave him a small smile as she answered the orderly, "I don't know how you do it, Orderly Hammond–apple pie and custard, indeed."

"Now here's me thinking the same thing about you, Sister." Hammond gave an overlarge wink at Hardy, as he pushed the trolley in his direction.

"I'll try to be as quick as I can. I know you are very tired now." Sister Reed smiled down at him and released her hold on his arm. She then turned to the bowl of water Hammond was holding, making ready to attack the dressings coating Hardy's body.

*****

Until that moment, Hardy had only felt tired. Now he was exhausted. The simplest task had him gasping for breath. Frustration at his plight replaced bland acceptance. Yet the fragmented memory–of the hand in his, autumn leaves, and

Hand of Glory

flames—lingered. It became part of his new existence, as did the dressing of his wounds.

*****

Other wounded arrived and departed, dispatched to the larger hospitals on the French coast or back to Blighty. Yet Hardy remained. Twice a day doctors peered at his leg in its cradle and mumbled at the sisters, ordering this and that. The gas blisters on his flesh began to heal. The gashes from the barbed wire became red-lipped scars. Even the bullet wound in his thigh responded well to treatment. However, the broken leg worried them. It did not yet worry Hardy. He was still struggling to accept that he was alive, not gone, not stuck in his mental purgatory, the hell where he, in the small hours, still wondered if he deserved to be. Maybe if the leg had been lost it would have been something towards a down payment for his release, a balm to ease the guilt.

The short day was dying. A three-day-old newspaper, barely read, lay on Hardy's chest. The harsh acetylene lamps had been lit, and the black stove in the heart of the round tent glowed red. Hammond was dishing out the latest instalment of the seemingly never-ending flow of tea. Sister Marshal was instructing a new VAD nurse in her duties with regard to applying the dressings that constantly needed changing. Hardy could just see the tip of the woman's toe from under her ankle-length dress; it was tapping in rhythm with her words.

And Sister Reed? He was sure she should still be on duty. Hardy looked round, trying to find her among the shadows clinging to the edges of the tent. There. She stood by the bed of a young soldier whose arm-stump she had re-dressed earlier. The thick pus from the wound had coated her hands as she'd washed the torn flesh. No rubber gloves to spare. Yet she had not flinched. Her total concentration had been on caring for the young man. Hardy wondered at this brand of courage: hers, the other nurses, even Hammond's. The man was in his forties, thin, stoop-shouldered, and with the flattest feet in all England, he would have you believe, yet he was tireless in his care for others.

Nurse Reed's grip on the young man's hand was firm, her reddened knuckles whitening slightly as he returned the pressure, his breathing laboured, eyes focused on something no one else could see.

Hammond went to her side. "You be needing a chair, Sister?" She shook her head. He nodded in reply to her unspoken command and quickly left the tent.

The young man's breathing slowed and his eyes half closed. The sister's grip tightened and a soft smile came to her lips. Hardy felt his own breath hitch in his chest. The youth was dying. Not screaming or pleading, just fading away, his agony perhaps deadened by morphine.

A doctor hurried into the tent, his boots clattering on the scrubbed wood floor. Sister Marshall and the new VAD nurse were positioning a small screen round the bed. It was only shoulder height; Hardy could plainly see the doctor's resigned face, and the nun-like wimple that covered Sister Reed's brown hair. What purpose the screen? All here had seen death before. Messy. Violent. Bodies shattered beyond recognition in the blink of an eye. Or slow and lingering despite all efforts to prevent it, like the boy on the bed. Was the screen a token nod to old ideas of dignity? Perhaps. Who could say?

The doctor took his leave as briskly as he had arrived. Hammond and the new VAD nurse served the evening meal. Hardy's eyes continued to glance now and then at the white fabric that marked Sister Reed. He was not the only one. Each man in the tent did the same, exchanging glances with his fellows, their thoughts written on their faces.

Hand of Glory

The lad's going.
It could be me next.
Sister Reed's holding his hand.
Will she hold mine the same?

Hammond began his evening rituals of turning down the lamps and banking the stove for the night, before making the final cup of tea for his charges. Sister Reed's head vanished for a moment. She must have bent down. The screen rattled as she moved it to step out. Hammond, his chores abandoned, came to her side. His hand squeezed her shoulder for a moment. She smiled in thanks and glanced round the tent, then she left, the heels of her shoes tapping out a sad rhythm.

Hardy watched Hammond move behind the barrier that separated the dead from those still alive. Not much time passed before both body and screen were gone and another soldier, expelled torn and bloody from the battlefield, lay on the bed.

*****

Hardy woke to the distant pounding of artillery. He listened for a moment. They were British guns. A push was on in this sector. More men would soon be dancing among the wire.

Lamps were turned up. Figures hurried into the tent from the darkness outside. The beds quickly emptied. Men were wrapped in blankets and placed on stretchers. The bundles of their few personal possessions were placed by their feet, or where their feet should have been. A soldier stood in the doorway, a clipboard in hand. As each man on a stretcher passed him he ticked the paper before him, making sure each patient was accounted for.

Hardy felt the stretcher give a little under his weight as it lifted. The two men transporting him hurried down the duckboards between the rows of tents. He had not had time to say goodbye to those who had cared for him these last few days.

How many days? Hardy tried to count them as his stretcher slid into an ambulance. As the vehicle moved off he still had no idea. It could have been two days or twenty. All had blended together, indistinct from one another... except for the day he had seen Adams.

The journey in the ambulance was short. Before dawn Hardy was lying on board a hospital train bound for one of the big hospitals on the coast. He smelled the smoke from the engine wafting into the open door, heard the slam of doors and a guard's whistle. So familiar, yet at the same time painful. A vision of an event from his old life warped and twisted by the war.

"Want a cigarette, old boy?" A man was looking down at him. He was leaning over the edge of the bunk above Hardy. Hardy was lying on the middle tier of three bunks on the right side of the train, his feet towards the engine.

"The sisters might object," Hardy replied, looking up at the bewhiskered countenance of the man in the bunk above.

"Nonsense, they wouldn't deprive a man of one of life's little pleasures, I'm sure," the man answered. His hand, a lighted cigarette in it, reached down towards Hardy.

Hardy took the cigarette and inhaled, feeling the smoke curl round his tongue and drift into his lungs. He exhaled slowly, watching the fine, off-white plume nestle against the bunk above.

The man chuckled. "Seems we're off to the seaside. Where ladies in large blooming hats promenade, or is that Frog generals?"

"I really don't know," Hardy replied, somewhat confused, as he felt the train jolt and shudder, then lurch forward.

"Soon see, eh?" the man said, giving a broad wink at the nursing sister approaching down the centre of the train.

Chapter Three

"Fucking Officer's tart," Archie rasped as he hobbled away into the dark. The maze of bobbing lights surrounding the convoy faded away. The pit of his stomach was on fire; he felt his balls had been driven up into his chest. *Damn that bum-bent-over-for-officers corporal.* Archie stumbled into a crude cemetery to the west of the main dressing station. He knocked against a wooden cross, dislodging the tin helmet hooked onto the top. The helm tumbled off, hitting the sodden earth with a dull squelch. He fell to his knees on the damp earth mound, his right hand resting on the crooked arm of the cross.

He fumbled in his tunic pocket, pulling out a crumpled packet of cigarettes. Archie lit one and drew in the smoke, feeling it settle his nerves. *Nearly got rolled up there. Fucking tart's fault.* He would have silenced that tosser of an officer and been out of there with no one the wiser. The sod had seen him top Tennant. He had cottoned onto him at the dressing station. It had been his plan to get tagged as having a Blighty and be shipped home, and then vanish. Now he had to fall back on the remains of Jim's plan.

"*It will work, Arch,*" Jim said.

The familiar voice in his head told him everything would be alright. It had done so a dozen times since he had crawled out of no man's land. But Archie still had doubts.

He stubbed the cigarette out on the arm of the wooden cross and glanced around, trying to get his bearings. The faint noise of vehicles came from the east. That would be the main dressing station in this sector. He was to the right of it, so he needed to keep going the way he was. Across another road that fed the front line, then another couple of miles southwest and he would be safe. The road would be the worse if the Hun decided to shell it. There were bound to be men moving up before dawn. He would just have to chance it.

Archie got to his feet. Then he stopped, sensing something–or someone–behind him. His hand went to his bayonet as he looked over his shoulder, eyes straining in the night to pick out whoever it was. Nothing. He shrugged his shoulders and began to move on.

Jim had found the bolthole. He'd had the knack with the Frog lingo and had found out where a chap could fence his stuff and maybe disappear. Jim'd had it all worked out with the Frogs, but then that fucking lieutenant had stuck his oar in and Jim had copped it in the communication trench.

The road was empty except for the remains of previous travellers. Burned out vehicles, carts, and the bloated carcasses of horses and men loomed out of the night. The terrain under his boots changed. Stone cobbles, mud-slick, making his gait awkward and awaking the dull, lingering pain in his groin. He stopped, glancing round: he must be close to the farm by now. Yes, there it was. Fingers of brick and beams lanced the faint light of dawn. A cock crowed from the shattered heart of what had been a barn. Archie pulled out the officer's revolver he'd snagged back at the shattered convoy and entered the rubble that once had been a farmhouse.

"Hurry up. Be dawn soon."

"I bloody well know and, besides, you're dead, Jim," Archie said under his breath, half-heartedly trying to deny the voice he

Hand of Glory

heard. It no longer lurked in the shadows of his thoughts; it trickled through his waking mind, advising and guiding, a constant presence. It was Jim: it was taking care of him.

Down into the cellar he went. The stairs stank of piss, reminding Archie of the yard of the back-to-back house he and Jim had lived in as children. Daylight crept down after him and across the dank floor, touching the door to the right. Archie banged on the rotting wood with the butt of the revolver. The dull sound echoed round the shadowy hole. He banged again, a short rhythm. Three short and two long. *Had the Frogs moved on?* They were not from round here. From further south, Jim had said. They worked up and down the line. Here today, gone tomorrow. Had the redcaps got wind of the place and rolled them up?

He started to swear, then stopped at the sound of a bolt being drawn. The door opened a chink. His fingers tightened on the revolver. He began to sweat. Maybe he should've kept going? No, the redcaps would've got him for sure. It was not just thieving now; he'd topped that tart of a corporal and been seen doing it. They would have him walking to the wall at dawn.

The barrel of a rifle poked through the gap.

"It's me, Archie, Jim's brother. You remember?" The rifle barrel came out further. "Fucking hell, you've done well out of us, look..." He thumped his pack with his other hand. The door opened a bit more. He could see the shape of the person holding the gun. It was not the big chap he'd seen when he'd last been here; it was feminine. Not the madam—she was as broad as a bandstand; must be the daughter. "Look, Mademoiselle, don't mean you any harm." Archie lowered the gun and forced himself to smile. "Me, Archie, you, fence." He said the words slowly, over-mouthing each one.

The girl spoke fast in her own language to someone in the room, never taking her eyes, or the rifle, off him. The rasping voice of Madam answered; from her tone, Archie gauged she was both curious and concerned. The girl spoke again, blowing at the wisp of black hair that dangled in front of her eyes. Madam cursed. The girl winced. Archie did not know exactly what the madam had said, but he knew enough to know it was not very ladylike.

He began to think he would have to force his way in when the girl said, "You swear by our saint, no harm." Her English was heavily accented. "Our saint, St Nicholas."

"Oh, aye, bloody him," Archie replied, not getting at all what she was on about, but wanting to get into Madam's little hidey-hole as soon as possible. The light pouring down the stairs had widened its beam. It was past dawn. The redcaps would be out in force. He could almost feel them breathing down his neck. He glanced for a second back up the stairs, again sensing someone or something there. A shadow flickered and then vanished.

"Nowt there," Jim dismissed Archie's fears.

How the hell did he know? Jim couldn't see anything anymore.

"Put gun away," the girl said, waving the rifle.

"Right," Archie said, not sure he should.

"Do it!"

"You as well."

The girl nodded and lowered her weapon; Archie did the same, tucking his into his belt. She opened the door, and with a tilt of her head indicated for him to come in. Archie felt a wave of relief at getting this far and entered the den. The light was dim and the air stale. Archie could feel the occupants of the large room watching his every movement.

The sound of a table dragged across the floor behind him made him glance back. The girl was there, handing the rifle to a large, pasty chap who sat down on the table now blocking the door. Archie gulped; the rifle in the man's hands was casually aimed at his back. "Fuck!"

"*Oui. Allez, viens,*" the girl said. She came to Archie's side, her slender hand motioning for him to move deeper into the rank room.

Sitting at a small table close to a pot-bellied stove, the girl's mother was wrapped in a large black shawl, the fringes of which matched the red tablecloth. Her ample rear spilled over the sides of her stool. Archie saw her piggy eyes narrow, then widen, as they caught sight of his overstuffed pack. Her right hand placed an over-large playing card on the table. She looked at it, then at Archie, a smile cracking her rouged face. She indicated for him to sit opposite her.

Archie sat down, his pack hugged to his chest with one hand, the other on the pistol in his belt. The girl poured wine from a dirty green bottle into an equally dirty pair of glasses. Madam took one glass and swilled the wine round. She spoke to the girl, the words rasping in her throat, and then waited for the girl to translate.

"My mother doesn't trust you. You are not Jim."

"Jim's dead. I want the deal she worked out with Jim just for me now. Disappear, and not into some hole with me boots taken. More than enough in here to cover her expenses, and, besides, I got a way of making more if she's interested." *Bloody Frogs, don't know when they're onto a good thing.* He wished he were sitting before a good old-fashioned, dishonest, Black Country fence, not some card-reading French madam. A chap back home would jump at the chance of getting a cut on the profit from what was at the very bottom of the pack.

The madam took a mouthful of the wine and smacked her lips. She picked the large card up off the table, flicked it under Archie's nose as she spoke and then slammed it down on the table. The girl's eyes widened at her mother's words.

"My mother says you are the King of Cups." The girl stopped, searching for her next words. "Upside down—dishonest, a thief, you care only for yourself. She not trust you."

Archie gave a sharp laugh, his face jutting forward. The scars round his right eye split open and blood trickled down his cheek. "Aye, am a bloody thief. Dishonest, course I fucking well am. Care only for me own, as do you, which is the way it should be." He winked at the girl. She was changing his words into Frog. Best not rub her up the wrong way too much. "As for trust, well, if there's profit in a partnership, who needs it?" Archie shifted in his seat. Damn Frogs were annoying him more and more. He had half a mind to go, chance it going further back and find a Belgian fence in Ypres. He looked back at the chap on the table by the door. Big, yes, but a barrel of lard, not so quick on his pins, and the girl was in grabbing range. The mother was all bluster: she would let him go if a gun was under her daughter's nose. Or would she?

The voice of Mademoiselle telling her mother what he had said brought his gaze and attention back to the woman opposite him. She grinned and nodded her head; her fingers picked up the card and placed it back with its fellows. She then made her intentions plain by waving her arms and spluttering a stream of words: she wanted to see what was in Archie's pack.

He had her interest, but he also knew he had to be careful. He slowly undid the pack's straps and began to pull out his booty. As he placed the items down, he sorted them out neatly. Rings, cigarette cases—a number of them silver with matching, inlaid Vesta matchboxes. Penknives, watches—some, fobs with chains, others, the new wrist type, the preserve of officers, as were the silver tops of five walking canes. Silver medals of various saints on chains, along with lockets of silver and gold containing cut-down pictures of loved ones and snippets of hair. Coins and notes: French, Belgian and English.

Hand of Glory

"*Quel trésor!*" the Madam said softly.

Archie dug out the last few coins from under the cloth-wrapped prize that lay at the bottom of his pack. "More than enough?"

The madam picked up one of the lockets, peering at it closely, and then addressed Archie. Her daughter cleared her throat and translated her mother's words. "Yes, more than enough. I will not cheat you."

"Really?"

"No!" the mademoiselle protested before her mother, adding, "You mentioned a way of getting more–how? You are not in the trenches now; you are not going back if you want the deal my mother did with Jim."

"Fucking right I'm not going back. As for getting more, if–" Archie stopped, and picked up the untouched glass of wine before him, taking a small sip. He didn't like the stuff. It was worse than drinking vinegar. Give him a decent pint of beer any day. He suppressed a shudder at the taste and gave the madam a harsh smile as he put the glass down. He took his cigarettes out and lit one, blowing smoke rings towards the madam, and then leaned his arm on the edge of the table. The ash fell from the cigarette, peppering the black cloth.

"If...?" Mademoiselle repeated.

"If you get me what I need to finish a small job I have to do, and find *us*," Archie stressed the word, "some good places to pick over. Officers' quarters, battalion headquarters, posh Belgian and French houses, that sort of thing."

"*Merde!*" Madam swore, then forcefully continued, leaving Archie in no doubt she thought him a bloody fool. But he knew he was not. He had a secret and knew what to do with it.

"Shut up, you fat cow! You know what a Hand of Glory is? The Hand that opens doors for you? Keeps folk out of your hair while you're robbing 'em blind? You're a thief, think you might.

Jim said you lot work more or less like we do. Well, I got me the makings of one in here. Hand of a hanged murderer. That's a hard thing to get hold of; you know it is. You lot, like us, don't fucking top murderers in public anymore, and jailors are bloody difficult to bribe. You get me the rest of the doings and we're in business."

"Well done, Arch. You hooked the old bat good and proper. Now we get started," Jim chuckled.

The madam's whole demeanour changed. Archie swore she'd understood him. She bent forwards as well; Archie could smell her sour breath and knew her eyes were on his pack. *"Main de Gloire?"*

"Aye, Hand of Glory."

"Show me," the madam said, her words even more heavily accented than her daughter's.

"So you fucking well understand me?" Archie asked. Damn bitch. He took another pull on the cigarette and dropped it to the floor, squashing it under his boot.

"I know enough to know you are lying."

"Not fucking lying." Archie looked at his pickings on the table. If he made to leave he would have to kiss them goodbye, at least; might not even get out in one piece.

Archie put his hand back into his pack and drew out the cloth-wrapped remains of Lieutenant Tennant. The length of torn khaki shirt was smeared with yellow mud off the battlefield. The layer cracked, fragments flaking off and peppering the table. The smell of it made Archie curse under his breath. *Never fucking well going back, never.* He would cut up all here and go down doing so, rather than go back into that shit-hole. He began to shake with anger as he unwrapped the hand of the lieutenant. As the fabric fell off the fingers he was not the only one swearing. Madam was as well; she wildly crossed herself.

Hand of Glory

"Look, the fingers are already like a claw," Mademoiselle Marie said. It was true. Each finger, and even the thumb, curled upwards towards the palm. He would have to do little forcing of the flesh when it came to fitting the wicks for the candles. Archie smiled as he remembered how the lieutenant had grabbed at his hands as he'd tightened the garrotte.

"So you have a hand. Can you make it? Can you use it?" Madam asked, though a soft smile on her face hinted that she might actually believe he could.

"You get me the saltpetre, salt, long peppers and a good, large earthenware pot, and I'll show you," Archie said, setting his trophy down among his ill-gotten gains.

"It will cost you, cash." Her hand waved over the pile of Belgian currency.

"I bloody suspected it would."

*****

It had been fourteen days since Archie had deserted, and five since he'd seen the sky. The rumble of guns that day had driven all of them outside. The threat of being buried alive had encouraged even Madam to heave her fat carcass up the steps. But it had been the German trenches that were being bombarded, so the mismatched group had quickly scuttled back into their shelter. Archie had claimed a spot by the west wall of the cellar as his. It was here, near his bedroll, that he hunkered down and checked the pot's contents.

The hand had been in there for nearly two weeks. During this time Archie's uniform had gone into the fire of the pot-bellied stove. He now wore a local labourer's gear and, grudgingly, a decrepit pair of French boots. When a red cap stopped a fella he suspected, he would look at the man's boots first. They were the one thing most deserters did not get rid of. Worn-in boots were comfortable: you did not give them up easily. Bloody foolish. Archie had kept some bits of his kit tucked into a haversack, which lay on top of his bedroll. The main item was his gas mask. He wasn't going to let that go, not this close to the trenches. Ditch it later. The revolver, too, was shoved in there, but his bayonet he kept in his belt. He did not trust the Frogs, and they certainly did not trust him. It'd been a funny old few days, but Archie was not laughing. The sooner he made a good killing with the Hand, the sooner he was on his way back to Blighty.

"Too true, Arch. Use them and lose them," Jim agreed.

"I have the wax and wicks," Marie said.

Archie looked up at the girl through the smoke of his cigarette. She was thin, big-eyed and dark-haired. Not like the lasses at home, that was for sure. She wiggled when she walked like the whores in Ypres. And, like many of the whores, she was sporting a black eye. Her mother had a hard hand; so, too, had her brother. "Good." Archie glanced past the girl to her mother, who sat, like she always did—a big, fat spider hunched over the table. "I need a large pan as well."

"On the stove." Marie gestured toward the source of the only heat in the cellar. Her foot tapped, dress lifting slightly so Archie could see the smallness of her ankle in her high-laced walking boot.

"Bloody expensive, them," he commented, as he gently lifted the dried remains of the young officer out of the pot. The hand had taken on a dark sheen. The skin had withered, shrunk tight to the bones. Archie had removed the hand regularly, squeezing it in a cloth, draining the blood and fluids out of it, just as he remembered his grandfather had said needed to be done. Then he had put it back in and covered it with warm ashes taken from the fire each night. It had now begun to take on the consistency of old, un-oiled leather.

Hand of Glory

"The bourgeoise, Madame Tour, gave them in payment for the séance. She was so pleased that her old husband came to speak to her about where his money was."

Archie had no idea what a séance was, or what the girl was on about, but he knew she was mocking the madam who had given her the boots. "You mean you wheedled them out of her. Get anything else?" Archie placed the hand on a piece of cloth he had put ready and wrapped it up carefully.

"Some ribbons and a good look at her valuables," Marie answered, laughing.

"So you were looking the fucking place over?" Clever girl– her mother was taking their loose partnership seriously.

"*Oui*. She has many things, and officers are often billeted with her; the house is large."

Archie nodded in reply, picked up the wrapped hand, wax, and lengths of wick, then walked to the table by the stove. Here he placed the items down, ignoring Madam's glare. He took out his bayonet and chopped up the wax, dropping it into the pot on the edge of the stove. The wax started to melt. Archie watched it carefully; he did not want to burn it.

Bound to the Hand as it is bound to me.

Serve the Hand as it serves me.

Give to the Hand what it desires; it in turn will give wealth to me.

As long as me and mine are true, protected and safe all shall be.

Jim chanted in the darkness deep in Archie's mind, repeating the words over and over as Archie unwrapped the hand and tied lengths of the wick to each digit. Each word vibrated in Archie's skull. His jaw ached; the muscles in his right cheek ticked and throbbed, beating time to the rhythm of the words that only he could hear. Carefully, he dipped the hand into the melted wax, coating it.

"Take your time with it. Allow each layer to air dry for a minute or so before dipping it again," Jim said, breaking off from his incantation for a moment.

After each immersion, Archie found it was harder to catch his breath. His muscles ached across his neck and shoulders, as if he were carrying a sixty-pound pack. The air around him smelled stale, as foul as a ten-foot-deep dugout, and it was changing colour to a musty yellow. Archie began to panic. Gas, it was mustard gas. He swore it.

"Easy, Arch–nothing there," Jim said, trying to soothe Archie's fear.

He was just in the cellar. Nothing was different. He couldn't shake the feeling of being lost in the sickly, billowing clouds–off-course, and watched. There was a figure in the clouds, walking towards him. The wax-coated hand slipped in his grasp. He scrambled to keep hold of it. Jim cursed him, *"No gas. No figure. Just the Hand and me. I will keep you safe if you and yours serve the Hand."*

"Serve the Hand," Archie repeated, not knowing if he said the words aloud. He tightened his grip and forced his shaking hands to continue. Slowly he worked on the hand until all the wax was gone, elongating the fingers until they resembled candles.

As Archie finished, the familiar voice faded away, leaving him shaking. A cold sweat lathered his back, even though he was standing by the pot-bellied stove. He coughed, rolling his shoulders to relieve them of the ache that lingered in his muscles, and placed the finished Hand of Glory down in front of the madam. He looked at her and asked, struggling to keep his voice level, "What do you think?"

"It looks like one." The madam leaned over the wizened remains. "Smells!" She pulled a face and heaved herself up from her chair.

Hand of Glory

"That it does. Smell a bloody lot more when the candles are burning," Archie laughed. A memory he was sure was not his surfaced in his mind: the light of five small flames illuminating a weatherworn face.

Marie arched an eyebrow questioningly, as if she were going to say something, but her mother forestalled her with a wave of her hand. The girl flinched, moving back out of range. "So we test it, yes?"

"At that Madame Tour's place?" Archie asked, winking at Marie. The strange memory was gone and his confidence in himself had returned, increased twofold. He felt bulletproof, as if he could take on the bloody world and win.

Madam spat out a stream of words at her daughter, droplets of spittle peppering the air like machine-gun bullets. Marie shuffled backwards, her eyes almost pleading with Archie to interfere.

"Here, don't you get fucking ratty at the lass. Just mentioned the séance, whatever that is," Archie snapped, picking up the Hand, cradling it like a child. Stupid bitch, she'd be lost without the lass running her errands. The woman could not make it up the cellar stairs in one go. As for the large chap– Madam's son, Henri–lazy bastard did nothing save fiddle with the watches Archie and others had brought in.

"You not know séance?" The madam sounded surprised.

"No, some sort of bloody parlour trick?"

"Yes, my daughter can talk to the dead and people pay her for it." The madam gave a shrill laugh.

"No bugger can do that. The dead are gone... That's it. You pretend to be like a gypsy at a bloody fair?" Archie laughed as he figured out what the girl'd been up too.

"My daughter is no gypsy. She does not work fairs."

"No, just the houses of rich ladies with dead husbands. Fucking brilliant." Archie winked again at Marie and noticed her blush. Well, that was a surprise; maybe he had a friend here? Maybe more than a friend? Then again, maybe not.

*****

Green fields. Houses in one piece. Archie tried not to grin. This was the ticket. No more mud, no more "yes sir, no sir," no more officers and their tarts for him. He inched his haversack higher on his shoulder and began to whistle. The tune earned him a smile from Marie and a glare from her mother. The old bitch he took no notice of, but the lass he did, matching his pace to hers and giving her a wink.

They were gone from the bolthole before dusk the day after he had finished making the Hand of Glory. Madam had ordered Marie to pile their belongings onto a large handcart and off they'd gone across the torn landscape towards Ypres. It had taken the British Army three years of hard, bitter fighting and innumerable corpses to cover the same ground in the other direction, from Ypres to Passchendaele. By dawn the thieves rested in the outskirts of the city. Even so, the slow pace bothered Archie, but they could only go as fast as Madam could waddle.

For a few coins they exchanged the handcart for a larger one with a lop-eared donkey in the shafts. Madam rode from then on and the pace picked up. So did the rain. It came down hard, bouncing off the road. Archie could feel it working its way through the thick wool of his coat.

Archie nearly panicked the first time a column of troops appeared on the road. His fingers twitched, itching to get hold of the revolver. He was not going to go back. *"Of course you're not,"* Jim said, his words comforting, a soothing balm on Archie's plagued thoughts.

Hand of Glory

Jim was not the only one offering help. Marie grabbed his arm and told him to look down. Just ignore the poor sods going up. He did, and the battalion just marched by, intent on their own misery. Archie laughed at being taken for just another no-account, uprooted Frog. He smiled and murmured his thanks to the girl.

They were soon so far behind the lines that the only soldiers they saw were those with thick braid on their hats, driven round in cars. Senior officers' country.

Madam called a halt at a crossroads to allow a convoy of ambulances to pass. On the mound of grass in the middle of the junction sat a small shrine to the Virgin Mary. Archie looked the shrine over. It was swamped with offerings. The bedraggled remains of flowers and candles mixed with sodden scraps of paper that had once been photographs. Nothing worth slipping in his pocket; not even the remains of a couple of candles were worth the effort.

"We go right," Marie said over the drone of the vehicles. She did not seem glad to be coming close to their destination. Archie peered through the gaps between the passing ambulances. Through the rain, he made out a straggling line of houses not even numerous enough to constitute a village.

Henri tugged on the protesting donkey's halter and the cart lurched across the road. He took to hitting the wretched animal, Madam encouraging him. Down the road they went, rattling along the line of houses. Archie broke into a dogtrot to keep up. He started to curse. Daft Frogs, where were they going? The cart turned sharply to the left, its metal-rimmed wheels grating as they hit the cobbles of a small yard attached to the end house. Marie shut the gate behind them. Madam heaved off the cart, shouting, cursing and trying to hit Henri round the head at the same time.

Henri dodged his mother's blows, protesting as he struggled to tie the wet rope to a post. A dog started to bark, then another. The donkey brayed and bucked in the traces, its small hooves scrabbling on the cobbles. Pummelled, near trampled, when he finally managed a knot Henri threw up his hands, cursing unintelligibly.

Marie had moved from the gate and now stood by Archie, her shoulders rounded, as if she were trying to make herself smaller. Archie knew Marie feared both her mother and brother to some degree, but now she was almost trembling. Her eyes shifted across the scene in the yard, then to look at a small man about fifty years old standing in the doorway of the house. The man was looking at Archie—not just *looking,* but giving him the once-over. Now who was this when he was at home? That soon became plain when the man coughed loudly and both Madam and Henri stopped in their tracks. Well, well… must be the boss.

"Careful," Jim whispered.

Archie nodded in agreement. He had Madam on his side, but Monsieur was another kettle of fish. The old man had a hardness around his eyes that reminded Archie of his own grandfather.

*****

Archie sat on a bench in the corner of a large kitchen, smoking the last of his cigarettes. His belly was full, his boots off, and his eyes were on Madam and her husband. He knew he was the subject of their conversation. The odd glance and wave of the hand in his direction told him so. Jim concurred. Marie's worried looks told him other things. Buggers were going to top him once he proved the Hand did its job. It made sense. "Why train a monkey to do the job, when you can do it yoursen?" Jim used to say. Only Archie was no Frog's monkey. He intended to do a job on them. The only question was when.

Monsieur turned in his seat, his small, hard eyes sparkling in the lamplight. "Tomorrow night we visit Madame Tour's abode, yes?" The man's English was clear, almost officer-like.

Archie's lip curled. The man looked like an officer, even. Had he been one? If he had, then it would make Archie's plan even sweeter. "Aye." Archie patted the pack on the bench beside him. Make them feel at ease. Make them think he didn't get what was going on.

"Good. Marie?" The girl jumped, almost dropping the plates she was clearing off the table. "You finish. Feed the dogs, then get some blankets for our guest." Monsieur spoke in English, making it plain to Archie he considered himself the boss.

The girl nodded and continued her work as her parents and brother retired for the night. Archie bent down and put his boots on, checking the laces as he did so. He then just continued to sit on the bench, his mind going over his plans. Now and then he looked at the girl, smiling when he caught her glance. Oh, yes, she wanted out. She feared and hated both her parents and her brother. She would help and be grateful. Marie was the cleverest of the lot of them, Archie saw it. He was not the only one; he could hear Jim chuckling as he shared Archie's thoughts.

The fire in the hearth faded, its warmth now barely reaching Archie. He could smell the ash as it wafted upwards in the wake of Marie's passage across the kitchen. The young woman stood before him, a blanket clenched to her chest. She looked round, then opened her mouth as if to speak.

"You're going to tell me they mean to fucking well do me in?" Archie leaned forward to take hold of the blanket, gently pulling on it. It fell from Marie's hands. She sniffed and nodded her head. Archie stood, still holding the blanket, and moved close to her. "You like me?" He was pretty sure she did. He had gone out of his way to be kind to her. The girl had gone without any affection for so long, she was well on the way to being putty in his hands.

She nodded.

"What if I said I liked you, too, and mean for both of us to get out of here tonight?"

Archie let go of the blanket. It fell to the floor between their feet. His hand went up as if to touch her bruised cheek. She flinched back. "Won't ever bash you, promise."

"No good. They stop us," Marie said.

"Won't be fucking able to," Archie said. He didn't want a bunch of Frogs on his tail stirring up the country; it would bring out the redcaps, sure as eggs was eggs.

"You would? *Pour moi?*"

Archie could see on her face she was figuring it out in her mind, deciding which way to jump. She was torn between her dread of those upstairs and going on the run. He hoped it would be with him. He didn't want to top her as well. She would be better off with him, of that Archie was sure.

"Yes," he replied.

Marie chewed her lower lip. Archie could see the panic in her features. The fading light of the fire made her eyes larger, her face thinner. Marie's hand came out and touched his face. Her small fingers traced the freshly healed scars under his right eye. His left hand came up and covered Marie's, squeezing it and bringing it down. For a few moments both stood still, then Marie's hand squirmed in his.

Archie smiled. "Best get going, then?"

"*Oui.*"

Archie watched for a moment as she began to gather things. Bags and baskets were found and food and bottles put in. Pleased she was getting on with things with a will, he turned to

Hand of Glory

his pack. He took out the Hand of Glory and walked to the remains of the fire. Taking a twist of paper from a small jar on the mantle, he lit the candle on the end of each digit. A thick, oily smoke began to rise from each of the sickly flames, blending into one thick column which hovered over the upturned palm. Archie took the Hand and held it tight. He began to chant and his inner demon brother joined in. For a moment he swore he felt his grandfather's hand on his shoulder, as he had when the old man had taught him and Jim the rhyme. The old sod would be proud of him.

Open each door lock to the dead man's knock.
Fly back bolt and bar.
All not move.
Sleep still all who now sleep.
And all that awake now be as the dead
For the dead man's sake.
O Hand of Glory, shed thy silver light
And direct us to our spoils tonight.

The column of smoke shimmered as if in a gentle breeze. Then it broke into fine tendrils and spilled into every corner of the room. It crawled under doors and wove up the narrow staircase in the corner. Archie was filling with a cold confidence that he could do anything and get away with it, as he had the murders of Tennant and the corporal. Shadows of this and all of his past actions hung amid the candle haze. Then the flames on the fingers brightened suddenly, banishing them all, save one: a shadow figure which refused to be dismissed. Archie ignored it; Jim said it was of no importance, and he believed his brother. The smoke from the candles now contained fine threads of silver, which snaked across the room and up the stairs. Just as Jim's comforting presence had said it would, the Hand showed the way for him and all those sworn to him, as long as he held to the bargain.

Archie smiled and looked at Marie. She had stopped what she was doing. She held her hands clenched to her mouth, her gaze on the Hand of Glory. "Don't worry. You stay close to me. Just follow where it bloody well points."

Marie nodded and walked with Archie towards the line of silvered smoke that hovered against the wall close to the fire. Here the soiled wallpaper was torn away from the wall and fluttered in the hell-made breeze of the flames. Archie reached out with his free hand and tore it further. He then removed the rough piece of wooden board the wallpaper had been covering. Cut into the brick was a ragged hole. Marie's small hands reached in and pulled out small, wrapped bundles, which she quickly placed into one of the baskets on the table. From hiding place to hiding place in the house they went, discarding anything too large to carry easily.

Up the stairs the smoke led them. Marie clung to Archie's arm. "You go back. I'll deal with the tossers." He felt the girl's grip loosen and then tighten as she continued with him upstairs. He smiled. She had bottle, the lass had.

The line of smoke parted into two and vanished under doors set three feet apart on the landing. Archie reached out for the handle of the one on the right, his fingers slipping on the cold metal. His grip tightened and the door opened. It was Henri's room. Marie's brother lay sprawled on his back across filthy sheets. His mouth was open. His clothes were in disarray and he still had one boot on. An empty bottle of brandy was trapped between the other boot and the top right leg of the bed. The silver trail of smoke led under the bed. Archie motioned for Marie to go forward as he pulled his bayonet out from its sheath on his belt. Marie got down on her knees and fumbled under the bed, which vibrated to her brother's snores. The dull clank of cheap china echoed round the room as Marie dragged out a chamber pot, watch chains hanging over the side. Archie hitched his head sideways, indicating for her to leave. Marie

Hand of Glory

came to her feet, the pot clenched tight in her hands, and scurried through the door.

Archie approached the bed, setting down the Hand of Glory on the stained bed linen. He then took a sure hold of Henri's hair and pulled his head back, tilting his double chin up to expose his fat-covered neck. Archie's bayonet came forward, drawing a deep red line across Henri's pale flesh. Blood spurted. A swift, high fountain of red arched across the bed. It splashed across the Hand of Glory. The flames guttered for a second, then burst higher, becoming dark-ringed. Henri's eyes opened wide. His eyelids fluttered and then stilled, as his blood fell from a wild flow to a mere trickle. Archie coolly wiped the bayonet and his hands on the trailing edge of the sheet. He then picked up the Hand. For a moment he heard Henri's dull voice blending with the lieutenant's pleas and the distant voices of those he and Jim had robbed on the torn and bloody battlefield. He shook his head, dismissing such fancy. Such imaginings were not part of the world he knew and understood. The voices stopped.

"Done, as easy as pie. Like killing a rat, nothing more," Jim congratulated him. Archie felt no concern about what he had done. It was part of the bargain. Rob, kill and allow the power behind the Hand to reap its own pickings. Yet again a figure of yellow smoke refused to leave. It trailed along the soiled wall, vanishing only when the sick light from the Hand splashed across the peeling wallpaper.

Archie stepped back out onto the landing. Marie was there, standing by her parents' door. "Best you go downstairs," Archie said. "Go. Start getting the bloody stuff out of the house and into the cart."

Marie made to speak, then gave him a thin smile, her wet lips shining in the light of the Hand. Archie listened to the rattle of her footsteps on the stairs as she went down, and then turned his attention to the other room. As he entered the foul-smelling place the flame on the thumb of the Hand of Glory died. One of them was awake. Archie was not worried; the dark confidence in him would not let him falter.

"Asleep or awake, they will be as the dead for the dead man's sake. Unable to move, but aware of everything," Jim crowed in amusement. Archie felt laughter bubbling up in his chest in response. It was not of his making, but came from a darker, blacker place than even his mind. It burst from his lips as he saw the whites of Monsieur's eyes reflecting the remaining four flames of the Hand of Glory.

The man lay in the bed next to his wife. Archie again set the Hand of Glory down, this time between his two victims. He pulled off the sheet covering their bodies and began to cut it into strips, all the while aware of Monsieur's eyes on him. Something inside him took delight in the terror the man's orbs held, amused by it. Taking the strips of sheet, Archie tied the hands and feet of Madam and Monsieur, Frog fences, to the top and bottom of the grimy brass bedstead. Archie then held a length of sheeting to the flames of the Hand and shoved it between the two trussed-up victims. He picked up the Hand and walked to the door. Here Archie stood until the bed and its contents were well alight, then he turned and went downstairs.

Marie was just carrying the last of the bags out the door. She looked at him, saying, "Do we harness the donkey?"

"No, we pull the cart ourselves. It isn't large. The donkey'll need looking after and feeding. Besides, we'll get us a fucking vehicle as soon as we can." As he spoke, Archie put the Hand of Glory on the table. Taking up the milk jug, abandoned there after the meal, he poured the remains of the contents over the Hand. The flames suddenly died, and with them the cold blackness that had descended on him. He felt frightened, far more than he had done in the trenches. He swore the figure he

Hand of Glory

had half seen before was there in the stairwell. It was no longer made of yellow smoke, but was a man with hooded eyes who looked at him. His heart was pounding so loud he swore he could hear it. He felt again the splash of Henri's blood on his hands, and smelled Monsieur's fear as he had tightened the torn strips of sheets.

"Enough!" Jim bellowed.

The fear vanished, along with the shadowy figure. Both banished by the power in the familiar's voice. Archie filled with a feeling of exultation. He had done it! Fucking well used the Hand of Glory! He had got hold of more loot in this one job than he had in a lifetime of normal thieving. Archie began to chuckle as he dried and wrapped the Hand carefully before putting it in his pack.

By the time he and Marie had dragged the cart to the crossroads, flames were consuming the roof of the house.

"Which way?" Archie asked.

Marie smiled and pointed southwards, saying, "What sort of vehicle will we get?"

"What sort do you bloody well fancy?" Archie replied.

Chapter Four

County town of Stafford–England
Saturday–28th October–1922

Hardy occupied a corner table in The Bear public house, with his back to a leaded window that overlooked Greengate Street. He half turned in his seat. The glass pane behind him was streaked with condensation; he went to wipe it off to see outside, so he could add the inclement weather to his list of excuses, but instead just traced a finger down it. Like all who had lived in the morass that had been Passchendaele, he disliked the damp. Rain and mud had been the enemy as much as the Hun. For a second he caught a glimpse of his reflection in the crooked mark left by his finger. Eyes pale, the grey almost washed out, surrounded by lines that by rights should not have been there for another twenty years. His features were narrow, framed by fine, light brown-coloured hair that always flopped across his forehead. Not different, or special, just not quite sure of what sort of man he was, and it showed.

On the table in front of Hardy was a pint of bitter he had bought half an hour before, barely touched. Next to that lay the change from the half-crown given in payment. However, these items were not the subject of Hardy's gaze. A line of medals was

Hand of Glory

laid on the table, instead of being pinned above the breast pocket of his suit.

He did not want to wear them. Did not feel they meant anything beyond the fact that he had survived. Since being medically discharged from the army in June 1918 he had struggled with the matter of doing what his family and others expected, just as his left leg had struggled in its thwarted efforts to move again as a leg should. Over the past four years his leg at least had become better at doing what was required of it.

He had tried, damn it. Hadn't he agreed to go back to university? That had been a mistake. The way the fresh-faced third-year had stood there, lecturing him on what was expected of those in their first year of living in the yellow stone quad. The boy with his unlined face knew nothing of what the real world was capable of doing to you. Like going over the top first and leading your men. Being responsible for them and failing. Living on while your men were left dead in the mud.

One term had been enough for him to realise these boys' dreams of the future were not his. His were long lost and replaced by ones of dead men, flaming trees and a hand held, the latter strangely comforting–painful, yet if not visited upon him, missed.

He had returned home to Stafford in September 1919 to find that a cousin, deemed medically unfit for army service, had succumbed, with his young, promising family, to the *"flu."* His house, land and income had come, surprisingly, to Giles. For a few months Giles had lived up to his mother's hopes. Then she, too, had taken ill with the Spanish influenza and never got to live in the small manor house some seven miles away from where Giles was now seated. So Giles, who before had been of the poorer branch of the family, now had a comfortable income for doing absolutely nothing. He was twenty-eight, but his life was over. No matter that he still rambled through it.

"You going to drink that?"

A trilby landed on the table next to the medals. His friend James Parker placed his own pint on the table beside Hardy's. James rubbed the right side of his moustache with the metal split hook that had replaced his left hand and sat down.

"I suppose I'd better." Hardy gave a half-smile and took hold of the pint, raising it to his lips.

"And put them on." Parker's metal replacement hand tapped on the medals. James rarely wore the "human" replica hand he'd been given on his last visit to the Queen Mary's Hospital at Roehampton. He had told Giles he preferred his split hook. Had said, with a wink, it was handier, and, besides, people made the mistake of underestimating him, as if the loss of his hand had diminished his intelligence. That, Giles knew, suited James down to the ground. He was far from the bumbling detective inspector that littered popular crime novels.

"Is that an order, sir?" Hardy asked.

"You wouldn't bloody obey me if it was. I don't know what junior officers are coming to these days." Parker took a long pull of his own pint, leaving a thin layer of froth on his moustache.

"Most didn't live long enough to become anything."

"So put the damn things on for them, not for those who'll be there gawking today. Wear them for all those whose names are on that bit of stone and can't stand about freezing their balls off in Victoria Square."

"They should never have let you over the Shropshire border." Hardy's fingers plucked at the silken ribbons on the medals.

"They didn't. I tunnelled my way in." Parker clawed the air with his replacement hand. "Besides, the wife's family live here, and a wife needs her family." A pained grimace twisted Parker's

Hand of Glory

face, then he laughed, though Hardy was not quite sure that in this instant his friend was joking.

"I thought you came over to torment me." They were in many ways opposites. Parker's irreverent humour had jarred at first, but Hardy had soon come to realise that, in his way, Parker was as turned around by his time in the trenches as Hardy was. For Parker, the jests kept the memories away; Hardy envied his friend's defences.

"No, that is merely an additional pleasure." Parker finished his pint, stood up, and shrugged. Giles knew the shrug was not a comment on their conversation, but the way in which James triggered the opening of his split hook. The array of cords, straps and elastic that criss-crossed James's chest and shoulders allowed him to pick up his hat with his claw and deftly place it at a rakish angle on his head. He stood there, waiting.

Giles picked up his medals, pinned them into place, placed his overcoat over his arm, and stood up. They were not the only ones leaving The Bear; a steady flow of men drifted out of the door and onto Greengate Street. They spilled out over the narrow pavement and across the road. Here, in the shadow of the large, overhanging upper floors of the Tudor high house, the crowd paused for a moment, then began to move up Saint Mary's passage towards the church and Victoria Square.

Parker was looking round, searching for familiar faces in the gathering crowd. "Don't envy uniform today, shepherding this lot." Parker waved at a knot of figures standing by the gate to Saint Mary's Church. Parker's wife and in-laws of various ages stepped out from the shade of the skeletal trees that overhung the narrow cobbled walk and made their way through the crowd. Hardy began to drop back. He did not want to be swept into the collective bosom of the numerous female members of Parker's extended family. Parker glanced back and nodded, a smile of understanding turning up the ends of his moustache. He moved forward through the growing crowd, shooing his approaching family back towards Victoria Square. One of the ladies peered under Parker's outstretched right arm. Her eyes were on him—Hardy felt them. Questioning. Then she was gone, as the crowd surged round him. The torrent of people dragged him along and down the side of the railings that surrounded the churchyard.

The expanse of Victorian monuments on the other side of the barrier was quiet and deserted, left to the attention of sparrows and curled autumn leaves. Hardy found himself pinned to the railings under a yew tree at the end of the graveyard. Ahead of him lay a crest of hats topping a wave of dark coats. The day's event had already begun.

In the centre of this undulating mass was a white, four-sided marble column. On top of this stood a bronze statue of a Tommy, a rifle in its right hand, in its left a tin hat raised in a cheer. The man of metal drew Hardy's eyes. He blinked. For a second the figure's pose changed. Still gun in hand, still hand upraised, but falling backwards, the tin hat tumbling off a head shattered by machine gun fire. Hardy shivered and pressed back against the metal railings. Hands on the spikes. The metal bit into his flesh. His suit jacket caught. His coat began to slip down his arm and snagged on the railings. Again, he hung on the metal, images of what was not there superimposed on the scene before him.

As the mayor and distinguished visitors gave their sombre speeches, Hardy heard the rattle of orders. The hymn "Abide with me" began. The voices raised in song turned into the shouts of men surging across no man's land. The brass of the band became the vibrating tones of distant guns firing down the line. The hymn faded away. The two minutes' silence followed. The rows of hats before him now all bowed in remembrance of those who had not come home. *They all should be standing*

Hand of Glory

here. Not just me. All of them. Hardy's head began to pound with self-loathing. He shook as the past took over from the present.

The wire binding him.
The flash of explosions above the shattered ambulance.
Adams fighting to protect him.
The sound of the corporal's voice that day in the hospital tent. "You have to, for all of us."

"Why?" Hardy's lips repeated the question he had asked. His left leg arched, the set bones grinding flesh, as if broken again. He felt as though it could barely hold his weight.

"Because." A voice echoed from under the shade of the yew tree next to Hardy, the word spoken by a shadow that lurked in the corner of his eye. He tried to swallow, but his mouth was dry, his sight blurred by the torrent of tears welling there. The shadow moved forward: a figure flickering in and out of the silent crowd. *Impossible.* Nevertheless, it looked like Adams, his smelly held lightly in his hand. Boots coated in mud. He moved with ease through a crowd that was not aware of him, or of the other soldiers that had formed out of the watery beams of sunlight dappling the square.

The Tommies moved in and out of gathered family and friends. They wore gentle smiles of farewell on their lips. Cigarettes in their hands, their jackets off and their soft caps at jaunty angles. Saucy postcards exchanged and ogled at, letters and parcels passed about between them. Their faces relaxed, no strain of battle narrowing their young eyes, off duty for good, now their work was finally done.

A number of the figures made their way through the crowd and gathered round the monster of marble newly erected in Victoria Square. For a moment they each stood before the roll of names, then faded away. Gone home. Others held back, the strain of battle creeping back into their features. Adams was among them. His right foot shifted forward and was blocked. A dark mist began to rise from five points of light before Adams and the rest of the men.

"Because?" Hardy repeated, straightening himself up, unaware that the crowd before him were dispersing.

"Of the hand within the hand." The reply was faint, lost in the rat-tat of voices commenting on the service.

Hardy's long-held breath was driven from him. *No.* He raised his right hand, now bloody, and watched the red lines trickle down his palm and puddle along the cuff line of his shirt. The hand. His hand? *No.* The hand in his? *No.* He would not block them. Nor would the hand held in the swirls of his dreams, waking and sleeping. That hand gives comfort. Aid. *Whose?* A hand within the hand. Five flames. Dark mist. A Hand.

"Your hand?"

A woman's voice cut through the melee of chaos drowning him. The visions behind his bruised eyes faded. Sand washed by the sea. Yet an imprint remained. Why had he, after all this time, seen Adams's shade again? Hardy coughed, struggling to find his voice and reality. He felt drained and exhausted.

"Your hand?" The question was repeated, as he felt his bloody wrist taken hold of and his hand lifted up for inspection.

"Your gloves, Agnes," Parker's wife said, her pale complexion drawn, marked by the cold and the emotion of the event.

"Are just gloves, Elizabeth." Agnes wound a white handkerchief round Hardy's hand in a businesslike fashion. "I think you need a cup of tea as well."

"Tea, the nation's cure-all. Are you in the habit of offering it to strange men, Agnes?" Parker chuckled from behind the two women standing in front of Hardy.

Hand of Glory

Agnes did not reply. A sad smile crept across her face. She let go of his hand and stepped back, her own hands lightly clasped before her.

Hardy looked from one woman to the other, then to Parker standing behind them with his father-in-law. What to say? How to act? What was expected of him? "I... Yes. Tea. Where?"

"Jenkinson's, Giles. I have a table reserved. The others will be there by now," Elizabeth said as she inched the black, fur-trimmed collar of her coat up round her neck.

"Then off we go." Parker waved his split hook with a flourish, and the two women and his father-in-law moved off. Parker did not follow them, but stayed by Hardy's side. "Bad?" Parker reached out with his hand of flesh and blood and squeezed Hardy's shoulder.

"Very." Hardy looked at his friend's hand, then into his face. There was no false sympathy there, just a depth of mutual understanding of a journey taken together and re-visited in the cold sweat of nightmares.

Parker's hand came away, dropping down to Hardy's coat where it had dragged off his arm onto the floor. He took it and shook it out, offering it to his friend. Hardy rolled his shoulders and took the coat, putting it on. He pulled the wool fabric tight, trying to block out the remains of what he might have seen. It made no sense—why Adams, why now? Had the day's events opened up the old wound, the blame he would always feel for Adams's death? "For a moment it was so..."

"Fucking real?" Parker finished the sentence for him.

"Yes..." Hardy began to move back down the side of the railings.

"They always bloody are."

*****

"Who is Agnes, by the way?" Hardy asked as he opened the door to Jenkinson's Café.

"Oh, Agnes is Elizabeth's cousin. Her mother, Elizabeth's aunt, has sent her over to us so Elizabeth can get her married off to some poor, unsuspecting Staffordshire man."

"And what does this Agnes think of that?" Giles asked, shaking his head in amusement.

"Well, being a bit of an independent madam, and a nurse to boot, she's ignoring Elizabeth's efforts and got herself enrolled in a midwife's course at the hospital, to fill up her time till Elizabeth gives her up as a lost cause," James Parker replied. He beckoned to the approaching waitress. The girl bobbed a small curtsey to the newly arrived gentlemen and took their coats, quickly showing them to the rest of the large party.

"Good, then I will ignore Elizabeth's efforts as well." The penny had dropped as to why he had been invited to join the party. It was not the first time he had been the "extra gentleman" at Elizabeth's gatherings. Since his mother's death Elizabeth had decided it was her duty to get him married off. Hardy had no desire for such a thing. He could barely cope with still being alive at the beginning of each day.

Giles sat down at a table heavily laden with a majestic high tea. Dainty sandwiches, scones awaiting jam and cream, and the cakes that made Jenkinson's reputation as the place in town for tea, called for his attention. He pulled at the handkerchief round his hand.

"Has it stopped bleeding?" Agnes asked from across the table.

Giles peered under the stained edge of the fabric. "I think so."

"Good, but keep the handkerchief on until you get the chance to wash and dress it properly." Agnes nodded in thanks to Elizabeth as the woman placed two sandwiches on her plate.

Hand of Glory

"It's not that bad."

"Doesn't matter if it's bad or not. Oh, I am sorry. Old habits die hard." Agnes suddenly looked very flustered.

Giles felt a twinge of amusement. There was something familiar about the young woman. But then, she looked like most other young women of her class. Her hat was fashionable, trimmed with ribbon, and it kept her short, dark-brown hair firmly in check underneath. Her dress—high-necked with long sleeves, the colour a dark blue-black with white piping—was entirely suitable for the day's sombre occasion. She could be interchangeable with any of the women seated at the surrounding tables, but for one thing: she seemed different, as if something had happened in her past to change her in a way Giles could not put his finger on.

"All this gossiping and you haven't been introduced properly. How modern, so risqué," James said between bites of his sandwich.

"James..." Elizabeth sighed. "Giles, this is my cousin, Agnes Reed. She's staying with us for a time. Agnes, this is Giles Hardy, formerly a captain in the East Staffs."

"Reed?" Hardy repeated the word, as his mind filled with cracked memories. A head covered with a nun-like wimple, half glimpsed behind a screen. The stench of Dakin's solution. The pain of damp dressings being removed. Adams standing at the bottom of his bed next to... *Her?* Sister Reed? The tilt of her head as if acknowledging the ghost. "Sister Reed?"

"Well, now, you're not going to tell me you two have met before?" Parker asked. He scooped up a large dollop of strawberry jam, and deposited it on his plate. The jam splattered, small, sticky crimson droplets dribbling over the edge of the plate, soiling the white tablecloth. Bright as blood. Hardy's eyes flickered from Agnes's face to the cloth and back again. Her gaze, too, drawn to the stain. He watched her shudder slightly, her hands dropping from in front of her. He imagined them twisting on her lap.

"Yes," Giles answered, positive it was she. Sister Reed who held the hands of dying men, who did not let them move on alone. Kneeling in the mud with Adams. Standing with the young officer in the tent. Hand within the hand. He felt sick. *Stupid*. Not possible. The illusion had nothing to do with her. It was all in his mind. He coughed, trying to clear his thoughts. Part of him was still on the wire, no matter how he reasoned it.

"No... I'm not sure. It's impossible to say if we did. There were so many. Faces. Names. It was years ago. I can't remember," Agnes garbled. Her eyes were looking down, not meeting his, and her mouth was a firm line.

She did remember. Hardy knew she did. Her eyes said so. She would never forget, like him, like Parker, like all those dragged by fate through those Flanders fields.

"I am sorry, Miss Reed. I didn't mean to upset you. As you said, it was years ago and it's quite understandable for you to not remember one face among so many."

*****

Giles did not address Agnes directly again; neither did she, him. It was as if they were both trying not to remove dressings from half-healed wounds. He took his leave as soon as it was polite to do so.

As he drove down the narrow lane that took him through Stowe-by-Chartley, the newly risen moon danced along the top of the high hedge. *Flick. Flick.* Shimmer of light. Hypnotising. The smell of a newly lit Woodbine cigarette filled the small Austin Seven.

Flick.

A burst of moonlight suddenly illuminated the curls of smoke over the head of his ghostly passenger.

Hand of Glory

"Captain, you frightened that lass."

Hardy braked hard; the car slithered and stalled. Hardy cursed, knowing he would have to get out now to wind the starting handle. "I didn't mean to," Hardy answered, addressing the ghost as he would have done the man. His hand went out to take the vaporous cigarette offered to him. He placed it to his lips, drawing in, feeling smoke that could not possibly be there fill his lungs. He handed it back to the shade of his friend.

"I know that. A good lass. Means well. Always has, always will do. Got guts, too," Adams said as he took back the cigarette.

"Why?" Why had the ghost decided to start haunting him, demanding his help with its strange quest? Or was it the events of the day? Had the unveiling of the memorial stirred up the twin demons of guilt and loss in the depths of his mind, creating the spectre?

Adams coughed, as if the smoke from the non-existent cigarette were troubling his lungs. He looked at Hardy, his ghostly eyes narrowing. "It's coming to a bloody head, sir, after all this time. We've got a good chance to get it damn well done for good."

"Get what done?" Hardy asked, confused and angry, cursing under his breath at the nonsense of it all.

Adams did not answer. The smoke from the cigarette gathered against the windscreen. Flames flickered. Red-hot. The gothic window of tree branches. Fingers entwined in his. The cold metal of a ring on a small finger. Hardy screamed and the illusion shattered. He slumped back in his seat, staring out of the windscreen at the night-wrapped lane that led to his home. How long he had been sitting there he did not know. His mind tumbled over and over, stressed to breaking point. Was he really here? Still in Flanders? Or, as one doctor had tried to put it, in a mental retreat where all his fears and perhaps hopes played out: a self-created purgatory?

Hardy took in a deep breath as he fought his way back to reality. He fumbled with the door catch. The door swung open, allowing the chill night air to swirl into the vehicle. Hardy got out and stamped his feet to rid himself of an unearthly chill. He closed the door and walked to the front of the vehicle.

As Hardy bent down to unclip the starting handle, the dull crack of a shotgun drifted across the fields to his right. He flinched, almost flinging himself to the ground at the sound, then cursed his stupidity. Poachers in the copse behind the manor, perhaps; more likely, Mathew Adams, George's son, taking a shot at a fox to protect the pheasants he had spent the year rearing.

Mathew, now seventeen, was the gamekeeper for Hardy's small estate and for two of the neighbouring farmers. The farmers made a tidy sum from taking out small shooting parties during the autumn and winter seasons, over their land and Hardy's. Though Hardy had not taken up any of the invitations to join the shooting, he had enthusiastically endorsed the suggestion that Mathew be employed in his father's old position. He had also managed to persuade Betty, George Adams's widow, to take the position of housekeeper at Caston Manor, though it did mean he daily ran the gauntlet of her disapproval. When she had accepted his offer Betty had used her favourite term for anything that did not meet her standards. She had informed Giles that both he and the manor were *"going to wrack and ruin,"* and that she had her work cut out getting both back into shape. At least he had tried to do something for Adams's family, to repay the debt in some small measure, though he truly believed it could never be settled.

Hardy inserted the starting handle and cranked it hard. The car engine burst into life. He returned the starting handle to its clip and got back into the car, wondering if the ghost that had haunted him earlier would still be sitting there, but no. The car

Hand of Glory

was empty save for the lingering smell of a cigarette. Hardy sighed and put the car into gear to continue his drive home.

The moon shifted higher in the sky, cutting the straggling line of houses into moonlit pictures as Hardy drove the car round the small village green. He turned left at the far end of the houses and down an even narrower lane towards the impressive-sounding Caston Manor. As he pulled up before the house, a figure walked across the front of the dwelling, cutting through the twin beams of the vehicle's headlights. For a second Giles thought it was Adams. His mind was so full of his dead friend that he expected to see the man's shade again. But it was George's son, Mathew. The young man stood in the hazy beams, a shotgun broken open and set in the crook of his arm. He held up his hand and placed it over his eyes, shielding them from the white glare of the car headlights.

Hardy switched off the engine and opened the door, calling to the young man as he stepped out. "Busy night, Mathew?"

"Aye, a bit. Been a bit of a damn rum day, all told."

"Yes it has. You were in Stafford?"

"Me, mum, and the others. We went with mum's cousin, Taffy. He runs a pawnshop in town, you know. Mum thought it would be proper for us all to be there, though she said me dad would have been surprised at all the fuss and money spent on that there memorial." Mathew pushed back his cap, scratching at the thick thatch of hair underneath.

"Yes, he would," Hardy smiled, adding, "You going up to Chartley Moss?"

"Aye, sir, going to check the copse on the edge of it. It's what you, Mr Baker, and Mr Howard pays me for," Mathew laughed.

"I see, and would you be feeling like a nightcap later?" Hardy asked.

"You'll be sound asleep by then."

"No, I don't think so. A night cap and a bite, eh? If there's anything in the pantry."

"'Course there is. Me mum brought up a nice pie earlier for your supper, under the impression that you most likely forgot to eat while you were in town."

"Well, you can tell her I didn't forget. I had tea with Inspector Parker and his family." Hardy smiled, enjoying the small banter.

"Aye, well, I know you can take care of yourself, but me mum, that's another matter. She don't think any man can take care of himself." Mathew gave a wink, nodded respectfully to Hardy and moved off.

Hardy stood there watching Mathew walk back down the lane towards the gate of the old sawmill. Only when the young man had faded into the darkness did Hardy turn and go into the manor.

Chapter Five

The train juddered. Smoke poured past the window. Archie sighed and tapped at the soot-stained window with a silver-topped cane, his frustration at the wait beginning to show. The train was stuck two hundred yards from the station, waiting for the points to change and allow the London to Liverpool express to slip into Stafford Station.

The town was on the main west-coast line and it was a wealthy one, with its businesses a mix of heavy industry, footwear and agriculture. The Victorians had turned the small halt into one of their gothic wrought-iron confections, which now straddled six lines. Archie had come home more by chance than choice. It was the next town on the west-coast line, that was all. One more place ticked off his list of places to do over. He no longer belonged to this town, a place that had trapped him as a child and led him, along with his brother, to snatch at the idea of war as an escape. It had been from this very station that he and Jim had embarked on their adventure to see a bit of the world and line their pockets at the king's expense. Jim had died, blown to bits, and them bits buried in Flanders mud. However, Archie had returned to Blighty with more than his pockets lined, and aiming to make more.

He looked at his travelling companion. Marie had a Frenchwoman's taste for the finer things in life. She was no longer the poor French peasant girl who had been at the beck and call of her brutish family. Her hair, though long, was now piled up on her head and covered by a very fashionable soft pink felt hat. Her knee-length coat was of a matching colour. The hat was trimmed with a deeper pink ribbon, the same shade as her cube-heeled leather shoes and matching handbag. Marie's lips were red-wine shaded, eyes smoky-black, the makeup smeared above and below the lashes, enhancing her "foreign," exotic look.

The lass could and did charm the coins out of her marks' pockets with a blink of those big eyes. Just a hint here and there. The way she shifted the table during a private séance with a nudge of her leg and foot, the way she could change the pitch and tone of her voice—she had them eating out of her hand. She was the all-seeing Madame Marie, and at times she was a bloody pain, but Archie had no doubt he could handle her.

"Of course we can deal with her," Jim said, fat cat yawning. Archie frowned at the words. It was he who dealt with Marie, always had. Jim did nothing, but just muttered now and then. Sometimes the babbling helped, but often it did not seem to. He was the boss, not Jim. Jim's restrictions chafed. They were an ill-fitting collar he was getting loath to wear.

A whistle blew and the train moved forward, then pulled up in a cloud of steam against the platform. For a moment a tint of yellow shimmered through the plumes of steam that drifted past the window. Archie stiffened in his seat, his eyes searching the dissipating column for the shadow face that he knew would be lurking there.

"There's nothing there, never been nothing. Besides, you and those that serve you hold to the bargain made with the Hand. So, even if there were something, it couldn't harm you." Jim's reply was bored. He sounded petulant at being disturbed

from his rest by Archie's old, irrational fear. Archie's frown deepened; Jim never bloody well understood. Archie did. If Jim existed, then maybe the sod in the yellow smoke did.

"I know, I know..." He was still not bloody convinced by the same old words. For five years he'd had this sense of being followed and watched. No matter how many times Jim said there was nothing, Archie could not shake the feeling, and he trusted his feelings. If he hadn't, then he would not now be listening to his brother.

He coughed, trying to clear his thoughts, and stood up, taking his coat from the seat by his side and slipping it on. Marie handed a well-brushed bowler hat to him. Archie gave her a wink. Marie blew him a kiss and waved her gloved fingers at him. He took the hat and placed it on his head, carefully, not wishing to disturb his hair. His red curls, neatly trimmed and slicked back with pomade, completed the look of a well-heeled gentleman. Archie on the outside was far removed from the ragbag, backstreet lad who had left the town nearly eight years before. He extended his hand to Marie. She took it and stood, smoothing the front of her coat with an almost casual brush of her hand.

The sound of doors slamming echoed down the carriage. Just as Archie reached for the door to the compartment, it was opened by a thin young man, his Adam's apple bobbing against his spotless winged collar as he spoke. "Porter has the cases, Boss, and I spotted Kevin waiting for us on the platform."

"Good, Will. And Lilly?" Archie asked.

"Faffing around as usual; thinks the porter will hop it with the bags. She's standing there giving him the evil eye."

"He might. I do not trust porters. Lilly knows this. They are all thieves if they get the chance," Marie said as Archie handed her down from the train.

"Aren't we fucking all," Archie said as he joined the other members of his small robber band on the draughty expanse of the platform. Lilly Wainwright was standing close to the porter, who was loading the party's cases onto his trolley.

"Take care. Don't you scrape the leather," Lilly instructed, ignoring the porter's rolling of his eyes.

Will had joined her and stood cracking his knuckles in boredom. Archie caught Will's gaze with his own and the lad shuffled his feet, giving a grin to his employer. A guard's whistle blew and the train behind them began to move off again, the engine chugging slowly at first, then building up speed as it continued its journey north.

"Boss." His third employee approached the party. Archie's eyes narrowed. Kevin Jones was a well-educated bugger who set Archie's teeth on edge. If he were not so damn good at his job, Archie would have ditched him long ago. Oh, he trusted Jones all right. It was just Jones's superiority—it reminded Archie of bloody officers like the late, unlamented tosser Lieutenant Tennant. Kevin Jones was a former schoolmaster who had found that the illegal use of his education earned far more money than attempting to beat Latin into the heads of small boys. The sodding problem was Jones never let others forget he was better educated than they were. That he was, Archie conceded, but not as sharp, no, sir.

"Of course he's not, and you have me," Jim laughed, before settling down again in the dark loam of Archie's soul, to rest.

"Jones," Archie acknowledged the man. Another train was coming up to the platform in a cloud of acrid-tasting smoke and steam. Crowds on the platform ebbed and flowed round the group.

"The journey was not tiring, I hope?" Jones asked, as he bowed to Marie and removed his hat to reveal a shiny bald spot in the midst of his thinning brown hair.

Hand of Glory

Archie answered, "It bloody well was. We've been sitting outside the station for God knows how long."

"Yes, well, I believe it was due to the additional local trains put on today."

"Something going on?" Archie waved to the porter, who had finished packing up their luggage. The man nodded and began to push the trolley towards the exit.

"Take them over to The Railway Hotel. We have rooms booked there under the name of Adams," Jones said. "Will, Lilly?"

"Aye." Will tugged on Lilly's arm and began to walk quickly after the porter.

"No need for that, William." Lilly reached up and straightened her hat. "I'm coming. I don't need telling twice."

"You were saying, Jones?" Marie asked.

Archie took Marie's hand and tucked it into the crook of his arm, repeating her words as they walked out of the station.

"Yes, they are unveiling the Borough War Memorial this afternoon," Jones said.

Archie was not surprised; the things were sprouting up like mushrooms across the country. Why would Stafford be any different? Yet the thought of the memorial brought back parts of the past which Archie did not wish to relive. He had managed to get out of that hell by the skin of his teeth, and there was no way he was going to let the army reclaim him. They would if they could. They would put him against a wall and shoot him for what he had done. "So folks have been putting bits in the local papers about their dear departed, then?"

"Oh, yes." Jones fumbled in his jacket pocket. He pulled out a crumpled notebook, glancing at the ink-covered pages. "I have made notes of all the larger columns and done quite a bit of research. The local head librarian was most obliging when I told him I was writing a book. He personally found me the back issues of all the local newspapers for the last eight years. I thought it best to cover all of the war years and the duration of the Spanish Influenza outbreak, this being the county seat and all." He snapped his book shut and peered across the road to The Railway Hotel. The large establishment stood a mere hundred yards from the station. It was a four-storey Victorian monument to the enterprise and power of the railway companies.

"Good, though I must not seem to be too specific at the public meeting. We will go over things this afternoon. But I say now, I will do only three private sittings here," Marie said, as she stepped out from under the elaborate wrought-iron canopy that marked the entrance to the railway station. Here taxis jostled for customers, their exhaust fumes curling round the feet of the small party.

"What the fuck?" Archie snapped.

"The place is small." Marie waved her free hand in the air, indicating that she was not impressed. "The bourgeoisie will all know each other. We will have the same people at the séances if we do more. Even with three there is that risk. They will talk, especially after the first of our other *evenings*." Marie stressed the word. "Those, too, we must limit more than normal–two, maybe three at the most."

"Now hold on a bloody minute," Archie spluttered in protest.

"Don't get side-tracked by the past and the fact you're in this place again. Marie's right, you bloody fool!" The venom in Jim's words physically shook Archie.

"*Non*, Archie. We must be careful, *homme de ma vie.*" Marie brought her free hand up, gently touching his scarred face. Archie could feel the warmth of her hand through her cotton gloves.

Hand of Glory

"I wanted to make 'em all fucking pay," Archie began, trying to explain to her and Jim, realising the reason he had really come back, even though he'd sworn it was just because it was the next town on the route. He and Jim had lived in the back streets of this town. Two small boys of no more account than stray dogs: ignored, half-starved, stealing what they could to survive after their grandfather had been arrested. He wanted the town to pay. That Jim had rebuked him so viciously rankled. Archie had thought Jim would understand: he was no longer a small-time crook, but a boss. He was the master of a Hand of Glory; he could–*would*–make the sods pay, and pay double.

"I know," Marie leant forward and kissed his cheek, then let her hand drop as she moved from his side and into the hotel.

*****

Archie let himself out of the double doors, and stood on the steps of the hotel for a moment to get his bearings. Lilly and Will, their jobs done for now, had taken themselves off to find a picture house or a tearoom to sit in. As for him, well, he had got the fidgets sitting listening to Marie and Jones going over the details Jones had gleaned from his few days in the town. All the mumbo jumbo did not interest him at all. Archie knew the séances turned a good profit and gave them a lead-in, but, dammit, they bored him silly. He decided to take a walk. Partly out of curiosity, to see if the town was still the rear end of nowhere he remembered it to be, but more because he wanted to swagger his way into The Swan or The Bear and show them all he was as good as, if not better than, any here now.

He stood debating which way to go to get to the town centre and its *gentlemen's* public houses. Should he go down Newport Road to the new library, then left towards the Royal Brine Baths? Stafford stood on a lake of brine. The baths were an offshoot of the salt business; the brine was pumped half across the town for folks to lie in for medicinal purposes. That was not the only service offered at the baths. His grandfather had taken him and Jim there every Saturday morning. Two pennies each paid for the hire of a bath, soap, and a towel. A good scrub once a week was his grandfather's motto when it came to personal hygiene, and both he and Jim had begrudged those pennies like anything. They would rather have gone to the Saturday morning flickers at the picture house across the road. Archie smiled at the thought, then shook his head. Jim was in his mind a lot today, more so than normal. It was being here again, it had to be. It had woken things in his memories that he thought he had forgotten. Archie found he did not like it.

"Neither do I," Jim remarked. The tone was so cold it made Archie hitch up his shoulders as he suppressed a shiver.

Archie stepped down onto the pavement and became swamped in the flow of people making for the station; they seemed to be coming from the direction of Saint Mary's Church. Something going on? He tapped the shoulder of a man and asked, "Something up?"

"Been a service in Victoria Square. They've been unveiling the war memorial," the man replied, the medals on his chest chiming slightly as he turned to answer Archie.

Of course, Jones had mentioned it. He wondered if Jim's name would be on this memorial. Should he go look? No, no point. Jim was dead. Yes he was, and his name should fucking well be on that memorial. Jim had died in that muck just like all the others. Bugger it, he damn well would go and look. Archie turned on his heel and walked quickly in the direction of Saint Mary's and the square that lay on its west side.

The afternoon was darkening as he pushed his way through the crowd to where it was thinning out, near the memorial. On the western edge a brass band were putting their instruments onto a large handcart. The flags of the newly formed branches of the British legion were being furled and covered. A clergyman, his white robes flapping round his ankles, was taking one last look at the column of marble before disappearing to whatever entertainment the town's civil dignitaries deemed appropriate for the officiating parties.

Archie felt his lip curling. *Officers–those good for nothing tossers and their tarts.* He moved closer to the memorial, his eyes running over the statue on top. Stupid. Look at the sod. Nothing to damn well cheer about, being dead. It looked like brass. It must've cost at least a thousand quid. More money than bloody well sense. His gaze dropped down to the lines of names on the marble. Alphabetical order. Name. Rank. Regiment. On and on. Then one name–it stood out from the others. Hawkins, James, Pvte, Second Battalion, East Staffs. It was Jim's. Archie felt a lump in his throat. Jim should not have been on this bloody stone. They'd been going to skip that night. If it hadn't been for that sod lieutenant putting Jim on a charge. *Tennant.* The fucking bugger's name was engraved by Jim's, sitting on the line opposite. Of all the sodding coincidences. The sod was still hounding Jim even now. Archie lashed out with his walking stick. It slammed into the marble, hammering hard at the deeply cut name of Tennant. Jim chuckled, delighting at Archie's anger.

"Here, what do you think you're doing?"

"Sorry, it was just an accident. I was just pointing at me brother's name and me hand slipped," Archie said as he half turned to see who had spoken. Just his luck, a bloody plod. The policeman stood, hands on his hips, just a few paces away.

"I see. Your brother was out there, then?" The plod's manner mellowed.

"Aye, so was I," Archie replied.

"Were you, now?"

"Yes, from 1915 right through to Wipers and all that mud," Archie said as he stepped away from the memorial. "With the East Staffs."

"With Captain Hardy?"

Bit nosy, this plod. Did the sod not believe him? "No, Captain Mellor and Lieutenant Christian Tennant. Good man, Tennant, you had to hand it to him." Archie winked at the plod.

"Aye, he was a good young man from what I've heard," the plod replied and began to move off.

The daylight had almost gone now; so, too, had Archie's desire for a drink. He needed to get back to the hotel, to find out if Tennant's family still lived in the area. If they did, Jones would have them on his list. They would've put a couple of inches in the papers about their *dear son*, the bugger that got men killed for no good fucking reason. As he walked back, Archie's cane tapped out a rhythm while he made his plans. He was going to do Tennant's family over. He began to laugh. He would pinch the shirts off their backs, so he would... and the way to their stuff would be lit by the hand of one of their own. He sensed Jim gathering himself to speak. He was going to object, he knew. Up to now Jim had always had the last say about the jobs they did, but this time Archie was determined, too. "No, this time *I* sodding well choose, you understand?" He tensed, waiting for the creature's rebuke, but none came. Archie smiled as he mounted the steps into The Railway Hotel.

Chapter Six

Sunday–29th October–1922

"Mother doesn't like a knot behind, Aunt Agnes," Victoria said as she peered at the needle full of coloured thread that Agnes had just handed her. "She says it makes the fabric lumpy."

Agnes looked at the crumpled, stained scrap of fabric in the girl's hand and wondered how Victoria's mother, Elizabeth, would notice a knot among all the misplaced and caught stitches. "I know, but it's a small one and easily hidden." The girl smiled at Agnes's remark and set about drawing the sun-yellow silk through the fabric, her small tongue poking out of the corner of her mouth as she concentrated.

Traditional Sunday afternoons and the ritual of doing nothing after lunch still lingered in this house. Agnes's cousin, Elizabeth, had been brought up a Methodist, and as such the cannon of not doing any work that was not absolutely necessary on the Lord's Day had ruled her childhood. Nothing meant no housework or pottering in the garden. Even sewing was limited to embroidery. No mending of clothes or sheets on a Sunday. Though books other than the Bible were now read, and pictures such as the flower–well, it was supposed to be a rose that Victoria was working on–were sewn rather than Bible quotations, Elizabeth still insisted it was a time of rest for all under her roof. Cook, housemaid and the children's nurse had the afternoon and evening off. One was permitted to walk in the garden, or even, if a male member of the family would oblige and keep you company, go to the town park. Mainly Sundays were comprised of reading, sewing, talking and being bored out of one's mind. Well, that was how it felt to Agnes. She had not even been able to wrangle a duty day at the hospital. Matron had noticed that of all the trainee midwives, Agnes worked more Sundays than the others. Interfering woman. Agnes enjoyed her work. She had gotten out of the habit of doing nothing in September 1914 and did not intend going back to idleness willingly. For all the horror and turmoil she had witnessed in France, it had opened her eyes to many things. She had come to realise what was actually possible for a woman to do, if the woman in question had the courage to do it.

"Oh, pooh!" Victoria exclaimed, throwing the embroidery away in annoyance. The mauled fabric landed on the brass rail of the fire surround and lay there, flapping gently before the fire. Agnes laid her book down on the small table beside her chair and got up to rescue the girl's work. She picked it up and tugged at its edges gently in a vain effort to straighten it. "You know, perhaps if you put it aside for a while…"

The girl turned her head and looked out of the sitting room window at the rain-drenched garden. A wistful look came over her young features. "Just wish it would stop for a bit."

"Don't think it's going to, Vicky. Looks like it's set in for the day," Agnes said as she walked back towards the girl and offered the fabric back to her. "Anyway, it will soon be time for tea, and you can then help me make the toast on the fire."

"And the crumpets?" Victoria's face brightened as she took the embroidery and folded it up, placing it in the small bag that lay by her feet.

Hand of Glory

"Oh, one for a challenge, are we?" Agnes asked and held out her hand to the child.

"I promise I won't drop any of them in the fire." Victoria took the offered hand and they both made their way out of the room.

Tick, tick, tick, the steady beat of a metronome echoed down the hall. To Agnes it measured out the lethargy of the day. The very fact of doing nothing chafed at her nerves. It was stupid, really. When she'd been in France she had often longed to be able to sit down for a while and do nothing. Yet now she had the chance to do exactly that, she hated it with a vengeance.

She had continued to nurse until late 1919; then her parents had decided she'd done far more than was required and should return home. She had tried to tell them no, but they had not listened. They would not listen. She had wandered round her parents' house, bored–even more bored than she was now–until two things had happened which offered Agnes a chance of the independence she craved. Elizabeth, one of her cousins, had invited her to keep her company during her latest confinement. Secondly, a maiden great aunt on her father's side had died and left Agnes a small inheritance. Agnes had grabbed both opportunities like a drowning man thrown a fraying rope.

The money had allowed her to enrol in the midwifery course here at the general hospital. It also guaranteed her a small but liveable income once she had finished her training. No one could possibly object to an old maid of twenty-six setting up home by herself and doing a quite respectable job helping bring children into the world. Perhaps being there at the beginning of life would also help balance the books for all the times she had held a dying man's hand in France, or so Agnes hoped.

"No! No! Again, Edward, again!" Elizabeth admonished.

The metronome stopped. Then started. Then stopped, as Agnes pushed open the door to what Elizabeth called her music room, which held her pride and joy: a very large, ornately carved upright piano. Victoria began to giggle at her elder brother's discomfort. Agnes gave the girl's hand a squeeze to catch her attention, in the vain hope she could forestall any sibling bickering. But it failed.

"Like to see you do better!" Edward snapped.

"I can," Victoria said.

"Now, you two, please–it's *Sunday,*" Elizabeth said, straightening up in her chair.

"Yes it is, and it's nearly tea time," Agnes added.

"Super! Crumpets!" Edward took Agnes's remark as a signal that his lesson was finished and quickly closed the piano lid, knocking the sheet music off as he did so.

The fluttering sheets caught the eye of his eighteen-month-old brother, Charles, who gurgled, abandoned his wooden building blocks on the carpet, and began to crawl towards the descending paper. Agnes scooped him up and sat him on her hip. Charles protested for a moment, then, his gaze caught by the ribbons on the neckline of Agnes's dress, decided to try and eat them.

"Yes, crumpets. Edward, look, why don't you and Victoria go and get the trays cook has left set up in the kitchen and bring them through to the front parlour? Then we can begin toasting."

"Be careful–don't drop anything," Elizabeth called after her disappearing children, adding as she stood and reached out to take her youngest offspring, "Thank you, Agnes. I don't know what I would do without you."

"You'd cope very well, as you know, Elizabeth," Agnes said as she disentangled Charles's fingers. She half-heartedly tried to smooth the now damp ribbons down before handing the young man over.

"Perhaps," Elizabeth laughed as she settled her son on her own hip. "Though I do enjoy your company in the evenings when you're not on duty, there's no doubt about that. Besides, James has no qualms about me even going to the moving pictures with you."

"I see, so that was the reason you wanted me to come and live with you for a while. So you could go ogle at Rudolph Valentino whenever you wanted to."

Elizabeth burst out laughing, her bobbed blonde hair bouncing round her delicate features. "I would have you know I am a married woman, and pregnant." She patted her slightly rounded stomach. "Still, he is so captivating in *The Sheik,* isn't he?" Elizabeth's face changed, becoming serious.

Agnes winced; she knew what was coming next. Elizabeth was going to mention a subject which had caused the only disagreement they'd had of late.

"Agnes, please, won't you reconsider coming on Tuesday?"

"I really would rather not; it's not as if you need me, even as your pet chaperone. Your mother is going, and your friend Mrs Warner." She did not to want go through this argument again. Elizabeth was so practical in so many respects, yet in this matter of her brother's loss she clung to straws. Christian was dead. Elizabeth and her mother should let him go. It did no good to hang onto false hopes. You had to let them rest. To do otherwise was cruel. She knew in her heart it was the right thing to do.

"Agnes, there is no need for that tone. I thought you understood. If there is the smallest chance... Just to find out where he lies? Madame Marie comes highly recommended."

"You know where he is. Where all like him are. They are buried somewhere in that mud!" Agnes snapped. Charles began to cry. His small face was twisted with concern, as if he sensed the tension between the two women.

"That was uncalled for," Elizabeth replied, both her eyes shining with tears. "I don't understand you. You of all people. You were there. Yet you deny it sometimes, like you did to Captain Hardy. Why?"

"No, I don't! I just said I didn't remember him," Agnes retorted. But she did remember him, as she remembered all of them. The problem was that for her in many ways it had been the best of times.

At the outbreak of war Agnes had been surprised that she'd managed to persuade her parents to allow her to volunteer as a VAD. Had her parents expected her to come running home after her first sight of a wounded man, like Sybil Claymore had done? The poor girl had only walked half way down one of the wards in an officer convalescent hospital near Brighton when she'd been taken with a fit of the vapours. The girl had been a self-diagnosed invalid ever since.

Did Elizabeth think of her like that? Damaged by what she had seen and done? Yes, there had been bad times. More than once after her shift she had been asleep before her head touched the pillow, yet finding that after an hour she woke, totally exhausted yet unable to fall back to sleep. Her hands had become red-raw from constant washing, her feet hot and swollen from standing for hours on end, and her eyes often red from the fumes of the Dakin's solution and hard held-back tears. The heartache of knowing that, for some, despite all the care, all the devotion, there was nothing that could be done.

Yet all the pain and anguish of those years was wrapped up in memories of happier times. The fun of an impromptu concert put on by members of the hospital staff. The friendships. The silly jokes. The celebration of birthdays and Christmases far away from home, and making it special for others and yourself. The sharing of good news from home, both with fellow staff, and, more importantly, with patients. The saying goodbye to men who had survived all that the trenches could throw at them and who were now going home. The knowing that what you were doing was vital, and, more importantly, others believing you were capable of shouldering the responsibility.

She could not bring herself to look at her cousin's face. The grief Elizabeth held onto was there, and she had just added to it. "I'm sorry, I didn't mean..."

"I know," Elizabeth, said. "Just think about it, please?"

Agnes nodded.

Tuesday–31st October–1922

She should not have agreed. The small function room in The Railway Hotel was slowly filling up with what seemed to be all of Elizabeth's acquaintances, each one having to be acknowledged by the tilting of one's head and a fixed smile. Was this event by invitation only? The middle class may not have had a monopoly on grief, but they did have money to spare in the pursuit of the nonsensical–which this evening was as far as Agnes was concerned. In fact, she considered it a folly of the highest order. It had to be a confidence trick of some kind.

Agnes did not believe in ghosts, or any other kind of wandering spirit that sought to make contact with the living. She had seen men–even fellow nurses–die in the war. Now, during her midwife training, it was newborn children and their mothers whom she saw dying. It was hard; you felt totally distressed and undone at the loss of a life. One felt regret and anger at not being able to prevent death, but one did not see ghosts after. No one came back. What lay beyond, if anything did, was to be discovered when it was one's turn, which was the way Agnes believed God wanted it. The Almighty had certainly not given her any reason to believe otherwise.

Was everyone here clutching at straws? Alternatively, were they just curious? The former she could understand, even if she did not approve. Grief affected people in different ways. Agnes did not expect people to forget those they had lost. One could not do that. She did not. However, to stop living, to wrap oneself up in the memory of that moment of loss, was self-defeating in her eyes. It certainly would not be what those who had departed this life would want their loved ones to do. As to the latter, well, ghouls would be the most polite word she could think of for such people. She had come across those before, when she was on leave during the war. They wanted details, the gorier the better, and were offended when Agnes had refused to feed their addiction.

"Quite a gathering, is it not? I knew Madame Marie would have a good turnout. She is so talented," Charlotte Warner said as she reached out her hand for a leaflet, nodding her thanks to the young woman who was giving them out. This assistant was soberly dressed, but her blonde hair was cut in the latest fashion: short, level with the bottom of her ears, and not a wave in sight.

"Yes, it is. You think that maybe this time...? I mean it is All Hallows' Eve, and–" Elizabeth answered, only half finishing her sentence as she took two of the papers and murmured her thanks to the young woman before placing one of the sheets on Agnes's knee.

"I am very sure. When I spoke to Madame Marie in Bath she said it was the distance that had prevented my mother from reaching out to us. Perhaps that is the reason Madame Marie is here. She was so upset when she could not help me."

Agnes brought her left hand up to her mouth to cover her snort of derision. All Hallows' Eve, of all things. What was Elizabeth thinking of, for goodness' sake? It was all folklore and balderdash. As her gloved fingers dropped again to her lap they brushed the leaflet and sent it spinning to the floor underneath the chair in front of her.

"Here, let me give you another, miss." It was the young assistant. "I am sure you will find it interesting."

"I'm sure I will," Agnes replied, knowing full well she would not. She deliberately placed the leaflet under the handbag on her knee, eyeing the protruding corner as if it were a snake.

"Of course," the young woman continued, "and if you have any questions, please feel free to ask me. My name is Lilly." Lilly tilted her head in a friendly fashion, which did not match the fixed, bored smile on her face. Agnes had seen the same expression before on the faces of the young women in France who'd hung round the bars and cafés. Totally mercenary, the friendliness there just a pretence. It had allowed them to get into the wallet of some unsuspecting Tommy, by promising something they were not going to deliver.

Lilly hovered for a few moments, as if waiting for Agnes to speak. When she did not, the young woman struggled to smother a pout and moved on. Agnes's gaze again dropped to the leaflet, resisting the desire to crumple it up and throw it with its fellow beneath the chair in front. She gazed round the small function room. The rows of chairs were placed in an arch, with a table and chair at the midway point of the two arms, which stood three feet from the far wall. This table faced an aisle that separated the rows at the midway point. The way it mimicked the layout of a church altar and congregation was not lost on Agnes.

As she watched, a thin young man in his early twenties, very nattily dressed in a pinstriped suit and with white spats on his shoes, was lighting a series of candles positioned on elaborate, free-standing holders around the room. Strange–perhaps Madame Marie believed the spirits preferred candles to the newfangled electric lights which hung overhead. As if to confirm Agnes's thoughts, the lights above her head went out.

The buzz of conversation in the small function room stopped for a second, then started again, becoming slightly louder as people commented on the change. The room corners were now darker, the plaster roses on the ceiling lost from view. In the soft, shifting candlelight the interlaced patterns on the floral wallpaper rippled, reflecting in the puddles of light on the highly polished wooden floor. A strange smell began to waft through the gathered audience from an ornate metal container on the table.

"Incense, for cleaning the room," Charlotte said as she stood and began to remove her coat. She carefully folded the garment and draped it over the back of her chair before sitting down again.

"I prefer a good, strong disinfectant," Agnes said under her breath, earning herself a glare from Elizabeth.

"It is not that sort of cleaning, dear Agnes," Charlotte said as she leaned forward and smiled at Agnes. "It is to remove any bad influences."

"Oh, that explains why I feel the sudden urge to leave." Agnes was already out of patience with this performance and it had not even started.

"Agnes, please." It was her Aunt Vera, Elizabeth's mother. "Why are you so against this? If we have even the smallest chance of finding out..." The older woman's words died, choked off by hard-held emotion.

"I am sorry, Aunt Vera, Elizabeth, I just can't... and, well, I don't think Christian would have approved. He was very modern-minded," Agnes muttered her apology. She was sorry for upsetting them, but she was not sorry she had spoken out. This all felt so wrong. She picked up the paper from her knee and began reading it, trying to distract herself. The urge to say

Hand of Glory

something else warred within her, as she ploughed through the mumbo jumbo concerning Madame Marie and her tireless work in contacting the dead. This, plus the encouragement to donate money to Madame so she could support a group of poor French orphans, made the whole thing stink higher than a kite.

There was no denying the passion in Elizabeth's voice as she spoke. "Yes, he was, which is exactly why we should try. He would see it as a challenge to accepted beliefs, just as he saw all the new advancements in science. If Christian could put our hearts and minds at rest and show us, then he would do it."

Agnes sighed and resigned herself to being the one, outvoted voice of reason.

Chapter Seven

Why was he here? Hardy tried to reason out the matter as he parked his car against the railings surrounding Victoria Park. He sat for a few moments, listening to the ticking of metal as the car engine cooled. The train station on his right was ablaze with light, which picked out a haze of smoke tumbling up into the night sky. A train was departing, its mournful whistle seemingly declaring its reluctance to leave. Hardy felt the same unwillingness to abandon the relative warmth of his vehicle. He did not believe in ghosts. No, that was a rather ludicrous statement. He had, if he were to believe his own senses, been in the company of one particular shade very recently. On the other hand, could it have been just a mental aberration? *Was he mad?* Still stuck on the wire? Was he dead and everything he had experienced since merely his slow progress through purgatory?

"Rather dramatic thinking, that—worth sixpence of anyone's money," Hardy said aloud, mocking his own thoughts. He ran his gloved left hand round the steering wheel. Yet the feeling of doubt still lingered. Even though to all outward appearances he had accepted his survival of the war, the nagging fact remained that the wire still held him mentally, chained to events that had happened in a Flanders field five years before.

Hand of Glory

A flash of headlights in front drew his attention. A large car had drawn up in front of The Railway Hotel. The driver was trying with difficulty to park the vehicle as close as possible to the pavement. After chugging backwards and forwards for a minute or so the driver decided to give up and switched off the engine. A quartet of female figures disembarked and stood for a moment under a streetlight. He watched them shake out the creases in their coats and reposition their hats. Then, as one, three of them turned and walked towards the steps of the hotel. The fourth did not move, as if she did not want to go in. *Know how she feels.* Then the fourth figure put back her shoulders and walked after her companions.

"Well, if I am going to go, I best get moving." As he got out of the car his left leg began to ache as if it were averse to taking his weight. He turned and locked the car, then stamped his foot, trying to encourage the limb to cooperate. It did, after a fashion. Of late the injured leg had gone through stages, from struggling to cope with even the slightest movement, to being able to undertake a five-mile walk without so much as a twitch of pain. At first he'd believed he had developed the king-sized version of a weather ache, but had found out that the symptoms did not correspond to changes in either precipitation or temperature. Perhaps it was his state of mind that triggered the leg's unpredictable reactions? He shrugged his shoulders and began to walk towards the hotel.

The warmth in the lobby of the building made him undo his coat as he walked up the stairs in the direction of the small function room on the first floor. He was not alone. A gentle stream of figures flowed round him, all a lot more eager than he to reach their destination. He removed his trilby as he reached the open door. He stood there for a moment, inching the brim of the hat round in his gloved hands. The soft swish of the leather against the fabric counterpointed the rising level of voices coming from inside the room.

A cough sounded behind him. Hardy turned, and there stood a man in his early forties, slightly balding, glasses balanced on his nose. The man was looking at him. Then he spoke. "Are you entering, sir?–as we would like to close the doors."

"Yes, of course," Hardy replied, moving into the room.

The smell of incense caught at the back of his throat, making his eyes water. He slipped onto the end seat of the back row on the left-hand side. It gave him a good view of the table at the head of the room, and an even better view of the side profile of the young woman on the end of the fourth row from the front on the right-hand side. It was Agnes Reed. Sister Reed, the former nurse who had denied knowing him when he knew she did. Was she as unwilling to face her past as he was to leave his? He peered through the shadowy candlelight at the women with her: yes, it was Elizabeth, Elizabeth's mother and, *God*, Charlotte Warner. He had no liking for the woman. The times he had been in her company he had been hard-pressed to keep his temper. She was middle class to the bone. The woman was obsessed with maintaining her position in local society and looking down on the rest of her fellow citizens.

In the trenches Hardy had lost what little belief he'd had in the class system. The mud and pain had been a great leveller of men's abilities and self belief. What on earth did Mrs Warner want with a séance? It was not from some spiritual need, he was sure. That said, he still did not know why he had come. He took off his gloves and placed them with his hat on the empty chair beside him, waiting for the event to begin.

He did not have to wait long. A draft of air told him that the door behind him had opened again. The rustle of silk confirmed the entrance of at least one person. Like everyone else in the room, Hardy turned to look at the new arrival. A woman had entered, dressed in black, in a style more suited to the turn of

Hand of Glory

the century. In fact, in a manner Hardy had seen a lot of in France. She wore the dress of a widow: black silk heavily laden with lace, the hem of the garment trailing on the floor. The woman's hair was long, piled up on her head, again in a fashion long discarded by most of the women in the room. Fine lengths of lace and black ribbon hung from the twisted confection. All this, Hardy assumed, supported the idea that Madame Marie was of mature years. Nothing could be further from the truth. She was very young, barely in her early twenties.

After Madame had walked past Agnes Reed, he saw the former nurse's expression change from one of surprise to one of suspicion. He felt his lips twitch. So, Agnes had her own doubts about the forthcoming event. His smile was noticed: Agnes nodded her head in recognition as she looked back, past the young woman, to him. Well, this time she did admit she knew him, as the suspicion in her features changed to puzzlement. She'd opened her mouth to speak when a small bell began to ring, drawing her gaze forward to the group now standing at the front of the room.

The young woman with the blonde hair was standing next to Madame Marie, gently ringing a small bell. Two gentlemen, one in his early twenties and the older one Hardy had seen previously, began doing the same. The conversations in the audience died under the spell of the silver chimes. Madame Marie waved her hands through the billowing cloud of incense, then sat down. The bells stopped and Madame's three assistants moved behind her.

"We shall begin," Madame Marie said, her voice thickly accented. Madame picked up a pile of thick cards and placed them out on the table, then just sat there. The silence began to lengthen. People shifted in their seats. An odd cough and the tap of shoes on the floor sounded out. The hairs on the back of Hardy's neck began to stand up as he felt the tension in the room rise. It was nonsense, mere hokum. Suddenly Madame

Marie's body jerked as if she'd been shot. Her arms flailed about, her head went back, then she was still. A gasp went round the audience. Hardy found himself joining in.

Then Madame Marie began to speak. Her voice changed pitch with each set of jumbled sentences. Deep, almost a man's, then high, whining like a spoiled child. The most surprising thing was that her French accent vanished. Her voice now varied from upper class English with a nasal twang to almost a perfect mirror of local working class. Then names, places, dates, and piteous cries streamed into the verbal concoction Madame Marie was mixing. Then she began to thrash around again, calling out in her own voice for them, whoever they were, to be patient. The blonde woman caught one of Madame Marie's upraised hands and held it tight. Madame Marie sobbed and sat bolt upright, her young face tearful. She gulped, nodding in thanks to her companion, and reached out her other hand for the glass the older man was now offering her.

Madame Marie took a sip of the liquid and handed the glass back to the man. Then she spoke as if she were in pain. "There are many here tonight, so many. Did anyone hear a name, something? Answer, please—help me make the connection for you."

Hardy could hear the collective hiss of hard-held breath exhaled by his fellow members of the audience. They were all spellbound, totally caught in the moment. Yet Hardy felt completely detached from events, as if all he had just witnessed were mere play-acting: interesting, but not real at all. As first one hand, then another, raised, Hardy heard a cynical snort from behind him. It was accompanied by a plume of smoke that wafted over his shoulder. He knew that smell. A Woodbine cigarette. Adams's favourite, *old coffin nails*. He glanced round, half expecting to see Adams, but the ghost of his friend was not there. There was just a fast-dissipating cloud of twisted cigarette smoke. Yet the impression that Adams's shade had

Hand of Glory

been here—and was not impressed by Madame Marie's performance—remained with Hardy as he returned his attention to the continuing séance.

A woman was speaking of a dead child, voice quaking with emotion. Madame answered, her tones childlike, uncertain. The woman sobbed, thanking the medium. The process was repeated, again, again. Sometimes Madame's answers were vague. Then, to Hardy's surprise, now and then her remarks contained solid information, which drew gasps from the audience as the knowledge was confirmed by one or more persons. It was as if Madame Marie were spinning a web, entangling all in the room in its fine, binding threads, which drew more from the audience than was given away by Madame Marie.

It was all a trick. Did the others not see? Yes, the woman knew a few details about the families of those here, but nothing that was not common knowledge or could not be gleaned by asking a few questions locally. Yet the majority of those here took her parading of this knowledge as proof of her lauded gift. His face flushed with anger. Real ghosts were not worried about naming who should have their three-strand pearl necklace, like the phantom of Charlotte Warner's mother, who was supposedly currently whispering in Madame's ear. Hardy knew the real dead just wanted to go home and rest. As Adams did, like all those he had seen on the day of the unveiling of the memorial. He picked up his hat and gloves and made to stand, then stopped as he heard Elizabeth Parker's voice. No—she of all people could not have swallowed this perversion.

"Madame, one name you mentioned... " Her voiced faded a little. "Christian."

"*Oui*, Christian. He is a young man in his prime. Pale now, and in the uniform. He stands close to you." Madame Marie's voice quivered. She shifted in her seat, her eyes looking fixed, not on Elizabeth, but somewhere at the back of the small function room. Hardy felt a chill. At him? No. Her gaze was directed behind him. He was sure she was looking at someone by the door. Hardy looked back. A long, twisted shadow of a man was falling through the half-open door. Someone *was* there. Whoever it was was not just listening, but conducting the whole performance. For, as Hardy watched, the head of the shadow nodded and Madame began to speak again.

"He is an officer? A young, brave lieutenant?" Madame stopped, awaiting confirmation from Elizabeth.

"Yes," Elizabeth said as she stood up, ignoring Agnes, who was reaching up a hand to restrain her cousin.

"Mud, he is telling me of the mud and the shell-holes. It is so cold. He is lost there."

"Oh, my son!" Elizabeth's mother sobbed, falling into the arms of Charlotte Warner amid gasps from the rest of the audience.

"He wants to talk to you, this brave Lieutenant Tennant."

"You know he don't give a damn about the likes of you or me. Time he was fucking well topped." The words exploded in Hardy's mind, like a star shell which illuminated a single memory long pushed down into the depths of his mind.

A shell-hole.

Water up to his chest, rank and sickly.

The bite of the wire.

The murder on the rim.

"Hand of Glory, hand of a hanged murderer!"

The sight of the butchered lieutenant's body rising from the shell-hole as Adams and the others had pulled him free. The way the lieutenant's face had surfaced, mouth open, as if speaking. A gasp of air bubbling from dead lungs. A sound. Words forming. Impossible, but he heard them now. *"Hand within the hand. Five flames. Dark mist."* No. Hardy screwed up his eyes, trying to blot out the vision. He drew in a breath, relieved that the nightmare scene from the past had stopped flickering on the screen of his thoughts. Hardy opened his eyes and found his relief was short-lived. The ghost of Adams was standing in the aisle between the chairs. Mud ran in runnels off his puttee-encased legs, staining the polished wooden floor and gathering in the seams of the boards. The corporal was nodding, as if confirming what the voice of the murdered lieutenant had said.

Hardy found he could not expel the air he had taken into his lungs. He could not breathe, just like those men who had sunk beneath the foaming, foul mud of no man's land. His feet scrabbled to find purchase on the floor, as he heaved himself up and staggered to the door. He forced it open, colliding with the owner of the shadow, and for one moment he came face to face with the man. Yet he did not see him. Hardy only saw mud and felt the wire binding his chest ever tighter.

"Easy on," the man said, as his hands went out to steady Hardy's stumbling flight.

Hardy batted at the man's hands, dropping his hat and gloves as he stumbled past. Down the curved staircase he went, his shoes slipping on the carpet. His left leg suddenly gave way. He fell forward. His right hand snapped out instinctively and he grabbed hold of the curled and carved wrought iron that held the banister. The metal bit deep into his palm, opening up the recent and old wound. Hardy called out, swearing as he swung sideways and hit the banister, doubling over the polished wood at his waist. For a moment he hung over the edge, looking down to the lobby of the hotel one floor below. Then he heaved himself back and collapsed hard on his rear onto one of the wide steps. The breath that had been trapped in his lungs raced out, leaving him gasping. Hardy dropped his head into his hands, ignoring the dampness as the blood from his cut hand smeared his brow. He tried to breathe again, but his body refused to cooperate. Then the air poured in, expanding his chest, and, as it did, the sights and sounds of the past went back into the battered old footlocker deep in his memory.

"That poor old hand. This will be the second handkerchief of mine you've absconded with; you'll be getting quite a collection of them if you continue. Though I must add, I am very much obliged to you for providing me with an excuse not to go back in there quite as soon as I would have had to." It was Agnes Reed. She was sitting on the step next to him, his hat and gloves on the step between her feet. The fingers of her right hand came up and began plucking at his in an effort to release their hold on his forehead. Hardy allowed her to take his hand in hers. He watched her place it on her lap and wrap the small, white square of linen round it with professional precision. "You'd best go and wash your face. You look as if you've been in the wars. I'll sit here and look after your things." She gave him a broad wink, tapping her fingers on the top of his trilby hat.

"My leg–it gave way," Hardy mumbled.

"Not surprised, seeing the speed with which you were bolting out of there; wish I'd had the courage to do just that. I had to plead I needed the ladies' room."

Hardy gave her a half-smile.

"That's better," she said in her best nurse's voice.

"Still giving me orders, Sister Reed?" he asked as he sat there, his hand still in hers.

"I'm sorry, I should have... " She blushed as she spoke, chewing her lower lip in a rather attractive fashion.

"I understand," he said. Wanting to comfort her, he turned his hand over and took hold of hers, suddenly becoming aware of how their two hands moulded together.

"No, it wasn't like that. It was just everyone would have started asking silly questions. I don't mind talking about it. It was a special time for me, but for you it was different. I was...

Hand of Glory

well, useful. I was doing something important, not only for others, but for myself. People don't seem to realise that. They talk about the sacrifice we nurses made, but it was far from that, at least for me."

"I see," Hardy replied, wondering what she actually meant. She had been changed by the war, that much was certain. It was plain Agnes considered it a transformation for the better. It might be pleasant to find out more if she would let him. It had been a long time since he'd been interested in another person in this way. Now, faced with the slight prospect of actually wanting to get to know her, he was unsure how to go about it. He found the smile on his face widening for some strange reason, and his hold on her hand tightening.

"Hand within a hand. Hand of Glory?"

The thought struck him so unexpectedly, he did not realise he had said the words aloud until Agnes repeated them. "Hand of Glory?" She frowned. "I've heard that phrase before somewhere."

"Have you?" he asked, his eyes searching her face, his interest in her changing in nature.

"Yes, I'm sure, but I can't quite put my finger on it. It will come back to me," Agnes said, her frown increasing. "It was in France."

Hardy felt a chill steal up his spine. Everything went back to those muddy fields of France and Flanders. "France?"

"Yes, I think it was something I read." The sound of other voices now began to trickle down the stairs. "The meeting has finished." Agnes suddenly changed the subject and glanced down at their joined hands. It was Hardy's turn to blush. Silly. He had nothing to feel embarrassed about. He released his hold on her. She picked up his hat and gloves and stood up.

Hardy placed his damaged hand on the banister and heaved himself up. Both Agnes's hands came out as if to steady him. He looked at her, his eyebrows raised. "Still playing the nurse, wanting to give me a hand?"

"I don't play." She sounded annoyed.

"I'm sorry. I didn't mean–" Hardy said as the noise in the corridor above them increased.

"No need to be. Oh, we are beginning to talk nonsense, aren't we?" Agnes gave a giggle.

"Very much so, with hands playing a large part, and you still have my hat and gloves in yours," Hardy said as he felt the pain in his left leg suddenly ease. *Strange.* The weakness was gone.

"Oh." She began to hand them to Hardy, then blurted out, "It was a story!"

"What was?"

"The Hand of Glory! I can't remember details, but one young officer had a book with it in. It was when I was stationed on the coast, before I was sent to the advanced dressing stations. We, the newly arrived nurses, that is, were considered too cack-handed for anything other than basic tasks, so we were often put to reading or writing letters for the wounded awaiting evacuation to Blighty."

"Cack-handed?" Hardy repeated, trying not to laugh and not succeeding.

"Oh, you… " Agnes said, and laughed herself. "I would have you know my time in France widened my vocabulary considerably."

"I bet it did, but try not to use it too much in front of Elizabeth," Hardy said.

"Too late for that." As she spoke, Agnes was looking up the staircase. "I think Elizabeth is looking for me." The tone of her voice told Hardy that Elizabeth would not be pleased with Agnes for absconding from the séance.

"I'd best come and explain you were being my Florence Nightingale again." Hardy made to take her arm.

Hand of Glory

"Sanfairyann!" Agnes retorted.

"Agnes! Of all the times, too—such language! *Ca ne fait rien.* 'It was nothing'? It certainly was something. Have you no sense of decorum? Giles, I can't begin to apologise." Elizabeth's mother, Mrs Tennant, spoke from above them.

Hardy began to try to answer in Agnes's defence, but found he was laughing. Not the cynical or self-lacerating laughter which since his time in France had come more than often from his lips. No, this laughter was clean, honest and open. He was not the only one. Agnes, too, was laughing. Her green eyes crinkled at the corners, making them more attractive.

Chapter Eight

Friday–3rd November–1922

The soft whoosh and pop of the gas lamp as it was lit filled the small kitchen. Taffy's eyes narrowed slightly as they adjusted to the illumination. He liked gaslight. The soft, yellow glow did not hurt his eyes as much as the newfangled electric light bulbs. Even bright sunlight made him wince these days. But he was lucky, and he damn well knew it. Others had not been so lucky when that cloud of yellow mustard gas had rolled across no man's land in 1917. The gas had clung to anything it touched. It burned lungs, skin and eyes. Days after, it still did. Kit became contaminated. Bloody gas masks were no good.

Taffy felt his lungs tighten, as they always did in the morning. Be better with a cup of tea inside him. A good brew always put the world to rights. He coughed as he put the kettle on, not just a clearing of his throat, but a rasping hack that seemed to come up from the bottom of his boots.

"Bloody Huns," he muttered. They had ruined him, and Taffy was not about to forgive and forget. He had been the best: quick, clean and silent. Now he could barely walk from his home in Greyfriars into Market Square without coughing up half his guts. Then there was the matter of his eyes. What good

Hand of Glory

was a cat burglar who needed bottle-bottom lenses to see an arm's length in front of him? Gone were the days of swiftly scaling walls, dodging round corners and playing cat and mouse with the local coppers. Even in the trenches there had been times when his skill had saved his–and other lads'–bacon. Those were the days, alright. He did not regret joining up. Just because he'd been a thief did not mean he was not as patriotic as the next fella. Just the bloody Hun had not played fair.

The kettle whistled and Taffy Holbrook turned his attention back to his tea. As he made the brew he warmed his hands on both the teapot and his china mug. Taffy felt the cold. It had crept into his bones in the trenches and he had never been able to banish it.

Soon, mug and toast in hand, he set about opening his business. On his release from His Majesty's forces Taffy had gone legitimate, or rather had decided to make use of his keen sense of what was valuable. He had moved away from Swansea and settled in Stafford. It made sense; he had cousins here. They were good, honest, hard-working folk. It made it easy for him to slip into the town and settle down. He still moved the odd bit for the local petty criminals. Small stuff: watches, jewellery and suchlike. Nothing that he would not move in the legitimate side of his business, he made a point of that. What was one watch among a few dozen? Unless it was engraved with the name of the owner, of course. He never touched anything that was marked in that way; those were too bloody easy for the plods to trace.

Taffy took a large swig of tea and felt the warm liquid move down his throat, easing the tightness there. He placed the mug down by the side of his breakfast on the shop counter and unbolted the grating fixed to the wood. Moving this to one side he could then open the counter and walk into the shop proper. There were no goods for sale here. Taffy did not run that type of shop. He was a pawnbroker, and a damn good one.

Susan Boulton

Taffy undid the locks on the shop door, then slipped the blind up on his window and turned round the sign hanging against the inside of the glass. It was barely six o'clock on Friday morning, but he knew that he would be very busy before long. Fridays always were; like Mondays, it was a day when folks realised they needed a little extra cash.

Taffy had just made his second brew of the day when the small bell on top of the shop door tinkled. A man walked in, his hobnail boots clattering on the wooden floor. His flat cap was tipped forward and his neck muffled by a thick scarf, the ends of which were tucked into his jacket.

"Morning," Taffy said as he settled himself on the high stool behind his metal screen. He pulled on a pair of knitted half gloves and laced his fingers, patiently waiting to see what his customer had brought.

"Morning," the customer answered and fumbled in his jacket pocket. He rubbed the objects he removed with his fingers before placing them down in the metal tray.

Taffy did not pull the tray through the slit in the bottom of the grating. He did not have to look closely at the items to gauge their value; it was not much in monetary terms, but to the man in front of him they represented four years of his life. Taffy owned a similar row of medals. He had worn them last Saturday when the memorial in Victoria Square had been unveiled.

"You sure now, Bob?"

"Am sure," Bob replied and rubbed his unshaven chin.

"Look, why don't you leave them until after Armistice Day?"

"Can't afford to, Mr Holbrook. Now, if you don't mind..." Bob pushed the tray towards the opening.

"Very well, Bob." For a moment he thought to offer the half-crown as a loan, then thought better of it. Bob would be

Hand of Glory

insulted. Men like Bob did not want charity; they just wanted the chance to earn a decent living.

Taffy inched the tray through and removed the medals, replacing them with the silver coin. Bob pulled the tray back and pocketed the money. He nodded in thanks and took his leave. Taffy sat for a moment after the man's departure, then took a paper bag and carefully wrote on it in thick, black pencil the type of goods and the name of the owner. The doorbell rang again. The sound of not one pair of feet, but three, echoed round the small room. The tap of metal on wood brought Taffy's gaze up from his task; he coughed, cursed and gave a smile that had no greeting in it whatsoever.

"Been busy, Holbrook?"

"Friday morning, Inspector, always busy. What can I do for you? The week tapped you out? I can do you a nice price for that gold hunter watch of yours." Taffy ignored the glare of the young constable on the left of Detective Inspector Parker.

"I'm sure you can," Parker replied, his metal claw hand tapping first the tray, then the counter. "As I said, been busy?"

"I don't know what you mean, Inspector." Taffy's eyes narrowed. What did the sod want? Stumpy Parker did not concern himself with the odd day's work of a half-grown pickpocket that sometimes passed across Taffy's counter.

"Don't you?" Parker moved forward until the tips of his boots were against the bottom of the counter. His clawed hand reached out and grabbed the metal grating that separated him from Taffy.

As Taffy watched, the metal began to bend outward under the pressure of the claw. He began to cough. He could feel the blood draining from his face. Spittle formed on his lips. He pulled a handkerchief from his pocket, shook out the large folds and wiped his mouth, trying to ignore the dots of red that appeared on the white linen. The spasm stopped, but it left him gasping for air. His sight misted with pain. He pushed his left index finger up under his glasses and rubbed first one eye, then another.

"Yes, I fucking well do, but look at me, Inspector bloody Parker, just look. I cannot even twitch without coughing me bloody guts up. Jerry did for me, right and proper, the bastards. I am retired."

Parker let go of the grating and stepped back, a soft smile on his lips. "So I heard, but then, again, you might have thought the Warners' a soft target, Mr Warner having charge of the collections to date for the poppy appeal."

How dare this arse-wipe Parker think he would steal from the lads, his fellow ex-soldiers? "Sod you, Stumpy Parker!" At the venom in his voice, the two constables with the inspector moved closer to the counter. "You think I would do that? You can go to hell in a basket."

"So there's no reason for these lads to take a look in the back or upstairs?"

"They can take a look with pleasure, so they can, but they won't find any bloody thing belonging to the Warners. Their sort don't do any business with me." Taffy spat. "I served like you, Parker, did my bit. I wouldn't take money I knew was meant for lads worse off than me–or you, for that matter, Inspector–even if I were bloody well starving."

"Had to ask, Taffy. You're the only one I know round here with the knack of getting in unseen."

Taffy's eyes widened. What game was the bugger playing at now? Was Parker trying to get him to admit something? No plod gave you such details. He could tell Parker was waiting for an answer. Taffy did not oblige.

"Aye, well, let's hope no one comes through that door with something they *found* that used to belong to the Warners, eh?"

Hand of Glory

With this Parker put the tip of his claw to his trilby hat, tipping it back on his head.

Taffy still did not reply.

Parker sighed and nodded to his two constables. The men turned and left the shop. Parker followed, stopping in the doorway, as if debating whether to say anything more. "Taffy, what happened at the Warners' would make even what the likes of you got up to once upon a time look lily-white."

"Fucking hell," Taffy swore as the door closed behind the inspector. Whoever had done over the Warners' home must have left someone cold on the floor. *Bloody idiots.* That sort of thief gave everyone a bad name. Taffy had prided himself on being a gentleman thief. He'd only taken small-yet-expensive stuff. He'd loved the challenge of getting it without leaving a clue for the plods to go on. It had been part of the thrill.

Some murdering sod had decided to set up business here in town and topped a mark. The police would turn the whole place on its head. They would give no one currently in the business— or retired, for that matter—any peace. Taffy knew he would not be the only one having a visit from Inspector Parker today.

He needed another cup of tea, that was for sure. As he made his way into the kitchen, Taffy felt a wave of anger rise in his chest. The sods had stolen money from the lads; they'd caused the plods to question his *retirement.*

Taffy banged the kettle down on the gas cooker. The water splashed out, running down the sides, hissing as it hit the flames. As Taffy watched the kettle come to a boil he made up his mind. He would find out exactly what had happened at the Warners'. He would check if the inspector had been telling the truth. Then, depending on that, he would do some sniffing around. Or give Stumpy a piece of his mind for yanking his chain. Not that Taffy thought it was a joke: even Parker would not abuse the memory of the lads in one of his little pranks.

Susan Boulton

*****

The day went slowly for Taffy. Every spare moment he had, he went over Inspector Parker's visit. By five o'clock in the evening he'd decided enough was enough. He usually stayed open until seven o'clock, but not tonight. By quarter past five he had locked up and was on his way across town, his thin frame wrapped in a large overcoat, with a thick scarf wound round his neck. A bowler hat was pulled down over the tops of his ears, the black rim framed by a layer of Taffy's blonde hair. Every five dozen steps he coughed, pushed his thick glasses back against the bridge of his nose, and steeled himself for the next five dozen.

He made his way into Market Square, glancing at the police station on the ground floor of the Guildhall as he walked close by. He nodded at the young policeman standing by the door. The plod, his double-breasted coat done up tightly under his chin, returned Taffy's nod. Taffy knew Inspector Parker would be informed of his being out and about earlier than usual. He did not like the idea of being Parker's snout, but the matter touched on the lads' honour—if Parker was right about the money taken. He moved down the side of the High Court buildings, making for North Walls. As Taffy got closer to his destination, the buildings he passed changed; there were no more smart examples of civic pride or thriving places of business. The windows of the small shops were stained, the streets narrow and dark. The back-end of nowhere, that was for sure.

A rough-painted sign swung above a pair of open gates. The air in the street was heavy with the smell of wet hops. A barrel rolled out of the small yard, clattering against the cobbles as it wobbled to join a number of others by the offside rear wheel of a small dray. The horse in the shafts snorted as Taffy walked

Hand of Glory

into the yard. He made for the far side, in the direction of a one-room pub attached to the small brewery.

The door to The Hole in the Wall was ajar. It was not quite opening time, but Holbrook knew they would be serving a few select customers. He pushed the door and watched the last of the fading daylight trickle across the sawdust-covered floor. He stepped in.

"Damn me, what you doing out this early? Something up?"

"I just fancied a bit of your company, Mavis," Taffy replied and took his glasses off, wiping the misted lenses on the cuff of his right sleeve.

Mavis flicked the tea towel in her hand along the bar. "Flatterer. Well, get close to the fire and I'll bring you a pint over. How about some pie as well, me duck?"

"That would be right nice, Mavis." Taffy fumbled with the buttons of his coat, making his way across the room to the fireplace. He took off his coat and carefully folded it, placing it on the seat of the chair next to the one he intended to sit on. His bowler hat followed, but his scarf he kept on. He settled down, nodding in greeting to the other early customers.

"Here you go, love." Mavis placed the pint and pie down in front of him.

"Thanks, Mavis. Got a few moments? And, by the by, how you doing?" he asked as he picked up the pint and set it to his lips. The smell of the freshly drawn beer filled his nostrils. He felt a cough begin and quickly set the pint down, bringing his hand back up to cover his mouth as the spasm took over.

"Got a few. Not much doing yet, and I'm better than you by the sounds of it. You should take better care of yourself, or let someone else do it." She pulled a stool from a nearby table and straddled it, bunching her long skirt between her knees. "You need someone to rub goose fat on that there chest of yours more than once a week."

"You volunteering?" Taffy quipped.

"Why, you cheeky devil."

"Seriously, Mavis. You're a fine lass and you know how I feel."

"'Lass'–been a while since I was called that. Won't see thirty again. I'm too old for walking out." Mavis's laughter increased, a warm smile spreading over her face.

"Still plenty of life left in you for a gallop, let alone a walk. More than there is left in me."

"Don't you talk like that, me duck." Mavis laid her hand on his arm. "Just you need to take care of yourself, for my sake if no other's."

"I suppose so."

"Suppose nothing. You best do it." Mavis's fingers tightened on his arm and her eyes searched his face. "What's got you so gloomy?"

"I had a visitor this morning."

"Bloody hell, that sod covered some ground. I think he poked his nose into every corner of the town before noon."

"Been here as well, then?"

"Aye, told him straight I'd not heard anything. Not sure if the bugger believed me, but it was the truth. From what I heard later, whoever did it took even Mrs Warner's new Persian carpets."

"What? You're joking, Mavis," Taffy spluttered, his eyes widening.

"No, I am not." Mavis moved closer to Taffy; the stool grated on the stone floor and her fingers dug into his arm. A tangled wisp of her brown hair had fallen out of the bun at the nape of her neck. As she moved closer it brushed his cheek. Taffy could smell lavender soap and hops. "They, whoever they were, went through the place like the bailiffs."

Hand of Glory

"Well, I'll be." How the hell had they done that? Were the family away? Couldn't've been, least not from what Parker had hinted at. Taking even carpets? Stupid. They would've had Warner down on them with his shotgun. Oh, was that it? Had Warner taken a pound of shot from his own gun in his chest? No, that would've made the *Evening Sentinel*. The paperboy would've been shouting about it when he'd come across Market Square.

"Aye," Mavis agreed. She pushed back her stool and got to her feet. "Now, you eat that pie. No more flesh on you than a sparrow, Taffy Holbrook."

Taffy smiled as the woman moved back to the small bar. He had found out a bit, but he had his doubts as to whether it was gospel. Mavis loved a tale, and the taller it was the more she believed it. Still, there would be others in tonight who would perhaps know a bit more. One thing puzzled him. Parker had in his roundabout way said that someone had snuffed it during the burglary. Taffy had taken that to mean the thieves had topped someone. Maybe they hadn't. "Sod it..." Taffy swore as he felt his chest tighten. He began to cough and stopped himself, to speak. "Now, then, Bert, stop measuring me up."

"Sorry, Mr Holbrook, didn't mean to. I mean... just looking, I mean staring, I mean, oh, bugger..." the tall, thin young man at the next table gabbled. He was dressed in a dark suit, a little rubbed round the cuffs and half a size too big. His winged collar had come undone on the right side, and his face was as grey as that of any of the folk who'd graced his father's marble slab.

"Been a bad day, has it?" Taffy gave the young apprentice undertaker a smile and waved a hand for Bert to join him by the fire.

"You could say that, you could," Bert replied, shaking his head. He uncurled from his stool and came over, the beer slopping from his pint glass as he set it down on Taffy's table.

"Well, a couple of pints, a warm fire and Mavis's pie'll take care of that." Taffy signalled Mavis, indicating that he required two more pints. She nodded in reply and soon two glasses and more pie appeared on the table. At first Bert did not want to eat, but with Taffy's cajoling he soon tucked in. Taffy had seen the look in the young man's eyes before. The lad had seen something out of the ordinary. It was worrying at him like something stuck between his teeth. Couldn't just be the sight of a corpse. Bert was third generation undertaker. He'd been at home with the dead as a boy, as Taffy had been with shinning up drainpipes.

As the evening progressed Taffy made an effort to talk to the young man, trying to draw out of him what had shaken him so, partly because Taffy was of the opinion that if a chap kept things bottled up they would only get worse until they couldn't be contained. He'd seen it in the trenches. Been there himself. He talked about things now, to Mavis mainly, but he talked about them. Besides, his gut was telling him Bert's reluctance to talk might have something to do with what had happened at the Warners'.

Taffy got Bert talking about the Rangers' match last Saturday and where the team stood in the Birmingham Combination league. What was on at the picture house and who was courting who among the young folk of the town. By the end of the evening, when Mavis called time, Bert's face was glowing more from the beer than the fire and he was talking freely, his conversation jumping all over the place. "Not frightened of dead bodies. I've seen lots of them. Can't harm you, but, bugger it, Mr Holbrook, I hope I don't see one like that again. It fair shook me up; even Dad did a double take."

"Like what?" Taffy asked, as out of the corner of his eye he saw Mavis shooing the last of the other stragglers from the small pub.

Hand of Glory

"Like that. As stiff as a board, the old gent was, and sitting on the indoor privy, his hands gripping the seat so tight you'd think they were glued to it. Shit himself well and truly as well, all over his nightshirt. That didn't bother me—it was the look on his face, Mr Holbrook."

Mavis had joined them and was sitting on the other side of the young man, tutting and patting his right hand where it gripped the edge of the round table.

"His face, Bert?" Taffy prompted.

"Horrible. All twisted. Like... like he'd been frightened to death." Bert took his pint and drained the liquid. He wiped the drips from his mouth on the sleeve of his suit.

"Well, I'll be. What would do that to a man?" Mavis asked, shaking her head.

"Don't know, Mavis, but there wasn't a mark on the old man. Me dad said his heart must've given out when the buggers surprised him on the privy. But I've seen gents whose hearts have given out, and they don't look like that. He was shit-scared to death, I swear it." Bert banged the glass down and stumbled up from his stool.

"You going to be alright?" Taffy asked.

"Aye, just got to get round the corner. Not had that much."

Taffy's eyebrows rose at this. "Sure?"

"Sure, Mr Holbrook, and thank you," Bert replied as he lurched towards the door.

"Me pleasure, Bert. Tell you what, me and Mavis'll walk with you to the gas lamp and make sure you get into your dad's yard." As he spoke, Taffy got up and picked up his coat. He began to cough, and cursed as he pulled on the garment. Maybe the lad might let slip who he was talking about. Taffy had a good idea. It fitted. The younger Warners certainly would not have allowed the knowledge that the old Mr Warner had died on the privy during a robbery to become common knowledge.

"No need," Bert mumbled as he swayed by the door.

"Every need," Mavis said as she joined Taffy in guiding the young man out the door and down the cobbled street.

Taffy stood alongside Mavis under the gas lamp, as Bert got his bearings. "Good night, Bert. I hope tomorrow isn't as bad as today was for you."

"I bloody well hope not, Mr Holbrook," Bert said, as he decided that his father's yard was behind him, not in front. He tried to straighten himself up, half tripped, swore and walked into the shut half of the double gates. He staggered backwards. Both Mavis and Taffy started forward. Bert waved them back. "I'm alright, don't worry. It's just that look on old Warner's face keeps coming back to me." Bert's voice faded away as he vanished into the depths of the undertaker's yard.

"It'll fade, don't you worry," Taffy said as he exchanged surprised looks with Mavis. *Well, damn me, so that's it.* Not only had the buggers stripped the house, they'd frightened an old man to death on the privy.

"Well," Mavis remarked as she tucked her arm into Taffy's. They walked back to the warmth of The Hole in the Wall.

"Well, indeed, Mavis," Taffy said as he shut the door behind them and turned the key.

Mavis laughed at his actions. "You staying, then?"

"You want me to?"

"Aye, if you want. What Burt said, do you...?"

"Yes, but it doesn't make any sense. Robbers that can strip a house with the folks still in it, and frighten an old man to death in the process..." It didn't feel or sound right to him. There was something more, something that had Parker worried as hell and had set him stirring folks up to find out what was going on.

"Not much that does make sense, love," Mavis said, and she leaned over and gave him a soft kiss on his cheek.

Chapter Nine

"Easy with that there carpet. I don't want it to arrive in London fucking damaged." It was taking too bloody long to get this finished up. He had already dispatched Lilly and Kevin back to The Railway Hotel, to get things sorted out for the private séance, as things here were dragging on.

Archie was standing, overlooking the disposal of the last of the goods he and his little band had acquired the previous night. They were being wrapped and boxed up, and would hopefully be on Friday's noon train to London. Once there, they would be delivered to his special warehouse to await his return to The Smoke. Archie had more than enough money to be able to wait and move the goods when the market was at its best. Besides, it was better to hang onto them for a while. He had learned that the hard way in France. Him and Marie had nearly got caught in Paris trying to move some stuff too soon after a job, and had had to abandon a pile of loot there.

"Am being careful, Boss." William Clover winked at Archie as he gave the rope holding the thick brown paper round the rolled carpet one last tug. Cheeky young bugger. Get any sharper, he'd cut himself. *Need to keep an eye on him.*

"All is done, *oui?*" Marie asked. Archie looked round. Marie stood framed against the morning light that trickled through the half-open doors of the small lock-up he had rented behind the Lotus Shoe Factory. She looked lovely; Archie smiled.

The road outside the lock-up was always busy. No one would notice a lorry shifting stuff, especially not on a Friday morning. The factory opposite had been churning out shoes and boots by the hundreds since early Monday; lorries here were ten a penny, running up and down.

"If you act legitimate, then folks don't see what's under their bloody noses," Jim said.

"Aye, nearly," Archie replied to Marie's question as he gestured for William to grab one end of the rolled carpet. The young man obliged, and between them they carried it to the vehicle. William lodged his end on the tailgate and then jumped up into the lorry. Archie pushed from his end, but even with trying the extra-long parcel at an angle it would not quite fit. Archie gestured for William to shift a few of the other parcels and they laid the carpets down the middle of the lorry.

William got out of the lorry and dusted his hands, slapping the palms across one another in a satisfied manner. Then, whistling, he walked back into the lock-up and picked up a length of rope from the floor. He then set about tying the handles of the rear doors together. "That should hold it, Boss, no problem." He made to walk round to the cab of the lorry, but Archie beckoned him to come back into the lock-up for a moment.

"You're going to have to deal with him sooner than later. The lad's getting too bloody cocky." Archie ignored Jim. If anything, it was he who was getting too cocky. He could deal with Will without Jim's interference.

"What is this?" Marie came to Archie's side, a pile of torn, off-white paper in her hands. She was angry. Her right foot was tapping and her dark eyes mere slits. She thrust the paper at Archie. He took it, spreading first one sheet out, then another.

Hand of Glory

They were spoiled address labels. Archie turned to face William.

"Lilly spoiled a couple of the addresses on some of the parcels. She had to re-do them," William answered, giving his employer a sickly smile.

"So sure of himself, positive you'll believe him. Well, Willy boy is about to learn his mistake in thinking that, isn't he, Archie?" Jim said.

Archie agreed, but did not comment so to his companion.

"That does not sound like Lilly. She has a good hand," Marie said.

"No, it bloody well doesn't." Archie grabbed hold of William's jacket lapels and thrust his scarred face into the young man's.

"Time to remind William smart arse who's boss."

"Yes, fucking me..." Archie said under his breath, the words directed at his brother, who did not show any sign of hearing them. Just as he had not remarked on Archie ignoring him since the other day, when, for the first time, he had openly disagreed with him.

"Now, Boss..." William began, as Archie pushed him backwards, nearly lifting him off his feet. William's hands grabbed hold of Archie's arms, his fingers digging in. Archie ignored the pain. William began to struggle, his hands now striking at Archie's arms. His face whitened in fear at the lack of effect his blows were having. Archie slammed him against the rear wall of the lock-up, enjoying the sharp cracking sound the youth's head made as it bounced off the brickwork.

"An answer, *oui?*" Marie said as she began to close the lock-up doors.

"She was all of a shake. It was seeing that old geezer dead on the throne like that," William babbled. "I told her it didn't bloody matter. It was just a few labels. I told her you wouldn't dock it out of her money. She was worried you would."

"Not telling me a fucking whopper, are you, Will? Want us to turn the lorry over and check your stuff back at the hotel?" Archie slammed William against the wall again. The force made the young man's jaw snap shut.

William's tongue came out streaked with blood. He licked at his lips. "Be my guest, Boss. Won't find anything, I fucking swear it!"

Archie could feel William shaking. The faint light that was coming from the crack in the doors caught on the sweat beading the young man's forehead. The bugger could still be lying, but Archie doubted he would find any of the stuff, even if Will had taken it into his head to swipe any. Will was smart. When he came to think about it, the young sod would not have left labels lying around. Archie let go of William. The youth stumbled, as if his legs had gone weak. He made a half-hearted attempt to straighten his jacket. His eyes flickered from Archie to Marie and back again.

Archie felt a smile twitch his lips. *That's taken the wind out of the young cock's sails, and no mistake.* Maybe Lilly just had the shakes a bit. The old fool popping his clogs at the sight of the Hand had been damn hard luck in some respects. However, Jim protested this line of reasoning: the power of the Hand had wanted–no, *demanded*–a death last night. Archie had to concede that an old man with a weak heart had been a less messy offering than someone he'd needed to knife. That would've gotten the plods well stirred up.

Still, Archie knew they would be digging a little deeper into the robbery than normal because of the old fart snuffing it. Maybe they ought to postpone the next one? No. That one he wanted so much he could taste it. Besides, these country coppers would not find out anything about him. Archie had made sure he'd kept clear of any of his old contacts here. An outside job was a rum one to crack, and not even the Yard had tumbled his little game over the years.

"Alright, let's get this stuff to the station. Then I want you to bring back the lorry and park it up in here for now. I don't want it left on the street. After that you can get some kip; won't be needing you until later this evening."

"Right you are, Boss," William said. His voice shook.

"You do not trust him?" Marie asked softly as Archie shut the doors of the lock-up.

The faint smell of a Woodbine cigarette wafted under Archie's nose. He pushed open the door again, peering in, the feeling of someone being there tightening his chest, making it hard for him to breathe. He could sense his brother sighing at his old irrational fear. On the ground near the door was a still-smouldering stub, black ash smeared on the concrete. His, had to be, or William's; both of them'd been smoking as they worked. It couldn't be anyone else's. He took a step in, crushing the remains of the cigarette under his heel. A thin tail of yellow smoke rose as he lifted his foot, making Archie shudder. He quickly moved outside again and shut the door, trying to dismiss the sensation as bloody nonsense, but not quite succeeding.

"I trust bloody nobody." Archie threaded the hook of the padlock through, snapped it shut, then tested it by giving it a sharp tug.

"Not even me?" Marie frowned, then laughed, "But then you love me, don't you? That is different, *non?*"

"Very different," Archie said and playfully slapped her bottom in response to her flirting.

"Such a naughty man," she giggled. She climbed into the lorry alongside William, blowing Archie a kiss as he took the starting handle and slotted it into the crank.

A nod from William told him he was ready, so Archie jerked the metal rod, once, twice. The engine burst into life. Archie could feel the vibrations in his arm reaching down to the bone. *Thump, thump.* Just like the shells in France. *Thump.* He shook his head. Done and gone; he had escaped. He'd got clean away from that sodding hell. He pulled out the handle and replaced it in its holder, then nodded to William to start the lorry moving. He jumped in beside Marie as the lorry sped past.

"Show off!" Marie laughed as he put his arm round her. Archie leaned back in the seat, his eyes straying to the rows of terraced houses as they slipped by.

"No, am not. Jim was, not me," Archie said as the lorry turned onto Gaolgate Street.

"You are thinking a lot about him lately?" Marie gave a soft smile; her hand came and rested on his knee.

"Aye, this was our sodding home turf. Our granddad died in that fucking place, for all I know." Archie's thumb jerked to his left at the large expanse of twenty-foot-high brick wall they were now passing. The small, narrow windows of the prison's upper floor could just be seen. The thin, late autumn sun bounced off the glass, turning the bars behind to silver.

"Bit of a bloody rum place, that, nearly in the centre of the town and all," William commented.

"Might as well be on the sodding moon," Archie snapped as the unwanted memories of his childhood flooded his mind. He fell into a sullen silence, mentally counting and licking his wounds, real and imagined.

"Put a sock in it, will you?..." Jim began, but Archie ignored him; they were *his* memories.

"Jesus!" William swore, his hands spinning the large steering wheel first left, then madly to the right. The lorry veered sharply across the road. Archie heard the thump of William's boot as he hammered the footbrake, hard. All three of

Hand of Glory

them shot to the right, slithering on the long leather seat. A loud bang from the rear of the lorry filled the cab as it rocked on its sparse suspension. Marie screamed. The vehicle continued on its new track in a screech of rubber, coming to a halt facing the way it had come. Archie's right hand clung to Marie's waist, striving to hold her back as she slid to her knees on the floor of the lorry. His left hand grabbed the narrow dashboard, arm locked tight, bracing himself back into his seat, trying not to join Marie on the floor. The engine rumbled, the metal hood juddering, as if expressing its own shock at the event.

"You young bloody arsehole!" Archie bellowed. "Marie?" His hands went down to help Marie back up onto the seat. She slowly came up, her whole body shaking. Archie put his arms round her, hugging her. He was surprised to feel the thud of his own heart. If she was hurt he would have it out of William's hide.

"A shitting man on a bike, he came out of bloody nowhere." William's hands left the steering wheel. He clenched them tight, then straightened his fingers and ran them through his hair.

"Mon Dieu!" Marie exclaimed, her eyes widening in fear. "You did not hit him? Please, Archie, look, please..."

"He better bloody well not have!" He released his hold on Marie and jumped out of the lorry. As his feet hit the ground, Archie's eyes began scanning the scene of their sudden stop. The lorry had spun round one hundred and eighty degrees, coming to rest in front of The Elephant and Castle Hotel at the end of Greengate Street.

"Buggering hell!" Archie swore as he walked round the front of the vehicle and down the driver's side, peering underneath. He hoped not to find a crushed bike and its rider under any of the wheels. There was nothing, save for the dying plumes of dust kicked up by the sudden braking of the lorry, all of which had a tint of yellow in them. The sick yellow of the mist that had hung over no man's land.

"Lucky, you was. He cut right across you. Never even bloody well stopped. Then he just vanished down the road. That's idiots on bikes for you. Dangerous buggers. Think they own the road. You've made a mess of your lorry rear, though. Looks like you clipped the drinking fountain beneath the clock." A man on the steps of the hotel was pointing with his pipe stem to the four-dial clock that stood high on its plinth in the centre of the square.

"Fuck!" Archie ran to the back of the lorry. As the lorry had spun, the half-open doors had caught on the protruding horse trough on the water fountain. The driver's side door had been ripped off and the other was just hanging on by the lower bracket. That was not the worst of it. A number of parcels lay strewn in the arc of the lorry's passage, and they were attracting the attention of a number of children.

"Bugger off!" Archie waved his fist at the children, who laughed and thumbed their noses at him as they ran off. "Will, get out here now! I want this bloody mess cleared up, then you get me and Marie back to The Railway Hotel."

Archie suddenly felt a ripple of fear beginning to grow. A man on a bike, vanishing; puffs of yellow smoke; their little game nearly burst right open because of a stupid accident. Archie felt a sick feeling begin to grow in his stomach, and for the first time Jim did not tell him it was nothing. Jim was quiet, and unreachable. Sulking, perhaps because Archie had ignored and gotten angry at him. Or perhaps Jim felt he did not need to say anything. Maybe it was just an accident. "I still want everything on the midday train. Then you get the bloody doors on this van repaired."

"Aye, Boss." William began picking up the parcels and putting them in the lorry. Archie slipped off his jacket. He

Hand of Glory

walked to Marie's side, slipping the garment round her shoulders, then hugging her.

"My knees, I think I have skinned them," she said softly, trying to smile up at him.

"I'll get a quack to look at you. I can afford it. Look, you sit back in the front while I help Will shift the stuff, and maybe we should think about cancelling that bloody séance night."

"*Non*, I know how much that one means to you."

*****

Archie closed the paper on his knee and glanced round the gentlemen's lounge of The Railway Hotel. It was only two o'clock, but the daylight outside was already fading. He was having second thoughts about the séance tonight. Things had started to go wrong the moment he'd stepped off the train. He should've known it. It was this armpit of a place; it had it in for him. He'd never had any luck when he'd lived here. Coming back only allowed the place to have another go at him.

"*Foolish thoughts,*" his brother remarked. "*We're safe—you, me, and the Hand—and able to do what we want.*"

"We bloody well are. Just bloody well be quiet for once. I keep my part of the bargain to the Hand, don't I? I don't need you lecturing me."

Jim was going to say something in reply, Archie could sense it. Then he didn't, leaving Archie wondering why. Jim knew he still wanted his revenge. Then there was that Captain Hardy, the one whose corporal tart had roughed him up the night he'd made a run for it. Hardy had been at the séance. He'd run full tilt into him in the doorway. Archie had recognised him in an instant. Had Hardy recognised him? He doubted it; those toffee-nosed buggers never did notice you except when they put you on a charge. He had watched the captain after, just to make sure, and seen him sitting on the stairs with a woman. The captain was chatting her up. All calf eyes, he was. Hardy's mind had certainly not been on shopping Archie to the plods.

Not that he was any different when it came to Marie. Archie gave a snort. Women did that to you. They messed with your head. The doctor had pronounced that Marie was fine, just suffering a bit of shock from the suddenness of the accident. The quack had advised that she should rest for a while. Archie had insisted she do so and had left her lying tucked up in bed. He did not want to risk her. Marie had chosen between him and her family. He'd said he would look after her, and a boss kept his promises to those who stood by him. His granddad had said only threaten when you needed to make a point, as he had with Will.

His eyes narrowed as he thought of William; that lad was hiding something, of that he was sure. Young bugger was as nervous as hell. Maybe something that should've been in one of the parcels was not. Grown sticky fingers, had he? Was he alone in this? Lilly? Oh, she had taken quite a shine to Will, that much was for certain. She might be helping him, or maybe she was up to something herself. Then it might be Kevin. No. He didn't have the stomach. He knew Archie would have it out of his hide. Then, again, maybe all three of them were in on it together. They were laughing at him behind his back. *Fuck it.* It was this place. It had him doubting his own people. Or was it the voice inside? Had he not, with Marie, hand-picked all of them? Archie rubbed his chin, trying to clear his mind of doubts, but not succeeding. He folded up the newspaper and laid it on the arm of the chair.

"There you are, sir," Kevin called as he entered the lounge. His hat and coat were damp. The wool fabric across his shoulders had begun to steam.

Archie's eyes snapped open. He did not like the sound of Kevin's voice. The bugger was worried about something.

Hand of Glory

Kevin moved to Archie's side, his eyes glancing round the room. "Might I suggest we talk privately, sir?"

Kevin turned and walked quickly to the door of the lounge. Archie followed the man through the lobby and out into the street. Kevin put up his large, black umbrella and held it at an angle in an attempt to cover Archie. Archie ignored the man and stood at the bottom of the hotel steps, waiting for him to speak.

Kevin cleared his throat and tried not to look Archie in the eye. "I think we might have a problem, sir." Archie did not answer, merely raised an eyebrow. "I was in the library this morning and..." Again, Kevin stopped, licked his lips, hesitated, then continued, "There was a lady at the desk asking about some information she had requested on folklore and stories. I also remember seeing her at the séance here at the hotel."

"And?" Archie asked, his eyes narrowing. Typical–the man never said anything right out.

"The Hand was mentioned; she seemed very interested in any information about it."

"What the fuck?" Archie's hand lashed out and grabbed Kevin by the front of his coat, dragging him across the few inches of pavement between them. "Who was she?"

"I questioned the librarian, but he was hesitant to say."

"But you did find out?"

"Yes, a Miss Agnes Reed."

"Well, find out bloody more. Everything, in fact, even down to the colour of her sodding bloomers," Archie hissed into Kevin's face.

"It will take me a day or so. I will have to make enquiries with people of a dubious nature, and it will cost," Kevin spluttered, his glasses slipping down his nose.

"Then bloody well do it, and make sure you cover your tracks," Archie snarled and turned to go back into the hotel. As he did so he stepped right into the path of Lilly. "Where are you going?" He glared at the young woman.

"Out, sir, to the chemists for Madame Marie." The young woman sought his gaze and held it with her own, as if daring him to contradict her.

"I see…" He leaned forward. "Had some trouble with the labels, Will said?"

"No," Lilly replied, frowning. "Did he say I did?"

"He mentioned it." Had the sod been lying, covering his tracks and blaming Lilly? Maybe he should take the bugger back to the lock-up and have a further talk with him.

Lilly gave a small laugh, then shook her head. "Silly boy, it wasn't the labels I had trouble with, it was the pen. It leaked all over my fingers and ruined my cotton gloves. I got quite angry about it."

"I see. The pen, eh?" Archie repeated, not believing a word that was coming from her pretty mouth. She was up to something; he could smell it.

"Yes, the pen, and, sir, it's getting late. What with everything that's happened, Madame will not be pleased if I don't get to the chemist's before it shuts."

"Best get off, then." Archie stood aside to allow Lilly to pass. She hurried down the steps, drawing the collar of her coat up against the rain, and set off at a smart pace down the road. Archie stood there watching her for a few minutes, then turned and went back into the hotel.

Chapter Ten

Agnes applied the brakes and gently slipped off the saddle as the bicycle rolled to a stop. Her two travelling companions waved at her as they continued on. Constance shouted after her, saying she must be mad, preferring the library to her bed. Agnes smiled and waved back.

She lifted the edge of her thick nurse's cloak and glanced down at the watch pinned to the breast of her uniform. It was quarter past nine. She pushed the bicycle up onto the wide pavement before the new library. For a moment she was tempted to lean it against one of the two Grecian columns that supported the neoclassical dome covering the grand entrance of this latest symbol of civic pride, but thought better of it. Not really the done thing. Instead, she parked her vehicle with the other bicycles on the side of the building, to the left of the main door. Taking her bag out of the basket, she walked towards the door, noticing that it was beginning to rain harder. She made her way through the large, brass-trimmed doors of the library. The building smelled of polish, books and dust. She always noticed the smell of places: must be her nurse's training. Smells told you a lot about what was going on. As she gazed round the main room she became aware of someone watching her. The library clerk who stood behind a large oak counter was looking in her direction.

He coughed.

Agnes smiled.

He coughed again.

Agnes frowned.

The man mouthed some words.

Agnes's frown deepened.

The clerk mouthed the words again, slowly, "Miss, your feet."

Agnes looked down. It seemed every puddle she had biked through had left a layer of muddy water on her shoes and stockings. "Oh, bugger!" she said, in far more than the whisper she'd intended it to be. "Sorry." She made a show of wiping her feet before she stepped onto the well-polished floor of the library.

The man gave a faint smile, which widened slightly as she approached the counter. "Miss Reed?" he said softly, his over-large Adam's apple bobbing between the crooked wings of his collar.

"Yes, how did you—?"

"Your uniform. You were wearing it when you made the request. Besides, the request was quite a challenge."

"But you have managed to track down the story?" Agnes placed her bag on the counter.

"Oh, yes, it was part of a collection that was quite popular before the war. People seem not to be interested in such works now; perhaps extracting the humour from the verses is too much of a struggle compared with the ease of watching a moving picture."

"So you have a copy for me?" Agnes said, trying not to laugh at the man's pomposity.

"Yes." The clerk turned and studied the shelves behind him. "Here it is." He lifted the leather-bound volume from the pile and placed it down on the counter, pulling out the card. "*The*

Hand of Glory

Ingoldsby Legends, by the Rev Richard H. Barham. The tale with the Hand of Glory in is called 'The Nurse's Story'—how apt."

"Indeed," Agnes remarked, her eyebrows rising.

"I also have two books on English folklore that might contain some information." The clerk turned again, adding two more books to the first.

"I see. Thank you."

"You will be taking them all?"

"Of course." Agnes opened her bag and peered in to find her purse.

"It is still raining?" the clerk asked as he flicked open the metal case of an inkpad and proceeded to ink the date stamp.

Agnes frowned as she pulled out her library card from her purse and placed it down on the desk. She just wanted her books, not small talk. "Yes, it is."

"I see." He made a show of stamping the books, then positioning them carefully in front of Agnes. "You have a bag."

"Yes." Of all the nonsense. The man was fussing about the books getting wet.

"Will they fit? One of the folklore books is quite rare." The library clerk picked up Agnes's library card and wrote in flowing script the date and title of her books.

"Don't worry. I will make them," Agnes replied, winking at the man as she made a show of putting the books in her bag. The largest of the three was half out of the bag when she had finished, the gold letters on its spine upward. Agnes's hand came out for her card, her fingers twitching. The clerk opened his mouth to speak, then closed it. He handed her the card and tilted his head slightly. "Thank you." Agnes picked up her bag and left.

*****

"Of all the uptight, over officious, jumped up, jack-in-office..." The muttered words kept time with the swish of the rain tumbling off the front mudguard of Agnes's bicycle. The trees lining Weston Road were gaunt. The thin branches overhanging the road gave Agnes little protection from the rain. By the time she had wheeled her bicycle down the short drive of Elizabeth's house she was soaked to the skin. The book sticking out of her bag had not fared much better.

She sniffed and reached out for the wrought iron latch to the side gate. Her fingers slipped. The gate half opened, then started to swing back before she could push the bicycle through. "Oh, bugger it!" she said in frustration, and kicked hard at the gate. It swung back and hit the wall, rattling on its hinges as it came to a stop. Agnes nodded in satisfaction and managed to manoeuvre her vehicle round the back of the house, into a covered passage that led to the outbuildings. For a moment Agnes considered walking back to the front door and making a ladylike entrance. But she was too wet to bother with any pretence, so she pulled her bag from the basket of the bicycle and made her way to the kitchen door.

*****

"Oh, my dear!" Elizabeth's cook exclaimed as she dusted her hands of flour and came round the large table towards Agnes. "You look rather wet, miss."

"I feel it," Agnes replied as she put down her bag and began to shrug out of her cloak. She then attempted to peel her soaked, sagging hat off her head. The thick felt came away from her hair, making the damp, dark brown strands of her short bob stand on end.

A smile played across the cook's face as she worked at the rope holding the clothes rack high against the ceiling. As it dropped to shoulder height she tweaked off a large, white towel

Hand of Glory

and in one smooth movement hoisted the device back into place. "Here you are, miss. And may I suggest you get them boots of yours off as well, else you'll be coming down with a chill."

Agnes took the towel and began to rub furiously at her hair. She then draped the towel over her left shoulder and bent down to pull off her flat-soled ankle boots. Her stockinged feet were not much dryer, and kept trying to stick to the floor. "I'd best go and get out of these clothes." She picked up her hat, bag and cloak from the puddle they had made on the floor.

"I'll send you up some tea and toast, miss," Emily said as she picked up Agnes's boots and placed them before the firebox of the large, black-leaded range to dry.

"Oh, that would be lovely. Is Mrs Parker at home?" Agnes was hoping to get to her room without having to run the gauntlet of Elizabeth's disapproval.

"No, miss. She received a telephone call from Mrs Warner and went out in quite a tizzy, if you don't mind me saying."

"Oh." Agnes wondered what had gotten Charlotte Warner all of a fluster on a Friday morning.

*****

Dried, wrapped in her thick dressing gown and sitting by the fire in her room, Agnes was quietly enjoying her tea and toast as she thought about the books, two of which lay on her bed. The third was placed on the mantelpiece above the fire, where it was recovering from its soaking. She yawned and bit another piece of toast.

It was not that she would not have time to read the books over the weekend. She had two whole days off, as on Monday she started what she laughingly called her fieldwork. She was going to be working in the village of Great Haywood alongside the local nurse-cum-midwife. So she had better get used to getting soaked to the skin. She could be bicycling a good five to ten miles sometimes to visit a patient. That would be as far as Colwich and Little Haywood in one direction and Weston, Stowe, Hixon and Caston in the other.

"Captain Hardy!" she spluttered. He would certainly like to know she had managed to find the story. She should tell him before she crawled into bed. She placed what was left of her toast back on her plate and finished her tea. Then, taking hold of the tray, she stood and made her way downstairs to the kitchen.

Having left the remains of her breakfast with the cook, she retraced her steps into the hall. Now where would she find Captain Hardy's telephone number? She began to look through the two black books that lay on the hall table next to the large, black Bakelite telephone. Yes, there it was. The captain's number was on a page marked in Elizabeth's flowing hand: "James's friends." It lay between the pages that listed various businesses and the vicar and local doctor. Agnes wondered in amusement if Elizabeth considered James's friends better than tradesmen, yet not quite the social standing of the vicar and doctor.

She ran her finger along the entry, reading it aloud: "'Hardy, Giles, former Captain, Caston Manor, Weston 270. You will have to go through the operator. It is not a Stafford number.' Oh, Lizzy. Talk about stating the obvious."

Agnes picked up the black handset. A soft click was followed by a hum from the earpiece as she placed the device against the side of her head. It was heavy, and the mouthpiece was so large and curved it almost brushed her lips. She placed the index finger of her free hand in the dial and pulled it round. The ringing tone began, then was interrupted by a clear, polite female voice. "Operator here. Good morning. How may I be of assistance?"

Hand of Glory

"Err, yes, good morning," Agnes stuttered. She hated talking to thin air. "Can you put me through to Weston 270?"

"Putting you through now, caller," the woman said, and a sharp *tap, tap*, then ringing tone replaced the woman's voice.

"Good morning, Caston Manor." The voice was male. It sounded far away, the words cut by cracks and whistles.

"Captain Hardy, I mean Mr, I mean... Oh, bugger!" Agnes could kick herself as the swear word ended her burst of conversation.

"Yes, this is Giles Hardy." *Of course it was he.* "Who is this?"

"Miss Agnes Reed."

"Oh, my Florence Nightingale." She could hear the amusement in his voice.

"No, I am not."

"No?"

"No!"

"So you haven't rung to see if you can have your handkerchiefs back?"

"I don't want them back."

"Then I will treasure them."

Agnes felt herself begin to blush–very silly, really. "I really rang to..."

"To...?" Giles prompted

"To tell you that I have the book. The one with the story in, and a couple of folklore ones. The clerk at the library was very helpful and kind. Well, that's not quite true. He was helpful, but not kind. He was a bit of a jack-in-office, truth be known." The words came out in a rush.

"I see." He was beginning to laugh.

"It's not funny. I got soaked riding my bicycle back from the library."

Giles cleared his throat. "I am sorry. Can I come round and pick them up this morning?" She could sense a creeping note of tension in his voice, as if now faced with an answer he was a little unwilling to face.

"No."

"No?"

"I am going to bed."

"Bed?" She could hear him start to laugh again.

"I would have you know I have been working all night."

"And now you want to go to bed. I don't blame you wanting to. I would in your place. How about I come across late this afternoon, unless you're working this evening?"

"Not working till Monday." Agnes yawned. She tried to stifle it, and knocked the handset, making it crackle and hiss.

"Go to sleep, Sister Reed," Giles said softly. Then the telephone clicked and a droning noise followed.

"Well I like that, hanging up on me," Agnes muttered through another yawn.

*****

"Agnes, are you awake?" Elizabeth's voice fought through the pile of blankets over Agnes's head. Agnes groaned and turned over, pulling the covers up higher. "Agnes!"

"Go away. I'm asleep," Agnes retorted, and tried to place her feet back on the warm spot she had just moved them from.

"It's four o'clock and Captain Hardy is here to see you. Besides, I want to speak to you about this horrible thing before you go downstairs," Elizabeth said, shaking her.

"What!" Agnes sat bolt upright, throwing the covers off. "Dammit, I meant to wake up at about three. What horrible thing? There isn't anything wrong with the children, is there? James? My parents? Not you? Don't say the baby!" All sorts of things began to rumble through her mind. "I'd best go down and take the books to Captain Hardy first so he can get off, then come back and we can talk and get things sorted out." She struggled to the edge of the bed, looking around for her dressing gown.

"No, the children, James and your parents are fine. We're all fine." She patted her slightly rounded stomach before she reached up and lit the gas lamp on the wall by Agnes's bed. "And you are not going downstairs half dressed. Besides, Captain Hardy is speaking with James. I've asked him to stay for tea. You have time to get dressed, and I will talk to you about what has happened while you do so. I've had hot water brought." Elizabeth gestured towards the steaming bowl of water on the small marble washstand in the corner of the room.

Agnes slipped off the bed and pulled on her dressing gown. "Can I just go down the corridor...?"

"Oh, of course. I am sorry, Agnes. It's been such a day. My nerves are shredded to ribbons."

"Oh, my poor Elizabeth! I'll be back in two ticks." When she came back into the room Elizabeth was sitting on the bed. Agnes shrugged out of her dressing gown and walked over to the washstand. "So, what is the horrible thing?"

"Poor Charlotte." Elizabeth gave a sob.

"Oh, dear," Agnes replied as she picked up the soap and began to lather it. What had the redoubtable Mrs Warner been up to, then? Had she been woken because Charlotte Warner had broken a nail?

"Yes, it's terrible. Her beautiful home."

"Not a fire?" Agnes spluttered as she rinsed her face and felt around for a towel.

"No, a– a robbery!" Elizabeth shrieked the words.

"Bloody hell!" Agnes swore and dropped the towel she was holding into the water. It quickly became sodden. Agnes picked it up, wrung it out and placed it alongside the bowl.

"Agnes, there's no need to— Yes, I agree, it *is* enough to make you swear."

Agnes came to her cousin's side, sat down beside her and took her hand, trying to comfort her. "What was taken?"

"Charlotte is still putting together a list. However, I do know they took all of the silver, of course. Her own and her late mother's jewellery, including the pearl necklace. Those impressionist paintings Charlotte bought in France before the war. Cufflinks, tiepins, her coral-inlaid brush set. The Chinese vases—not that Charlotte liked them—and the new Persian rug she had just bought."

"What, they moved the furniture and took a rug?" It was incredible. How could a thief do that?

"No, silly—though they do seem to have taken everything of any value they could lay their hands on. The rug was only delivered late yesterday; Charlotte was going to get the servants to move the furniture this morning. I was going to go round to help her re-arrange her parlour. The rug was still wrapped and rolled up in the hallway. But it wasn't just what was stolen; it was what happened to old Mr Warner, Charlotte's father-in-law."

"No, he didn't? The thieves, they...?" Agnes could not finish the sentence. She had a sudden vision of old Mr Warner attacking the villains with a poker and becoming a victim of another type of crime altogether.

"No, he was on the indoor lavatory when... well, the shock of seeing them, it stopped his heart. Poor Charlotte found him the next morning."

"Oh..." Agnes did not know what to say. She suddenly felt the need to laugh. Not that it was amusing for the Warners, having the senior member of the family pass away while seated on the loo. Of course it wasn't. Well, actually, it was just something you expected to see at the pictures, with Charlie

Hand of Glory

Chaplin bouncing around the screen and everyone laughing at the absurdity of it. She gave a small cough and forced the laughter back. "You must give Charlotte my sincere condolences and ask if there is anything I can do."

"I knew you would say that. You have a good heart, Agnes. Now, you'd better finish getting dressed. James has to go back to work this evening. He is of course heading the investigation into this horrible crime, and we have the séance at mother's." Elizabeth gave Agnes's hand a squeeze and stood up.

"Aunt Vera isn't going to cancel the event, then?" Agnes found she was mentally crossing her fingers; the thought of attending another of Madame Marie's displays made her shudder.

"No, we did consider it, but as it is family only, a private sitting, I don't think there will be any objections from anyone."

Chapter Eleven

"Right bloody mess—never come across a crime scene like it before," James said as he flicked the ash off his cigarette end onto the hearth of the fire. "Tipped the place on its head. They must've made enough noise to wake the dead, yet no one heard a thing."

"Going to keep you busy for a while, then?" Giles asked. He had no liking for Charlotte Warner, but even she did not deserve this.

"Yes, though it's plain they were not local felons; they'll be hard to track. They won't shift the stuff through any local fences, either. Most likely back in The Smoke by now, counting their ill-gotten gains. In addition, I can't very well tag old Mr Warner's demise as a suspicious death and stir other forces up to look for them." James flicked his cigarette again, his annoyance plainly growing.

"Oh, well, you decided you must work for a living."

"This doing bloody nothing getting to you, old man?" James countered. He glared at what was left of his cigarette and threw it into the fire.

"It's not all it's cracked up to be, certainly," Hardy replied. James was right; perhaps it was the doing of nothing that had

Hand of Glory

him brooding too much. It gave the wire binding him to the past extra strength.

James laughed. "I wondered how long you'd stand it. You should set about getting that estate farm going again, though Baker might take objection to you earning a profit off your land instead of him. He's onto a good thing, renting those fields off you."

"Well, at least he knows about farming—I certainly don't." Having inherited the small manor, he had done nothing more than move into it.

Actually, he didn't live in much of it. Most of the rooms were still wrapped in dustsheets, though he had a feeling that Betty Adams had a plan of action to put things to rights. In fact, she had said that morning, "If you don't mind, Captain, I'd like to talk to you, if you have the time?"

"You can learn about farming, and, besides, there's the sawmill your cousin built. It was doing well during the war. Damn sure it need not have been closed, but your cousin was a rum one, so I've been told," James said as the sound of children's voices tumbled down the hallway and into the parlour.

"Remember, remember, the fifth of November, gun powder, treason and plot!"

"Wizz, bang!"

"Penny for the guy!"

The parlour door flew open. Victoria and Edward raced in, heading towards their father.

"What now?" he cried. "Not another crime to solve?"

"Been solved—they hung him!" Edward said, giggling as he dodged his father's hook hand, which swished over his head.

"And quartered him! What's quartering?" Victoria asked, a puzzled look on her face.

"Something not very nice, and not a good subject just before tea," Agnes said from the doorway.

Hardy got up from his chair. He gave Agnes a small smile and was surprised to find she returned it. She had forgiven him for teasing her on the telephone, it seemed. Though, if he thought about it, he was surprised he'd teased her in the first place. He was not a natural flirt.

"Story tonight, Father?" Edward asked.

"Sorry, old chap, I'm working. You'll have to make do with your mother," James said, and gently touched the top of Edward's head with his claw.

"Oh, pooh," Edward moaned.

"Well, young man!" Elizabeth said sharply from the doorway. She stood there, framed by the bright light in the hallway, the toddler, Charles, balanced on her hip.

"Sorry..." Edward said sheepishly.

"I should think so, old man," James said, trying to sound stern, but failing miserably.

"Now kiss your father goodnight," Elizabeth said and entered the room, walking towards James. Another figure took her place in the doorway, that of the nursery nurse. Nurse Gladys stood with her hands gently clasped before her, her gaze on her charges as they surrounded their father.

James bent down. Edward and Victoria each in turn planted a kiss on their father's right cheek. James then stood and leaned in the direction of his youngest child. Charles tried to grab the end of his father's moustache, as James's bewhiskered face came in range. James caught the child's podgy hand and blew on it. Charles chuckled.

"Enough, now," James declared, "Nurse Gladys is waiting." He winked at the children's nurse. The girl smiled and came to Elizabeth's side. She took Charles from his mother and escorted the two other children out of the room.

Hand of Glory

"Peace at last. They certainly wear you out," Agnes said dramatically, wiping her brow.

"I thought you'd been asleep..." Hardy said in a teasing voice.

"Well, I can empathise with Elizabeth and Nurse Gladys, can't I?" Agnes retorted.

"Like all good nurses do, and hold their patients' hands," Hardy said, and immediately regretted doing so.

Agnes's face paled. "Sometimes that's all you *can* do." A silence fell on the small group.

Elizabeth coughed, drawing everyone's attention. "Shall we go through for some tea?"

"Perhaps I'd better go. I do feel as if I'm intruding," Hardy said, his eyes on Agnes.

"No, please stay. I'm just being a bad hat," Agnes said.

"Aren't you just," James said, taking his wife's arm and leading her out of the room.

"I didn't mean to annoy you," Hardy said as he walked by Agnes's side down the hallway.

"You didn't," she replied, giving him a small smile as she increased her pace.

Hardy gently touched her arm, to gain her full attention and to halt her progress to the dining room. He had felt a barrier come down between them and found he resented it. He had begun to find out today that he could exist outside his all-encompassing purgatory when he was in Agnes's company, and was fearful that it would smother him totally again if she shut him out. "I did."

"Yes, you did, but not for the reasons you think you did." As she spoke, her gaze roamed over Hardy's face. He could feel its touch as if it were soft fingertips. He wondered what she was seeing. Nothing very spectacular, of that he was sure. Hardy did not consider himself handsome. In fact, he'd always thought he was rather a dull fellow.

"And what were the reasons?" As he asked the question Hardy felt a certain amount of trepidation. Did he want to know the answer?

Agnes glanced at the vanishing backs of her cousins and spoke, her voice lowering, "I saw you were going there again."

"Where?" He did not need to ask—he knew the *"where"* she meant—and added, his voice suddenly weak, "I'm sorry."

"Nothing to be sorry about. It just made me angry, that was all." Agnes's hand came up and touched his. He was still holding onto her forearm. He released his hold and slipped his hand into hers, again noticing how well they fitted together. His grip tightened and he felt the cold pressure of a ring on her small finger. The dream. Hallucination. The hand in his. Hand in the hand. Stupid. It wasn't real. Nevertheless, he welcomed the dream, as much as he welcomed the fact of being in Agnes's company. He let go of her hand suddenly and watched it swing down out of his grasp and to her side. The ring glinted in the gaslight.

"Your ring?" he asked, suddenly filled with a need to know. No, it was a fear of what he knew was not possible. She had not held his hand on the battlefield.

"Oh, the children bought it for my last birthday. I don't wear it much—it turns my finger green—but I wouldn't let them know for the world. They saved out of their pocket money to buy it."

"Tea?" Elizabeth had reappeared in the corridor.

"Yes, tea, then I must give you those books, Mr Hardy," Agnes said, walking towards Elizabeth.

"Giles, please," Hardy said, moving to join her, and adding, "I had hoped that perhaps we might spend an hour or two after tea going over them together, that is if Elizabeth does not object and that you, of course, have nothing else planned."

Hand of Glory

"Agnes, you can call me that–but you know my name. Silly... And... I... Oh, drat... Sorry, Elizabeth wants me to go with her to this séance at her mother's." From the tone in Agnes's voice Hardy gauged that she was not looking forward to it. He looked at Elizabeth standing in the doorway to the dining room. He hoped her matchmaking instinct might kick in and she would release Agnes from the event in favour of a few hours with someone she viewed as a potential suitor. Was he that? Was he courting Agnes?

"I–" Elizabeth said, and frowned. It was plain she did not want to release Agnes from her commitment for the evening.

"Well, I'm off duty all weekend. Perhaps late tomorrow morning?" Agnes replied as all three of them entered the dining room together.

"I'll see you then, then?" Hardy asked as he stood behind a chair at the dining table.

"What's this?" James said, trying not to laugh. "Giles, you poor soul, Elizabeth hasn't got you pinned down, has she? Agnes, shame on you for giving in so easily to Elizabeth's prodding."

"It's nothing; it's to do with some books I've managed to acquire for Giles."

"Well, you and *Giles* had better sit down–the tea's getting cold," James said, and burst out laughing.

*****

Hardy had reluctantly taken leave of Agnes. The conversation during tea had been haphazard. No earth-shattering disclosures, just everyday things. For a small space of time he had shrugged off the wire that held him mentally welded to the past. However, it had tightened again as he took his leave of Agnes, and he had seen her grow uneasy, too. He had sensed that the coming evening was going to be difficult for her. Should he have suggested he accompany her? No, Elizabeth had said it was a private reading, for the family only.

As he drove out of Stafford he wondered if Elizabeth and her parents were as caught on the wire as he was. They fought their way free of it from time to time, but in the end it always dragged them back into the mud. Plunged deep into that torn landscape where the future they had believed in had died with the young man who would have made it.

On a sudden impulse, Hardy pulled the car up close to the high hedge and stopped. He was at the cusp of the divide that led down into the Trent valley. Here use and time had cut the road deep into the side of the hill. It narrowed and twisted down into the valley, shadowed on either side by high stone walls supporting the earth banks. He got out of the vehicle and drew in a deep breath. The air tasted of an approaching English winter. Damp. Cold. Yet underneath there was the sense that this was not permanent, that it would end in a few months. Unlike the long winters in Flanders that had haunted the men in the trenches with cold fingers of finality.

He made to get back in the car, but the same unexplained impulse that had driven him to stop now made him move towards the large, five-barred gate on his right. Climbing over, he dropped down into the muddy edge of the field which ran along the side of the hill above Weston Hall. His feet squelched in the soft loam round the gate, then fell silent as he walked deep into the meadow. He passed huddled shadows that protested his presence with bleats and the shuffling of heavy, woolly bodies.

A rumbling sound made him stop. He turned and looked out over the night-shrouded valley, trying in the pale moonlight to see the source of the noise. There, on the floor of the valley, a train was running parallel to the faint ribbon of the river Trent. Sparks flew into the night sky from its smokestack. The rumbling increased as the train turned towards the moonlit river. Its whistle screamed as it went over a bridge. Hardy swore he could feel the hillside vibrating. The train was now so close to the bottom of the slope on which he was standing, he was positive he could hear the *rat-tat* of its iron wheels. Rumble. *Rat-tat*. Rumble. His eyes closed and the battered locker of his memories sprang open, allowing the wire to enmesh him and drag him under.

*****

"Tea, sir?–seeing you're awake." Corporal Adams offered him a tin cup. Steam rose from the brown liquid, forming a small haze in the dugout. Hardy laid the revolver he was cleaning down on the small table and reached for the cup.

"Careful, it's hot."

"So I can see, Corporal," Hardy said. He gingerly took the cup and placed it down on the table.

"Up early, sir?" Adams stood in the doorway of the dugout, his smelly slung on his shoulder.

"Those shells Jerry dropped on our left earlier woke me. I couldn't drop off again," Hardy lied. He had not been sleeping. He never did, no matter how tired he was, on the night before he had to lead men over the top.

"Aye, made a mess of the jakes and communication trenches behind B Company. A few men bought it as well, sir." Adams took a sip of his own tea.

"Wounded being moved out?" Hardy felt his chest tighten.

"Don't know, only know Corporal Jones said it was a bit of a mess."

"Always is, Corporal." Hardy picked up his mug and drained the hot liquid.

"Won't be tomorrow, sir."

"It's tomorrow now, Corporal."

"Aye, just shy of four o'clock, sir."

"So what are you doing up and about, Corporal? Not on duty tonight, are you?"

"Not as such, sir, but that sniper got another of our lads at dusk. Major wanted me to concentrate on getting him before he takes out any more."

"That will teach the new replacements not to take a bloody peek at Jerry," Hardy said harshly. No matter how much you tried to drum it into the new lads that came up, they still did it. Thought they were invincible, that the Hun would not get them, but he always did.

Adams looked at him. His mouth opened as if he were going to speak, then he closed it. Hardy knew he had been going to remonstrate with him, maybe say that such a comment was not like him. However, he was not the same man who'd joined the army three years ago. He had lost part of himself. It had been smothered by responsibility for the men under his command. He had changed, where Adams had not. The man was still the same: solid, part of the land that had made him, apart from it at present, but still connected.

"There's a low-lying mist across no man's land, sir. If it lingers after daylight..." Adams said. He leaned out of the door and poured the dregs of his tea onto the duckboards of the trench.

"Fingers crossed, Corporal," Hardy said, and went back to cleaning his pistol.

"You know, I remember one early evening at home. I was with Arthur Wright up on the hillside above Weston Hall. Full summer, it was. Been a hell of a downpour and we'd sheltered under a tree up there. Then the rain stopped and the sun came out. Hot, it was. The ground was steaming. Then I looked out over the valley. As far as I could see, a low mist had formed. The trees and houses stuck out of it, as if they were surrounded by

Hand of Glory

the sea, sir. The mist moved in waves, lapping round them. Not sure how long me and Arthur stood there watching it as it lifted. But it was a sight, sir."

"And, Corporal?" Hardy said sharply, as he snapped his revolver shut and laid it down.

"Just the mist over no man's land reminded me. Most things remind me of home, sir. Once we get back I'm not stirring out of that valley if I can help it."

"You sure we will get back, George?" Hardy said the man's name, forgetting the difference their ranks made for a moment.

"One way or another, Master Giles, we will. We will, I promise you that," Adams said.

*****

Hardy's eyes snapped open. The train had gone, but wisps of its smoke still lingered, illuminated by the pale moon. It tumbled along the river, joining with the mist that was rising off the water. He brought his hand up to his eyes and rubbed them. His cheeks were wet. *"Damn,"* he swore.

"Aye, 'damn,' but a beautiful sight." It was his ghostly companion.

"Yes it is," Hardy answered as he reached into his pocket and pulled out his packet of cigarettes. He offered one to the shade by his side. Adams smiled and took one, placing it over his ear as he looked from the night-wrapped view of the valley to his former commanding officer and friend. "You ready to go over the top one more time, sir?"

"Do I have to?" Hardy asked, feeling the wire tighten across his chest and hand.

"Not if you don't think she's worth taking a risk on." Adams pulled the cigarette from behind his ear and lit it. The flare of the match lit up his face. He looked cold, tired.

"You mean I have to go over the top to get her?" Hardy replied, puzzled.

"Nay, go over with her, to get the job damn well done, sir." Adams turned away from Hardy and began to walk off into the night. The lit cigarette fell from his slack hand, hissing as it hit the damp grass.

"Wait!" Hardy called. "Wait!" His left leg suddenly gave way and he fell onto the soaked grass. "Wait!" he called again as he bent double at the waist, his hands going out to break his fall. *Fingers into mud. Thick. Clinging. Up to his wrists. Elbow. The tree tops to his right burst into flame. Voices called his name.* He wrenched his hands up and fell onto his back. The trees were just dark skeleton fingers against the starlit sky. And the wire was dragging him down.

Not purgatory–it was hell.

It tempted him with the vision of life beyond the mud and wire–of Agnes, her hand in his–then snatched it away, leaving him up to his chest in the stinking shell-hole. Hardy put back his head and bellowed his anguish to the night sky.

Chapter Twelve

"Here we are, sir," Bright said as he brought the police car to a stop before the night-shrouded house. Inspector Parker did not move. Bright looked over at him. James could feel the young man tensing, as if he were about to ask a question. Today had been a rum one, and no mistake. It was not so much the matter of a robbery taking place, or the fact that he personally knew the victims; it was the manner in which it had been committed. It was as if a whirlwind had torn through the Warners' home, picking up everything of value. That the family had been home and had heard nothing would in other circumstances have Parker believing this to be an insurance swindle. He still had some doubts about the matter. Certain items stolen were the source of some family dispute between Charlotte Warner and her sister-in-law. Though he doubted either lady would resort to such desperate measures to have her own way.

"Sir," Bright repeated.

"Yes, I'd better..." Parker began, and reached over with his right hand to open the car door. He stopped and leaned back in his seat. "Warner said the doors were open, yet he, himself, had locked them?"

"Yes," Bright answered, running his hands round the steering wheel.

"Bolted? Keys put away?" The hook that had replaced Parker's left hand came up and began to tap on the side of his moustache.

"Yes, it seems very strange. Had to be inside help, one of the staff–" Bright began.

"Not necessarily, Bright. Though we will interview them again."

"One of the family?"

"Not in bloody financial trouble, are they? Least not as far as we know," Parker said. The desire for a cigarette sent his right hand fumbling into his coat pocket.

"Let me, sir." Bright pulled a packet out of his own pocket and offered one to his superior. Parker took it and nodded in thanks as Bright lit his cigarette for him.

"Very clever of you, Bright, buttering up the boss." He took the cigarette out of his mouth and picked at a small piece of tobacco stuck on his tongue. Parker looked at his young detective constable. In the faint light spilling from the windows of the house he could see the young man's grin.

"Best advice my granddad gave me, sir. As for the matter of the Warners' financial affairs, I've made a few enquiries. But it will be well into next week before we start to get any answers, bankers and solicitors being what they are."

"Gave you lots of advice, did he, your grandfather?" Parker said, laughing.

"Quite a bit, sir."

"Aye, he was an old-fashioned copper from what I've heard. He..." Parker's voice trailed off as a thought struck him. Everything about this robbery made the hairs on the back of his neck stand up. It was as if he should know who was responsible and how they had done it. An old memory, long forgotten, something he'd heard as a constable on the beat in

Hand of Glory

Shrewsbury... "Bright, I want you to have a word with your grandfather about the case."

"Sir?" Bright spluttered in surprise.

"He might have heard of something similar in his day. You know, doors being open and the like. Also I want you to look through any information passed to us by other forces regarding similar cases. See if they have any leads, or if anyone was arrested."

"Yes, sir."

Parker smiled at the unmistakable tone of resignation in Bright's voice. Well, the lad would not be the only one working all day this Saturday. "So, see you in the morning?" Parker took a large puff on his cigarette and held it firmly in his mouth while he reached over and opened the car door.

After the car had vanished down the dark street, Inspector James Parker continued to stand outside his in-laws' home. The day's events paraded again through his mind. Each one was reviewed, catalogued and then filed back into its place. Some were mentally marked with a tag: Holbrook's reaction, for one. James knew little went on in the town's criminal fraternity that Taffy did not know of, or get to hear about. Taffy might be retired, but he still liked to be in the know. Holbrook had been genuinely surprised, and, judging by his reaction, downright angry that someone had pocketed the monies collected for the poppy appeal. Hopefully, it would have the desired effect and turn Taffy into a long-nosed ferret with a mission. Whether Taffy would confide any information he turned up was another matter.

James sighed and turned down the path to his in-laws' front door. The lights were still blazing in the front parlour. The private séance was obviously still in full swing. This mumbo jumbo had been the source of additional marital discontent of late. James's only ally was, to his surprise, Agnes. That girl had her head screwed on right, and no mistake. The whole business stank to high bloody heaven as far as James was concerned. However, Madame Marie did not charge for her events, and, as the checks he had run had turned up nothing untoward, he was at a loss as to what to do. That his Elizabeth and her parents swallowed this hogwash galled the hell out of him. Expressing his displeasure had led to Elizabeth declaring him old-fashioned, even Victorian. He had retorted that if seeking to protect his family from charlatans made him Victorian, then so be it.

The ensuing pained silence that had developed between Elizabeth and himself hurt. She could not see why it was not possible to find the remains of her brother and put him to rest. James had tried to explain it, but Elizabeth could not grasp the enormity of the horror that men had fought and died in, over in France. Perhaps that was why Agnes had agreed with him over this séance business. She did understand. The young woman had seen it with her own eyes. "You're a lucky bloody dog there, Giles," Parker said out loud, as he dropped the remains of his cigarette onto the gravel drive and crushed it under his right heel.

James did not relish entering the house and becoming exposed to the heightened emotions that Madame Marie stirred up among the occupants. However, he had promised he would be here to escort Elizabeth and Agnes the seven hundred yards back to their house. He plucked off his trilby hat with his hook hand, tapped it against his side, heaved a sigh and stepped towards the front door. "Bugger it!" James turned sharply to the left and began to make his way to the rear of the large property.

Light from the kitchen windows traced patterns on the damp flagstones in the small rear courtyard. He could see the figure of his mother-in-law's cook, Jane, sitting at the kitchen table, her plump fingers round a thick pewter mug. James

Hand of Glory

rapped on one of the small panes in the window with the knuckles of his right hand. Jane jumped in her seat, hands flying to her flushed cheeks as her head swivelled round towards the window. Her face at first was covered with an expression of shock, then a smile began to turn up the corners of her mouth as she recognised the face on the other side of the glass. She wagged a finger at James, heaved herself off the chair, and shuffled to the kitchen door.

"Why, Inspector, you fair made me jump!" Jane exclaimed as she opened the door.

"That was the intention, Jane." James strode into the kitchen, throwing his trilby hat down among the muslin-covered plates on the large kitchen table.

"Why didn't you ring the front doorbell? Creeping round the back like that—I don't know why you did so." Jane shut the door and turned back towards the table.

"Don't you, Jane? Thought you knew all the family gossip," Parker replied, as he picked up the corner of the muslin cloth and peered under at the remains of the evening supper.

"I suppose I do." Jane's expression changed to one of concern. She reached up and pushed a stray strand of hair back under her mobcap, as she continued, "Not that I blame you—rum lot, this whole thing."

"An ally," James declared, as he pulled out a dainty sandwich from under the muslin and ate it in one bite.

"Would you like a cup of tea, sir?"

James's eyebrows went up.

"A glass of beer, perhaps?" Jane's head tilted in the direction of her own beverage.

"Actually, I fancy a shot of that nice single malt my father-in-law brought back from his last trip to Glasgow."

"Now, sir... Oh, very well—but you stay here while I go into his study." Jane's voice had taken on a conspiratorial tone.

"The old bugger got it under lock and key, has he?" Parker laughed and sat down at the kitchen table, pulling the plate of sandwiches free of the muslin and helping himself to more.

"Not exactly."

"Bet he's put a line on the bottle then, the old skinflint."

Jane did not answer him; she had vanished down the darkened hall that led to the family's rooms. James listened to her feet trip-trapping on the highly polished quarry tiles, then heard the tone of her tread soften as she stepped onto the carpet that ran at the far end, fading away as she turned the corner by the bottom of the stairs.

As he waited for the glass of single malt to wash down the sandwiches, James again mulled over the day's events. The only bright spark was that his friend Giles was finally coming out from under the cloud that had dogged him since the war. Well, as far as any of them had come out from under it. The war, James knew, hung like a millstone round your neck, dragging you back there whenever it got the chance. "Getting bloody morose," James chided himself and removed more of the muslin to see what else was left from supper.

"I've had enough of it, Will." A female voice unknown to him tumbled out of the darkness of the hall. James leaned back in his seat, then peered through the partly open door. Two shadowy figures, so close they were almost touching, stood in the corridor.

"Don't be sodding daft," a male voice answered, obviously the Will who had been addressed. The instinct that made James an exceptional policeman woke with a vengeance and he stiffened in his seat, totally concentrating on the conversation.

"Yes, I have. Do this, go there. She treats me like a skivvy. I have more smarts than her. She makes mistakes, time and again. I'm fed up of covering for her and being paid tuppence for it."

"You're paid a lot more than tuppence, Lilly," Will said.

"Not enough for the risks I take," Lilly hissed. "I tell you, Will, I'm off as soon as I can. I got plans. I don't need them. I can do better on me own."

"Lilly, don't go doing anything stupid, will you? Think it over. Talk to the boss." Will sounded anxious. James leaned further back. The chair tipped onto its rear legs. His ears strained to catch every nuance of the conversation.

"Do you think that'll do any good?" Lilly asked.

"It might do. Let me speak to him. Promise you won't do anything until I have."

"I'll think about it," Lilly said, and coughed loudly.

Had someone else walked into the corridor? Jane returning with his whisky?

"Is there anything I can do for you two dears?" Yes, it was Jane.

"Thanks, no. We're just waiting for Madame to finish saying her goodbyes to the family."

Well, well. It seemed Madame Marie's staff were a bit fed up. It might be worthwhile having a little talk with that young woman. The whole thing had to be some sort of swindle. Could he prove it? Then, again, would it be worth taking action? Making Elizabeth look a fool would not help the situation at home.

"Here you are, Inspector." Jane placed the glass of single malt down on the table before James. "I hope you have time to drink it, before…" There was the sound of a door opening, and muffled voices drifted down the corridor.

"No worries about that, Jane." James took hold of the glass and tossed down the contents in one gulp.

*****

"*Merde!*"

Marie's curse woke Archie. He grunted and turned over, his hand going out across the bed. Marie's side was empty. "What the fuck?" Archie mumbled and sat up. Mind fuzzy with sleep, he glanced around the room. Marie was sitting at the small table by the fire, the dying flames casting strange patterns on the hearthrug. It was late or early, Archie did not know which.

"What you doing, woman?"

"She is trouble." Marie waved one of the large tarot cards in Archie's direction.

"Take no mind of them bloody cards and come back to bed."

"Don't be annoyed. Listen to her," Jim said in a friendly manner, almost cajoling, as if trying to regain Archie's confidence.

"Bah! You do not understand. I saw her face at the séance tonight. She did not believe. She watched me. She is the Queen of Swords, upright. She will bear the sorrow and act." Marie cast the card in Archie's direction. It fluttered to the floor and lay there, an accusation he could not deny. She picked up another and glared at it. "The Moon, upright. Deception—she will trick us." Marie's grip on the card tightened and it twisted out of shape.

The lass had a right mood on her. No good trying to make her see sense—Archie knew that of old. She just got louder and forgot her English. Besides, sometimes she hit the mark with those blooming cards.

"How? Maybe it isn't her, this Agnes Reed, whoever she is, that's in the cards."

"*Non?*" Marie frowned, as if the thought had not occurred to her. She placed the bent card back in the pack. "Someone else? *Oui*. Maybe. Who?"

"Will?" Archie's thoughts returned to the young man. The more he thought on it, the more he felt the young bastard was lying about something.

Hand of Glory

Marie cut the cards and lifted one out. "*Non*, but... six of pentacles, he worries about a threat to his money. Us? *Non*. One of the others?"

Archie began to feel cold. The fire was almost dead, and a sickly yellow smoke was rising from the dying embers. He was sitting up in bed in an icy room, that was it. Nothing to do with the sodding picture cards, or faces in the smoke. He got out and walked over to the fireplace. Taking the coal scuttle, he tipped some of the contents onto the fire. The dying ash crumpled under the weight of the black lumps. A small plume of dark smoke began to rise, banishing the yellow-tinged one as he placed the brass scuttle down. He looked at Marie; she was waiting for an answer from him. "Kevin?"

She gathered the cards together again, and cut them. "*Non*, he is the Knight of Pentacles–dull, but trustworthy, for now."

"How about Lilly, then?" Archie asked. The coal on the fire began to hiss, as the flames released a small pocket of gas trapped in the black orc.

"She would not! She does what I say," Marie snapped.

"Ask the damn cards," Archie said and leaned down, bringing his face to within an inch of hers. "You believe in them, don't you?" The dark confidence he felt when he lit the Hand now bubbled and frothed under the surface of his thoughts. Archie could not resist the feeling; it made him powerful, clever.

If the lass were cheating on them she would regret it. Sworn to him and to the Hand, she was. His grandfather had given only two warnings about the Hand: *"Don't steal from others bound to the Hand with you, else the job will go bad, or let the Hand be taken up by someone you've crossed."* Jim had said the same. Simple rules, nothing fancy, yet they lay at the heart of the bargain.

"*Oui*," Marie said. She laid out a number of cards, face down on the table, placing the rest of the pack to one side.

"Well?"

Marie's lips formed a tight line and she flipped one of the cards over. Her intake of breath was sharp, as if it pained her. "Queen of Cups, reversed. She is a dreamer, not to be trusted. She will sell us out for a few bits of gaudy trash. I do not believe it, yet the cards…?" Marie's voice faded away. Her eyes came up to Archie's. He could see the uncertainty in them.

"So, we best keep an eye on her, then?"

"*Oui*," Marie said and reached out to turn another card, but decided against it. "Will, he knows?"

"I bet he fucking does," Archie snarled, a smile breaking out across his face, twisting the scars round his eye.

"You speak to him, *oui*?"

"Aye, tomorrow tonight, after we've done Tennant's place."

Chapter Thirteen

Saturday–4th November–1922

Mud—stinking. It filled his mouth. He coughed, trying to force the glutinous killer out of his mouth. His chest tightened and air rushed in, tainted with dust.

Where was he? The manor. In his late cousin's study, sitting in a winged leather chair to the right of the fireplace. *God!* What time was it? Giles tried to sit up and felt resistance. The mud he had lain in had glued his suit jacket to the leather. He heaved himself forward. The fabric ripped and he knocked over the half-empty bottle of whiskey by his right foot. The bottle rolled. Its golden contents rippled round inside, vanishing behind the label, then reappearing, catching the dying light of the fire. A soft chime cut the air as the bottle nudged the tiled hearth.

"Hell and shitting damnation!" Hardy dropped his head to his hands. It had been a bad night—no, a waking nightmare. His stomach rolled. His mouth felt dry. How much had he drunk?

"Now where did all this mud come from?" a voice sounded from outside the room. The brass handle moved and the door opened. A cascade of light entered, dancing around the plump figure of Betty Adams. "Oh, excuse me, sir. I'll come back later."

Hardy could feel her gaze on him and then watched as she looked at the bottle before the fire.

Hardy tried to clear his dry throat, gave a short cough, and replied, "My apologies, Mrs Adams. I did not want to make you extra work–I just had a little accident last night and…" His voice faded as Betty Adams's eyes narrowed slightly. She disapproved. Of course she would. Betty was a stern teetotaller.

"I understand, sir. I'll make some tea and a late breakfast for you while you get cleaned up." Betty's words were polite, but Hardy felt as if he had had a tongue-lashing from a sergeant major.

"That's a good idea, Mrs Adams," he said as he stood up. "Might I ask what time it is?"

"Gone eleven, sir."

"Oh, hell."

"Pardon, sir?" Betty put her hands on her hips.

"I'm late–well, not too late. I'm supposed to pick up a friend, return here, and show the manor. I thought maybe a late lunch and a bit of tea here, if that would not be too much trouble." *I'm garbling.*

"Well, I'm sure the gentleman won't mind waiting. Maybe you could use the telephone and tell him you'll be a mite late," Betty said as she entered the room and made for the windows, her hands reaching out to pull back the heavy drapes.

"If I do that she might think I'm crying off."

"She?" Betty's voice went up as she turned sharply to face him.

"Yes, a lady friend, Mrs Adams." As he spoke, Hardy walked towards the door. He had rendered Betty Adams temporary speechless, something George said he had rarely seen. As he moved down the passage to the wide staircase, Hardy was sure he heard the corporal chuckling.

Hand of Glory

*****

Agnes made no mention of him being late when he picked her up. Her answers to his pleasantries were short, containing as few words as possible. As they passed the church in Weston, Hardy decided to change tack with the conversation. "Was the séance that bad?"

Agnes turned and looked at him. "Worse."

"I am sorry," Hardy replied as he edged the Austin out of the tee junction by the side of the railway bridge, guiding the vehicle over before taking the next turning right, towards Uttoxeter.

"Nothing you need to be sorry for. I can't believe they can all be such fools, especially Elizabeth. Christian is dead. He died fighting in a war he believed in. He was proud of what he was doing, of the men he served with. Would it be different if they knew where he was buried? I don't know. However, with all this excessive hand-wringing and grief it's as if they're blaming him for going. As if it were his fault.

"They seem to be making themselves martyrs to the fact. Worse, it's as if they have to put on a show of grief, bigger and better than anyone else's. I can understand people wanting to remember what has happened, to think about those who died and what they died for. But people seem so wrapped up in this grief that they're forgetting we're supposed to be making a 'land fit for heroes.' To make sure that those lost in the so-called 'war to end all wars' didn't die for nothing. Not that we're doing *that* very well–things are worse now. Work is getting scarce. I find it shameful that the fact that a man gave four years of his life serving his country doesn't seem to mean anything to employers, and... Now it's my turn to be sorry." Agnes blushed to the roots of her hair.

"You have strong opinions, Agnes." They were now passing through Stowe-by-Chartley and motoring down Stowe Lane. The turning for Caston village was just round the bend.

"You don't approve of women having such."

"On the contrary. I just like to be able to get a word in edgeways in such a conversation." Hardy swung the wheel to the left and put his foot on the accelerator, increasing their speed.

Agnes gave a small laugh and sighed. Hardy glanced over, wondering if she was going to continue about the events of last night. Obviously not: her attention was on the detail of the passing hedgerows.

He throttled back his speed as they entered the small village and circled the green and its attendant gaggle of houses. The lane to the manor felt narrower, the hedges higher. The bare, finger-thin branches scratched at the car as it passed. The ruts in the road made the small vehicle rock. Muddy rainwater splashed its sides. On the left the half-open gate to the abandoned sawmill added to the feel of neglect, compounded by the view of the shabby appearance of the manor at the end of the short road.

Hardy stopped the vehicle by the main door and switched off the engine. They both sat there for a few moments, looking first out of the windows, then at each other.

"It looks like it could do with a lick of paint," Agnes said, trying to smile.

"To say the least." Hardy leaned forward, the brim of his hat gently tapping on the windscreen as he peered at his property. "I haven't really... I mean..." It was no good trying to make excuses. He had done nothing about the upkeep of the house or land since he had inherited it. The fact had never bothered him before, but now he felt a little ashamed.

"Does the roof leak?"

Hand of Glory

"No, thankfully, least I hope not—I haven't been on the third floor," Hardy said somewhat sheepishly as he got out of the vehicle and walked round to the passenger side. He opened the car door and held out his hand to her.

"What?" Agnes sounded surprised. "You haven't explored the place? Next you'll be telling me you've been living in just the kitchen."

Her hand slipped seamlessly into his as she got out of the car. His fingers closed. Again, the feeling of rightness flooded into his mind. He gave the gloved hand in his a squeeze, then let it go, shutting the passenger-side door. "That's not far from the truth. Up until recently it was the kitchen, one of the smaller bedrooms close to the top of the stairs, and my cousin's old study."

"And now?" Agnes, to his surprise, slipped her hand through the crook of his arm. They began to walk towards the house.

"Well, my new housekeeper, Mrs Adams, has made the breakfast room, as she says, 'halfway decent.' So I now eat in there, sometimes." Hardy guided their steps round the side of the house, towards the rear of the building.

"And you use the tradesman's entrance?"

"I can't find the key to the front door. I put it down somewhere when I first came, and..." Hardy started to laugh. It was so pathetic, it was funny.

"I can see why you hired a housekeeper. The poor woman has a job on her hands." Agnes looked over the rear of the building. "It could be a very nice and comfortable place to live, though a bit lonely if you were rattling around in it by yourself."

"I suppose it could," Hardy said as he opened the door to the rear passageway that led to the kitchen.

*****

As Mrs Adams and her daughter Hetty cleared the remains of their lunch, Hardy placed the books Agnes had acquired on the table. "I hope you don't mind us staying in here. I don't want to make Mrs Adams any more work by asking her to light a fire in the small parlour."

"Begging your pardon, sir, you couldn't have a fire in there even if you wanted one," Mrs Adams said as she swept the crumbs from the tablecloth with firm strokes of her hands.

"Oh?" Hardy asked, glancing quickly at Agnes, who was stifling a laugh.

"The chimney in there's blocked. So, too, are a number of the others. Mathew's going to bring his father's brushes down next week to do most of them, but the larger one in the main drawing room will have to wait until Arthur Wright can come and give him a hand."

"Well, maybe I could give him one, and is the state of the chimneys one of the things you wanted to speak to me about, Mrs Adams?" Hardy asked as he watched Agnes reach across for the topmost book.

"It is. There's a lot of work to do, sir, if you'll be living here for a while, that is." Mrs Adams lifted the laden tray, nodding her head at her daughter to leave the room ahead of her.

"Well, we'd best get things going soon, then," Hardy said.

The door closed on the redoubtable Betty Adams, and Agnes burst into laughter.

"I hope you're not laughing at Betty," Hardy said as he drew his chair closer to Agnes and sat down.

"Of course not. She's a practical woman who doesn't like the idea of a house like this, and its owner, going to wrack and ruin."

"So you think I'm going to the dogs, too, then?" Hardy picked up one of the books and glanced at its spine, then read

Hand of Glory

the title aloud. "*The Ingoldsby Legends*, by the Reverend Richard H. Barham."

"Not really. Just a bit turned around. And that's the book with the story in it." Agnes made a reach for the book.

"No, you don't." Hardy opened the tome, flicking through the pages.

"You don't know what you're looking for," Agnes laughed, trying again to take hold of the book.

"Then tell me." Hardy lifted the book above his head, daring her to reach for it again.

"Oh, pooh!" Agnes made one more half-hearted attempt to reach the book. "'The Nurse's Story.'"

"Oh," Hardy said, chuckling as he laid the book on the table, opened it and began to look for the list of contents. His fingers leafed through the pages. He could smell the paper. It had a slightly damp, dusty tinge to it. In fact, the edges were slightly water-stained. His right thumb traced the brown mark as he began to read the beginning of the story.

"That's my fault." Agnes pointed to the water stain. "It got wet on my way back from the library." Hardy did not answer. He was engrossed in what he was reading and quickly turned the page.

"Well?"

Hardy looked up from the book. "I'm sorry, I... Perhaps I should read it aloud."

"Perhaps you should."

"Very well. '*Malefica quaedam auguriatrix in Anglia fuit, quam demones.*'"

"That's Latin."

"Yes, I know."

"I remember skipping that bit, as I don't—"

"I'd better translate, then."

"That would be nice."

Susan Boulton

Hardy cleared his throat. He was not quite sure who was teasing whom, but it was enjoyable anyway. "There was a certain wicked witch in England whom demons dragged forth and, placing her on a frightening horse, carried off through the air. Terrible cries were heard for nearly four miles, it is said."

"A suitable beginning for a tale of horrible deeds."

"Indeed," Hardy replied, feeling the fun of the moment begin to drain away.

"Pray, continue."

On the lone bleak moor
At the midnight hour
Beneath the Gallows Tree,
Hand in hand
The Murderers stand
By one, by two, by three!
And the Moon that night
With a grey, cold light
Each baleful object tips;
One half of her form
Is seen through the storm,
The other half's hid in Eclipse!
And the cold Wind howls,
And the Thunder growls,
And the Lightning is broad and bright;
And altogether
It's very bad weather,
And an unpleasant sort of a night!
"Now mount who list,
And close by the wrist
Sever me quickly the Dead Man's fist!–"

As he read the poem, Hardy sensed the world closing in on him. Out of the darkening shadows of the late autumn day came visions of the men on the lip of the shell-hole.

Hand of Glory

Noose round the neck of the officer, the cry of his executioner. As Hardy finished the story he was struggling to breathe.

"Gruesome, don't you think?" Agnes said, getting up from her chair. "The daylight's going. Shall I light the lamps?"

"No gas here," Hardy said, mentally fighting to stay in the real world.

"Oil?" Agnes looked round and, seeing a lamp on the far end of the sideboard, made towards it.

"No, electric. My cousin spent a fortune getting the place wired and attached to the mains, not that it's totally reliable."

"So, where?"

"Oh, there's a switch on the right-hand side of the door, about shoulder height."

"I see it." Agnes walked to the switch and pulled the small black lever down.

A soft click was followed by a flood of light from the three bulbs set in the light fitting above the table. Yet the light did not fully penetrate into the corners of the room. They lay like the memories behind Hardy's eyes, heavy with menace. He closed the book and rested his fingers on the cover. His hand was shaking. He pushed it down hard onto the tooled leather in an effort to stop it. "Thank you for your help, Agnes."

"You're not going to look at the others? I mean if this Hand of Glory story is based on folklore, then... Besides, you haven't let me into the secret yet." She sat down again by his side.

"What secret?"

"Why your interest in the story, this Hand of Glory."

"My interest," Hardy repeated. "Do you think it's possible that...?" The words died in his throat. Agnes did not reply. She just sat there looking intently at him, waiting for him to continue. He did, his sentences sharp outbursts of phrases.

Bullets tearing at logic, releasing his memories into words for the first time.

"When I was in Flanders. When I was trapped in the mud. I saw two men kill their officer."

"I am sorry. I heard whispers of such things happening. We all did. It was very hard to believe. Then, again..." Agnes began. Hardy shook his head. She fell silent, her eyes narrowing with concern. For him?–he wondered.

"They garrotted him. Called him a murderer, said they were hanging him for killing others. Then one of the men took his right hand. Cut it off, calling it a Hand of Glory. I didn't cry out. I just watched as they pushed the officer's body into the shell-hole. I think the officer was your cousin."

"Dear God! But why haven't you...?" There was accusation in her voice, and it was painful for him to hear.

"I wasn't sure. I didn't know. I still don't, for certain... I can't remember clearly. I was hanging there for so long, half buried in the mud..." *And I still am.*

"But why Christian? He was a good officer. His major wrote my aunt. He said Christian was very keen to do his bit and..."

Hardy did not answer. Keen young lieutenants out to make a name for themselves, taking risks they didn't have to, were not well liked by the rank and file, as it was the men who took the brunt of the keenness. They preferred a diligent officer to an *out for glory boy* any day. "He died in no man's land?"

"Yes, leading a raiding party."

Hardy flinched and knew immediately that Agnes had seen his reaction.

"I see. That wasn't a well-liked duty among the men?" The pain in her voice levelled out. He marvelled at her courage. At her strength to just sit there and listen.

"It was bloody dangerous, and often as not a waste of time and men."

Hand of Glory

"And a *keen* young lieutenant would take on such a task as a way to prove himself, and..." Agnes's eyes dropped from his for a moment, then came back up, as if she were absorbing his knowledge of that time.

His mouth opened, but the words did not come. How could he say that in the confines of the trenches, the horror, boredom and moments of sheer terror magnified everything. A grudge became all-consuming. Any man, be he officer, non-commissioned, or simple private, could quickly become a personal enemy, seen as a Jonah by his fellows. He tried again, hinting, hoping she would understand, "Gain a bit of glory and run afoul of others, yes."

"Oh, Christian," Agnes sobbed. Both her hands came down onto the table and she clenched them into two small balls.

"As I said, I don't know for definite, but it was a junior officer from the East Staffs." Hardy's own left hand went out to her right one, taking hold of it. He felt her hand uncurl under his, felt the palm turn up and link with his. "I'm sorry, I didn't want to hurt you." Nevertheless, he knew he had.

"It's possible, dear God, it is. Thank you, Giles. I have an answer, but how do I tell my family? I totally understand how you couldn't say anything. My aunt would demand proof. She would want the names of the men involved, even demand something be done about it. Impossible to give, get or do. Maybe it is best just to leave things as they are, but my aunt and Elizabeth, they keep raking things over and over. That damn séance! Could telling them what you believe you saw hurt them any more?"

She had mentally spread the information out and checked it, as he had seen her do the tray of equipment in the hospital tent, years before. She did not like what she saw, but she faced it. Her green eyes were tearful. Her pain was only showing there, and he had caused it and was about to bring more. No, he could not do it.

Hardy looked away from her towards the window, but did not let go of her hand. The window faced north, and not even the weak autumn sun dappled the glass on the uncared for lawn. All outside was dull, the shadows lengthening across the field that separated the house from the edge of Chartley Moss. A fine screen of young birch trees ran there, their latticework of branches marking the beginning of the Moss, a floating peat bog that varied in thickness from a few inches to two feet, beneath which was water–bottomless, according to local tales. Yet Adams had known the Moss like the back of his hand. He had taken Giles and his cousin across many times when they were boys. Adams had shown them the open pools of water, the trees half submerged, rotting where they stood, and the dragonflies skimming across the strange, almost alien landscape.

Adams. The ghost haunting him.

"You ready to go over the top one more time, sir?"

"Not if you don't think she's worth taking a risk on."

"Nay, go over with her to get the job done, sir."

He turned back to face Agnes. "The man who killed your cousin, whom I saw take his hand, was a thief."

Agnes's eyes widened, but she said nothing.

Hardy ploughed on. "I think he believed in this." He tapped the book with the index finger of his free hand. "To him it was not folklore or superstition. He robbed the dead, the dying–not just of their possessions, but of their individuality, by scattering the very things with which they could be identified. He left them unknown and unable to go home. He killed my friend."

"Corporal Adams?" Agnes asked, then glanced towards the door, then back to him. She had remembered.

Hand of Glory

"Yes, Betty's husband. And I think the murderer is using the Hand now, to rob and maybe even kill."

"No, it's folklore. It doesn't—it can't—work," Agnes remonstrated.

"He believes it does. That is all that matters. Isn't that the thing with superstitions, countries, ideals, even ghosts? If you believe in them, you…" Hardy stopped talking and waited. For what? His personal ghost to put in an appearance to confirm his words? He could hear the clock on the mantle ticking. He was suddenly frightened that Agnes was just going to let go of his hand and demand he take her home. That she would say she never wanted to see or speak to him again. He could not face that now. He would be lost for good. She had become his link with what might be for him, and he did not want to lose her.

"If you believe…" Agnes slowly said. "Faith in a perverted idea… God save us from such men. Even so, where? No, you're not thinking…? Charlotte Warner's home? Impossible. Why here and why now?"

"Very possible. As to the here and now, well, coincidence perhaps?"

"James would think us both loons for even thinking such an idea as this."

"Yes, you're right. Proof I don't have. I just know what and who I saw, and what I felt," Hardy said, as a knock on the door heralded the arrival of Betty Adams with a tray of tea.

Chapter Fourteen

The rain had stopped by the middle of the afternoon. With an early onset of winter weather, the sky cleared and the temperature dropped. By midnight a thick film of ice covered everything. The puddles on the drive of the Tennants' house were small mirrors reflecting the approaching and very unwanted visitors. In the lee of the front porch Archie unwrapped the Hand and gave the cloth to Marie. The rasp of a striking match drew his attention away from the warped fingers of his treasure. Kevin had lit a wax taper and now stood at Archie's side.

Archie took the taper and set it to the fingers. Puffs of dark smoke rose from the wax-coated human remains. The dark, all-consuming confidence began to rise inside Archie's mind as he said the charm:

Open each door lock to the dead man's knock.
Fly back bolt and bar.
All not move.
Sleep still all who now sleep
And all that awake now be as the dead
For the dead man's sake.
O Hand of Glory, shed thy silver light
And direct us to our spoils tonight.

Hand of Glory

The fog of his breath mixed with the rising smoke from the Hand, thinning it and making the silver threads reaching out towards the door falter. His belief in the Hand wavered for a moment and a knot of fear began to grow in his gut. He heard his brother hiss, as if he, too, were afraid of the waning light of the Hand. Archie glanced at Marie. Her eyes had widened, and in the dull light of the Hand he could see the unease in them.

This was Lilly's doing, the bitch. The job was going to go bad. "Deal with it. I fucking will," he whispered. Jim echoed his words. As if in answer, the flames on the fingers flared brighter. The smoke from the Hand thickened and the voices of those trapped in the darkness moaned, cursing him. Archie laughed. Back bent, he slouched forward.

The sound of the locks clicking open of their own accord tumbled out into the night. "Be quick. Don't be taking any bloody big stuff. In and out sharp with this one," Archie said over his shoulder as he began to make his way into the house. The door began to close of its own accord. Archie blinked for a second; a shadow hand was on the edge of the wood, its fingers mud-stained and its knuckles white. There was someone there behind the door, waiting for him, for them. Archie pushed the door open again, hard. It banged against the edge of a plant stand, sending the potted aspidistra rocking. *Clack, clack.*

"Boss?" Will said as he inched down the darkened hall.

"Got a sodding bad feeling about the job, Will," Archie muttered as he looked again at Marie. The dark confidence was ebbing away again, and the silver trails of light in the smoke from the fingers were failing, twisting round in spirals that led nowhere. This job was going bad fast. Jim was screaming, telling him to flee. The door behind him began to move again, as if pushed from the other side. It grated against the plant stand and this time knocked the aspidistra off its pedestal. The pot exploded as it hit the tiled floor. Dirt flew up, taking shape as it did so. It was yellow-tinted, rolling and boiling like the gas that had blown across no man's land.

"Get the fuck out, now!" Archie bellowed. He moved quickly to the bottom of the stairs. "Lilly, Kevin, bloody shift your arses!" As he shouted, the thumb on the Hand of Glory went out suddenly. "Folks are bloody waking up for real!" They had to get out now. The figure half hidden behind the door was becoming solid; Archie could see the toe of one mud-covered army boot.

"Christ!" Will exclaimed as he came back down the corridor to the rest of the lower house, his arms full of loot. Archie had never seen the lad look so frightened. Join the club. The flames on the index and middle fingers of the Hand were spluttering, struggling to stay alight, then they went out with an audible hiss. The voice inside him howled and floundered around in the dark recesses of Archie's mind. "Get to the sodding lorry! You, too, Marie, and start the bloody thing. Move it, you buggers!"

Doors slammed open on the floor above them. Voices called out. More than two sets of feet were bolting along the landing towards the top of the stairs. The moonlight crept down the hall, running pale fingers over the pictures hanging on the walls. The light lingered on a photograph at the foot of the stairs. A smile was on the lips of the young man in an officer's uniform, but it was not a friendly one. And the expression tightened, the anger expressed moving, as the moonlight did, to the officer's eyes. The picture caught Archie's gaze as the figure of Kevin sped past it, racing Lilly for the door. It was that sod, Mr Out-for-Glory, Lieutenant Tennant.

"Bastard!" Archie smashed his fist into the picture. The glass shattered. The photograph crashed to the floor. As it hit the red tiles the hall burst into light. Harsh and brilliant. Electric light bulbs set in the ornate ceiling rose illuminated the

Hand of Glory

scene of the picture's destruction, just as the last two flames on the Hand died.

"By God!"

The blast of a shotgun from the top of the stairs.

A wave of small shot whistled over Archie's head. "Fuck!" Archie ducked. Crabbing forwards and tucking the Hand of Glory into his half-fastened jacket, he made for the door. The second barrel of the shotgun fired, followed by the sharp crack of the gun being broken to be reloaded. The shot slammed into the right-hand side of the doorframe and Archie's arm. He screamed, stumbling forward. He missed his footing as he lurched out of the porch. Down he went onto all fours, his fingers in the gravel of the path. His arm was on fire. It twitched with spasms of pain. *Not getting me. Never. Got out of the shit army. Get the fuck out of this.*

He flung himself to his feet and dodged sideways, fighting his way through a low laurel hedge. The gun discharged again. The thin branches tore at his clothes, then snapped, crashing to the ground in his wake. Across the front lawn he ran, his feet slipping on the ice-slick grass. More shouts. A blast of a whistle. Bloody plods. Must have heard the gun. The Hand tucked in his jacket clawed at him as if in fear, a child hanging onto a beloved parent.

The roar of the lorry's engine. Crash of gears. Voices bellowing. Another blast of the shotgun. The sound of his heart pounding in his ears. The hedge in front of him suddenly–gone. The lorry, its rear doors flung open, ploughed backwards across the grass towards him. He jumped, his fingers clawing at the metal edge of the lorry's open rear end. Hands grasped his arms. Fingers dug into his flesh through his jacket, detonating a new wave of pain as they dragged him onto the cold metal floor. The lorry lurched sideways and then tore forward. It careered across the pavement and swung wildly onto the road. The doors slammed shut, plunging the rear of the vehicle into darkness, and shutting out the sight of a shadowy, yellow-smoke soldier running after the lorry, rifle in hand.

Whoever it was will pay. Archie could not say if they were his thoughts or Jim's.

"Boss?" It was Kevin; he was shaking Archie's right shoulder. The movement woke the pain in his arm. It began to tear up the limb, taking away what was left of his breath and making him gasp.

"The sod filled me right arm full of shot."

"*Non!*" Marie wailed.

"Damnation!" Kevin let go of Archie's shoulder. Archie could hear him moving in the dark. Then a loud bang. A fist on metal. "Will, any sign of company?"

"No, but the buggers'll be crawling all over soon. I'm going to swing north out of town and pull up off the main road for a while, before heading back for the lock-up."

"*Non*, we must stop now. Archie is hurt. I must…" Marie's voice faltered as the dull flare of a wax taper illuminated her tear-stained face.

"I will light what I have. They won't last long, but will give us enough light to take stock." The ex-schoolmaster was kneeling on the floor of the lorry, his upper body swaying as the vehicle lurched to the left. The engine then slowed, settling into a steady pace. Kevin lit another taper, adding it to the other in his left hand.

Archie felt Marie begin to pull at the buttons of his jacket. The force of her assault ripped one from the fabric and sent it spinning. It landed with a soft ping on the metal of the floor. The Hand of Glory was revealed, lying on Archie's chest. Marie took it gingerly and set it aside. Then she began to inch Archie's jacket off his left shoulder.

Hand of Glory

"We'll get 'em for this." This time it was Jim's voice. It dripped hatred, acid, eating away at any doubt that lay in Archie's mind as to what must be done.

"We need more light," Kevin said. As if to underline his words, the tapers in his other hand began to splutter and fade. He bellowed, all the educated tones vanishing from his voice, "Will, how much longer?"

"Another five minutes. We're just clearing the town now."

"Make it now! Pull over!" Marie screamed. The weakening light of the tapers played across her bloodstained hands. She had ripped the gold cufflinks from Archie's shirt and torn the fabric open, exposing his pale flesh. A pattern of small, bloody holes marked Archie's upper arm, the red liquid running in rivulets into the bend of his elbow. Archie found his eyes drawn from one puncture wound to the next.

"No, the lad's doing the bloody right thing. Stop when it's safe to, then fucking sort things out."

"But you could be bleeding to death!" Marie sobbed, dabbing at the wounds with the remains of his shirtsleeve.

"I don't think so. It looks nasty, but most of the shot is only just under the skin," Kevin said as he waved the last lit taper close to Archie's arm.

"He is still shot!" Marie then broke into her native tongue, swearing and cursing. The vehicle turned, began to slow, then stopped. Archie heard the click of the hand brake, then Kevin's curse as the hot wax from the taper dripped onto his hand. The weak light died as the rear doors swung open.

"Bloody hell, Boss!" Will said as he stood there, the moonlight streaming in round him, picking out the faces of those in the rear of the lorry.

"Fucking right!" Archie said and waved his injured arm at him.

"Christ, they got you! Hell, what are we...?" His words failed, as Archie shuffled out of the van.

Archie's rage had burned through red-hot; it was now as cold as the ice coating the rutted road under his feet. He stood there for a moment, then rubbed his left hand over his wounded arm, feeling the thin leather of his fine gloves slip on the congealing blood. "Where is Lilly?"

"Not in the rear with you?" Will asked, taking a step back.

"Did the bitch rob us and then run out on us?"

Will's mouth dropped open, but no words came out.

"You bloody well knew, didn't you?" Archie took a step towards the young man. His blood-coated left hand came away from his wounded arm and reached out to the young man as if to grab him.

"Honestly, I thought she'd stopped after I caught her with those buggering labels."

"The labels." Marie hissed. She jumped down out of the lorry.

"What labels?" Kevin asked.

"We found a bunch of labels at the lock-up after the last job. Mister Will here said Lilly had spoiled them, told me she got the shakes over the old fart popping his clogs on the privy. Not quite the truth, was it, Will?" Archie took another step towards the young man, his left fist now bunching.

"Now, look, Boss, I was only... I mean, I thought I'd handled it. I caught her putting other labels on a couple of the parcels. I made her change 'em. I warned her. I told her she mustn't cream off you. She just didn't see it. She said she..." Will's voice trailed off.

"Pulled the wool over your eyes, Will, old chap. You should've kept an eye on what she was doing, rather than trying to see her stocking tops," Kevin said, the sarcasm dripping from his voice.

Hand of Glory

"Why, you...!" Will snarled, taking a step towards the ex-school teacher, his fists balled.

"Fucking pack it in!" Archie bellowed. "She took us all in. Bloody bitch could've been creaming off us for months. Slipped up, though, when you caught her. Should've come to me, Will, not tried to handle it yourself."

"I know, Boss, but I thought..." the young man mumbled.

"You'd handled it? She almost got us rolled up tonight. Wasn't enough to cream off us after she got greedy and pocketed something while on a job, and the Hand knew it."

"*Mon Dieu!*"

"You can't mean...?"

"Boss?"

"You all saw it sodding well fail." Archie's eyes narrowed.

"What we going to do, Boss? She's long gone, maybe on a train to London, even–" Will began.

"A train this time of night, here? No, she's holed up somewhere. She'll be waiting for the first train tomorrow," Kevin said, pooh-poohing the younger man's words.

"What time is it?" Archie asked as he half-rolled his right shoulder. The pain had dulled to a slow throb, matching the beat of the cold anger inside him.

Kevin pulled out his half-hunter watch and flicked the case open. "Coming up to one o'clock, Boss."

"We go back to the lock-up and stash the lorry. Tomorrow, Will, I want you to go over it with a fine-tooth comb. Make it as good as new and put back the license plates. Then you get rid of it. I want a car—a large, fast one. I want that bitch. But first, we walk back to the hotel and go in the way we came out earlier."

"Through the front door?" Kevin spluttered.

"Aye, we left our fancy togs at the lock-up, didn't we? They is expecting us back late from our evening out. We continue as if nothing happened. The stuff we took tonight, no way I'm having any of it within bloody forty feet of me. We dump it in the river, way outside town."

"With the tart's body for company?" Jim asked, then waited expectantly.

"Yes," Archie answered, already feeling his hands round Lilly's neck.

"Your arm, Archie?" Marie asked, her voice trembling.

"Can wait till we're back at the bloody hotel."

"But the gunshot pellets? A doctor, Archie?" Marie continued to protest.

"No quacks. You dig the fuckers out," Archie said, trying to give her a smile. The lass was worried about him. It was nice to see, but he had been hung out to dry by that little blonde tart, and it stung more than the shot wounds in his arm.

"But if we go back without Lilly?" Will asked, confused, stamping his feet to rid them of the cold.

"Ten to one she's already been back and gone again," Kevin said as he moved to close one side of the rear of the lorry.

"But surely that would make them suspicious?" Will continued.

"Like I said, girl's not stupid; no way she'd draw attention to herself like that. She would have another way in and out marked," Archie said as he nodded towards Kevin and Marie to get in the back of the lorry. "She'd have gone in, taken what she needed, and done a runner."

"Onto a train, like I said," Will began, as he held out his hand to help Marie into the lorry.

"*Non*, and she would know that we would watch tomorrow– bus, perhaps, on Monday. *Merde!*" Marie said, turning to look at Archie as she took Will's hand. She placed her foot onto the small metal step at the rear of the vehicle and began to get in. She was beginning to get mad–good. When Marie was mad she got on with things, in between getting louder and more French.

"Aye, maybe, but maybe she's lying fucking low for a bit. She'll wait until we've given up looking, or the plods begin to make it uncomfortable for us to hang around."

"But for that she will need money," Marie answered.

"Yes, she will." Archie did not say any more, but waved for Will to shut the door.

"We've been crossed. No half measures now, eh?" Jim asked.

Sunday–5th November–1922

Archie tensed as Marie began to peel back the stained linen binding his arm. The light of the short, late autumn day was already fading. He had hardly had any kip, plagued more by the thoughts of what had happened than the pain. He had put on a show when they'd gone down to Sunday lunch, but now, back in their room, all pretence had dropped. It was this shit place–it had always been bad for him.

He sat by the fire, Marie on her knees by the side of him. Will had brought more bandages, iodine, a thin-bladed knife and a small pan for boiling water on the fire. Where he'd got them from Archie didn't ask. The lad was throwing himself into any task asked of him, as if to make up for the blunder he'd made.

A couple of pieces of shot had resisted Marie's first attempt at getting them out. They could not leave them in. Archie knew that well. He'd seen it during the war, men thinking a small nick did not need seeing to, then their whole arm or leg needed chopping off. He hissed through his teeth, matching the sound of the gas lamp as Marie removed the final layer of linen. His upper arm was a lattice pattern of pockmark holes, linked by the yellow stain of the iodine. Some were mere grazes, others deep, made deeper by Marie's probing. All that remained of the lead was a small row of three silver balls just on the curve of his shoulder, submerged in raised, angry red flesh. Must've been the angle. Only piece of luck he'd had last night. The old sod had been at the top of the stairs when he'd fired and Archie's old jacket had been thick. Still, he'd been well peppered.

"Ready?" Marie asked.

Archie grasped the wrist of his right arm, holding it tight on his thigh. He looked at Marie and nodded. Marie brought up the small knife and sliced his flesh, twisting the length of steel slightly, so that it slid under the shot. Archie ground his teeth as the pain began. Small beads of sweat formed on his brow. Blood began to trickle down his arm. He felt the small ball of metal leave his flesh. The knife moved, attacking the next ball; again, the same progress, and again.

"All out," Marie said. "Iodine." The word was a warning. Archie braced himself again. Marie tipped the small bottle over the wounds and allowed the liquid to trickle over them and down his arm, coating the other wounds afresh.

"Fuck!" Archie hissed, as his arm tried to twitch away. The sweat broke out again on his brow and his guts rolled, leaving him feeling clammy and cold.

Marie placed a soft, folded layer of linen against the length of his upper arm and began to wind a bandage round it. By the time she'd finished Archie had begun to feel tired. Maybe a few winks would do him good, help him think things out. He stood and slipped on his shirt, then walked to the bed, lying down on it. He lay there, watching Marie tidy up. His eyelids began to droop. As they did, the old sensation of being watched flickered on the edge of his consciousness. The memory of the spectre that had chased the lorry loomed into his mind.

His eyelids snapped open. His mouth went dry as the sickly fear of being hunted began to grow. He raised himself up on his uninjured arm, glancing round the room. There was nothing.

Hand of Glory

Yet, deep inside, something told him otherwise. The figure was real and getting clearer each time. Whatever it was, it was getting stronger. Archie lowered himself back onto the bed, forcing himself to relax, and slowly sleep claimed him.

*****

A sharp rap on the door woke him. Archie cursed and sat up. As he moved, the pain of his wounded arm was at first sharp, then it faded to a dull throb. The room was darker; the gas lamp had been turned down. How long had he been asleep?

"Marie?"

"*Oui,*" she answered. She was standing by the door. "Who is it?"

"Me, Kevin."

Archie nodded to her to open it.

"Well?" Archie asked, resisting the urge to rub his wounded arm.

"Things getting sorted out, Boss. Will has shifted the lorry."

"No shot in the doors or side?"

"None we could find. We gave it a good going over and a clean, inside and out. Be hard-pressed to find even a partial fingerprint from it." Kevin shrugged out of his coat and placed it on the chair by the fire. He stripped off his gloves and held his hands to the blaze. "Damn cold out there today."

"Get the man a drink, me as well," Archie said to Marie. Her eyebrows arched at the rough request. As she handed the glass to Archie she looked hard into his face. He gave her a small smile. She sighed and got onto the bed and sat in the middle of it, her legs tucked under her.

Archie swilled the liquid round his glass, then took a sip. He was waiting for Kevin to continue.

"Will also has some feelers out for that car—not going to be easy to get in a place like this. It will cost."

"So it will bloody cost. You double-checked about when Lilly checked out?"

"Yes, Saturday afternoon. Told the clerk on duty her luggage would be left at the station, and she was catching the late London train after she'd been out with us. She was going to do a runner while labelling up the goods, I swear it. That means she had a bolt hole fairly close to the lock-up."

"Might as well be on the moon. Rows of back-to-back houses round there." The more he found out about Lilly's activities, the more his rage at her deepened. "What else you got to tell me?"

"Local buses start running about six o'clock tomorrow morning. However, those going any distance don't come into the bus station until at least nine. Trains going south start about six. Not be the only ones watching, so we have to be careful. The plods have a number of uniform hovering round the station and will most likely have some detailed to the bus station.

"Will is also making enquiries about which of the town's pawnbrokers might touch lifted stuff. Lilly won't know of any of the local fences, but she is not daft enough to take the loot to any old Jew." He stopped to draw breath. "And I have got some more information on Nurse Agnes Reed, as well."

"Agnes!" Marie hissed. "That is she, the one that watched. She is dangerous—I feel it." She sat up on her knees on the bed, her dark eyes hardening.

"Lilly'll move stuff sooner rather than later. Tam's and Robyen's are the only ones I remember, but might be a few more touch dodgy stuff now. With work getting tight, folks turn to lifting. Likely be round the gaol, North Walls or Greyfriars. So what else about the Agnes woman? We already know she's related to the Tennants and is a nosy, know-it-all little bitch."

Hand of Glory

"Seems she is walking out with a former captain, Giles Hardy, him with the gammy leg at the first séance."

"Fuck!"

"Archie, is it that bad?" Marie slid off the bed and came to his side.

"That sod remembers. Thought he didn't, but he does. Saw me, he did, the night I gave the bloody army the flick. I gutted that tart of a corporal of his. We—me and you, Marie, Will—check us all out tomorrow morning, early. Make a big show of it. Then double back with a local train and meet up at the lock-up." Archie began to sweat. A cold, clinging fear began to gnaw at his gut.

Did this Hardy know about the Hand? Had he seen or heard something out in no man's land? At the dressing station, the bend-over corporal had said something about Hardy being stuck on the wire. Had he seen him gutting Tennant? Put two and two together? He should not have got off the train at this sodding place. Then again, maybe it was the Hand that had made him? Had it sensed the danger, from Lilly, from Hardy? Yes, that was it. Both were knives at his back, waiting. Well he would remove them, cover his tracks, and move on.

Chapter Fifteen

"Will you go into the parlour now and sit quietly!" Elizabeth shouted at her two eldest children as she moved her youngest child from one hip to another.

"But–" Edward began, cocking his hands onto his hips and thrusting out his lower lip.

"Don't you 'but' me, young man!" Elizabeth retorted.

"Do as your mother says, both of you. If you behave for a little while I might consider taking you both for a walk to the park." Agnes hoped the carrot might work better than the stick Elizabeth was using. Victoria and Edward exchanged looks, then nodded, turning as one and making down the hall towards the front parlour.

"Really, Agnes, you shouldn't make them such promises," Elizabeth began, then Charles burst into tears. "Oh, shush!" Elizabeth began to sway gently, rocking her son.

"Here, give him to me." Agnes held out her arms for the child. Automatically, Elizabeth passed her son over. Charles's tears subsided to small hiccups and he began to take an interest in the lace trim on Agnes's dress, attempting to poke his fat fingers through the holes.

"Evil child," Elizabeth said, running her hand through her fringe.

Hand of Glory

"He's just sensing you're upset. Go rest. There is nothing you can do, is there?"

"But Mother needs–" Elizabeth began.

"Stuff and nonsense. Auntie Vera understands. Wasn't it she who insisted you come home? Besides, it's time that sister and sister-in-law of yours did a bit more. It could have been a lot worse, you know." It could have: Elizabeth's father, Martin, could have actually hit the robber. If he had done so, it could have ended up in court. They should be glad for small mercies, though James had said no English jury in their right minds would find him guilty of assault or, worse, murder.

"Maybe you're right," Elizabeth said, then sighed.

"I always am. Seriously, I can manage for the afternoon, and Nurse Gladys said she would be back by six." Agnes waved her free arm at her cousin, shooing her in the direction of the stairs.

"I don't feel right about that." Elizabeth gave Agnes a small smile and lifted her arms slightly as if surrendering to the force of Agnes's argument.

"She offered to stay. So did Emily and the maid, young Sally," Agnes said, increasing the wave of her hand.

"It's their day off. They shouldn't have to."

"Yes it is, but it shows how much they care for this family," Agnes replied. Elizabeth mounted the stairs; Agnes watched her go up. "Now, young man," Agnes said, turning her attention to the small child in her arms, "let's get you sorted out and in that perambulator. A good walk will do us all good–" She was interrupted by the harsh bell of the telephone. "Drat, who can that be?" The ringing stopped suddenly, and Agnes heard the voice of Emily, the cook, asking who was there. Agnes sighed and walked towards the woman, who stood in the hall, the dark handset in her hand.

"Mr Hardy, Miss Agnes–asking for you." Emily held out the telephone towards Agnes.

"Thank you, Emily." Agnes took the telephone, trying at the same time to keep the wire out of Charles's reach. "Now, please, off you go, and tell the others to go as well. I know how precious days off can be."

"Alright, miss, but we all intend being back earlier than normal this evening." With that, Emily turned on her heel, straightening her hat as she walked back towards the kitchen.

"Hello, anyone there?"

"Hello, sorry... I..." Agnes mumbled.

"What's wrong?" She could hear the tension in Giles's voice.

"It's... oh, dear..." Agnes said, realising her voice was shaking.

"I'm coming over." The words were swiftly followed by the sharp click of the telephone at the other end as he hung up. Just like that. *Well, of all the cheek.* No, not cheek–he knew something was wrong. *Am I so transparent to him?*

"Pooh..." Charles gurgled as he successfully reached the wire to the telephone.

"Pooh to you, too, young man," Agnes replied and began untangling him from the device.

"Are we going to the park soon?" Victoria had crept out of the parlour and was standing there looking at Agnes.

"In a while, yes. I have to get your brother sorted out, so why don't you go look in the kitchen? I think Emily might have left something on the table for you two."

"Cake, I bet. We always have cake when things go pear-shaped," Edward said with glee. "Will we be walking over to Grandfather's house? I want to ask him about him shooting the robber."

"No, your poor grandmother has enough to cope with at the moment."

"Oh, pooh!" Edward said and scuffed the floor with the toe of his right shoe.

Hand of Glory

"Pooh!" Charles repeated.

"So that's where your brother picked that up from."

"That's not all he's been trying to teach him to say," Victoria said over her shoulder as she skipped towards the kitchen.

"Tell-tale tit!" Edward retorted, sticking his tongue out at his sister.

"Put that tongue away, else it will fall out," Agnes said. "Then how are you going to eat the cake?"

"Really?" Edward asked, a frown creasing his young face. Agnes did not answer, just raised her right eyebrow. Edward giggled and trotted after his sister to see what sort of cake Emily had left for them.

Agnes shifted Charles back to her other hip and made her way upstairs.

*****

Agnes was just putting on her coat when she heard someone knocking at the door. "Get that, will you, Edward? I think it's Mr Hardy." Agnes finished putting on her coat and picked up her hat and gloves.

"Is he coming with us?" Edward asked as he pulled his woollen hat down over his ears.

"I think so," Agnes replied. She was not sure what to say to Giles. Had she sounded such a woebegone thing on the telephone, or had Giles just used it as an excuse to come? Maybe he had decided he was coming over before he had even rung. Oh, bother, this courting was confusing. Were they courting?

Edward opened the door. "Quick, out you go, children. We're letting the heat out," Agnes said, more sharply than she meant to.

"Going for a walk, are we?" Giles asked. He was standing in the doorway, his trilby hat in his hand, winter coat unbuttoned.

She had not noticed before how tall he was. She thought he must be nearly six foot, and he was light in build, well, compared to someone like James, but strong. No, strong was the wrong word. Giles had that air of a man battered by events that would have crushed a lesser soul. Resilient–yes, that was the word. He had survived and fought on against the memories, the mud that still tried to claim him.

"Yes, if you don't mind. I promised them, and Elizabeth needs to rest," Agnes said, setting her gloved hand to the silver handle of the perambulator.

"Is that what this is all about?" Giles asked as he stepped aside to let the two elder children pass.

"Wait at the gate, you two," Agnes called as she steered the pram out. She nodded to Giles to close the door.

"Have you a key?" he asked.

"Of course. I don't lose them."

"Ouch, hit the mark with that one." Giles pulled the door shut, pushing it gently to check it was closed.

He walked by her side as she pushed the perambulator down the gravel path. She could tell he was waiting for an answer to his earlier question. "No, it's not Elizabeth, though I am worried the shock might affect her."

"What has happened?" Giles asked, his gaze searching her face.

"Grandfather shot a robber!" Edward obliged with the answer as he swung on the gate.

"Edward, he did not shoot a robber, he shot *at* one," Agnes corrected him.

"Same difference," Edward said. He jumped off the gate and began to hop down the pavement, his sister, Victoria, joining him.

"It is not..." Agnes began, increasing her pace.

"So, tell me," Giles said softly.

Hand of Glory

It all came out in a rush, the words tripping over themselves in their haste to exit her mouth. When her telling of events finally spluttered and died they were in the park.

Giles did not answer her; it seemed his attention was elsewhere. Edward and Victoria were examining the thin layer of ice on the edge of the sluggish river and poking it with sticks.

"Take a couple of steps back, both of you. That bank is slippery," Giles said.

"Yes, Captain," Edward replied and gave the man a sharp salute, then tapped his sister's shoulder. "You're it!" He dashed off down the icy gravel path. Victoria giggled, slapped her woollen-mittened hands together, and followed

Agnes was stunned. Had he not heard a word she'd said? She felt silly, and a little angry. Giles reached out and took hold of her left hand, taking it off the handle of the perambulator. He squeezed it and looked into her eyes. He did not speak. She realised he did not have to. That gesture, the look, told her he understood—her anger, her pain, the confusion she felt about what had happened. How it had hurt—her, her family—and how she was coping with it all by being practical.

"Thank you," she said softly and returned the pressure, noticing for the first time how well their hands fitted together.

"Good job there's no park keeper about at the moment," Giles said, drawing her attention to the two children racing between the empty, dug-over flowerbeds.

"Well, I can't see a 'keep off the grass' sign. Is it possible it was our thief, I mean the one you believe has the Hand? ...Oh, I sound totally gaga."

"No, only partly gaga," Giles replied and let go of her hand briefly to allow her to turn the perambulator down the next length of gravel path, before he reclaimed it.

"You're certainly not one for flannel, are you?"

"Never had much practice at it, and, yes, it might be our thief. Only this time your uncle was a much lighter sleeper."

"So the Hand does not work. I mean if they are using one. It's just a vile superstition anyway," Agnes said.

"Yes and no. You said earlier that your uncle could not move at first, even though he was awake," Giles said and waved to the children, indicating for them to return.

"Yes, but that could have been just shock at hearing—"

"Possibly, but then the accounts in the folklore books tell the same tale as the story. *'Asleep or awake, be as the dead for the dead man's sake.'*"

"Those words are horrible. I still find it hard to believe. Are you going to tell James? I mean, it might give him a clue as to who...."

"Not yet—I'm still not sure." Giles sounded vague, as if he were again drifting off, going back to the mud. Had he remembered something more? A name perhaps?

"But you are going to tell him?"

"Tell who, what?" Victoria asked as she took hold of the silver handle of the perambulator.

"None of your business, young lady," Agnes said, adding, "It's starting to get dark. We should be getting back."

"Can we go back through Victoria Square? I want to have a good look at the memorial. Father promised he'd take me, but..." Edward's voice trailed off and he kicked at the ground with his right shoe.

"You're going to take the toe out of that shoe," Agnes said.

"Careful, Edward, she's using her nurse's voice," Giles said, winking at the boy.

"Has she used it on you as well?" Edward asked, as they made their way out of the park and up the slight bank towards Victoria Square.

"Oh, hundreds of times!" Giles replied.

Hand of Glory

"Why, you!" Agnes tried not to laugh, but found she did anyway.

The square was empty. The remains of the poppy wreaths laid at the memorial's dedication–bedraggled, damp and covered with ice–clung to the bottom of the marble. The bronze statue no longer looked patriotic, but accusing. The soldier of metal gazed round the empty space, as if asking why he'd been abandoned.

The sound of a hymn came across the graveyard from St Mary's Church. Agnes did not recognise the tune. It was more of an orchestral piece, almost lilting. Very different from the normal *boom, boom* that accompanied most hymns. The words, too, were unusual. She looked across to the church. Its arched, stained glass windows were blazing with light, reds, greens, and blues dappling the gravestones surrounding the building. It was almost surreal, and added to the poignancy of the words as they faded in and out.

"*I vow to thee, my country... Perfect, the service of my love... The love that stands the test... That lays upon the altar... the love that pays the price... makes undaunted the final sacrifice.*"

At first Agnes thought it sounded patriotic, another rallying hymn for king and country–as if they needed another to encourage young men to die in mud. Then she realised it was a lament. For those who had made the final sacrifice for their country, for others, in a war that was supposed to have been the war to end all wars.

The second verse of the hymn started. Edward was reading the list of names on the marble pillar in time to the tune.

Adams, George.
Boulton, William.
Hawkins, James.
Hobson, John.

Tennant, Christian.

West, Norman.

"And soul by soul and silently her shining bounds increase, and her ways are ways of gentleness and all her paths are peace."

"Do you really think it was 'the war to end all wars'?" Giles asked.

Agnes bit her lip and slowly shook her head.

Giles sighed. "Then was it all for nothing?"

"Do you think it was?"

"I asked you first." His gaze flicked from her face to the two older children, who had lost interest in the memorial and were now hanging over the railings of the church, trying to see what was written on a toppled gravestone.

"No, not for nothing. Nothing is ever for nothing. Maybe we are too close to it to see all that will come from it, but the world has changed a lot because of the war. Many things are different because of it. People have changed. I know I have. Perhaps future generations will see things better than we do."

"Will they just see the waste and nothing else?" Giles asked and looked down at the baby, Charles, where he lay sleeping in the perambulator. "Will he and Edward have to fight another war because of it? Because we failed to win a good, lasting peace?"

"If they do have to—and I pray that they won't—I hope it's because if they didn't fight, the world would be a worse place for everyone."

"So if the world is a better place now, then we didn't fight for nothing," Giles replied, turning her words on her.

"I didn't say that. I can't judge what the war made of the world at large. I only know what it made of my world. I am sorry. I didn't start the war. I didn't send men to die in the mud, but I am who and where I am now because of it. I will never go

Hand of Glory

back to what I was for anyone, not even you." As she spoke, she turned the perambulator and started to push it towards the church, calling to Victoria and Edward as she did so.

"Agnes," Giles called. She stopped and looked back at him. He was smiling. "I like you the way you are."

"Oh..." Agnes spluttered, blushing.

"Can we go home now? I'm cold," Victoria said, pulling on Agnes's sleeve.

"Of course we can. Let's see who gets there first," Giles said.

"I will!" Edward shouted as he began to run.

"At walking," Giles called after him.

"Oh, pooh and bother!" Edward said and stopped, then giggled as his sister walked past him, her steps extra long.

"Thank you," Agnes said, as Giles fell into step alongside her.

"No, thank you." He paused, then said, "I'm going to Whittington Barracks tomorrow. I called my old major this morning—he's still in the army. I... well, I want to check something with him. We're having lunch. May I see you tomorrow evening?"

"I don't know. I was supposed to be shadowing the local nurse in Great Haywood for the next four days. Perhaps if I speak to Matron when I report tomorrow morning and tell her what has happened, she might postpone it for a day or two, at least. But that will mean I might be working next weekend."

"No peace for the wicked?" Giles quipped. He took hold of her hand again, and raised it to his lips.

"No good at flannel, indeed," Agnes said, laughing.

"No good at all," Giles said. He dropped her hand and took hold of her shoulder, stopping her mid-stride. He bent his head and gently kissed her on the lips. For a moment Agnes thought of pushing herself away, then she returned the kiss, feeling a large pang of regret when he lifted his lips away from hers.

Chapter Sixteen

Monday–6th November–1922

"Bob'll need 'em for Saturday, Mr Holbrook. It being the eleventh and Armistice Day. Besides, I don't wear it. It gives me the creeps, if I'm honest." The woman crossed her arms under her shawl. Her small, black straw hat was lopsided on her head, and two lengths of hair had fallen out of the bun at the nape of her neck. She looked worn out. For the men who had managed to survive and their families, the land fit for heroes was not turning out to be one. Jobs were scarcer than they had been in 1914, wages were lower, and the employers thought they still ruled the roost. Well, Holbrook had a feeling that soon they would get a shock.

"Well, mourning jewellery is falling out of fashion a bit, but the jet round the edge is beautifully carved. Whose is the hair inside, by the way?" Holbrook asked as he turned the brooch in his hand. Under the thin film of glass was a plaited and twisted length of hair, almost corn yellow in colour.

"I honestly don't know, Mr Holbrook. Certainly wasn't me father's hair. Me mother kept it wrapped up in tissue most of the time when he was alive, though she wore it a lot after he died. Is it worth the half a crown, Mr Holbrook?"

Hand of Glory

"I would say it's worth a pound, Mrs Griffiths."

"Goodness, you can't be serious?"

"Very serious, Mrs Griffiths. I would give you back Bob's medals, and seventeen and six as well." The brooch was only worth half of what he had said, if that. However, Taffy knew he could pull the wool over Mrs Griffiths' eyes far better than he could over Bob's. She wouldn't mention about handing over the brooch, either. Most likely claim she'd done a bit of extra washing for a couple of neighbours to get the medals back. Seventeen and six would go a long way in that household. "Now, would you be pawning it or selling it, Mrs Griffiths?"

Mrs Griffiths chewed her bottom lip as she thought on the matter. "Selling it, Mr Holbrook. I won't miss it."

"Very well," Holbrook replied, and slipped off his high stool. "Just give us a moment to find Bob's medals." As he walked through his small kitchen towards his storeroom, a spasm of coughing hit him. He stood there, hanging onto the small table, hearing nothing but his hideous struggle to breathe. As the fit died down, the soft tinkle of the bell on the top of his shop door crept to the edge of his hearing. Had Mrs Griffiths changed her mind? He glanced back through the door. No, she was still there. He could see her shadow across the counter. Another customer, then? Late one, too. It was nearly seven o'clock in the evening. Seems he would be late for his pie and pint tonight.

He found the packet he was looking for and returned as quickly as he could to the front of his shop. "Here you are, Mrs Griffiths." He placed the medals on the tray, along with seventeen and six from the till, and slid it under the grating.

"God bless you, Mr Holbrook," Mrs Griffiths said as she put the medals, along with the money, into her handbag. As she took her leave, Holbrook was looking over his next customer. *Well, well,* he thought, *what have we here?*

Susan Boulton

The young woman waited until the front door closed behind Mrs Griffiths, then approached the counter. She was well dressed. Her small felt hat had a small, rounded peak pinned back to the bowl of the hat with a long, shiny hatpin. The matching dark coat was well tailored and expensive. Not his normal customer, that was for certain.

"I wish to sell some jewellery that has come into my possession." Her accent was not local: below Watford Gap, maybe even London. Holbrook felt the hair on the back of his neck rise.

"I see, but wouldn't it be better to approach a jeweller, madam? Given time he could get you a better price than I could give you."

"I don't want the hassle. And I'm sure the price you will give me will be rather good. I made a few enquiries before I came to you." As she spoke, she glanced back towards the door, then licked her lips. Dry, were they? Looking out for the plods, was she? Or someone else? He had half a mind to tell her to hop it; he wanted nothing to do with her or her goods.

He began to cough, fumbling again for his handkerchief. As he held the cloth to his mouth, she spoke again, sounding impatient and very cocksure of herself. "Well, you interested or not?"

"I am interested." Yes, he was. "Let's see what you've got, miss." Stumpy Parker would need proof if, as he began to suspect, she was involved with the robberies. The shock of what he was considering doing nearly brought on another coughing fit. Shopping in a fellow thief? But then he felt the anger in him harden. He was retired, thinking of settling down with Mavis. This woman, and whoever she was working with, had come here without a by-your-leave, stripped two houses, scared an old man to death, and, more importantly, made off with money that was for the lads. Sixty pounds of donations for the poppy appeal they'd lifted. She deserved all the beaks would throw at her.

The young woman opened her handbag and pulled out a brown paper bag. She tipped the contents onto the tray. The jewellery fell with a harsh clatter onto the metal. Holbrook pulled the tray through and prodded the mass with his right index finger. He picked up his jeweller's glass and placed it in his eye socket. Then, carefully, he lifted one of the three rings out of the pile. A ruby, set round with four small diamonds, fifteen carat gold–not too bad at all. He inspected the two others. One, a man's signet ring, thick, with a crest cut into the gold; the other, a delicate weave of silver inset with small emeralds. *Very lovely. Wonder if Mavis would like that?* Two fine gold chains with lockets of different shapes and sizes were laid out carefully on the polished wood of the counter next to the rings. Finally, he lifted the remaining piece of jewellery. It was a three-strand pearl necklace. Each strand was longer than the other. One was very short, almost a choker, the second, double the length, the third, nearly double again. The sort of thing you saw Queen Mary wearing in the newsreels. He ran the pearls through his fingers, then rubbed a number of them against his teeth.

"They are real," the young woman said sharply, looking down her nose at him. *A right one, here.*

"I don't doubt that, but..."–Holbrook spanned a number of the pearls with a small pair of callipers–"they're cultured, not natural. You'd need to be royalty to afford a necklace like this of natural ones."

"Then they aren't worth anything?" The woman sounded annoyed. Her fingers began to tap on the edge of the counter and her pretty lips twisted in anger.

"I didn't say that." Holbrook laid the necklace down and stifled a cough.

"So, how much for the lot, then?" The woman leaned forward as she spoke. Her lips now formed a smile, and her eyelids batted a couple of times. Trying to charm him, was she? Used to getting her way with men, was she? Well, not this one. Her sort left him cold.

"I would reckon fifty guineas." Holbrook took off his jeweller's glass and polished the lens on the edge of his waistcoat.

"That all? I was looking for nearer a hundred." The woman pouted in annoyance. Holbrook could hear her foot tapping.

"Nowhere near. A fifty is as good a price as you would get from any of my competitors."

"Seventy-five?"

"Sixty, and that's my last offer." Holbrook knew it was a fair offer, most likely the best she'd had all day. It was plain she'd been doing the rounds and he was her last call.

"Very well."

Holbrook nodded and turned to the small safe behind him. Placing his body between the door of the device and the young woman, he quickly twisted in the combination and then withdrew two small bags of guineas. Carefully, he emptied them and counted the coins, returning some of them to one of the bags and locking it in the safe. He then transferred the agreed amount into the other bag, placing it on the metal tray. The young woman took it quickly and placed it in her handbag. It was plain she wanted to be on her way.

Pushing his latest purchases aside, Holbrook undid the grating and was raising the counter when the woman clicked shut her handbag. He stepped through the gap. As he made his way to the door he gave a wry smile of amusement when she glanced back at him, her face creased with suspicion. Her hand was on the doorknob.

Hand of Glory

"It's getting late—time I shut up shop," he said by way of explanation as he took the door from her and held it open so she could leave. "Goodnight, miss."

"Goodnight," she replied as she hurried out the door and into the dark, rain-drenched street. The temperature had risen during the day as dark clouds had rolled in from the west. Holbrook didn't know which he hated more, the damp or the cold. He stood for a while, watching the young woman vanish into the darkness, then stepped back inside his shop.

With care, he locked the door and turned his shop sign to "closed." He placed the gentleman's signet ring and the pearl necklace on one side on the counter. The rest of the items he placed in his safe and locked it. They were his fee. He intended to hand the girl over to Inspector Parker all right, but he was not going to be out of pocket by sixty guineas. Besides, the necklace was unusual. It was bound to be on the top of any list of what was missing, same as the gent's ring. These he put in a brown envelope, carefully folded it, and placed it in his waistcoat pocket.

"Cup of tea first, I think, before we go looking for Stumpy," he said aloud. Not that he was looking forward to trailing into Market Square in this weather, but he owed it to the lads.

*****

Holbrook felt uncomfortable. *The bloody proverbial Daniel in the lion's den.* Only he was an ex-cat burglar, and the den was the main police station situated under the Guildhall in Market Square.

"Well, then, what can we do for you, Mr Holbrook?" the desk sergeant asked, looking up from his incident book. The man was standing behind a large wooden desk. The harsh electric light made the buttons of his uniform glitter, sending thin, crackling beams across the white paper of the open pages.

Holbrook cleared his throat. "I wish to see Detective Inspector Parker, if you don't mind, Sergeant."

"I'm afraid the inspector is no longer here, but if you come back in the morning…"

"Too important to leave overnight, Sergeant."

The sergeant's thick eyebrows went up, nearly disappearing into his hairline. "I see. So why don't you tell me?"

"Begging your pardon, Sergeant, but no—this is a matter for the inspector only. It's with regards to the events of last Thursday and Saturday nights." He was getting cold standing here. There was a hell of a draft coming under the door, and the coconut mat before the desk was damp from a great number of size-eleven police boots wiping themselves on it.

"Well, that puts a different light on it, doesn't it? The inspector's doing his rounds, so to speak. So he could be anywhere about the town, though I do know he was meeting Captain Hardy—I mean, Mr Hardy—for a drink in The Bear later." While speaking, the sergeant had leaned forward over the desk and lowered his voice, as if telling Holbrook a military secret.

"My thanks, Sarge."

"You best not be wasting the inspector's time, Mr Holbrook."

"I won't be."

*****

The Market Square was awash with rain. It splashed across the pavements, making them shine in the pools of light under the gas streetlights. The dark bulk of the High Court building lay just across the square from the police station. Its shadowed windows, like the blind eyes of justice, were just waiting for the next customer to be brought before them. Holbrook shuddered and turned his back on the monster building, walking as quickly as he could down Greengate Street. By the time he reached The Bear, he was shaking and near breathless. He clutched the sill of the window that looked out onto the street and stood there, fighting to regain his breath. *Damn gas. If...?* No good thinking on ifs. No regrets about doing his bit then, none now. That lass and those with her had taken from lads who were worse off than him. He straightened up and walked into The Bear Inn.

*****

"Hello, Lilly," Archie said as he stepped out of the shadow.

"Boss, I..." Lilly began.

"Been bloody silly, Lilly, haven't you?" Archie hefted his cane up, dropping the heavy silver top into the palm of his left hand. One tap. Two taps. His anger increased with each tap.

Lilly turned to the right and began to run towards a small alley. Another shadow uncurled from the dark and blocked her path. Lilly skidded to a stop, her chest heaving, then turned and began to run back in the direction of the street corner which led to the pawnbroker's. But another figure was standing there. Female, her right foot tapping slowly on the cobbles. Lilly gave a snarl and swung out with her handbag as she ran at the figure. Archie nodded to Kevin to close in. The man answered with a grunt and began to run.

"*Non*, I think not," Marie said, her voice a mere whisper, barely audible to Archie above the *rat-tat* of Lilly's heels. As she spoke, Marie's hand lashed out. A splash of light from a window caught on the thin length of steel in Marie's hand. The knife ripped open Lilly's handbag as it swung outward in its small, low arc. The contents spilled out, rolling away into the darkness. Lilly tossed the remains at Marie and launched herself at the woman, her right hand going up to her hatpin. Before Lilly could draw it from the fabric, the stiletto knife in

Marie's hand was swinging back, its arc now high. The tip of the blade slashed the back of Lilly's hand, cutting through the thin leather of her gloves. The snarl on Lilly's lips turned to a scream as the path of the knife moved upwards, taking off the lobe of her ear, complete with gold earring.

"Bitch!" Lilly shrieked, her hands first going to her ear, then out, clawing the air as she lunged forward.

"No, you bloody well don't!" Archie dropped his cane and grabbed the young woman from behind, pinning her upper arms to her sides. Her feet lashed backwards, sharp heels ramming into Archie's shins. He winced, cursed, and felt his grip on her loosening. "Hit her! Shut her the fuck up!"

Kevin hesitated.

"Coward!" Marie spat at the man and slapped Lilly's face, once, twice. The young woman's screams turned into sobs. Archie could feel her struggles weakening, but no way was he going to let the bloody bitch go. She would run if she had the chance. His fingers tightened, digging deep into her flesh.

She stopped resisting and began to drop to her knees. Archie leaned forward to keep his hold on her, then Lilly surged up. The back of her head hit his chin, slamming his jaw shut on his tongue. His mouth filled with blood. Pain surged through the lower half of his face. He spat, the blood running down his chin. Damn bitch had caught him hard. He gripped her arms even tighter.

"*Non!*" Marie picked up the dropped cane and rammed the silver top hard into Lilly's stomach. The girl went limp suddenly. Archie sensed the fight had gone out of her for now. He let go of her arms and she dropped like a stone to the cobbles. Marie stood over the downed young woman in triumph, the cane gently swinging in her hand.

"Get the bloody car, Kevin—now!" Archie snapped.

Hand of Glory

Archie wiped his mouth, then reached into his pocket, drawing out a length of bailing twine. He bent over the young woman curled in a ball on the wet street and forced her onto her back. The faint light from the distant street light caught in her eyes. All hell's fury was there, and directed at him. She coughed and spat at him. Archie dragged her arms forward and laced them together at the wrists.

"Boss, the pawnbroker, he's on the move." It was Will; he appeared in front of the small tableau, his eyes widening as he took in the sight of the battered Lilly.

"Bastard," Lilly hissed. "I'll get you for this. You sold me out. We could've run together after doing the first house. Been miles away in London, stripped their warehouse and shopped them in to the rozzers. I had it all planned. I was going to make something of myself, not spend the rest of my life wiping *her* arse."

Archie saw the pity for her begin to die in Will's eyes. He made to speak, but the arrival of the car stopped him. "Take her back to the lock-up. I want to know how much she's bloody well creamed off us before I deal with her for good. You said that pawnbroker was on the move, Will?"

"Aye, Boss," Will said as he helped Kevin put the girl into the car. "I watched him through the window. He put some of the stuff she fenced in an envelope. Me guess is he's going to shop her."

"Well, he'll be heading for the police station, then, in Market Square. I'm going to trot after."

"Take care, Archie," Marie said as she handed him his cane and got into the car.

"You as well, lass," he said, and blew her a kiss. The car moved off. Archie looked round the narrow street. How many net curtains had twitched during the last few minutes? Quite a few. None would say a thing, though, if the plods actually got

Susan Boulton

round to asking folks about any strange goings on. He knew what people were like in this part of town. Keep your nose out, else get it broken. Archie spat, clearing the taste of blood from his mouth, and moved off at a trot to catch up with the pawnbroker.

Chapter Seventeen

Hardy thought on the events of the last few days as he drove towards Lichfield. The Hand of Glory. Agnes. The robberies. Adams's ghost. It was a jigsaw, and he was at the centre of it. Not that he understood why. He most certainly did not want to be in this gathering maelstrom. The only part of it he was glad about was Agnes.

It was after he had driven Agnes home on Saturday that he had decided to ring his old major, now colonel—Grives-Thomas. Hardy hoped the man might be able to dig into the regimental records of the East Staffs, a regiment now defunct. It had blossomed out of the "pals" battalions raised in the county on the wave of the patriotic fever that had swept the country in 1914. Raw recruits sprinkled through with regulars and territorials from its two larger, older sister regiments: the North and South Staffs. The baby East Staffs had fought alongside its older siblings from 1916 to early 1918. In the aftermath of the great German push of spring 1918, when the two battalions of the East Staffs were just ragged remnants of what they had once been, the remaining men had been absorbed into the other two county regiments. The East Staffs was not the only "pals" battalion to suffer this fate. The action was a logical one from the army's point of view, but it might make the task he had set Grives-Thomas a bit harder.

Hardy had remembered a name, or rather a part of one. *Hawkins*. As he'd stood with Agnes yesterday by the war memorial in Victoria Square, Edward had been reading the names on the memorial. He'd only been half listening, but when the boy read out the name Hawkins, it had jolted him. Had the man who'd killed Adams taken this Hawkins's name? On the other hand, was he Hawkins's brother or cousin? Families had seen all their menfolk join up, serve and die together.

He could see the large Victorian barracks through the now bare hedges as he approached. Ahead was a sentry box on either side of the road. The sentry came out of the box on the left-hand side as Hardy slowed the car. The soldier stood, rifle across his chest, his gaze on Hardy's vehicle.

"I have an appointment with Colonel Grives-Thomas; my name is Giles Hardy, Captain, formerly with the East Staffs, Second Battalion."

"I see, sir. If you will wait just a moment," the sentry said, not changing his stance. His hand rested on the uppermost part of the butt of his rifle, two fingers across the trigger. The man nodded to his opposite number, who vanished into his hut. After a few minutes, the man came out and signalled to his companion to allow Giles in. "Very good, sir. Will you take your vehicle through about a hundred yards? Pull over to the right, then wait. The colonel will be sending someone to escort you up to the mess."

"Thank you," Hardy said and eased the car into gear. The soldier waved again to his companion and the wooden pole blocking Hardy's path swung up.

By the time he'd parked his vehicle, gotten out and locked it, a smartly turned-out soldier was approaching him.

Hand of Glory

"The colonel's compliments, sir. If you will accompany me?" the soldier said, his well-rounded vowels echoing towards the parade ground where they were more at home.

"Of course, Corporal," Hardy replied. The soldier nodded, snapped round, his boots rasping on the concrete, and began to march off. Hardy followed, his left leg at first protesting the quick movement.

Together they moved up the long drive towards the mess. The towering memorials to the fallen of the regiments whose home this was stood at one end of the parade ground, marking the entrance to it. Hardy wondered how many men would march past these gleaming white towers in the coming years, and if they would even notice them. Would the columns over time become part of the background, seen but unseen, remembered only on one day a year when poppies lay at their base?

Down the side of the large expanse of the parade ground they walked, deep in the shadow of the Victorian façade of the main building. Narrow, high windows gazed out across the expanse to their counterparts on the opposite side. A number of soldiers of all ranks moved swiftly in and out of the various red brick dwellings, but none put a foot on the parade ground. Hardy wondered if a regimental sergeant major was lying in wait somewhere, just in case some soldier thought to shorten his journey by daring to dash quickly across the tempting open expanse.

"Sir." Hardy's escort had come to a stop by a small set of steps which led up to a heavy oak door. The man was waiting for Hardy to precede him.

"Thank you, Corporal," Hardy said, moving up the steps and into the hall of the building. The smell of cigar smoke laced through with polish lingered in the doorway. The corporal followed him in and caught the attention of one of the white-gloved mess stewards. "May I take your coat, sir?" the steward asked.

"Of course," Hardy replied. The man draped the coat over his left arm and held out his right, indicating for Hardy to walk into the mess.

The walls of the corridor were adorned with reminders of the regiments' moments of glory, from the sporting fields to the bloody ones of battle. Photographs of young men clothed in uniform, their faces innocent, unmarked by the fate that had awaited them in Flanders.

Hardy found the smell of the cigars almost overpowering now; it marked a barrier that he had forgotten existed, between enlisted men and officers. He began to wonder if he should have asked Grives-Thomas to meet him out of barracks. Being here was beginning to reattach the burden he had carried in the trenches, that of other men's lives. It began to swamp him, pushing him under the mud and binding him with wire. He drew in a breath, trying to clear his mind.

"Ah, there you are, Giles!" Grives-Thomas's clipped accent cut through Hardy's rambling thoughts. "A gin, eh, Giles? Not far enough off twelve for anyone to call foul?" Grives-Thomas held out his hand to Hardy, a smile on his face. Hardy noticed the man was still straight-backed and trim. He looked a good ten years younger than his age, except for the lines round his eyes. They gave the impression of having been squeezed tight too many times to block out sights they did not want to see.

"A gin would be good," Hardy replied, and took Grives-Thomas's hand, shaking it.

"Two gins, then," Grives-Thomas said to the young mess steward, then indicated a table set by the window. "We have a while before luncheon is served. Thought we could go over things here, rather than in my office."

"You've found something?" Hardy asked as he sat down.

Hand of Glory

"Easy on, old boy, let's not rush things. How are you? I only saw you briefly at the dedication of the memorials here, back in September. How is Civvy Street?" Grives-Thomas sat down on the opposite side of the small round table. His right hand went to the large, brown envelope on the polished wood before him. His fingers picked at the edge of the brown paper, folding a small section over and smoothing it down flat under his thumb.

"Not bad, though I wasn't a career soldier like you. I always expected to go back." Stupid thing to say. It was impossible to go back. He was falling into the old pattern, saying what was expected.

"You had the makings of a damn good one." Grives-Thomas gave a sigh. "Jerry got too many good chaps, of all ranks. No wonder the country is in the state it's in today, and as for Ireland…" The man shook his head.

"The regiment been posted there?" Hardy asked as the steward brought the drinks.

"Yes, Belfast, and I don't doubt they'll be posted there on and off for the rest of this century," Grives-Thomas said as he took his own drink and sipped it.

"Surely not?" Hardy remarked, falling into the old trench banter.

"Surely yes!" Grives-Thomas replied in kind. "Now…" He set his glass down and took hold of the brown envelope. "I've had some notes typed up from the regimental diaries and company reports of the time. Interesting reading. Surprised myself how much I'd forgotten. The boredom and routine, for one. Strange how the mind homes in on the stuff you would rather forget, while forgetting the normal hum-drum."

"Yes, bit like being trapped in a never-ending circle," Hardy said slowly, as he took up the glass before him and drank it far more quickly than he'd intended too. He set the glass down, his tongue licking the droplets of gin and tonic away from the corners of his mouth.

"Yes, that's it. Damn strange, anyway." Grives-Thomas pulled out a small sheaf of papers. "Seems there were two brothers in B Company by the name of Hawkins. Rum buggers, by the look of it. A number of charges each. Nothing serious. The usual stuff that most men run afoul of in the army. Until October 1917, that is. Captain Mellor took Lieutenant Tennant's report quite seriously. He also did a bit of looking into it himself as well. Put the one brother…"–he shuffled the pages–"on a charge, and sent him down the line on the night of the 28th October 1917. There was a short period of heavy shelling and the communication trench behind B Company got a pasting. End of James Hawkins and a few other men."

"What was the charge?" Hardy asked.

"Theft. I thought it strange at first. Most captains deal with that sort of thing themselves. Soldiers will pocket the odd thing if they get the chance. It often pays to look the other way. A dead man hasn't much use for a good penknife, or a tin of bully in his pack. You know as well as I do that most companies have a man capable of acquiring anything if the company find themselves diffy come inspection time."

"This was different?"

"Very. A methodical and systematic looting of the dead."

"And the not so."

"Yes. The thought of stripping a dying man of everything he owned, even perhaps putting an end to the chap to stop him from shouting for help, would sicken even the most hardened Tommy. I suspect that one of the reasons Mellor had the man sent back to battalion was to protect him from the rest of his company."

"What about the brother?"

Hand of Glory

"Well, seems James Hawkins said his brother was not involved. No proof. No sign of any stolen goods in the man's possession. Not seen looting. So not charged."

"Anything at all on the brother?"

"Archie Hawkins. Reported wounded about the same time as you, 31st October, then accused of murdering Corporal Adams and looting the dead in the remains of the ambulance convoy."

"And?"

"Nothing more. He deserted. In fact, he totally vanished. Which is unusual–he should have been rolled up pretty sharpish. He was not that far behind the lines."

"Had help?"

"More than likely. He must've had a funk hole he could crawl into. By the by, why all the interest? I know Adams was a friend of yours, but after all these years?"

"I think Archie Hawkins has come home and is up to the same old tricks."

"By George!"

It had been a simple statement. One based more on feeling than facts, but Hardy was sure it was the truth. It had been a long time since he'd been so positive of anything. He glanced outside the window. A small group of soldiers under the command of a corporal were marching onto the parade ground. Arms sloped, feet perfectly in time. The corporal glanced back towards the building. For a split second the man's face and form blurred, reshaping themselves. It was Adams, a smile on his face. Hardy gulped and reached out for the glass in front of him. As his fingers touched the glass, the corporal's features no longer bore any resemblance to his dead friend.

"So what do you intend to do about this, then?"

*****

Susan Boulton

Grives-Thomas's question rattled in Hardy's thoughts for the rest of the day. It was still battering away when he took his usual seat in The Bear that evening. He turned the pint glass in front of him slowly round its own axis as he mentally rehearsed the words he was going to say. The harsh sound of coughing brought Hardy out of his thoughts. He looked up. Before him stood a man in an over-large overcoat and bowler hat, his neck swathed in a thick woollen scarf.

The man's voice was low, a harsh whisper which tumbled out of damaged pipes. Yet his Welsh accent was undimmed. "Captain Hardy?"

Someone he had served with? He didn't recognise the man, but that was not unusual. The faces and voices blurred in Hardy's memory, drowned in the mud. The man was a former soldier, of that Hardy was sure. He had a rattle in his voice that said gas. "Yes, can I help you?"

"You're meeting with Inspector Parker tonight? The desk sergeant at the station said you were."

"Yes."

"You've known the inspector long?"

"A few years," Giles answered, frowning as he tried to understand the reasoning behind the man's questions.

"But you are an old soldier, like him? Like me?"

"Yes. Though I think you had it a bit worse than me." Could it be the Welshman was trying to see if he could trust him?

"There were more had it a lot worse, Captain."

"True enough. What is it this old soldier can do for a fellow old soldier?"

The man nodded, as if Giles had given him the answer he was looking for, and undid his coat. He reached inside, pulled out an envelope and placed it on the table next to Hardy's pint of beer. "I want you to give him this for me. Tell him he can find me at Mavis's place. Important."

Hand of Glory

"Is this to do with...?"

"It might be." The man cut him short, fumbling with his coat buttons, re-fastening them.

"I'll tell him the moment he gets here."

"Thank you."

"You sure you don't want to have a pint? Take the weight off your feet for a while?" If he could persuade the man to stay, it would save time.

"Am sure, Captain. Got me tea and a few pints waiting for me at Mavis's place."

"Goodnight, then..." Hardy left the words hanging, waiting for the man to supply a name. On an impulse, Hardy stood and offered the man his hand.

"Taffy Holbrook," Holbrook said and took Hardy's hand, shaking it.

"Good night, Taffy, take care of yourself," Hardy said; he released Taffy's hand and sat down. He then took the envelope and put it in his jacket pocket.

"I will, Captain, I will." Holbrook put his bowler hat back on and made his way towards the door.

Hardy's hand strayed to his jacket pocket. He patted the fabric, trying to feel what was in the envelope. He should have been more persuasive. He had just let the man leave. *Stupid.* "Damn and bloody well blast it!" Hardy swore, not realising he had done so aloud.

"You've been spending too much time with Agnes. Your language is getting as colourful," James's voice boomed out as he made his way towards the table. "Now, is that pint mine, or do I have to fight my way to the bar to get one?"

"No time for pints," Hardy said, a rush of relief at Parker's early arrival flooding through him. He stood up and grabbed his coat, throwing it over his shoulder.

"Always time..." Parker began, then his eyes narrowed. "What's wrong?"

"Something might just be right," Hardy said and nodded towards the door of the public house. Parker turned on his heel and strode to the door, Hardy on his heels. Once outside, Parker turned to Hardy. The light from the half-open door played across his face, illuminating the questions written there.

Hardy reached into his jacket pocket and pulled out the envelope, handing it to James and saying, "A man called Holbrook brought this for you. Said you could find him at Mavis's place."

James took the envelope in his good hand, feeling its contents though the brown paper. His eyes widened and he handed it back to Hardy. "Open it, will you, Giles? Let's have a look-see."

From the sound of his words, Hardy believed James already had a good idea of what they would find. He took back the envelope and carefully tipped the contents into his cupped right hand. The signet ring fell into the hollow of his hand. Cold. Metallic. The rope of pearls tumbled over the sides and sought to escape through the gaps in his fingers. Parker's hook hand swooped down and fished the pearls up. A soft *click, click* sound followed their ascent.

"Mrs Warner's mother's pearls, and..."–James looked down at the ring in Hardy's hand–"my father-in-law's ring. We've got the stupid buggers. They must've fenced some stuff through Taffy for some reason. They could not have picked a worse one to use. Taffy's an old soldier and proud of it. It got right up his Welsh nose that they took the takings from the poppy appeal." As he spoke, he opened his coat pocket with his good hand and lowered the pearls in, indicating for Hardy to drop in the ring. Once the purloined goods were safe, Parker set off at a brisk

Hand of Glory

pace. Hardy fell in alongside him, wondering how long his leg would allow him to keep up.

"Do you really think they're that stupid?" Hardy asked. They had left the brightly lit Market Square behind and were walking down the narrow street that led to North Walls.

"No, I don't, but they might not have any other choice now but to fence some stuff here. They made a right muck up of it Saturday night. One of them was hit; there was blood on the doorstep. Not much, but the wound might have been bad and forced them to go to ground somewhere in the town until they can move on. They would have needed money..."

It sounded very logical. For a few moments as they walked Hardy almost believed that the robbers were hiding in a corner, just waiting to be rolled up by the police. No. It was not that easy. Archie Hawkins was not that stupid. He was cunning. A devil. *Or in league with one.* Where had that thought come from? Hardy shook his head. He needed to tell Parker about Hawkins. About the Hand. Tell him everything he and Agnes had pieced together.

"Nearly there. Damn well lucky, that's what we've been." Parker sounded annoyed and relieved at the same time. "What the–" Parker began to run. His undone coat flew out behind him, as his hook hand pulled at a string dangling from the breast pocket of his waistcoat. The whistle on the end of the string was quickly put to his lips. Ahead of them, partly illuminated by the light spilling out of a yard, a man was beating another to the rain-slick cobbles. A bowler hat, the brim crushed, fell from the victim's head as he went down.

Holbrook. Hardy began to run, trying to keep up with Parker, but his leg would not oblige. The strength began to drain out of it. His breath rasped in and out. His chest tightened. The sharp sound of Parker's whistle was answered by another, then another. Holbrook was on the ground. A man was standing over him. A woman screamed. The attacker looked in the direction of the scream, then towards the fast-approaching Parker. The man backed off, vanishing into the dark, pursued by Parker.

*****

Hardy came to a ragged stop by the prone figure on the cobbles. He bent, hands going to the knee of his left leg, pressing hard as he tried to force it to stop shaking. The woman who had screamed was kneeling by the side of the man on the ground. A straggling line of men led from the scene back through the yard doors, into The Hole in the Wall. Their voices rose and fell as they debated what to do. The woman sobbed. Hardy straightened up and surprised himself by taking control.

"Get a doctor, now!" he shouted to the milling men. "A light, so we can see what we're doing, and a stretcher of some kind. We can't leave this man lying on the cobbles." The small crowd still continued to hover. Hardy pointed to a man on the far right of the group. "You, get a doctor, now. You two,"–Hardy pointed again with his index finger–"light and stretcher, now." The men jumped, as if his finger had poked them in the ribs, and began to move.

The woman looked up at him, her eyes full of tears. God, was Holbrook dead? Hardy placed two fingers under the thick scarf round Holbrook's neck, feeling for a pulse under the man's jawbone, close to the ear. He had done this so many times before. In the mud. On the duckboards of a trench. Among the strands of wire. Praying for the smashed remains not to be still alive. Hardy's eyes closed. The soft thump of a pumping heart pressed against his fingers. He sighed and tried to give a smile of reassurance to the woman as he removed his hand.

He leaned closer, trying to see the damage done to Holbrook's head, but figures blotted out what light there was.

Hand of Glory

Four tall men, made taller by their helmets, stood there, one demanding to know what had happened. As Hardy opened his mouth to speak, the blast of Parker's whistle carried back to the scene of the crime. One of the policemen nodded to the youngest of his companions, then ran on with the other two in the direction of the sound. The young constable who stayed looked round the scene while ordering that the makeshift stretcher be placed down, close to Holbrook.

"What happened, sir?"

"This man left a message that he wanted to see Inspector Parker. We, the inspector and I, were on our way to meet him here when we saw him being attacked."

"I see, sir," the constable said, pulling out his notebook.

"Do you?" Hardy muttered as he moved after the disappearing stretcher.

"Now, sir..." the constable chided as he followed Hardy into the single room of The Hole in the Wall. Holbrook rested on the largest of the tables there. His scarf had been removed, as well as his coat. The well-rounded woman who'd screamed and rushed to Holbrook's side was gently cleaning the blood off the side of his face.

"Looks like Mr Holbrook's bowler took the worst of it," a thin youth dressed like an undertaker remarked, turning the battered headwear in his hands.

"Let me have a look at that," the constable said, snapping his fingers. The hat was handed over, inspected, then placed down on a nearby table. Notes were duly made on its condition by the efficient young constable, who then returned his attention to Hardy. "And you are, sir?"

"Giles Hardy."

"And you are a friend of the inspector?"

"Yes," Hardy tried not to snap at the constable. Where was the doctor?

"I see, and the inspector continued in pursuit of the criminal?"

"Yes, I bloody well did, Jenkins, but the sod gave me the slip. Damn alleys round here are like a rabbit warren! Off you go and join Sergeant Tamms outside. He's organising a search of the area, though I don't think it will do much good. I swear the bugger knows the place better than we do," Parker said from the doorway. He then huffed like a steam train, bending near double in an effort to relieve the pain in his side. "How's Holbrook?"

Hardy walked over to Parker. "Alive, but unconscious. Nasty bang on the head, face bruised and cut something rotten. I think his bowler hat saved him from worse."

"Let me be the judge of the man's condition," an officious voice said from behind Parker. Parker stepped forward out of the doorway to allow the doctor in. The man's winged collar was unfastened on the left side and his coat hastily donned over shirt and braces. A fine line of foam marked the edge of his chin and his round glasses were misted.

"Of course," Parker said as he watched the doctor set down his bag and begin his examination.

"I suggest you get rid of this audience, Inspector, and if I could have some hot water, my good woman..." the doctor said.

The men who had surged back into the bar did not wish to leave at first, but Parker's glare and the return of one of the constables made them decide it would be better to have an early night.

Hardy took a seat and observed the scene. Parker joined him. Hardy opened his mouth to speak. Closed it. Rapped on the table with his fingers. Sighed.

"Out with it," Parker said as he took out a packet of cigarettes and offered them to Hardy.

Hand of Glory

"How did you know?" Hardy asked, taking one and placing it in the corner of his mouth. He reached into his pocket and drew out a box of matches, lighting both his and Parker's cigarettes.

"You're fidgeting like my Aunt Fanny, so give me your opinion of this."

Hardy coughed. "I think I know who's behind these thefts and the attack on Holbrook."

"Oh?" It was plain to Hardy this was not what Parker had expected to hear.

"Hear me out, James. Just give me a few minutes while you wait to see what the doctor says about Holbrook." Hardy tried to keep his voice level.

"Very well, but if Taffy there starts to come to, then your theories can wait."

Hardy began with the events in Flanders. As he spoke, his words gained a life of their own. The idea of a man believing in, using, a Hand of Glory. That man being local, come back to take some perverse revenge on Tennant's family, and perhaps on him. At first, James had worn a look of polite disinterest, barely tolerating the conversation. Then, as Hardy laid out more and more information, Parker's manner changed.

"So there it is. I don't believe in the power of this so-called Hand of Glory." As he said the words, Hardy felt the untruth of them. There was something evil and it had to do with this Hand of Glory. He saw ghosts. No, Adams was not a malevolence, and neither were the others he'd seen at the memorial. *Just lost.* What was preventing them all going home was the evil thing. *Nonsense.* It was all in his mind.

"But you believe this Hawkins does?" Parker's voice was barely audible.

"Yes, James. We both know how belief, faith—or even the lack of it—can affect a man, or bring him through." *Or make a*

232

man do terrible things. Hardy could see the words he'd left unsaid reflected in Parker's eyes.

"You have the notes from Colonel Grives-Thomas?" Parker asked.

"Yes, in my car." Giles frowned, adding, "You don't believe me."

"I didn't say that. Just let me have the papers and I'll do a bit of digging around. It won't do any harm."

Hardy was annoyed now. Was everything he'd said being dismissed? He shifted in his seat, banging his left foot, trying to get some sensation back into his cramped leg.

Before Parker could answer, another voice entered the conversation. "Wasn't a man." The words were followed by a hacking cough.

"Easy," the doctor said, laying a hand on Holbrook.

"Easy?" Holbrook repeated, fighting to speak through another coughing fit. "No time for taking it easy!"

"Inspector, I would like to have Mr Holbrook removed to the infirmary. I wish him to have an x-ray to confirm there is no damage to his cranium." The doctor drew himself to his full height and pushed back his spectacles against the bridge of his nose.

"Not getting me in front of one of those machines," Holbrook said and tried to sit.

"Nonsense, an x-ray won't harm you," the doctor huffed.

"Bugger that, and, Mavis, leave off. I need to speak to the inspector."

"You stubborn old fool," Mavis muttered, but aided the man to sit. His face was bruised, eyes sunken deeper in his head than when Hardy had first seen him in The Bear. His thin blonde hair was matted with blood and his thick-lens glasses hung at an angle across his eyes.

Hand of Glory

Parker had risen from his seat when Holbrook had first spoken. He stood waiting, the metal hook of his hand opening and closing.

"Not going to choke me with that, are you, Stumpy?" Holbrook asked, the left corner of his mouth twitching.

"No, though what did you mean, 'not a man'? Looked like one to me." Parker placed his hook hand behind his back, holding it with his flesh hand, and rocked on his feet.

"Not on about the one that clobbered me. That, at a guess, would be her boss. Silly bitch was skimming. Could tell it a mile off when she brought that stuff to me. I'm out a few guineas as well, doing this favour for you." Holbrook's smile widened, then faded, as he began to cough again.

"Sorry, Taffy, you coming to me got you a beating," Parker said, then frowned. "Damn it, we need to get to her before he does. Need to check at The Bear, see if anyone noticed someone acting a bit strangely. Constable!" he shouted to the young man by the door. Hardy could see Parker had something to work on now. He prayed James would not forget what he had told him.

"Aren't you going to ask me what she looked like?" Holbrook asked, dabbing at his mouth with an over-large handkerchief.

"Keep up with that cheek–" Parker began.

"What did she look like, Taffy?" Hardy asked, forestalling the outburst Parker looked ready to unleash on the Welshman.

"Blonde. About five and a half feet. Good looking. Expensive coat and hat with a silver hat pin. Hair cut in a bob. Not local– south of Watford Gap, I'd say, and full of herself."

"Right. Did you hear that, Constable?" Parker asked as he moved with purpose towards the door. The young man nodded. "You go get Sergeant Tamms and Detective Constable Bright for me. We have a young lady to find. Also, I'm going to leave a constable here, keep an eye on you, Taffy." Parker grinned widely, scoring his own hit in the game of words with Holbrook.

The turn of events had left Hardy feeling abandoned. He'd kept his word to Agnes and told James. He was even more convinced now that the thief was Hawkins. Had James even really listened, though? Hardy shook his head.

"Giles," James said, placing his hand on Hardy's arm, "just don't start turning into Sherlock Holmes with regards to this matter, now promise me. I said I would do some digging and I will, but right now…"

"I understand," Giles said, trying to smile.

Chapter Eighteen

A dull chink of light trickled out from under the door of the lock-up. Archie rapped twice with his cane and waited.

"Archie?"

"Who did you fucking well think it was?" he said, annoyed at Marie for stating the bloody obvious. Behind Archie, the high narrow windows of the Lotus factory blazed with light. The nightshift was well underway. They needed to have dealt with Lilly and be gone before six the next morning, else someone might see something. He heard the floor bolt lift. The wood grated on the concrete floor as it opened. He entered and walked over to Marie's side. His shadow played over the floor. Arms elongated, stooped back. Marie took a step back as the shade approached her feet, as if reluctant to allow it to touch her.

The Rover Coupe was sitting in the centre of the lock-up. The driver's side rear door was open, showing the fine red leather that covered the interior. Lilly was still in the back seat, watched by Kevin who was standing by the front of the vehicle. He was dabbing at a scratch on his cheek.

"Lilly been leaving her mark?" Archie asked.

"Bitch! I was only trying to make her see reason. All she has to do is tell us how much, then we clean her up and let her go."

"Like hell you will!" Lilly spat, moving further back into the car. Her face was streaked with blood. It ran in crusted rivulets down her neck from her sliced ear. Her bound hands lifted to the damaged lobe, then she covered her face with them. She began to sob, her shoulders heaving.

Will moved forward and leaned inside the car, his hand on the door, left foot on the running board. "Listen, Lilly, you put us all at risk the other night. Boss shot. Just te–" Will's words turned into a scream. High pitched, girlish. His face went slack, as he staggered back for two steps. He then fell to his knees with Lilly's long hatpin up to the hilt in his chest. Lilly surged out of the car, pushing the crumpling body of Will out of the way as she made for the door of the lock-up.

"She killed Will! Make the bitch pay! She has destroyed your gang, left you wide open to the plods. Rip her apart!" Jim roared. Archie felt his anger rise. Will's scream died away, replaced by Kevin's bellow as he moved to catch the toppling body of the young man.

"Christ! The door's open." Kevin's cry broke the lock on Archie's muscles. His head spun round. He swore he had pushed the door closed. He had, but the wood had jammed on the uneven concrete. It was still ajar. If Lilly reached it, one good yank on it and she would be out into the night. Then all hell would come crashing down. She would go to the plods and spin a tale. Bloody tart.

Archie surged after her, throwing himself bodily through the air and rugby tackling Lilly. He hit the back of her legs with his left shoulder. The wounds from the shot screamed out with renewed pain. He felt her knees buckle. She fell forward, her head hitting the door and sliding down the wood. Six inches before her head hit the floor, her body convulsed. It stiffened in his grasp, then went limp. She began to scream, but the sound died in her throat. Archie lay there, his arms wrapped round her legs with his head on her thighs. Something trickled against his arm.

"*Merde!* She... Her right eye. The floor bolt on the door has gone right into it," Marie said, her voice a harsh whisper. Archie looked up. Marie was crouching by Lilly's head.

"Dead?" Kevin said.

Archie was not sure if it was a statement or a question. He let go of Lilly's legs. They flopped like dead, white fish onto the floor. He knelt there, just looking at her.

"I think she is," Marie answered and kicked hard at the girl's head. It lifted with a soft plop from the bolt that had lanced it. Lilly's body rolled onto its side. Archie shuddered. He had seen hundreds of dead, even topped a few in his time. So had Marie. But not like this. Not as bloody stupidly as this. He had meant the girl to pay all right, but now they had lost whatever she'd skimmed off them. He continued to sit there as Marie pushed the door firmly closed. Her feet left a trail of half-formed footprints, from where she had stood in the spreading puddle of blood.

"That fucking bitch killed young William." Kevin was sitting on the floor, Will's body in his lap, rocking.

Archie looked from Kevin to Marie. They were waiting.

"You are the boss," Jim whispered.

"We have to get sodding rid of them," Archie said slowly.

"No, not Will. You can't just dump him," Kevin pleaded, tears running down his face.

"You want to get bloody rolled up?" Archie asked. Soft bugger. It was a shame about Will, even Lilly, the stupid cow. But when it came down to his skin... He looked hard at Kevin, waiting for his answer.

"No, but... This has gone..." Kevin's voice faltered, as he gently laid the body of the young man down on the floor.

"...tits up," Archie said, trying to think his way through this mess. No way was he going to trust Kevin with getting rid of the bodies. The man was plum ready to scarper, and no mistake. It was up to him and Marie. "Kevin, I want you to take a wad of the money we have and hire some muscle, first thing."

"Boss?"

"Hire them to make sure that pawnbroker won't be telling the police anything. I didn't have time to finish the job—bloody plods came out of nowhere. Then I want you to get on the first train to London in the morning. Get to our place and sort out the stuff stacked there, then sell it, sharpish. We are going to America."

Kevin got to his feet. "What about...?"

"Me and Marie will sort this place out, don't you worry. We'll join you as soon as we can. I'm trusting you with this. Don't you let me down." Archie looked hard at the man. Kevin's mouth was opening and closing. Sweat and tears trickled down his pasty face. He returned Archie's gaze, nodding slowly, then roughly wiped his face with the sleeve of his jacket.

Archie opened the passenger-side door of the car and pulled out his briefcase. He took a wad of white five-pound notes from the bag and counted out six, giving them to Kevin.

Kevin hesitated, then took the offered money. He then gave both Archie and Marie another nod and walked to the rear door of the lock-up. Here Kevin glanced back at the murder scene, sniffed, made to speak, then vanished into the night.

"Will he double-cross us?" Marie asked. She turned her foot, watching as the red stain on the edge of her shoe began to dry and turn a rusty brown.

"Do you think he fucking might?" Archie rubbed his chin. He was tempted to set fire to the place, car and all, but that would lead the plods to start asking questions. All they needed was someone to give a description of Kevin, who'd hired the place, and the trail would end at his door. Bloody place: he should've stayed on the train. Then again, even with all the ructions and upset, it had shown up Lilly's little game and put him in a position to get rid of the only person who knew about him. Hardy.

"*Oui*," Marie said, her eyes hardening.

"So do I, but I don't want another bloody body round here. I can see right through Mr Clever-dick. He won't hire any muscle. He'll just make for the train station late tomorrow—late afternoon is my guess. Thinking we'll believe he's in London by then. Kevin doesn't think anyone has brains but him. Anyway, I'll be right behind him, whichever train he takes."

"*Bon*, now we get rid of this." Marie's hand waved over the scene of carnage, as if it was so much dirty laundry. "Then we leave this place for good? Tomorrow?" Her lip curled. Marie had not been fond of the town from the beginning.

"In a day or so we'll kiss this arsehole of a place goodbye, but I've got a couple more things to clear up first. That bloody pawnbroker shut up for good, along with the only fella who can really put his finger on me."

"Hardy?" Marie hissed. "And his little whore? Why bother? Just vanish—nothing they can do."

"No. Hardy, he saw, he knows, I fucking swear it. Just him. Do him and drive our way to London," Archie said softly as he took Marie in his arms. She came, grudgingly. Archie could tell she disagreed with his plan. She wanted out of this place now, but she didn't say anything more.

Tuesday–7th November–1922

There he was. Archie could just see the balding head of Kevin as the man removed his hat and made himself comfortable. He had guessed the bastard's plans spot on. The bugger was going north. Liverpool. Kevin sat in a first class carriage, hard against the window. It was nearly three in the afternoon; already the sun had begun giving up its battle against the coming darkness.

Archie looked down the platform towards the guard. Yes, he was about to wave his flag. He rubbed his eyes. He was ready to drop. He hadn't been able to sleep since Sunday night. Anger was driving him on, fuelled by Jim's encouragement. Archie had trusted his gang, hand-picked them, and they had all stabbed him in the back. *"Betrayed the Hand,"* Jim reminded him. *"Not something you do, cross the Hand."*

The guard raised his whistle to his lips. Archie removed his cigarette from his mouth and dropped it to the floor, twisting it under his heel. He walked quickly towards the train. The carriages were already moving as he slammed the door behind him. He had fifteen, maybe twenty minutes before the conductor reached first class. They always started down in third, which, along with second class, was pretty full. First was another matter. Typical Kevin. If the man had any sense, he would've opted to travel in second or third, and Archie would not have been able to get near him. Archie smiled. *Stupid bugger.*

He felt the train pick up speed. Archie was standing in the small junction between the last of the first class carriages and the buffet car. He glanced through the glass of the door. The waiters were preparing to serve afternoon tea. Kevin would be along any second. Habit. Archie had watched him before. The bugger hated going in late for a meal. He was frightened he'd be fobbed off with re-heated grub. Typical schoolmaster, always trying to get his nose first in the trough.

Archie walked across the width from outer door to outer door at the junction of the carriages. He then opened the door to the privy situated on the right-hand side. Yes, it blocked off the view of the outer door on the right for anyone coming out of the buffet car or first class carriage. He closed the door, walked back to the left side and waited. He did not have to wait long.

"Hello, Kevin," Archie said as the man walked out of the first class carriage.

"Boss, I..." Kevin spluttered as he instinctively moved away from Archie towards the right-hand side door. Kevin's lower lip trembled; beads of sweat began to trickle off the top of his bald spot.

"I..." Archie mimicked, stepping towards Kevin, forcing him against the outer door of the train. "Got something of mine, haven't you?" Kevin fumbled in the inner pocket of his jacket. Archie pressed close to him, snatching at the door of the privy and opening it behind him, sealing them off from prying eyes.

"Yes, I mean..." Kevin blathered, pulling the white five-pound notes from his wallet. "I was going to Liverpool to get the tickets. I thought, yes, I thought it would be safer to travel from there."

"Did you?" Archie said, snatching the notes from Kevin's trembling hands and shoving them in his jacket pocket. He leaned forward, dominating the small man, physically pushing him against the door. As he reached round the trembling man and caught hold of the door handle he could feel Kevin's breath against his neck and the vibration of the train. Archie felt a rush of excitement mix with his anger. His fingers began to twitch as he jerked the handle down. The door slammed back, its hinges screaming at the force. Smoke-laden air rushed in, snatching at hair and clothes. Kevin swayed backwards. His hands came up, grabbing hold of Archie's jacket. The sod knew what was going to happen. Archie braced his feet on either side of the small gap as his fingers uncurled Kevin's from the fabric of his jacket. He paused for a moment, holding Kevin's hands, then forced the man back. Kevin screamed and shouted. His feet scrabbled on the metal floor. For a moment he hung suspended in the air outside, then Archie released his hold. Kevin's nails raked down Archie's hands. He ignored the pain. Then the man dropped from Archie's sight. He tumbled down the side of the train, caught in the juggernaut's wake, his screams becoming lost in the thunder of the train's wheels on the tracks.

*****

Archie left the train at Crewe, hopping on a southbound train within minutes. The journey back to Stafford took longer than the forty minutes it had taken to reach Crewe. An accident: a body on the line. People in third wondered, cursed and peered out of the windows, hoping to get a look at the grizzly scene. Archie took no notice and gave the evening paper his attention. No mention of any bodies found in the River Trent. Still, it was early days. If there was still nothing reported by the weekend, they would be in the clear. Will and Lilly would be bloated and fish-nibbled by then. He and Marie would be in London, or even on their way to the States. They had money, no need to work for a long while. They could become pillars of American society. Archie began to chuckle at the thought. The chuckle turned into a yawn. He was dog-tired. The slow, jolting, stop-start motion of the train was sending him to sleep.

He fought to keep his eyes open. His head nodded forward, hitting the open paper. Bugger. He snapped awake. The muscles on his face stretched down, elongating the scars round his eye. The train began to move faster, the carriage rattling. Archie eased his buttocks on the hard wooden seat, pushing the middle of his back against the rear of the bench. Outside, the darkness frothed with red sparks from the engine, as if the mechanical monster were celebrating its freedom to eat up the miles.

Hand of Glory

Again, Archie began to nod, his head dropping. He slept and dreamt. The figure in the yellow mist was dogging him, making a tally of his actions. Hunting him. A sniper on his tail, with a well-oiled smelly brought up to a shoulder, its sights on him. He moaned and his head slipped sideways. The sharp pressure of a foot on top of his brought him awake with a curse. The carriage was seething with people struggling to the doors. "Where?" he asked, his mouth dry, the shimmering shape in the yellow mist still lingering in his mind.

"Stafford," a man said over his shoulder. He was struggling to pull down a battered suitcase from the netted rack above the seats.

"Thanks, mate," Archie said and stood up, throwing his newspaper down on his abandoned seat. For some reason he reached over and helped the man remove his suitcase from the rack. The man thanked him. Archie's face split in a smile. Archie followed him off the train, making his way out of the bright lights of the station into the darkness of the streets.

Chapter Nineteen

Friday–10th November–1922

"Tea, sir?" The muffled voice of the duty sergeant came from the other side of the door.

"Please, Sergeant Tamms, and some of that bacon I smell frying."

"Yes, sir—one or two rounds, sir?"

"Two rounds, please."

Parker heard the rough scrape of Tamms's boots on the floor as the man began to turn away. "Oh, Tamms..."

"Sir?"

"Is young Bright here yet?"

"Yes, sir. Detective Constable Bright is just going over the reports that came by special delivery, sir, on the early milk train."

"Was the special delivery from London?" James asked, standing up and reaching for his jacket.

"Bristol, I believe, sir."

"Good!" Parker answered and strode to the door, opening it and stepping out into the main corridor of the police station. "Bright! Where're you hiding?"

Hand of Glory

"In here, sir." Bright's face peered round the edge of an open door ten paces further down the corridor.

"Right, show me. What have we got?"

"Looks like a dead end, sir," Bright said, placing the buff-coloured folder down on the desk.

"You sure?" James picked up the folder and began leafing through it.

"Your tea and bacon butties, sir," Tamms said as he came into the room and placed Parker's breakfast on the edge of the table.

"Thank you, Sergeant," James said, picking up a sandwich and taking a large bite.

"You're welcome, sir. Would you like something to eat, too, sir?" Tamms addressed Bright as he turned to leave.

"No, thank you, Sergeant, but I wouldn't mind a cup of tea." Tamms nodded and left the office. Bright turned his attention to his superior and James could see the unasked question in the young man's eyes.

"I got caught up in those old files and, well, it wasn't worth going home." The answer sounded false, James knew it. He wondered why he was explaining the matter to his detective constable. Was he feeling guilty? Dammit, no, he was not. He had a nasty case of robbery and assault to solve. Running the gauntlet of Elizabeth's disapproval was not going to help him solve it. After the bungled robbery at her parents' home, Elizabeth had taken it into her head to blame him. He hadn't caught the thieves after they had robbed her best friend, so the horrible event at her parents' house lay at his door. Perhaps it was her pregnancy which was making her prone to such fits of temper, or maybe she had always been like that and James just hadn't noticed before. Without Agnes around to offer her voice of reason, Elizabeth had taken her accusations to new heights on Monday night when he'd come home in the early hours after the attack on Taffy. James had used the same event as an excuse not to return home since, saying the case needed his undivided attention.

"Any luck, sir?" Bright asked.

"Some. Thank your grandfather for me. I think we now know who the culprit is, but it's a matter of putting a face to him. Any luck with any of the local photographers? Most took photos of local lads before they shipped out."

"Not yet, sir. As to Bristol, the report states they did have similar robberies, but they arrested a local chap for the crimes." Bright pointed to the folder in Parker's hands.

"Sir?" It was Tamms. He stood in the doorway, left hand on the door handle.

"Seems we've run out of tea. Hard luck, Bright," Parker quipped and threw the file down onto Bright's littered desk.

"Never run out of that, sir. Just had a telephone call from the constable at Great Haywood."

"And…?" Parker asked.

"Couple of bodies have been pulled out the Trent by Essex Bridge."

"The bugger they have!" Parker swore, wondering what he had done to deserve this addition to his caseload.

"Yes, sir, and one of them bears a resemblance to the description of the young lady that–" Tamms did not finish his sentence as it became lost in Parker's bellow for Bright to get the car.

*****

The bodies had been taken from the river and placed on the bank. Two pairs of feet stuck out from beneath a sheet of oilcloth. One wearing shoes with spats, the other pair naked, with painted toenails. Short lengths of rope bound the legs of both. James could not take his eyes off the twine and the damage it had done to the woman's ankles. It had cut deep into her pale, bluish skin.

The slap of wet cloth cut the silence that had fallen over the scene. Bright had pulled back the fabric that covered the male body: young, thin-faced. Dark hair plastered to pale blue skin, bloated and slightly distorted. However, there was something familiar about him. Or was it just the fact that he was another dead young man, like all the other dead young men he'd seen in France?

Empty. Face and form. It had struck him the first time he'd seen a dead body. The blank stare. The relaxed muscles of the face. Even in sleep, he thought, a human face retained the imprint of the soul that lived within. In death, that was gone, leaving behind just the flesh. Nothing to be scared of, yet people often were. James sensed the fear in those watching today. Villagers who'd heard talk of bodies in the river and come to see for themselves. Some were more ghoulish than others and were feeding like leeches on all the gory details they could obtain. The local village police sergeant and constable stood in front of the straggly line of onlookers, their backs to the bodies on the river bank.

"Been in the water a couple of days by the looks of 'em," said one of the local boatmen who'd brought the bodies ashore. "They've become waterlogged–although, the river being cold, they're not as bad as they could be. The stone of the bridge cut a couple of the bricks loose by the look of it, so they floated up. Lucky, that. I bet if the rope to the bricks hadn't been caught on the side of the arch they wouldn't have been spotted before spring."

"Thank you for your assessment, sir, but if you don't mind..." one of the constables said, stepping in front of the man and blocking his path.

James said nothing. His hook hand hovered over the young man's chest, touching something metal that seemed to be pinned there. "Bright, is this what I think it is? I don't want to remove it, just confirm it for me."

Bright stepped forward. "I think... yes—it looks like a large seed pearl set on the top of a long hat pin. Could be silver, sir, judging by the setting round the pearl."

"The other end of it's in his heart, I would say." James's hook hand tapped the young man's chest, then picked up the end of the wet cloth and re-covered him.

He walked round and pulled at the cloth covering the other victim. "Oh, shitting hell!" He stood upright as if he'd been stung. The woman's wounds were washed out and swollen from the river water. Strands of her blonde hair fell into the hole where her right eye should have been. James was sure that whatever had caused that injury had killed her. "I think both would've been dead before they were put in the river. She matches the description of the girl we were looking for?" As he asked the question, James knew what the answer would be. Damn waste of a life—two lives—and it ran his investigation into a brick wall.

"Yes sir, in her early twenties. Five foot, five. Dark, well-made coat, hat with silver hat pin, blonde hair cut in..." Detective Bright's words faltered.

"Yes, Bright, I think we've found her, and perhaps an accomplice. Seems their boss didn't take kindly to anyone skimming off him. We have murder to add to the charges, eh?"

It was obvious the murders of these two were linked to the burglaries. *Joined by the Hand of Glory.* Giles had lent him the book with that particular story. Much of it had matched what Bright's grandfather had said yesterday.

And there they stand,
That murderous band,

Hand of Glory

Lit by the light of the GLORIOUS HAND,
By one!—by two!— by three!

The Hand of Glory always had a band of five, the leader, his witch and three henchmen, those who did the Hand's dirty work. And it always ended badly. Evil begat evil and you reaped its twisted reward. James saw again the face of Bright's grandfather, Colin, as he'd said those words. The old man had been leaning on a rake, the smoke from a small autumn bonfire of leaves curling round him before dissipating into the red glow of the sunset. The old man was a human bridge of memory to a time believed by many to be gone, but it so clearly was not.

The old ways. The mix of superstition and reality still lingered in the country, even now. The industrial nature of the Great War, as it was beginning to be called, had in a strange way reawakened a need in people for explanations of the horror, other than being what the human hand had created. Pseudo-science. Spirits, mediums and… "Shit!" James bent down and roughly pulled the cover off the bodies again. Crouching low, he looked hard at the two forms, trying to match them to a vague memory. That of two figures who'd stood talking in the passage at his mother-in-law's home on the night of that damn séance. He'd been made a fool of and played like… He should've put this together before now!

"Sir?" Bright asked.

"We… I… Fuck it! The bloody séance. Madame Marie!"

Bright's face whitened as the enormity of what his superior was saying dawned on him. "They'll be long gone, sir."

"I know, but we… dammit it… we need to try… Put it all together. If I can't string the buggers up, I bloody well want to give another copper the chance."

Chapter Twenty

"Here we are, sir," the young constable said as he turned the car engine off. Hardy gave a small nod of thanks and opened his door. It was cold. Frost had coated the road outside the police station. Hardy shivered, more from apprehension than cold. Parker had not telephoned him asking to meet him, he'd sent a car. This was official. It was also just shy of fifteen minutes to midnight.

Was it to do with their conversation of Monday? Possibly, Hardy supposed. However, Hardy was pretty sure by now that James did not believe a word of it. They hadn't spoken since then. James had even cancelled their mid-week pint in The Bear. Hardy had begun to think he'd offended James. On Monday, Parker had listened intently to what Hardy had said, and for a while Hardy had been convinced he was taking him seriously. Nevertheless, afterwards, Parker had been dismissive. Now he'd summoned Hardy in his professional capacity and Hardy was confused.

"Will be warmer inside, sir," the constable assured him as he walked with Hardy to the door of the police station.

"You on duty for the rest of the night, Officer?" Hardy asked.

"For my sins, sir, yes. If you would be so kind as to wait by the front desk, I'll go and tell the inspector you're here."

Hand of Glory

Hardy unbuttoned his coat and removed his hat. He stripped off his gloves and placed them in the centre of the upturned bowl of the trilby, looking round the room as he did so. The desk sergeant was busy writing in his book. The scratch of his pen punctuated the hiss coming from the valve of a large, cast-iron radiator on the far wall.

"Thank you again, Mr Holbrook."

Hardy looked to the left at the sound of Bright's voice.

"My pleasure, Detective Constable Bright," Taffy replied.

"Nice to be on the right side of the law for once, eh, Taffy?" Bright said, winking at the desk sergeant as he stepped aside to allow the small Welshman to pass.

"Got bloody cocky since Stumpy allowed you to wear a suit to work, haven't you?" Holbrook snorted as he moved towards the outside door.

"Beats walking the streets, Taffy," Bright said and nodded to Hardy. "If you would come this way, Mr Hardy, we're ready for you now."

"Royal 'we,' is it? Stumpy better watch his back." Holbrook coughed. Not the racking cough Hardy had heard before, just a gentle clearing of the throat. The man's colour was also better. "Hello, Mr Hardy. Stumpy dragged you out of bed as well?"

"Never quite made it to bed, Mr Holbrook. You look well, considering the events of the other night."

"Aye, bloody strange. That thumping I had must've shaken me innards up for the better," Holbrook replied and placed his bowler hat firmly on his head.

"The rewards of the just, Taffy," Bright chuckled.

Holbrook leaned towards Hardy as he walked past. "If that lad's tongue gets any sharper he'll cut himself."

"I heard that, Taffy."

"I know you did. Take care in there, Mr Hardy," Holbrook said as he vanished out into the night.

Hardy turned his attention to the waiting officer. "I'm all yours, Detective Constable Bright." The young man stood aside to allow Hardy to walk into the main part of the police station.

Hardy found himself in a corridor flanked by the various oak doors and opaque glass windows of numerous offices. Some were in darkness. In others, faint human shapes moved about in the lighted interior. The sounds of voices, feet and the occasional slam of a drawer sounded around him as he and Bright walked down the corridor.

Parker stood waiting at the far end of the corridor, by the entrance to a small flight of stairs which led down to the cells below. He gave a slight nod in recognition. "Thank you for coming, Giles."

"My pleasure, James. If I can be of any help...?" Hardy left the question hanging.

"We shall see." Parker smiled and pulled out his packet of cigarettes, offering one to Hardy. Hardy took one, watching the quick movement of Bright's hand as he flicked his lighter open to light his superior's and Hardy's cigarettes. Parker inhaled deeply, then blew out a long plume of smoke. "I need you to cast your mind back to the séance you attended at The Railway Hotel."

"Yes." Hardy felt a small chill begin at the bottom of his spine.

"Did you get a good look at those involved?"

"You mean those who attended?"

"No, those performing." Parker spat the words out, as if even speaking them left a sour taste in his mouth.

"I think so," Hardy replied, wondering where all this was leading.

"Think you could identify any of them?" Parker glanced down the stairwell into the inky darkness of the lower levels of the police station.

Hand of Glory

"Possibly."

"Good. Bright?" Parker indicated that the detective constable should precede them down the stairs.

Hardy stepped after, Parker following behind.

"What is going on, James?" Was this connected to the Hand of Glory? He shook his head. He should stop trying to link everything to that. It was becoming an obsession; no, it was one. He *had* to know. It was all tied to Adams, his personal ghost, to the mud and his lingering purgatory.

Hardy suddenly looked forward, over the head of Bright, as the stairs turned to the right. There was a shadow moving in front that had nothing to do with Bright. It moved quickly ahead, but by the time Hardy had reached the bottom of the stairs the shadow was nowhere to be seen. The tile-lined corridor of the cell area was devoid of any shades, the creatures hesitant to soil the dark blue expanse of shiny ceramic that covered the walls. Yet Hardy felt the figure that had entered before them was still here, waiting, and expecting something.

"If you would continue to the end of the corridor, we have a room there which we use as a temporary morgue," Parker began.

"Morgue?" Hardy repeated, his feeling of unease growing.

"Yes, I want you to look at two bodies and tell me if you recognise them."

"Then will you tell me–?"

"What it's all about? Well, as much as I can. I owe you that," Parker said.

"What?" Hardy began, then he smiled. James had believed him. A feeling of vindication and relief rose in Hardy's breast, banishing his sense of unease for a few moments.

Hardy followed Bright into the room. In here, both floor and walls were tiled: dull, off-white, the shine scrubbed off. His footsteps echoed. A tap set in the wall dripped in a ragged rhythm into a metal bowl. The place stank of disinfectant. Two waist-high, narrow tables stood in the centre of the room, their contents covered in oilcloth, the fabric stiff, bending round what was beneath. Hardy recognised the shapes. What lay under had once been human, but was now reduced to meat and bones. His hand came up to his mouth and nose, as if he was subconsciously erecting a barrier to the stench that was not yet present. The smoke from his cigarette curled round his face. The sense of unease came back hard, physically hitting him in the stomach. He felt sick.

"You alright, sir?" Bright asked as he moved to the end of one of the tables.

"I'm fine," Hardy said and dropped his hand, not feeling anything like. "Old habit. You don't forget the stench."

"Oh, I see," Bright replied and looked towards Parker. The man nodded and Bright peeled back the cloth from the face of the corpse. A young man. Dark-haired. Narrow of face. Eyes half closed, the orbs beneath misted. Muscles round his mouth slack. Lips pulled back from white teeth. So familiar. Seen a hundred times. More. Hardy closed his eyes, trying to cut off the tumbling memories of torn and battered bodies strewn across no man's land.

"Not one of ours, sir. Theirs." The voice ragged, bitter. Adams. Hardy opened his eyes. Adams stood at the head of the table, his army jacket undone, thumbs tucked into his braces. Head bare, eyes tired, face strained beyond imagining.

"Why?" Hardy said. In life Adams had not been so dismissive of the dead, no matter who they were, even when plying his trade as the company sniper. Had becoming a ghost stripped him of part of his humanity, leaving only the horror that still drove him to walk in this world?

Hardy wanted to laugh at the inanity of his thoughts. He was trying to analyse the thoughts and emotions of a ghost, a creature he wasn't even sure existed outside the twisted labyrinth of his mind.

"Now that is the question, isn't it?" Parker said, pinching out his cigarette and dropping it into a bucket by the side of the wall. "Do you know him?"

Adams's eyebrow arched. The ghost also wanted an answer to the question, it seemed. Hardy looked again at the corpse, mentally placing the features against the blurred memories of nearly two weeks ago.

"Yes... no. I can't be sure..." Hardy began. Adams shook his head, disappointed at the answer. "What do you want from me?" Hardy's voice shook, the strain clear in the rising tones.

"Easy, Giles," Parker said, coming to Hardy's side.

Hardy took a deep breath and plunged again into the flickering memories of the night of the séance. The smell of the burning incense mixing with traces of a smouldering Woodbine cigarette. The sound of bells. Figures, half in shadow, standing by a table. Guttering candles. The feeling of being duped and used. The barely suppressed smirk on the face of a young man. Hardy looked a third time at the corpse. The memory face became overlaid on the slack, death-pale one before him.

"Yes, at the séance he was one of two—no, three—men who were with the medium. Him..." Hardy's hand waved in the direction of the corpse. "An older man, balding, and another, who stayed in the shadows."

Parker nodded, and indicated for Bright to re-cover the corpse.

Hardy looked again at the ghostly member of their group and said bitterly, "Does that satisfy you?" Adams did not answer, merely looked with slowly misting eyes from one fabric-covered body to the other.

"Not, quite, sir," Bright said, glancing quickly at his superior, his face coloured with concern.

"I know this is hard for you, Giles, but I just need you to take a look at the other one. Then we'll get Bright here to make us a cup of tea," Parker said, trying to sound matter of fact, but failing. The tension in the room had heightened. Did Bright and Parker somehow sense they were not the only observers, or was their unease caused by what lay under the other cloth?

Bright moved round the other table. His hand hesitated for a moment, then he tweaked the oilcloth down. Blonde hair, curling on the ruined brow of the young woman. Soft wisps, floating up, filled with static. One blue eye, misted, yet wide and staring. The other, gone. A ragged hole of washed-out flesh. Meat cut on a butcher's slab. This time there was no uncertainty. Hardy felt his breath catch in his throat. He understood the tension now. So young, so beautiful, and so mutilated. The girl who had handed out leaflets at the séance. Her lips were no longer coloured bright red. No supreme confidence in her eyes.

"It's the girl. What did they do to deserve this?"

"Made a deal with the devil," Adams said softly, his right hand unhooking from his braces to gently touch the young woman's brow. The strain round his eyes softened. The mist in them cleared for a moment, then it returned. Adams's eyes were now opaque. Dull white gems that saw nothing. "We all have a choice, sir. They made theirs with open eyes, as did we when we went to France. Difference was, we believed what we were doing was right and our duty. They knew from the beginning what they were doing was wrong, but they did it all the same and enjoyed it."

"Both killed, just the same," Hardy said, answering the ghost. *Duty and choice. Good and evil. Degrees of grey. No matter what, they all are killed in the end.* Hardy could not prevent the rambling, bitter thoughts from forming. His eyes closed for a moment, and he did not see Parker's nod as the man expressed his agreement, as if Hardy's statement referred to the bodies.

Adams shook his head, denying Hardy's unspoken thoughts. "True enough, Master Giles, but least when you go doing your duty as you sees it, you have a right to go home, not get sucked down as a down payment for another's rotten handiwork." Adams's hand left the young woman's brow and began fading into the wisps of cigarette smoke lingering in the room.

Sucked down. Swallowed. Mud. Hell. No difference between the two. You were lost forever. Yes, there had been anger in Adams's voice, but, more than that, desperation. What battle was Adams fighting in the shadows? For how many? How many other victims were ensnared with him? Hardy's stomach churned harder than before; his right hand went again to his mouth, while his left pulled at the handkerchief in his pocket. "Sorry," he mumbled, trying to explain. "You'd think I would've become used to this sort of thing."

"I wouldn't trust a man who ever did," Parker answered and touched Hardy on the shoulder, indicating they should go. Hardy nodded in reply, retracing his steps to the ground floor of the station.

*****

The first cup of tea placed before Hardy went cold, abandoned on a desk. He watched the surface of the liquid in his cup vibrate to the rhythm of the typewriter. The three layers of paper and the two inner leaves of carbon rattled along the carriage, as each word spelled out the earlier events of the evening. Once typed, Parker took the sheets, the carbon paper staining his fingers as he separated them. He asked Hardy to read and then sign. Hardy did so.

The second cup of tea arrived, was half consumed, then forgotten again. Parker made Hardy repeat everything he'd said on Monday night. Bright recorded each word in his notebook, glancing now and then at Parker, who nodded—whether underlining what Hardy had said, or indicating to Bright he agreed with some unexpressed opinion of the young detective, Hardy could not be sure. Then the typewriter was employed again, the notes transferred into cold metal imprints on off-white paper. Hardy sat, his gaze roaming round the room. He looked at his watch. It was two-thirty in the morning. As each master and copies came off the clacking machine, Parker picked them up. He checked them, then passed them to Hardy. Hardy had trouble reading the maze of letters. They danced before his eyes, forming patterns which burst into confusion each time Bright hit the return lever to send the carriage of the typewriter back. Finally, a neat pile of paper lay on the desk. Parker picked up a pen and offered it to Hardy. He took it, feeling the cold metal of the fountain pen as he rolled it between his fingers. His hand shook as he lowered it to the paper. Before, the words had all been in his mind. But now, set down on paper, they had a power he had not imagined they could have. He clenched his hand round the pen and signed, the ink spluttering from the nib.

"Need a breather, I think. It will give Bright time to make us another cup of tea, eh, Giles?"

"Yes, a breather would be nice, and if we're going to have another drink…" Hardy left the words hanging.

"'Course, old chap. Need to water the lawn myself. Let me show you where, while Bright works his magic with the tea," Parker said, moving towards the door.

"Extra strong, sir?" Bright asked as his superior left the room.

"Oh, indeed, Bright, indeed," Parker laughed, and indicated for Hardy to walk back down in the direction of the cells.

Hand of Glory

Hardy lingered by the door of the office on his return. He felt both reluctant and impatient. He reached out, turned the doorknob and entered, to be greeted by Parker expressing his delight.

"Biscuits as well, Bright. You are getting efficient. Just what I need to soak up this tea," Parker said. He took one of the golden brown circles off the plate at the centre of the table. Bright smiled and sat down next to him, taking up his notebook and pencil again.

Hardy, too, sat down and took hold of the steaming cup of tea. He sipped at it, then coughed. It was strong, all right. At a guess, he would say it was fifty per cent brandy. "Nice tea."

"Thought you'd like it. Keep us awake a bit longer, eh? Right—now we have your theory of events down officially," Parker said, biting at the biscuit in his hand. The crumbs fell, peppering his waistcoat. Parker brushed at them with his metal hook, leaving faint trails in the fabric.

"My theory of events? Does this mean we can...?" Hardy began

"Get on, of course. I gather you realised that the young woman downstairs is the same one who pawned items from the robberies."

Hardy nodded. "Yes, I had gathered that."

Parker cleared his throat. "The young man was, we believe, her accomplice, and also a fellow employee of the medium called Madame Marie. You were not the first today to identify them as such."

"No?" Hardy asked, breaking Parker's flow of words. He wanted to know who else had identified them, but realised Parker would not say.

"No, but you are the last. As I said earlier, I have, I hope, some answers for you. Bright, for his sins, has most of it written up. The one thing that's annoying the hell out of me is that I seriously doubt I'll be the one to bring the ringleader to justice. He, I believe, is long gone from here, back to The Smoke. Hopefully Scotland Yard will be able to trace him from the information we've pieced together. One good thing is we've smashed his little game to pieces."

"You mean the séances?" Hardy asked slowly as he took another sip of the tea and brandy mix, feeling the alcohol burn its way down into his stomach.

"Yes! Jesus, Hardy! What a way to case bloody jobs—people actually inviting them into their homes. Makes me shudder to even think of it—and having my own family..." Parker sighed, coughed, and continued. "Anyway, I bet when we dig deeper we'll find Stafford is just one in a long line of towns to have been targeted by this gang."

"I suspect so." Hardy gave a thin smile in agreement.

"Yes, I felt sorry for the manager of The Railway Hotel. Went quite pale when we were questioning him about his former guests. Got some good descriptions of the other three off him, and cleared up a supposed accident on the railway line between here and Crewe."

"What?" Hardy asked, startled, and sat forward. This he had not expected.

"Yes, sir," Bright said, flicking through his notebook. "A man fell from a Liverpool-bound train about three-thirty on the afternoon of Tuesday, 7th November. He had a ticket bought here in Stafford in his pocket, and a receipt from The Railway Hotel. He—"

"Was the other man, the middle-aged one?" Hardy asked. The enormity of the scale of events was almost unbelievable. Yet Hawkins had not hesitated to kill before, why would he now?

"Right you are, Hardy. Seems yon boss of the operation had decided to dismiss his employees, cover his tracks and vanish.

Hand of Glory

The hotel has the girl leaving on Saturday, then the rest leaving on Monday morning. The hotel porter confirms putting their bags on the first London express. Yet we know they were still here on Monday night." Parker tapped the table with his metal hand, as if underlining each point.

"The girl selling the pearls, and the attack on Holbrook?"

"Correct."

"So what happened? I mean... can you deduce...?" Hardy began.

"I believe the rest of the gang caught up with the girl, and by Holbrook's statement it's pretty clear it was her hatpin that killed the young man..."

"Hatpin?" Hardy interrupted.

"Yes, a long, silver hatpin had gone right through the young man's heart. Something a gentleman in Mr Holbrook's trade would take notice of. It was quite an expensive one," Bright said, flicking back a few pages in his notebook.

"So, I would say there must have been a scuffle, and she most likely stabbed out at the man, maybe didn't mean to kill him. Then my guess is all hell broke out, and the girl was killed. The police surgeon suggests that her eye and brain were pierced by something long, rounded, and most likely metal. That left the boss with two bodies to dispose of. The dumping of them in the river at Haywood shows he has some local knowledge. He most likely believed the bricks would hold them down for a while."

"And the older man?" Hardy asked as he shifted in his seat. He felt a trickle of sweat break out on his brow.

"Possible he got the wind up and ran for it," Bright said, looking in the direction of Parker for confirmation.

"And his boss caught up with him on the train and–"

"He was alive when the others were killed?" Hardy asked.

"Yes, we believe so, which brings me to the identity of the leader of our little gang."

"Hawkins." Hardy said flatly, a statement, not a question; he knew in his heart it could be no one else.

"Yes, it all points to him, and the description you gave me of the man fits that of the husband of Madame Marie, though he was not using his own name, of course."

"What name was he–?"

"Adams."

"The bastard!" Hardy's fist hit the table. All the pent-up emotion that had been brewing since he'd arrived at the station suddenly burst. For Hawkins to use the name of one of the men he had killed to cover his game was *evil*. There was no other word Hardy could think of.

"Quite. I am sorry if I gave you the impression I didn't believe you, Giles."

"The Hand, you know... I don't... It was just..." Hardy began.

"Yes, I understand. It's an old legend among thieves. Not that many put any stock in it today. But this Hawkins's grandfather–who, incidentally, brought up Archie Hawkins and his brother, James–was old-fashioned. In fact, in 1906 he was sent to jail for a number of crimes that included the bribing of a prison officer and the desecration of a grave. Bright's own grandfather has been very helpful in this. He remembered the arrest and such legends from his time in the force, plus the store the older generation put in the likes of them."

"He enjoyed your visit, sir, and was very pleased that he could be of help."

"Grave? Prison officer?" Hardy knew he was rambling.

"Murderers are these days buried inside the prison walls after they are hanged, so the only way..."

"My God..."

Hand of Glory

"Yes, so it's plain the young Archie Hawkins got to know about this so-called 'Hand of Glory' from his grandfather. That he made one, or attempted to do so, and perhaps uses it during the robberies he commits in the belief that it works, is very possible. It sickens me."

"And Madame Marie?" Hardy asked, wondering why the young woman had hitched her fortunes to a man like Hawkins.

"Is French, as far as we can tell. It all makes sense. According to the army, Hawkins vanished. Most likely the woman hid him. A thief or fence herself. A lot worked behind the lines during the war."

"So you think they're gone?"

"Too clever to hang around. Though if they are caught, and I hope they are, it's quite possible that you will be called on to identify Hawkins."

"So that's that?"

"Yes," Parker said and stood, half stretching, as if suddenly his body had realised what hour it was.

"I..." Hardy began, not wanting to stop the discussion now, yet understanding that as far as Parker was concerned everything had been neatly tied up. Hardy stood, aware he had been dismissed.

"Been a long day, but I feel we've broken the back of this case, eh, Bright?"

"Yes sir," Bright said, and flipped his notebook closed.

"Well, one more thing. Would you mind running Mr Hardy here home? Then you can take yourself off as well." Parker took out his cigarette packet and offered one to Hardy. Hardy shook his head, declining the offer.

"I suggest, sir—" Bright said.

"That I do the same? Aye, I will. Just a few more bits to do. What time is it, by the way?" Parker looked round the office, searching for a clock.

Bright pulled back the left sleeve of his jacket. "Coming up to five-thirty, sir."

"Hmm... I might check in Taffy's on the way home. He's bound to be open about six to catch any lads going in for work. I just want to check he has nothing else from the robberies behind his counter." Parker's face creased in a smile.

"That's not very trusting, James. Taffy Holbrook has been very helpful to you, and is out of pocket on the whole thing," Hardy said, taking hold of his hat and gloves.

"Taffy would never let himself be out of pocket, Giles."

*****

"Least I can do is offer you some breakfast," Hardy said as he got out of the car.

"Well, all right, then, sir," Bright said.

"Please call me Giles. I've never been at ease with 'sir,' even in the army." Hardy closed the car door and waited for Bright to join him.

"Not sure Inspector Parker would like that," Bright replied.

"What James doesn't know won't hurt him," Hardy said and began to walk towards the rear of the manor, smiling at the sound of Bright's chuckle behind him.

"Looks as if someone's up already," Bright said, pointing at the light spilling from the windows of the kitchen.

"That will be Mathew. He's the gamekeeper I share with the other landowners round here. He tends to call in for breakfast." As he spoke, Hardy let himself into the scullery, and then into the kitchen proper.

"Morning, Mr Hardy. Tea?" Mathew pointed to the large teapot on the table.

"Not stewed, I hope?" Hardy replied.

Hand of Glory

"'Course not. Want some toast as well?" Mathew asked, removing the lightly browned slice of bread off the toasting fork and adding it to the pile on a plate on top of the black range.

"Just a light snack, eh, Mathew?" Hardy remarked as he took two more cups off the large kitchen dresser and placed them on the table.

"Was tempted by the bacon hanging in the scullery, but me mother would have me guts for garters if she caught me eating that." Mathew winked and placed the plate of toast onto the table.

"She won't even let me help myself," Hardy replied as he sat down and began buttering the toast, indicating to Bright to help himself to a cup of tea.

"She is a one, me mother," Mathew said, laughing as he placed another thick slice of bread on his toasting fork. He sat down by the range, holding the fork and its contents close to the red-hot grill of the fire.

"Yes, she is," Hardy agreed, pushing the plateful of buttered toast in Bright's direction. As his hand came back to his side, the door to the passage slowly opened. Hardy frowned, wondering how on earth it was doing that. He made to stand up, but found he could not. Bound tight. Muscles locked against his will, held more firmly than he'd been in the mud of Passchendaele. What was happening? The answer came: brutal, horrific. Deep inside he'd believed, even though he'd tried to reason against it. Floating as if unsupported, a clawed, twisted mirror of the hand that held it entered the room. Two sickly flames flared, one on the thumb, one on the small finger. The jet-black smoke undulated as it rose, wafted by an unearthly breeze.

Chapter Twenty-One

Holbrook locked the door to his shop and pushed the keys deep into his coat pocket. It was late, well past midnight. He unwound his scarf as he shuffled into the rear kitchen. He gave a shiver. Damn cold was gnawing at his bones. Should he have gone back to Mavis's? Perhaps, but he needed to be open early tomorrow. Going back to The Hole in the Wall meant another walk across town in the morning. Holbrook still ached from the beating, and though his breathing had eased he did not relish two such journeys within a couple of hours of each other.

Off came his gloves, joining his scarf and hat on the small table. He picked up a box of matches. Turning the small box in his fingers, Holbrook walked the few steps to the gas cooker and ignited a ring. The warm, yellow glow of the burners picked out Holbrook's surroundings, making them both familiar and strange. He lifted the kettle off the back of the cooker, shaking it. Yes, there was enough water in there for a brew and to fill a hot water bottle. He felt his chest tighten. Holbrook braced himself for the onset of a spasm beginning deep down in his lungs and a fight for his breath. It began, then died away, his lungs expelling just breath.

"Well, bugger me! That beating right cleared the rubbish." The day after he had been attacked, Holbrook had been locked in a grim battle with his own body. He had struggled to breathe. His rib cage still ached, not only from the beating, but also from bout after bout of coughing. He had sat on the edge of Mavis's bed, a bowl locked between his knees as the yellow, blood-flecked sputum spewed from his mouth. Holbrook had thought he was a goner. Going to drown in the stuff, just as others had on the bottom of a trench. By evening, the coughs had become short, dry hacks. Brandy laced with honey had dulled his senses and he had fallen asleep. He'd slept as he had not done for years. Curled like a child, deep in the depths of Mavis's feather mattress.

"Maybe I should have gone back to The Hole."

Tea poured, cup firmly in one hand, candle in another and the cloth-wrapped hot water bottle under his right arm, he walked slowly up the narrow stairs to his bedroom. The room reflected Holbrook's tastes and comforts: the large brass bed was piled high with blankets and topped with a thick eiderdown. Heavy curtains hung from a brass pole with a curled fleur-de-lis on each end. Rugs covered the polished floorboards, protecting his bare feet against the cold. The furniture was elegant and well made, taken in payment of business debts over the years.

Holbrook shivered as the chill of the room penetrated his coat. He thought about lighting the gas fire for a while, then decided against it. He pushed the hot water bottle between the sheets of his bed and turned to the window, checking it was shut. With a tweak, he closed the curtains and began to prepare for bed.

The dregs of his tea finished, Holbrook slipped between the sheets. As he lay there, warming his sock-covered toes on the hot water bottle, he went over the events of the past few days. More excitement than he'd seen for years, and Holbrook was hoping there would never be a repeat of it. A quiet life was what he wanted. Still, he had made a bit of profit. The rings and lockets tucked in his safe would bring a tidy sum. With thoughts of the profit bouncing round his mind, Holbrook slipped into sleep.

*****

"What sort of business you in?" The words had been spoken five or more years before, but they crept, as if newly said, into Holbrook's dreams. He was again hunkered down in the lee of a tarpaulin stretched along the side of the trench. The cold and damp clawing at his limbs, the stink, almost unbearable, lodged in his nostrils.

He winked at the young replacement, "Oh, this and that, maybe a bit more this than that."

The youth smiled at Holbrook's answer and opened his mouth to speak. However, it was not his voice, but another's that echoed down the trench.

"Gas! Gas!"

Holbrook tried to move. He could not. The old fear. The nightmare. Gas!

"Gas! Gas! Shift yourself, Taffy!" A corporal appeared round the bend in the trench, the thick yellow gas swirling round his legs. The man's eyes, behind the scratched glass lenses of a gas mask, were looking right at him. Holbrook fumbled for his own mask and dropped it. Panicked. Bent and reached down through the ground-hugging death cloud. He could not find it. He stood up, trying to find air to breathe. His eyes were watering, his sight blurring; he went down onto his knees.

"Here you are, Taffy." The corporal was pulling the cloth mask onto Holbrook's face, the coarse fabric rasping against his skin. Holbrook began to gargle, the gas he had inhaled burning his throat. He began to cough. Hard. His lungs straining. The lenses of the mask misted up and he could not see.

Hand of Glory

"Move it, Taffy! Get yourself up, man! Shift!" The corporal was pulling at Holbrook's arm, dragging him up to his feet.

"Gas! Gas!" The corporal bellowed, his voice now unmuffled by his mask, as if his lips were against Holbrook's ear. Holbrook tried to move. He could not. His legs were trapped. Wrapped tight by something. He lashed out, and fell out of bed, suddenly coming awake, yet the corporal's voice still rang in his ears: "Gas! Gas!"

Holbrook lay on the floor in the darkness, straining with his damaged eyes to see. Then he heard it. A soft, gentle hiss. *Gas.* He tried to stand, but his legs had no strength. His sight, as bad as it was, became worse. It was fading.

"Gas!"–again the corporal's cry.

Holbrook fought against his growing languor and began to drag himself across the floor to the gas fire. His fingers dug into the thick rug. His hand brushed against the tiles of the fireplace.

"Gas!" the cry went up again.

Holbrook could feel the corporal's hand shaking his shoulder and forcing him to reach out his hand. Holbrook's thumb touched the gas pipe. His fingers, tiptoeing, followed, until they reached the small, cold metal dial. He turned it. The hissing stopped, but the danger was still in the air. Holbrook tried to stand. He suddenly came to his feet, a drunken puppet, then fell forwards, his hands reaching out to break his fall. He caught the heavy curtains. The weight of his body wrenched the brass pole off its brackets and it fell. One of the curled fleur-de-lis slammed into the glass, shattering it. The brass pole toppled through and hung out of the window. The fabric of the curtains billowed as the cold night air rushed into the bedroom, chasing the gas away from its intended victim.

Holbrook heard a curse from the street below, then a whistle, followed by the thud of a body against the door of his shop. He tried to get up, but could not. He just lay there, drawing in gasps of fresh air.

*****

"No answer," Inspector Parker said as he put down the telephone and looked round the ransacked shop. The safe behind the counter was open. The door smashed off. The hinges destroyed by hammer and chisel. Papers, boxes, and other discarded contents strewn on the floor. The trail of devastation led from behind the counter through the door, where Holbrook was standing, into his storeroom.

"Maybe he's in bed," Holbrook said, adding, "You going to pay for those calls?" Holbrook pulled the blanket round his shoulders tighter. He was cold. But this chill had little to do with the weather. That bastard boss had been here, turned Holbrook's shop over and tried to kill him. All the neatly labelled parcels and boxes in Holbrook's storeroom upended. His life's work trampled on. The door to the shop lay half off its hinges, where the shoulder of Inspector Parker had assaulted it. In the dark street outside he could just see the outline of a police car.

"I just saved your life. Good job I'd decided to call on you before I went home, wasn't it?" Inspector Parker bent to pick up a ripped-open packet with his claw hand. The war medals tumbled out of the brown paper, the inspector neatly catching them in his flesh and blood hand. "You take a lot of these in?" Parker's fingers closed on the row of three lumps of metal and their attached ribbons.

"Did you save me? Aye, perhaps you did," Holbrook sniffed, wincing. His nose was still full of the smell of gas. "As for the medals, I take in too bloody many. The lads haven't been done right by and you know it, Stumpy. I had laid them out last night

Hand of Glory

for this morning. Today is Armistice Day; the lads'll be needing 'em."

"And you make a tidy profit lending them out," Parker said.

"No, I don't!" Holbrook snapped, stepping into the shop, his eyes going to the safe. On the floor by the thrown-back metal door lay three guineas. The gold glinted in the artificial light of the hooded gaslights in the room. Damn gas! It'd nearly got him again. He felt a cough begin to build up in his throat; it was going to be a bad one. His old enemy was back with a vengeance. He fought the feeling, pushing the spasm away with all his strength. "I let the lads have them for nowt for the day. I bloody well served, too, you know. Now I got to get them sorted out again, as well as find out what that bugger took. Damn arse-wipe, he came back to top me. Tried to gas me! Robbed me! And here you stand, mister high and mighty bloody Inspector of Police, asking if I'm going to make a profit from the lads when you should be after him. Sure as eggs come from a chicken's rear end, that bastard'll be after the captain now, if he hasn't already got him. Captain Hardy knows him, doesn't he?" Holbrook watched with bitter delight, as the expression changed on Parker's face.

"How did you—?" Parker began to close his claw, as sharp as a tin opener.

"I wasn't totally out of it that night the bugger coshed me. I heard bits of what Hardy was telling you. Him saying he knew the sod," Holbrook's right hand came off the blanket, and waved round the room, "that did this, and if that bastard knows—"

"Sergeant Timms!" Parker called to the man by the shattered door to the shop.

"Yes, sir." The man turned, nodding to his superior.

"Get a couple of lads to help Mr Holbrook take stock of what's been taken and get his shop open."

The sergeant frowned at the order. "What about–?"

"Prints? I doubt there'll be any. It was the same chap," Parker said, moving back towards the telephone.

"Understand, sir, and may I ask, sir, where you'll be?"

"Captain Hardy's home." He picked up the large, black handset and dialled.

"That's another call you owe me for, Stumpy," Holbrook said, as the cough he'd been holding at bay broke through his barriers. It began in his throat, the airway constricting. His chest heaved. The acid taste rose. The rubbish in his lungs flooded up. He raised a hand to cover his mouth and squeezed his eyes tight. His body began to shake. Holbrook was aware of nothing but the hacking and wrenching that had taken control of his body. Sweat broke out on his brow. His eyes opened as he felt an arm go round him, supporting him.

"Easy, Taffy." Parker had finished his call and now stood embracing Holbrook, keeping him on his feet.

"Aye, damn gas'll still be in your system," Sergeant Timms said. "I'll make us a cup of tea, eh? Then we'll get started. You can sit there and play the boss, eh?–telling us all what to do." As he spoke, Timms moved through the open hatch in the counter. He tilted his head, indicating to his inspector that he would take care of Holbrook from now on.

Parker released his hold and Holbrook managed to stiffen his legs to stand on his own. He shuffled forward and bent down, his right hand reaching out to the shelf underneath the counter. The blanket fell from his shoulders. He pulled a wooden box out and placed it on the top of the counter. "Before you go I want you to take a look at this." Holbrook undid the small clasp on the box and carefully opened the lid, ignoring Parker's frown.

"Is that what I think...?" Parker began, his eyes narrowing as he looked at the contents of the box.

Hand of Glory

"Aye, ugly bugger, isn't it? A Dreyse." Holbrook took the snub-nosed German pistol out of the box and handed it to Parker.

"Semi-automatic. You have some ammunition?" Parker took hold of the gun and examined it closely.

"Just the three clips," Holbrook said, reaching back into the box.

"Well, I best take this into custody. We can't have such things lying around in your shop, now, can we, Taffy?"

"No, Stumpy, we can't."

Parker smiled at the use of his nickname and put the gun and clips into his coat pocket. He nodded goodbye to Holbrook, his hat slipping onto his brow. He pushed the offending hat back and swept from the shop, calling for one of the constables outside to come with him.

Holbrook was thankfully seated in his kitchen, while Timms made tea for him and the remaining constable. On the edge of the sound of the steam from the kettle, Holbrook could just hear the fading tones of the police car's bell. "What time is it?" he asked Timms.

The man looked at his watch. "Just gone six."

"You think he'll be too late? I mean..." Holbrook said.

"Well, the captain and Detective Constable Bright didn't leave the station until about five-thirty, so..."

"The bastard could've already been there, waiting for them," Holbrook said, feeling suddenly cold again.

Chapter Twenty-Two

The car motored down the lanes towards the small village of Caston. The frost had turned the rutted half-tarmac roads into a skating rink. The large car slithered from side to side, its wheels crashing through the layers of ice on the maze of puddles. Marie cursed as she worked the wheel, yet did not slow her speed. Archie was now sure she disagreed with him over the whole matter of Hardy. But he was boss and she had better start remembering it, else she wouldn't make it much further. Archie's gaze drifted from her shadow-wrapped features to the surreal landscape picked out by the bouncing beams of the car's headlights–the high hedges curving inwards and the gnarled, frost-burned grass of the roadside. Closing in. Trapping him. He shuddered. Bloody countryside.

Suddenly the road widened. Archie's hand snapped out and touched Marie's on the steering wheel. "Easy, we don't want to end up in a sodding duck pond."

"Which way?" Marie asked, slipping her hand from under his as if she no longer liked his touch. She turned the slowing vehicle to the left, tracking down a short row of night-cloaked houses. Archie's hand dropped back down to his lap, his fingers tapping on his knee. So, it was like that, was it? Just because it had got a bit sticky she had taken to moaning about how right the cards were. Well, they were wrong. She was wrong. He was the boss. He had the Hand and he was right.

"Down the side of the pub, least that's what that fella in The Hole in the Wall said. There!" The splash of the car's headlights sprang across a gap in the small row of buildings.

"*Merde!*" Marie braked hard, crunching the gears as she put the car into reverse. The wheels squealed in protest.

"Go easy—don't want someone fucking noticing..." As he spoke, Archie caught sight of a door opening in a small cottage on the right of the lane. Yellow light spilled out, illuminating a figure in the doorway who was taking hold of a bicycle leaned against the wall. Archie swore, a cold sweat beading his forehead. Was it that figure? No, he snorted in contempt. It was a country bumpkin up early to be off to work, nothing for him to worry about.

The lane to the manor was even narrower. The hazy outline of a building flashed past on the left. Marie cursed again and put the vehicle into reverse. Archie opened his window. The cold night air rushed in, turning his breath into plumes of vapour. No, not the manor: it looked like a long shed, open this end. The moonlight caught on the outlines of machinery. A five-bar gate was half open, and a dirt track vanished into the darkness alongside the building.

"Must be further up," Archie said and waved for Marie to continue. She slammed the gear stick into first; the car's wheels span on the ice and it shimmied sideways for a few yards. Marie straightened the vehicle's progress just as the lane suddenly widened. She swung the car round in front of the manor, sending gravel in all directions. In the lee of the house were the dark outlines of two other cars. The side of the smaller one was illuminated by the light from a window, not that it mattered: awake or not, Hardy was his.

Susan Boulton

"Keep the engine running–this won't take long," Archie said as he reached down by his feet, bringing the leather bag containing the Hand of Glory onto his knee. He dug deep into the bag, bringing out the officer's pistol from under his most treasured possession. Archie handed the bag to Marie as he released the lock and pushed down the barrel. The cylinder eased up, releasing the smell of gun oil. Six bullets. It would be more than enough. Not that Hardy would be a moving target.

He snapped the pistol shut and got out of the car, stuffing the pistol into his pocket. He then bent down and reached back into the car, snapping his fingers. Marie sniffed at the sharpness of his unspoken command and passed the bag to him. Archie took it, placing it on the roof of the car. Archie felt a knot of excitement gathering in his chest. A Cheshire cat grin split his face, crinkling the scars around his eye.

His fingers twitched, echoing the excitement he felt as he reached up and removed the twisted human remains from the bag. He cradled, petted and cooed over the Hand, his warped child. He laid it down on the cold metal of the car's roof and carefully lit the gnarled finger candles. Archie stood there for a moment, his scarred face illuminated by the sickly light, then he picked up the Hand of Glory and began to chant.

Open each door lock to the dead man's knock.
Fly back bolt and bar.
All not move.
Sleep still all who now sleep
And all that awake now be as the dead
For the dead man's sake.
O Hand of Glory, shed thy silver light
And direct us to our spoils tonight.

The wide front door of the manor opened. He looked down the wide corridor towards a faint glow of light. *Up early, are we?* His footsteps echoed down the wide hall, each one

Hand of Glory

proclaiming his command of this place and all in it. The smoke from the Hand clung to him. Then, slowly, it began to spread out, the silver threads in the unholy mist seeking treasure worth taking. Archie ignored them. As if sensing his feeling, the threads curled back and wrapped round his body, encasing him in a devilish light. He could smell the sour wax, tainted by the dark scent of long-dead flesh. He drank it in and allowed full rein to the dark thoughts that came to him when he used the Hand.

His stance changed. Back bent, crouched forward and scuttling, he made his way. His eyes were dark. A cold rush of excitement filled him. His face was split by a grin. The scars round his eye glowed. Faintly, he could hear the voices of those he had killed and robbed. They clung like rags, rotting away in the darkness that the Hand allowed him to tap. Soon there would be one more voice in his choir.

Each door off the corridor opened as he approached, inviting him in. He ignored the allure, as he did that of the curving staircase. The corridor ended, a tee junction with a narrower passage running left and right. Servants' territory. Archie sneered. Was Hardy slumming it, pretending he was no different from those he employed? Archie glanced first left, then right. The sickly smoke from the Hand wafted out from around him. It hung, undecided for a moment, then it undulated towards the left. Archie smiled and followed it. A door halfway down on the right side of the passage opened, spilling yellow light across the tiled floor. Yes, this was it.

Archie increased his pace, his hurried footsteps matching the march of his heartbeat.

"*Soon be over,*" Jim said.

Archie tugged the pistol out of his pocket. The metal was cold against the palm of his right hand, but not as cold as the Hand of Glory in his left. He swaggered into the room.

"Bloody hell, a tea party!" Archie said, and burst out laughing. The room was the manor kitchen, with a high ceiling and a brace of tall windows to allow the sunlight to illuminate the workplace. It was a mix of the old and the new. A coal-black range sat unsure of its place within a chimney space built for spit-roasting half a side of beef. In the centre of the large room was an equally large table, the top bowing inwards where thin layers of wood had been scrubbed off over the years. At the table were two men. A third, his chair pulled close to the grill of the large black range, held a toasting fork, complete with a slice of bread on the hot metal. Each was awake, yet was as the dead, for the dead man's sake. The snuffing out of three of the flames on the Hand confirmed the fact. Only their eyes betrayed their incomprehension and fear. The cold darkness in Archie lapped up the radiating emotion, savouring it.

"Lucky I got enough bullets, isn't it, Captain Hardy?" Archie set the Hand of Glory down on the table next to the teapot. He snatched up one of the slices of toast and took a bite. The thick layer of butter coated his lips, making them glisten.

As he munched his toast, Archie looked over the small gathering. Hardy, his back straight with his left leg out at an angle, as if he were easing it, his grey eyes narrowed, the muscles in his face straining. The bugger was fighting the power of the Hand; Archie could sense it. "Won't fucking work, old fruit!" Archie slapped Hardy across his face, enjoying the fact that the man's eyes flinched, but his body did not.

The other man at the table, his hand resting on the handle of a teacup, looked to be in his early twenties. His suit was new, the edges still crisp on his trousers. Must be some hanger-on of Hardy's, a bit of smooth to go with the rough who was burning the toast. Archie walked round the table and over to the range as he finished eating. He peered into the face of the youth holding the now-smouldering bread. Oh, yes, a right country bumpkin, this. Cheeks weather-burned, his hands rough, and

Hand of Glory

dressed in thick cord trousers with a woollen jacket a size too big. Doing his master's bidding and cooking his toast.

"Tosser!" Archie snapped and slapped the top of the lad's head with his butter-smeared hand. "Right—down to business! Poor Captain Hardy threw a bit of a fit and killed his friends over breakfast." Archie stepped back from the tableau and brought up the Webley revolver, taking aim at the young man sitting next to Hardy at the table. His index finger tensed. The scrape of a shoe brought his eyes up off his target to the darkened doorway across from him. "Stupid bitch, I thought I bloody well told you to stay in the c– Fuck!"

A bicycle pump struck him on the arm, making his hand jerk upwards. The pistol discharged. The young man toppled to the floor, his chair knocked over by the female whirlwind that had entered the room. No splatter of blood, brains and bone fell in his wake. The bullet had missed. It had gone high, shattering one of the windows. A torrent of broken glass fell. The scene before Archie broke apart, every figure now in motion.

Archie screamed. A raw sound of denial. The Hand of Glory was gone from the table. The darkness deep inside him frothed; it was a ball of maggots squirming on the rotten remains of Archie's humanity. The Hand was his! He served it and it served him. Now another held it. An enemy. He must get it back. All thought of his revenge on Hardy was gone, smothered by the spreading gangrenous wound at his core. He called out to Jim, but he had gone.

The gun in his hand came up again and he fired at the fleeing female figure as it plunged out of the doorway and into the passage. He missed.

"Fucking bitch!" Archie broke into a run, following her, not hearing the shouts of the men left in the kitchen. His breath burned in his lungs. Tears of anger, raw acid in the corners of his eyes. He had lost the Hand of Glory and he had to get it back. Nothing else mattered.

Chapter Twenty-Three

"Now, you rest and just concentrate on this young man for the next few days. Nurse Morris, or myself, will be back this afternoon." Agnes's fingers plucked at the soft blanket wrapped round the baby. His small face crinkled in protest at the disturbance. His colour was good and his lungs were strong. The labour had been a short one and Hanna Thorpe was young. Still, giving birth was a dangerous game, one that Agnes thought she would never tire of seeing, or of helping a woman achieve victory in. "You know to ring us, John, from the call box, if anything–and I mean anything–worries you."

"Aye, don't you worry. I or me mother will. Now I needs to get some breakfast meself. Soon be time for work," John said.

"Goodness, what time is it?" Agnes asked as she stood up.

John took an old fob watch out of the pocket of his waistcoat and squinted at it. "Coming up to quarter past six, Sister."

"At this rate it will be light before I'm back at Nurse Morris's home," Agnes said, looking once more at her charges.

"I'll see you out," John said, adding, "Well, go on, Linda, take a look at him."

Agnes smiled as she watched the girl take a step towards her mother and baby brother. Then Agnes collected herself and left the room, clattering down the stairs, John Thorpe one pace behind her. The new father helped her into her cape and passed her bag over, then walked to the door.

"A cold one this morning, Sister Reed," John said. He stood in the doorway watching her straddle her bicycle.

"Yes... I..." Agnes began, but her words were lost in the roar of a large car. The vehicle passed within a handspan of her, the running board on the driver's side almost brushing her leg. The light from the Thorpes' cottage picked out the pale cream of the shiny paintwork, illuminating for a second the face of the woman driving. "Madame Marie?" Agnes said aloud, unable to believe that the woman was here, now, driving towards Caston Manor and Giles. Giles! Everything they'd spoken of a week ago exploded in her mind, setting down a barrage of half-believed ideas that suddenly became cold, hard facts. The Hand of Glory. The man who used it had robbed and butchered people, a man Giles believed he knew and whom he thought was responsible for everything that had happened. Was he linked to Madame Marie and her warped séances? Perhaps Giles was not the only person putting together this horrible puzzle. The enemy was as well, and they were intent on removing any and all possible links to them.

She had to do something. She could be wrong, go bursting in on something totally innocent, yet she doubted it. Madame Marie was not the sort to make early morning calls, and Agnes doubted Giles would give her the time of day.

"John, ring the police—now!" she said, trying to control her voice.

"Pardon, Sister Reed?" John scratched his head, indicating his confusion.

"Ring the police and ask for Inspector Parker. Tell him to come to Caston Manor, now! Giles is in trouble." Such was the force of her statement John did not question her again. He

Hand of Glory

fumbled in his pocket, checking to see if he had a penny before dashing across the darkened green towards the lonely phone box. Agnes stood there for a minute, fighting the ridiculous idea of going up to the manor. "Oh, bugger it!" She began to pedal for all she was worth.

Down the lane she went, trying to dodge the larger dips in the road as they appeared in the thin beam of her small bicycle lamp. She looked skywards; the moon was still up. The large orb was low in the west, its faint light competing with the lightening of the eastern sky. She passed the entrance to the old sawmill. Ahead she could see the twin beams of the car's headlights cutting across the end of the lane. She slowed, slipping off her bike. Carefully she leaned it against the high hedge on the right and walked up the last few feet of the lane.

The car was sitting in the centre of the circle of gravel before the manor, its engine running. She was sure someone was in it. However, it was not the car, nor its occupants, that filled her with horror. It was the sight of the front door to the manor standing open. It was impossible. Giles had lost the key. *Now open lock. To the Dead Man's knock! Fly bolt, and bar, and band.* Dear God, was it possible, was it real? No, someone had to have forced it, the sensible part of her said. However, in the darkness before dawn another voice whispered inside her of foul deeds and twisted legends.

"Stop it, silly woman," she muttered. The sensible thing to do would be to wait for the police, but that could take ages and Giles, if... Oh, Giles. She could not abandon him. Maybe if she distracted the villains, Giles could... She stepped forward. Then stopped. The car. If someone were in there, they would see her. Was there another way to the manor? Yes, from the old sawmill. A track led from there to the copse behind the house, and a rough path led into the kitchen garden from there. She remembered it from last Saturday, when, in the last light of day, she and Giles had walked through the tumbled, unkempt gardens of the manor.

She walked back to her bicycle and turned it round, pedalling back to the half-open gate. She dismounted, carefully pushed her bike through and remounted. *Hiss. Snap. Rattle.* The chain had broken. She came to a sudden stop, slipping forward off her seat and narrowly missing the handlebars with her chest. "Of all the bloody things to happen!" She slipped her leg over and laid the bike down, taking the small battery-powered lamp from the front, and the hand pump. The latter she weighed in her hand. Yes, it would give a good whack if needed.

As she picked her way through the yard of the mill, she noticed that the dull line of light in the east had taken on a pink tone, banishing the stars in that quarter. A low mist clung to the frost-covered ground, parting as she ran down the rutted track. She was frightened. Just as she'd been the first time she'd heard the creeping barrage of German guns working their way across the British lines towards the maze of tents that made up the main aid post. She had not run from her duty then and she damn well wasn't going to now. Giles was important to her. "No, I love him." She had spoken the words aloud in a harsh whisper that came between one quickly drawn in breath and the next.

Suddenly she found herself at the rear of the manor, facing the open door to the scullery. Agnes felt sick. Should she go in? What she was doing was foolish to the extreme and she knew it. She should wait for the police. As she debated with herself, she found she was moving through the small, dark room, drawn by the glow from the kitchen.

Agnes stood in the rectangle of light that spilled into the scullery. The frame of the door was a barrier, one her foot was unable to cross. Fear and doubt began to war in her mind. She

Hand of Glory

could still turn round and go back. No one would question her decision, except herself. Agnes knew if she were in the kitchen and Giles out here, he would not hesitate. He would charge in. Over the top. For her. Was this her moment in the trenches? Time to go over the top. Not for country, glory, or some abstract moral idea, but for love and friendship. Was that not the reason why men, like Giles, had slogged through the mud of Flanders? She'd heard so many broken men say in hushed whispers, *"I couldn't let me mates down, Sister."*

"I won't let you down, Giles." Her hand tightened on the bicycle pump and for a moment it was if her hand closed on another, on all the hands she had held. All the comfort she had given, when there was nothing else she could do, was being returned to her.

"Easy, lass, pick your target and take your time." The voice was soft, low. Agnes was not even sure it was a voice. She knew she was alone, but did not feel it. Something was helping her and supporting her. Her love for Giles? The streak of stubbornness her mother had so despaired of? Agnes did not know, but she welcomed the feeling. She blinked and shook her head and looked into the kitchen.

"Easy," the voice said again. The pressure of a hand in hers, not the cold bicycle pump, impinged on her senses and cleared the fog that was trying to obscure her thoughts. It was time. Over the top. In an instant, Agnes knew what to do.

"That's it," the voice confirmed, and Agnes nodded her agreement.

Her grip on the bicycle pump increased—now it was a lump of metal, and ideal for the purpose she had in mind. Agnes took a deep breath and ran into the kitchen, throwing the pump at the round-faced man and pulling at the back of Bright's chair. The pump hit the arm holding the gun. His arm jerked up. The gun fired. Agnes ducked instinctively. One of the windows shattered. She snatched at the foul human remains on the table and ran for the door on the other side of the kitchen. She had to flee and draw the villain off. To him, the Hand was everything; deep down inside she sensed it. Remove the Hand of Glory and he was lost and off balance. Giles could deal with him, along with the others.

The gun discharged again, the bullet burying itself in the wall of the passage as Agnes ran for the open front door.

"Fucking bitch!" Shouts and running feet followed her. Agnes was sure one of the voices was Giles's, but she did not look back. She had to put some distance between herself and the villain.

Out onto the gravel she ran. Past the car. A female scream of rage. The answering bellow of the round-faced man. The gunning of the engine and the squeal of the car tyres on the gravel all thundered after her as she entered the narrow lane. The sun was now creeping over the horizon, streaking the dark sky with red-tinted, ice-white strands. Agnes's head turned; she looked for her pursuers. The car was roaring after her. The man stood on the running board on the driver's side, his hand gripping the roof, bellowing for more speed and cursing the woman who was driving.

God help her, she could not outrun a car. He had a gun. How could she have been so stupid? She would never reach the village!

She tried to increase her pace. Each breath burned her lungs and her side ached. She missed her footing and lurched to the side, as if pulled by an unseen hand towards the sawmill's gate. Yes, it was a chance, a slim one. She turned mid-stride, dashing through the gap in the gate and down between the buildings. For a moment she considered trying to hide in one of the sheds, but something was dragging her forward, into the field and back towards the manor and the copse of trees beyond.

Hand of Glory

The squeal of smashing wood told her that her hunters had seen her change of direction. The car swerved, sliding in the iced mud on the rough track. Its headlights danced across Agnes's path, casting her shadow in front of her. She was in the field now, the grass soaking her legs. Each breath was an effort and her body was shaking. The air was full of shouts, cries and the roar of engines and bells. She dared not look round. The crack of shots rang out. Agnes ducked her head instinctively. *Stupid.* Her back felt as wide as the side of a barn. How could Hawkins miss? Forward she went, to the left of the line of trees. Something was driving her there. Inside she knew if she reached that place she would be safe.

Suddenly the ground beneath her feet shook. She fell to her knees. A scream of metal filled the air. The bells stopped. She felt a whoosh of heat and the autumn-bare trees to her right burst into flame, banishing the lingering remains of the night. A voice she knew and loved screamed her name. She answered, her voice more a wail than words. A body hit hers from behind. Hands tore at her clothes, pulling her down. Agnes screamed and fell forward. The Hand of Glory fell from her grasp, vanishing from her sight. Her knees hit the ground and it gave way—she was plunging through into nothing. She was sinking. She thrashed around, her hands clawing at the wiry grass on the edge of the pit she had fallen into. Her fingers closed on a length of barbed wire. She clung on, ignoring the bite of the metal as she attempted to pull herself free.

"Bloody bitch! You stole the Hand! You'll fucking pay, you will!"

Agnes turned her head. She was not alone in the murky bog. The villain was floundering, a mere arm's length from her. He surged upward, fighting the glutinous hold of the muddy peat. His hand lashed out and caught hold of her cape, pulling her towards him. She began to sink, her chest going under, her shoulders. The man was laughing as he pulled harder. The sour peat brushed her lips. She screamed. Her hand tightened round the strand of metal as she struggled to pull herself up. Then a hand closed on hers, adding its strength. Someone was lying down on the edge of the morass she was in, reaching out to her.

It was Giles.

"I won't let you go," he said, and Agnes believed him.

Chapter Twenty-Four

"No!" Hardy screamed, his voice blending with Mathew's bellow as the young man surged up from his seat. They were free.

"What on earth was that? I mean, shitting hell and damnation!" Bright swore, scrabbling to his feet and lurching after the fleeing Hawkins. Mathew was hard on the man's heels, stopping only to snatch up his shotgun from the kitchen dresser. Hardy began to follow, his heart lurching at the sound of a car's tyres squealing on the gravel outside. *Had Hawkins just killed Agnes, and was he even now making his escape?*

"Not to worry, sir—the lass is giving him a run for his money, but she's going to need some help, so we best get moving."

Hardy's head snapped round at the sound of the voice. It was Adams. He was standing in the door to the scullery dressed in full battle gear, tin helmet at a jaunty angle, his smelly unslung. Adams nodded and jerked his thumb over his shoulder as he turned and set off at a run.

Hardy looked for a moment in the direction the others had taken, then at the empty door where Adams had stood. It was madness, yet... He had trusted Adams in life, why not now in death? He began to move. Hardy burst out onto the path behind the house, looking for a glimpse of the ghost. Adams was jogging into the walled garden. Hardy started after, praying his leg would hold up

As he reached the far side, Adams was at his side. "That's it, sir. Told you she was worth the risk—well and truly over the top now, both of you."

"But are we going to make it through?" Hardy panted as he stumbled out into the field.

Adams did not answer, merely picked up his pace, charging across the field towards the careering car. Its headlights bounced over the frosted grass, picking out the fleeing figure a few scant yards ahead of it. Hawkins hung onto the car's side, his feet braced on the running board, his free hand reaching out to grab Agnes. The air was full of sound: screams and bellows, the roar of the car's engine, and bells. Bells? Hardy looked in the direction of the sound. Two other cars burst into the field from the direction of the old sawmill. Police cars. A figure was leaning out of the window of the first one. Shots rang out. A rapid *clack, clack*. Hardy ducked, his old instincts taking over. His leg gave way and he fell to his knees, the frost soaking his trousers. He had failed Agnes. It was no good. He screamed. The Hand of Glory had claimed them both.

"That's it—stay still just a moment longer, sir," Adams said softly, close to Hardy's ear. He felt the cold weight of a rifle barrel on his shoulder, and the shock of the recoil sent him forward into the grass. As he fell, he saw the car pursuing Agnes swerve. The driver's side mounted the remains of a cart, half buried in the field. Hawkins was thrown sideways and tumbled away into the grass. The car hung on two wheels for a heartbeat, then toppled onto the passenger side, sliding into one of the silver birch trees on the edge of the wooded copse.

A wave of exultation pulsed through Hardy. He fought to his feet, forcing his leg to work. The leading police car began to

Hand of Glory

brake, then swung to the right, cutting huge divots out of the field. Its doors slammed open and figures began to emerge, heading towards the crashed car. Hardy feverishly looked for Agnes. Where was she? He couldn't see her, but he could see Adams. The ghost was standing by the gently spinning front wheel of the Rover. Adams held a lighted cigarette in his hand. The shade held the Woodbine up and looked at it, then let it drop to the ground. Flames tore skywards, consuming the front of the car and the birch tree it had rammed against. The fire spread unnaturally fast, setting the gothic window web of branches afire and banishing the dregs of the night. It filled the air with the smell of burning wood and leaves.

The figure of Hawkins rose from the ground, bellowing, "Marie!" He started towards the toppled car, then stopped, as if seeing the police for the first time. He swung round and did not look back again. He was after Agnes, Hardy knew it, a vile hound on her trail.

Hardy's breath hitched; he couldn't swallow. He'd seen this before. It had haunted his dreams, waking and sleeping, along with the hand within his hand, clinging on the wire between them, cutting, flesh and blood mingling.

"Agnes!" he screamed, knowing now it had always been her hand in his.

"Giles!"

He looked round in anguish. Two figures fell plunging to earth beyond the line of trees. *God, no—they were in the peat bog of Chartley Moss.* He began to run, ignoring the protest of his leg. He stopped at the half-rotten fencepost that marked the edge of the moss. A thick strand of barbed wire snaked out from the post, pulled taut across the peat. Hanging from it was Agnes, up to her chest in the bog—she had broken through the layer of peat.

"To the left, Mr Hardy!" Hardy spun round, expecting to see Adams, but it was George's son, Mathew. The youth was standing there, his chest heaving, shotgun broken and over his arm. Hardy could smell spent cartridges.

Hardy nodded and stepped to the left. The ground gave under his weight, shifting like the moving floor in a funhouse at a fair.

"Careful, one step at a time," Mathew said, as he joined Hardy on the edge of the moss. "For some reason it's thinner on this edge than the others. Follow the line of that fallen pine tree." Mathew pointed at the rotting length of wood. Hardy inched along, his gaze only on Agnes as she struggled to haul herself out.

"Bloody bitch!" Hawkins's arms came out of the bog and he slapped down his fingers mere inches from Agnes. He heaved again and grabbed hold of her, dragging her to him and pushing her down into the bog.

"No!" Hardy screamed as he threw himself down. He felt his elbows and knees go into the peat. His hand snapped out, grasping Agnes's fist on the wire and pulling for all he was worth. He would not let her be swallowed and lost in the mud like so many others. He shuffled forward and tightened his grip. He was aware of the bite of the wire and of his flesh tearing. Aware too, of the cold touch of the ring on her little finger.

"She's fucking mine, as are you, Hardy," Hawkins snarled, burying both fists in her cape and heaving her closer.

"Like bloody hell they are. Time to pay the piper, mate." Adams appeared in the morass, his arms round Hawkins, mimicking the way he had supported Hardy in the shell-hole. This time the ghost was not helping the man in his arms to get out—he was dragging him down. Other hands formed out of the peat, each one adding its strength. Fingers of mud clawed at Hawkins's hands, peeling them off Agnes's cape. Hawkins

Hand of Glory

screamed and thrashed about, ignoring the rope thrown to him. Others were in the bog now, holding onto Hardy, supporting him and encouraging him. A rope slipped round his middle, anchoring him.

Hawkins coughed, spluttering, as the foul mud of the churned moss filled his mouth. His hands fought upwards, then were dragged down.

"Bloody fool–take the rope!" Parker bellowed, pulling the rope back and throwing it again.

Hawkins twisted his head round, mud-filled mouth snarling, then his eyes widened, the scars round his eye red and torn, as if reopened. He screamed, bubbles of mud splattering from his lips as his head began to go under. Hardy shuddered as he watched Adams's hands press down on Hawkins's shoulders, pushing the man under the mud.

Suddenly the burning birch tree began to fall, leaving a flaming trail of cinders in its wake. The men on the edge of the bog scattered. Hardy's gaze was dragged from the site of Hawkins's death, skywards. There, etched in the pattern of falling embers, was a horse. All red-eyed, with hooves of steel, the demonic rider's hand reaching down and pulling up a ghostly shadow of Hawkins, screaming and struggling, to the crupper of the saddle. The last stanza of the poem he had read for Agnes just a few days before flashed through Hardy's mind.

When a queer-looking horseman, dressed all in black,
Snatches up that old harridan just like a sack.
To the crupper behind him, puts spurs to his hack,
Makes a dash through the crowd, and is off in a crack!
No one can tell,
Though they guess pretty well,
Which way that grim rider and old woman go.

"Dear God!" Mathew whispered as Hawkins vanished beneath the bog.

"Bugger has cheated the hangman," Parker snarled.

"Giles...." Agnes said, coughing, struggling to bring up her other hand.

"I won't let you go; the mud won't have you," Giles said.

"I know—is it over?" Agnes asked, as her other hand closed over his.

Hardy looked round. No ghosts or demons hung in the dawn sky. "Yes, my love, it is all over..."

*****

James stood in the large drawing room of the manor. No fire blazed in the hearth. The numerous chairs and tables littering the room were covered in dust sheets. Yet the room did not feel abandoned. It had the air of expectation, as if it knew that soon the covers would be removed, the fire lit, and its walls would echo to the sound of a family again.

"Sir..." It was Bright. He stood by the large door.

"Yes."

"Father Thomas is here."

"Thank you, Bright. Would you show him in?"

"Sir, and your wife wants to know..." Bright stopped, his cheeks reddening.

Parker sighed. He knew what she wanted to know. Everything. But that was something he couldn't do, not yet. He would have to at some point, but not today. "Tell her we will speak later. Say that for now Agnes must be her priority." Yes, that should do it. Elizabeth wouldn't question that. Though if the circumstances were reversed he doubted Agnes would give up so easily. He had envied the fact that Giles had found someone who understood what he—they—had gone through in the so-called war to end all wars, but that very fact made it impossible to pull the wool even partly over Agnes's eyes. Their relationship was going to be an interesting one, of that he was sure. And he believed it was going to be good for both of them.

Bright nodded and left.

Parker's attention turned to the item that lay, wrapped in his coat, on the table by the French doors that opened onto the gardens. In its time the table had carried afternoon teas, drinks and after-dinner coffee for the ladies of the house. Its makers would have been shocked at the thought that it now bore in its centre the last known human remains of one Second Lieutenant Christian Tennant.

"Inspector," Father Thomas said as he entered the room. His use of Parker's title was both a greeting and question. The priest was short and slender, his face lined, and his hair long, receded back from his forehead, giving him a natural monk's tonsure.

"Yes, Father Thomas. Thank you for coming," Parker said and held out his right hand to the priest. Father Thomas took it and tilted his head slightly to the left as he let go, the question of his requested presence hanging in the air between them. James knew Bright had been surprised that he had not sent for the Church of England vicar from Stowe, Hixon or any of the other villages, but had requested that Bright ask the priest from the small Roman Catholic church in Caston itself. Something at the back of his mind had told Parker that it would be the wiser choice. That a member of the clergy of the *"older"* branch of Christianity might have more knowledge of the item on the table. "You perhaps are aware of the events of early this morning?"

"It is a very small village. A botched robbery, I believe?" Father Thomas clasped his hands in front of his chest.

"Yes, and, well, an item has been recovered and I feel it needs to be placed in your care for the time being, until *we* can decide what to do with it." Parker indicated for the priest to approach the table. Parker joined him and carefully unwrapped the Hand.

"Well." Father Thomas's voice was a mere whisper as he looked at the Hand. The thieves' tool was blackened and wizened, the fingers upturned like claws, and narrow. No excess flesh remained on them. Each bone was etched with the rank remains of what once had been skin. The wicks on the end of each digit looked as if they had been recently trimmed. It was if the Hand were awaiting its new owner.

"You don't sound as surprised as I thought you might be," Parker said, watching as the priest carefully re-covered the Hand.

"I have been a country parish priest for forty years, Inspector."

Father Thomas obviously thought his statement was explanation enough. "So you know what to do? You see, the hand used to be—was—my late brother-in-law's."

Father Thomas nodded as he lifted the swaddled hand from the table. "And at some point you would like to lay it to rest? Give it a Christian burial?"

"Would that be possible?" Parker asked.

"In time, I believe, but for now this will be safer under God's roof. Would you be wanting your coat back, Inspector?"

"No," Parker said, with more force than he had intended.

"Very wise," Father Thomas said.

*****

Hardy sat in the window seat of the study, both arms round Agnes's waist. The back of her head was against his cheek. He could smell the liquid soap with which she had washed her hair. She was wearing his dressing gown, and was loath to leave him and change into the clothes Elizabeth had brought. The door to the study was open; through it the voices of Elizabeth and Mrs

Hand of Glory

Adams could be heard putting the world to rights. Not that Hardy thought it needed to be. He felt content and no longer lost in the mud. Yet one question remained unanswered. The ghosts that the Hand had trapped and prevented from going home, what had become of them?

"Giles?" It was James.

Hardy unwillingly removed his gaze from the exposed nape of Agnes's neck and looked at his friend. "Yes?"

"We have found the Hand. It was just on the edge of the moss where you went in, Agnes."

"I see." Hardy felt a chill begin to form at the base of his spine.

"I have arranged with Father Thomas for it to be placed in his church until it can be buried properly."

Agnes shifted in Hardy's arms as she turned towards James. "I think that is the best thing to do. Don't you, Giles?"

"Yes."

"Good. We are agreed, then," Parker said, rubbing the corner of his moustache with his hook.

"Yes, we are," Agnes said, and looked over her shoulder at Giles, smiling.

"Right," Parker said and began to turn, saying over his shoulder, "Oh, Elizabeth says it's time you got dressed, Agnes. You can't sit there showing the world your right thigh all day."

"What?" Agnes spluttered, her hands going to her side, pulling at the fabric of the dressing gown. "I suppose I should." She began to edge off the seat, carefully removing Hardy's arms from round her.

"Pity," he said as he watched her stand.

"I will soon be back," Agnes said, giggling.

"I hope so," Hardy replied and watched her leave the room.

Hardy eased himself up in his seat, stretching out his left leg. The clock on the mantelpiece began to strike. Eleven. It was eleven in the morning on the eleventh day of the eleventh month. Armistice Day. The brittle, late autumn sun danced through the window, catching his gaze and taking it outside. There, in the frost-bound field behind the manor, figures were moving. Jackets hooked on fingers and draped over shoulders, arms linked and soft caps at jaunty angles. All were moving in the direction of the sun. Their stance was one of ease, the men relaxed, at peace. Tennant was there, Hardy was sure of it. The young man was moving quickly as he raced to catch up with the others. One of the figures stopped and looked back. It was Adams. He smiled and nodded to Hardy, who returned the nod. Adams then turned away and began to move after his fellows. The outline of his figure began to shimmer, taking on the hue of the sun. The brightness made Hardy look away for a second. When he looked back, Adams had vanished.

The End.

Glossary of British slang

Bad Hat	A Scoundrel
Beaks	Magistrate/ Judge
Bottle	Courage
To Cop it	To Die
Diffy	Lacking needed items
Do a place over	Steal from somewhere
Do for someone	Hurt or kill someone
Fag	Cigarette
Flannel	Flirting
Get the wind up	Get scared, become alarmed
Jonah	Some with bad luck
Kip	Sleep
Plods	Police
Rozzers	Police
Rum	Strange
Scarper	Run away
Screw (Noun)	Prison guard
To shop someone	To report someone
Smelly	SMLE. Short Lee Enfield Rifle
Snuff it	To die
The Smoke	London
Tick	Minute
Tommy	British Soldier
Top Someone	Kill someone

About the Author

Susan Boulton

Susan Boulton, as in the song by The Police, was born in the '50s and came into the world 200 yards from where Tolkien spent time thinking about hobbits 37 years before. Having loved to read since she was very young, Susan began to wonder if she could actually write a novel. Once she tried she found it addictive. She's been writing stories, long and short, ever since.

Susan has lived all her life in rural Staffordshire and has a passion for the countryside, its history, its myths, and its legends, all of which influence her work. Her first novel, *Oracle*, is a steampunk fantasy of political intrigue. She's also published numerous short stories, including "Jac" (Dark Fiction Spotlight, 2010), "The Giving of Adela" (*Tales of the Sword,* edited by

Dorothy Davis), and "Death Won't Be Cheated" (*Malevolence: Tales from Beyond the Veil*, edited by J. Scott-Marryat, 2014).

Married with two grown daughters, Susan now puts her overactive imagination (once the bane of her parents and teachers) to good use in her writing.

Hand of Glory was inspired by Susan's combined interests in World War I (fueled by family stories of both her grandfathers), the many historical memorials throughout local villages, and a deep appreciation of the myths, folklore, and supernatural stories of her region.

If You Enjoyed This Book
Visit

PENMORE PRESS
www.penmorepress.com

All Penmore Press books are available directly through our website, amazon.com, Barnes and Noble and Nook, Sony Reader, Apple iTunes, Kobo books and via leading bookshops across the United States, Canada, the UK, Australia and Europe.

PENMORE PRESS
www.penmorepress.com

HEAVEN CRIES
BY
STEPHAN SILVA

Heaven Cries is a compelling story.

Captain Artemio Battaglia, a young World War II pilot, who when repulsed by the brutality of Mussolini's fascist state, joins a partisan band to fight the Nazi death squads that were terrorizing Italian citizens. Nicolas Gage, author of bestselling *Eleni* praised **Heaven Cries** for reminding *"us of the true spring waters of freedom: hope, kindness, courage, and love. In the dark light of recent events, this history is particularly relevant."*

Now available at Amazon, Barnes&Nobel, iBooks, and Kobo.

PENMORE PRESS
www.penmorepress.com

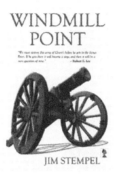

WINDMILL POINT

BY

JIM STEMPEL

Gripping historical fiction vividly brings to life two desperate weeks during the spring of 1864, when the resolution of the American Civil War was balanced on a razor's edge.

At the time, both North and South had legitimate reasons to conclude they were very near victory. Ulysses S. Grant firmly believed that Lee's Army of Northern Virginia was only one great assault away from implosion; Lee knew that the political will in the North to prosecute the war was on the verge of collapse.

Jim Stempel masterfully sets the stage for one of the most horrific battles of the Civil War, contrasting the conversations of decision-making generals with chilling accounts of how ordinary soldiers of both armies fared in the mud, the thunder, and the bloody fighting on the battlefield.

"We must destroy this army of Grant's before he gets to the James River. If he gets there it will become a siege, and then it will be a mere question of time." – General Lee.

Penmore Press
Challenging, Intriguing, Adventurous, Historical and Imaginative

www.penmorepress.com

Lightning Source UK Ltd.
Milton Keynes UK
UKOW06f0307100916

282613UK00003B/237/P